Praise for *New Yor...*

LORI
FOSTER

"Lori Foster delivers the goods."
—*Publishers Weekly*

"This fantasy plays out with sexy innuendos
and steamy love scenes throughout the book."
—*Romantic Times BOOKreviews* on *Jude's Law*

"Filled with Foster's trademark wit, humor, and sensuality."
—*Booklist* on *Jamie*

"Foster supplies good sex and great humor
along the way in a thoroughly enjoyable romance
reminiscent of Susan Elizabeth Phillips' novels."
—*Booklist* on *Causing Havoc*

"Foster executes with skill...convincing, heartfelt family drama."
—*Publishers Weekly* on *Causing Havoc*

"Suspenseful, sexy, and humorous."
—*Booklist* on *Just a Hint—Clint*

"Fans of Foster's sexy romantic comedies…
will find much to like here."
—*Booklist* on *The Secret Life of Bryan*

Also available from

LORI
FOSTER

and HQN Books

Heartbreakers
Fallen Angels
Enticing

LORI FOSTER
FOSTER
Caught!

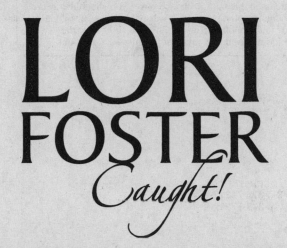

HQN™

HQN™

ISBN-13: 978-0-373-77312-1
ISBN-10:   0-373-77312-9

CAUGHT!

Copyright © 2008 by Harlequin Books S.A.

The publisher acknowledges the copyright holder of the individual works as follows:

TAKEN!
Copyright © 1998 by Lori Foster

SAY YES
Copyright © 2000 by Lori Foster

This edition published by arrangement with Harlequin Books S.A.

® and TM are trademarks of the publisher. Trademarks indicated with ® are registered in the United States Patent and Trademark Office, the Canadian Trade Marks Office and in other countries.

www.HQNBooks.com

Printed in U.S.A.

CONTENTS

TAKEN!

chapter 1

THE HEAT SWELLED within him until he thought he'd explode with lust. This wasn't what he'd expected, wasn't what he'd planned on. Her nipple stiffened under the gentle abrasion of his rough fingertips and Virginia groaned, thrilling him, turning him inside out with need. She twined her fingers in his hair and said with a touch of desperation, "Please."

Dillon felt the silky smooth, pliant flesh of her breast, heard her choppy breathing and soft plea, and he forgot his purpose. He forgot that he had ulterior motives, that he wasn't actually attracted to this woman.

"Dillon…"

"Shh. It's all right, honey." And it was, better than all right. It was incredible.

He pushed her coat farther out of his way and shoved her blouse higher. Her breast, full and firm and heavy, nestled against his palm, and more than anything, he wanted her naked. He wanted to see the color of her nipples by the scant moonlight coming through the windshield, to see the pleasure in her exotic hazel eyes, eyes that were usually hard with determination and arrogance but now were soft with pleasure and desire. For him.

He pressed open-mouth kisses to the smooth skin of her throat and breathed in her unique scent. He'd never noticed before that she had a unique scent. He'd never noticed how sexy she was, or imagined how hotly she would respond to his touch. She gasped and he whispered to her, soothing her as his fingers plucked at her nipple, rolling and teasing. As her entire body trembled with need, she moaned and he wanted to moan, too. This wasn't right, but it felt too damned right.

What had started out as necessary seduction now seemed amazingly like blind sexual need. There was no way he could deny his enjoyment of this little rendezvous, or the way his blood surged through his body to settle into an insistent throb in his groin. He was as hard as a stone, hurting with it, and Virginia was far too astute not to notice.

The car was cramped, but it didn't matter, and even though it was a miserably cold night, they were cozy, sharing the warmth of the heater and their combined sexual heat as the wind whistled around them. He knew that inside the mansion, the party was still going full blast. Lights shone from every window, sparkling across the snow-covered lawn, and the rumble of music drifted on the air. What he was doing, and where he was doing it, was dangerous, but he finally had her alone and he wasn't about to lose ground. He needed to push forward; too much time had been lost already.

For thirty-six years he'd been a mean, determined bastard—traits his father had instilled in him, insisted upon.

He never forgot his purpose, never wavered from his course. Tonight, though, right this minute, he couldn't seem to force the plan to remain uppermost in his mind.

He wanted Virginia lying naked on the narrow seat, wanted to fit himself between her soft plump thighs and slide deep, deep inside her. He wanted to ride her hard until she made those sweet little sounds again, until she begged him to give her what she needed.

"Dillon, wait."

Her tone wasn't authoritative now. It didn't carry the sharp cut of command it normally did. Instead, her voice was low, overcome with need, and purely feminine. As a man, he relished the thought of proper balance with this particular woman who didn't act the way he expected a woman to act, the way he needed her to act.

She whispered his name again, and when he ignored her, she tightened her strong fingers in his hair. Taking her reaction as one of encouragement, he worked her bra aside, nuzzling with his lips. Her breasts were extremely sensitive, and he liked that. He imagined how it would be to make love to her, to find all her sensitive places with his hands, his mouth, his tongue and teeth. He wanted to taste her, to draw her deep into the heat of his mouth, to suck her gently and then, not so gently, devour her.

He smoothed a hand over her soft, slightly rounded belly and heard her sharp groan. He needed to touch her, all of her. His fingers pressed lower, slipping between her thighs, seeking, probing, feeling the throbbing heat.

Suddenly, she jerked away. "Dillon, no."

He heard her gasping, heard the trembling in her tone. She pressed her head back against the seat and closed her eyes.

"I'm sorry. I can't do this."

Reality started to nudge his lust-fogged brain. *She* couldn't do this? He was the one who'd been forcing himself for the sake of his plan—at first. His sole purpose in coming to Delaport City, Ohio, had been to seduce her, and in the process gain answers. Reluctance was in no way the proper response from her to his lovemaking. In fact, it was so far out of line with his original intention that he scowled. "Virginia…"

"No," she said, shaking her head. "No, this isn't right. Hiding out here with you as if I'm ashamed. I shouldn't treat you so shabbily. Just because you work for the company and I have the authority to fire you doesn't give me the right to treat you with less than full respect."

As she spoke, her voice gathered strength and she straightened her silk blouse, pulling it down over her breasts. He tried his damnedest to catch a glimpse of that taunting nipple he'd wanted so badly to taste.

Then it sank in. She thought she was treating him badly because they were sneaking? They *had* to sneak, or his plan would never work.

He cupped her cheek. Long curls of titian hair had escaped their pins and now hung over her rounded shoulders. Those curls surprised him. Usually her hair was pulled up and tidy and he'd had no idea how long it was. Loose, it made her look almost vulnerable—not that anyone would ever think of Virginia Johnson in such human terms. It also made her seem very feminine. He toyed with a loose strand and it was incredibly soft against his fingertips. He wondered what she'd look like with it completely undone. That red hair of hers would frame her white body perfectly, maybe curl around her lush breasts, giving her an earthy, pagan appearance.

He shook his head at his meandering thoughts. He must have been too long without a woman, but then, he'd had other priorities lately. Namely, saving his brother's ass. He had to get a grip, had to remember the purpose of this little seduction.

He summoned up his most bland tone, the one he knew she wanted and expected from subordinates. "It's all right, Virginia. You can't be seen with me and we both know it. Cliff would be outraged and your reputation might be ruined."

She shook that stubborn head of hers. In the two weeks he'd spent cautiously wooing her, he'd learned Virginia Johnson had stubbornness down to a fine, irritating art, along with arrogance and a complete lack of business modesty. She knew she was good at making corporate decisions and she wanted everyone else to know it, too, even if she had to shove the fact down people's throats.

"I don't care what my brother thinks. He's a snob and we seldom get along anyway. He doesn't own me and he has no say over how I live my life."

"That's not the impression he gives." Dillon knew he had to speak carefully so he didn't give himself away. Deferring to anyone wasn't customary for him. He led his life in a unique fashion, following rules of his own making. He lived by a code of honor that was independent of the strictures of society. Except for his father and his brother, Dillon owed nothing to anyone. But Virginia was a bossy, powerful woman, damn her, and as used to calling the shots as he. He cleared his throat. "Your brother is very protective."

"Ha! He's a bully and I'm the only one with the guts to stand up to him, because I control the majority of the money. Cliff knows that without me, he'd destroy the company in a matter of weeks."

Even in the darkness he could see the ire on her face. She wasn't exactly pretty—at least, he'd never thought so before—and she was entirely too headstrong and self-contained. She enjoyed giving orders to everyone in her realm. She was also a bit too plump. Only, she hadn't felt too plump against him a minute ago. She'd felt soft and warm and comfortably rounded. He frowned at himself. "Virginia, I can't let you—"

"Can't let me?" she interrupted, one thin auburn brow climbing high as she met his gaze. "You can't stop me, Dillon. I always do as I please—you know that." With efficient movements, she rebuttoned her coat and started to open the door.

He caught her arm. From the minute he'd first forced an introduction, he'd damn near bitten holes in his tongue to keep from revealing his true nature. Sometimes the urge to put her in her place, wherever that might be, almost overwhelmed him.

She glared down at where his hand circled her arm, then slowly raised those incredible eyes to his in a look that plainly said, *You dare?*

The little witch might have the hots for him, but she

didn't want anyone telling her what to do, which probably accounted as much for her matronly status as did her excess weight and unremarkable features. Most of the men who worked for her steered clear because she frightened them half to death and they weren't willing to put their careers on the line. The rest simply weren't interested.

Dillon wasn't worried about his career. Working for the company was only a temporary sham, his way of getting close to her so that he could ultimately ruin her brother's destructive plans. But even if that hadn't been true, he would never have let a woman, any woman, dictate to him. There were easier ways to make a living than bowing under to the tyrannical rule of an iron maiden.

"Sweetheart, listen to me." He turned his secure hold into a caress to pacify her, and to some degree it worked. The only way he'd been able to get close to her had been to seduce her into wanting him. And seducing an iron maiden was no easy feat. He'd nearly depleted his store of ploys with her and he wasn't used to that. Women usually came to him easily enough, but Virginia had been so damn elusive his ego had taken a beating. Now the plan was more than a necessity; it was a personal challenge.

He'd finally been making headway, and then this. "Virginia, if you won't think of your own reputation, think of mine. If Cliff finds out about us, he'll fire me in a heartbeat. Is that what you want?" He had to keep their relationship secret so that later no one would suspect him.

She patted his hand in her condescending fashion. "Don't worry. I won't let him fire you. I hold controlling interest in the company. I have ultimate say over who goes and who stays."

He sighed, deliberately appearing put-upon. "I'm sorry, honey, but I won't have it. I'd look like a fool if I let a woman, any woman, defend me. People would start saying I was only after your money and—"

She waved a hand. "Nonsense. Everyone knows I'm never marrying, and that's the only way you could possibly get your hands on my money. We'd just be having an affair."

"Which is nobody's business but our own."

She frowned and he quickly retrenched, pulling together his frayed temper and gathering the remnants of his control. Why did she have to be so damn argumentative?

"I'm sorry," he said through gritted teeth, then managed to summon a calmer tone. "I didn't mean to yell at you. But what's between us is private. I want to keep it that way."

She still looked skeptical and he silently cursed her, while on the outside he did his best to appear hopeful. The damn shrew. What was it with this woman that she thought she had to control everyone and everything? Of course, he felt the same way, but it was different for him. He'd been raised to be cautious, to take control and guide the events in his life. His father's renegade life-style had carried over into parenting, and every survival value had been passed on. Dillon accepted his right to control as a means to protect those around him. It was what he was used to, the way he understood life.

Virginia had led a pampered existence, so she had no excuse.

Finally, she nodded. "Oh, all right, if you're going to be that sensitive about it, I'll keep our…association private. But I'm not going to make love in a car. It's ridiculous."

"Of course not." This was the opening he'd been waiting for, a culmination of two weeks' work and endless, nerve-stretching patience. "But we could take a day off, go somewhere private and indulge ourselves." He swallowed, then forced himself to say, "I want you so bad, honey."

Now that he wasn't kissing and touching her, only listening to the grating, overbearing tone of her voice, all lust had died and he was once again filled with cold deliberation. She would be a pawn in the scheme of things, used and deceived so he could accomplish his goals, but he had no intention of making Virginia a victim. Though she might end up slightly humiliated, he wouldn't hurt her. He would go only as far as necessary to stop her brother and save his own.

True to her nature, she was already shaking her head no. "I can't take any time off right now. Too much to do. Just come to my home tonight. We'll leave separately so no one will know, seeing as how your reputation is so important to you."

He wanted to smack her for using that sneering tone. Obviously, she wanted just an hour or two with him, a quick toss in the hay, not the commitment of an entire evening. Although it was foolish, he felt very insulted; she might as well have labeled him a stud for hire. His male dignity was sorely tried.

He needed enough time to gain her trust and find the clues to the deception that threatened to destroy his brother. But he couldn't do that if Virginia's brother found out they were seeing each other. He answered her honestly. "No. It's too risky. Someone might see me at your place."

She heaved a dramatic sigh and glared at him, her hazel eyes appearing gold in the dark night. "Are you sure you really want to do this? I mean, for a man who only a few moments ago was in the throes of lust, you're setting up an awful lot of obstacles. I've never known anyone so ridiculously sensitive or so overly cautious."

Through narrowed eyes he searched her face, not quite sure how to answer her and keep the peace at the same time. Though her brother stood as a figurehead, it was Virginia who actually ran things. She was the only hope his brother had out of this damn mess.

She sighed again and said, "I'm sorry. That was uncalled for. To be honest, I'm not quite used to this."

He could believe that. What man would pursue a dragon lady? When he'd been kissing her and she'd been soft and pliant and feminine, he'd forgotten how cold and domineering she really was. But what he'd learned of her other side had been accidental. Not many men had ever tried to get past the brambles to see what lay beneath. If it hadn't been for Wade, he certainly wouldn't have tried. That thought bothered him and he shied away from it.

"Virginia, I know this is complicated, but I don't see any other way...."

"Maybe we should just forget the whole thing. I'm not exactly cut out for affairs and it's getting entirely too awkward."

"*No!*" Damn it, he couldn't waste time backtracking now. Getting her this far had taken longer than he'd expected.

But here she was, lifting that damn supercilious eyebrow at his tone. He cleared his throat and had to clench his hands to keep from shaking her.

"What I meant," he said, painfully cajoling, "is that you can't change your mind on me. I need you too much." For good measure he kissed her again—then immediately forgot it was just for good measure and started enjoying himself. Her lips parted. Her tongue touched his.

Damn, but for a dragon lady she tasted fine—hot and sweet and sexy. Without making a conscious decision, he lifted his hand to that heavy breast again. Even through her sweater and coat, he could feel the softness of her as he kneaded her flesh. She moaned, and when he lifted his mouth from hers she whispered shakily, "Let me see what I can work out. I'll get in touch with you later in the week."

She had the door open before he could stop her, but it was just as well. The driveway was packed with cars and they could have been caught by anyone coming or going. He'd gotten so wrapped up in the job at hand he'd been careless.

No one knew who he really was and he had to keep it that way, because once he gained Virginia's confidence and ruined her brother's plans, Dillon would disappear. If anyone suspected him of having a relationship with Virginia, he'd fail. And his brother, Wade, would be the one to suffer.

chapter 2

WHEN VIRGINIA STEPPED back into the mansion, entering through the kitchen door, she ran smack into her brother, Cliff. He looked at her suspiciously.

"What were you doing outside?"

She pushed him out of her way and pulled off her coat. All that kissing and touching had her overheated. She'd rebuttoned the coat only as a sort of barrier, a way to shield herself from the overwhelming attraction and confusing emotions Dillon made her feel. Being so strongly drawn to a man wasn't something she was used to. And especially not a man like Dillon. She shivered in memory. "I was indulging in a secret liaison, of course."

"Ha, ha. Very funny." With his tone as bland as an angry brother could manage, Cliff glared at her. "Like any man would be foolish enough to tangle with you."

Virginia just shook her head. In one respect, Cliff was right. Men rarely pursued her—at least, not men who only wanted to have a heated affair. The term *sex symbol* had never been used to describe her, not with her excess weight and incisive personality. Men who wanted to try to marry her for her company connections showed up by the dozen each year, but their intentions were far from honorable or complimentary, which partially accounted for her ruthlessness. She'd decided to stay single because she couldn't find a man who suited her—they were all either immoral money grubbers or complete wimps.

She'd had high hopes for Dillon when she first met him. Unlike the other fools Cliff invariably hired, Dillon stood apart. His body was long and hard and honed, not the type of physique achieved in a gym, but rather the kind that came from hard work day in and day out, over a lifetime. With broad shoulders and thick thighs, he looked more than capable of taking on any physical task. And he wore a certain confidence, as if he possessed an alertness unknown to most men.

He had the kind of intensity that made a woman feel surrounded and closed in. It didn't threaten her—nothing did. She'd grown up a chubby, unattractive middle child who'd had to learn to fight for everything she wanted, including affection. She'd forced her way into the business and into her father's trust. After living through her parents' deaths and the battles for power that followed, she knew that very little in life had the ability to alarm her, including Dillon's pursuit.

Unhappily, Dillon was proving to be something of a pushover, just like the others. One little word from her, and he tripped all over himself trying not to anger her. Why couldn't she find a man who could deal with her head-on?

She was disappointed by his lack of backbone, but not

enough to call a halt to the affair. With any luck, Dillon might surprise her once he learned her bark was worse than her bite.

"Yoo-hoo, Virigina. Anyone home?" Cliff peered at her critically. "What are you up to that has you so distracted?"

Virginia sighed. "I'm not exactly in the mood right now for your prying or your sarcasm, Cliff. Shouldn't you be entertaining guests or something?"

"That's my line to you. We have important associates here tonight."

"Is that right? Such as your personal assistant? I saw Laura dutifully following you around earlier. In fact, she's probably looking for you right now."

Cliff stiffened. "Ms. Neil is no concern of yours."

In all honesty, Virginia really didn't care what Cliff did with his free time or his secretary, although she suspected he'd promoted Laura to personal assistant only as a way to get her in bed. In spite of her disapproval, it wasn't her business, so she just shrugged. "True enough. Now, what do you want, Cliff?"

"I want to know what you were doing outside that was so important you neglected your duties."

"We've been through this before, Brother." She kept her tone level, hoping to avoid a prolonged fight. She wanted to be alone so she could contemplate how to proceed with Dillon. "What I do with my life is none of your business. Stop pushing me or you won't like the consequences."

Just as she expected, Cliff fumed in impotent silence and then stalked away. It was a shame he'd been born first. It was a bigger shame her father had believed the company needed to be represented by a man, regardless of the fact that Cliff was spineless and shallow and lacked the necessary business sense. Just because they dealt in sporting equipment, her father felt a man would be a more traditional head for the company.

Virginia would have done a much better job of it. She'd learned the business from the sales floor up, working part-time at their three mall locations while taking business courses and acting as an apprentice at the main offices. She'd absorbed every nuance of the business, and she thrived there, but regardless of all she was capable of, she wasn't male and that mattered most to her father. At least he'd had the foresight to leave her a controlling interest. No, she wasn't the president, and she didn't interfere overly in the daily running of the business, but no major decisions could be made without her. And that one small stipulation in her father's will had garnered her near hate from Cliff.

Her brother had always been a petty child, and he'd grown into a petty man. Still, they used to be able to get along, to find a middle ground. Now she hardly knew him— or her younger sister, Kelsey.

Kelsey also held a share of the company, but she hated to get caught in the cross fire between Virginia and Cliff, and usually gave her proxy to one of the other voting board members. She threw herself, instead, into her college studies and her computers, taking great pains to separate herself from the family business.

There were times, like tonight, when Virginia wished she had the same options. It would have been nice to be just an ordinary woman for once. Any woman. Then she wouldn't have to question Dillon's motives in pursuing her.

He wanted her; she knew that. He couldn't have faked his reactions in the car. She'd been more than a little aware of his erection, heavy and full, pressing into her hip. But there was more to it than that, she was certain. And if it wasn't a part of the company he wanted, then what?

She'd read his file when Cliff had first hired him to oversee their security department, mostly because he didn't seem to be the typical Johnson's Sporting Goods employee. He didn't look as if he'd ever played a recreational sport in his life and every time he donned a tie, it seemed to choke him. No, with eyes so dark they almost appeared black, he looked more like a mercenary. Or a renegade. And his file had revealed that he'd never held a steady job for long. The man skipped around the country, and sometimes out of the country. It was for certain he'd been somewhere warm recently, because his skin was darkly tanned, contrasting sharply with the sandy brown hair that hung beyond his collar.

His qualifications and references had been excellent, plus he'd had some military training, so Cliff had hired him regardless of the way he looked.

Dillon knew his business. In the first few days he'd instigated additional safeguards on several levels, approved by Virginia, that would save the company substantial funds in the long run. Ruthless in many ways, he'd already fired two night guards, claiming that the men had been leaving their posts, playing poker and not paying attention to their jobs. Dillon wouldn't allow any dereliction of duty. He now did a personal background check on everyone hired under his jurisdiction, which encompassed all the company offices and the store locations, as well. He took his responsibilities seriously and expected the same of everyone else.

The intelligence in his dark eyes was easy to read, as visible as his strength and every bit as appealing. Even his disdain for her family's business seemed sexy to Virginia. But still, he was an enigma.

She'd give him one night, she decided. Even if he did prove later to be a swindler with ulterior motives, it wouldn't matter. She'd never get drawn in by a wimp, so there was no risk of a bruised heart. She wanted a man who could stand toe-to-toe with her, a man to be her partner in life, who was her equal in every way.

But Dillon, with his incredible body and incredible kisses, would work nicely for now to fill a terrible void. Her aching loneliness had lingered too long, and she needed a little attention, the kind only a man could give a woman.

No, she could never get serious about a man like him. But every woman had the right to a fantasy on occasion. And Dillon Oaks was six feet two inches of hard, throbbing fantasy material. He'd do just fine.

THE MINUTE DILLON opened his door, Wade pounced.

"What happened? How did it go?"

Damn, this was just what he needed. The entire night had been irritating enough; he didn't need to be accosted by his brother right now.

He shrugged out of his battered leather coat and kicked

off his low boots. "What the hell are you doing here? Are you trying to screw things up?" If anyone found out they were related…

"I was careful," Wade protested, looking wounded. "I took a bus to the corner and then walked the rest of the way. Besides, it's dark. No one could have seen me. Now, tell me what happened!"

His little brother, the personification of espionage excellence. What a joke. They'd been raised by different parents, and their upbringing and their outlooks on life couldn't have been more different. "Calm down, Wade," he said. "Nothing's happening yet. Hopefully, this coming week sometime."

"Damn it!" Wade began to pace, his turmoil the complete opposite of his usual, carefree lightheartedness. "What is the matter with that woman! No woman has ever treated you like this. Usually you're the one forced to turn them away."

Even though Wade's words echoed his own earlier sentiments, Dillon shook his head. "Don't be ridiculous. I'm no Romeo." Then he added with a frown, "And Virginia is no fool." A virago, but not stupid.

"Ha! She's a stuck-up bit—"

"Shut up, Wade." His defense of Virginia took him by surprise. He was automatically protective of women, the trait inborn, but of all the women he'd ever known, Virginia was least in need of his chivalry. Still, he didn't like the idea of using her this way, even if there wasn't any choice. Virginia had the answers he needed, and there was only one way to get them.

Fuming, Wade finally dropped into an overstuffed chair. "It has to be soon, Dillon. We're running out of time and I can't take much more of this. I keep having visions of being locked away in prison."

"I told you it won't come to that. I won't let it. If nothing else, I'll get you out of the country before that happens. You could come home with me to Mexico until I get things straightened out." Then he added, just to distract Wade, "How's Kelsey holding up?"

"She's got morning sickness." Wade looked ready to sink into the depths of depression. "She's sick and that damn brother of hers isn't helping matters by doing his best to separate us. He thinks that since I'm without a job and accused of a crime Kelsey won't want me. She's afraid to see me, in case he has me locked up right now. I have to settle for the occasional phone call and it's intolerable. At this rate, she'll be giving birth before we have a chance to get married!"

Dillon went into the kitchen and opened a can of cola, then began stripping off his shirt. For the sake of the party at the mansion and his scheme, he'd donned a dress shirt and tie. He hated ties. Wearing them to the office during the week was torture.

The lengths he went to for his brother.

Half brother, he corrected himself. They hadn't shared the same father, but Wade was still his brother in every sense of the word. Blood was blood, as his father had been fond of preaching. You didn't turn your back on a blood relative.

When their mother had died, leaving Wade alone, he'd made the effort to find Dillon, wanting him at the funeral, wanting to become a part of his life.

At the time, Dillon had just finished a stint in the military.

He'd been living the life of a loner, independent of everyone, even his father, with no clue as to where his mother had gone or what she'd been doing, and not particularly interested in knowing. He certainly hadn't heard that she'd remarried and birthed another son. All his father had ever told him was that she hadn't wanted either of them, and that as soon as she could, she'd abandoned Dillon. She'd turned her back on both of them, and that said it all. They'd never talked about her; given the circumstances, it hadn't seemed necessary.

Women had come and gone in their lives while Dillon was growing up, but none of them had been all that important. His father's relationships never lasted; women were just a necessary convenience for him.

Though he and his father were close, Dillon had never really understood his attitudes on some things.

Discovering he had a brother had taken him by surprise, but he liked the feeling of having someone around who would depend on him, who wanted to be close to him. He'd never felt the need to bother his mother with his presence, but she'd given him a brother and for that he was grateful.

Dillon took over the chore of helping Wade financially through college. He'd given him advice and concern in addition to loans. After eight years of keeping in touch and visiting whenever possible, they'd developed the kind of blood bond his father had always lectured about. They were brothers, and that counted for a lot.

Dillon stripped off his shirt, then dropped onto the

couch, propped his feet on the edge of the battered coffee table and downed his cola in one long gulp.

Wade shook his head. "Look at you! What the hell is wrong with that woman? Why doesn't she want you? I'd give my right ear to have a body like yours."

Dillon choked. "For Christ's sake, Wade, get a grip, will you?" He was well used to Wade's misplaced worship. He'd been putting up with it since the day they'd met, but he still wasn't comfortable with such open adoration.

"It's true," Wade persisted. "All the women at the company want you. The secretaries, the managers, every one of them! As long as I worked there, I never saw anything like it. The female corporate employees are usually so reserved, all buttoned-up businesswomen. Kelsey was the only one who ever paid me any mind. The rest pretty much ignored me. But they *all* gawk at you, and whisper behind their hands. Even Laura Neil, which is nothing short of a miracle."

"Why do you say that?" Dillon was aware of Laura's attention, but it had never felt particularly complimentary. More like wary curiosity.

"Since Cliff took notice of her, she hasn't left his side. She acts like a lapdog."

Dillon scowled at his brother's insulting reference to a lady. "Maybe she's just dedicated."

Wade snorted. "We used to have a thing going, you know. Before I met Kelsey. After we broke up, Cliff promoted Laura to personal assistant. I know he's not really interested. For him, her new position is just a convenience, keeping her close at hand." Wade said it with a sneer, emphasizing his dislike of Cliff Johnson. "Laura hopes he'll marry her, but it'll never happen. Maybe she's realized it, and that's why she's looking at you now. But then, as I said, all the women look at you that way. Kelsey told me some of the women even made bets about who would get you first."

Dillon could only stare. "I don't know about any bets."

"Trust me, the women know." Wade frowned in thought. "It's strange that Virginia is totally immune."

"She's not immune."

"Maybe Virginia's just not…you know." He bobbed his eyebrows suggestively. "Maybe she doesn't prefer men."

Anger surged through him, but he managed to restrain it. The explosive reaction didn't make sense, and he buried it deep, along with all the other confusing emotions he'd experienced tonight, thanks to one Virginia Johnson. "She likes men. There's nothing wrong with Virginia except that she's been given free rein too long. That and too many men wanting her money and not her."

"Not exactly a tough one to figure out." Wade's tone dripped with sarcasm. "Her money is the only appealing thing about her. My position in accounting only put me in direct contact with her a few times, thank God. She scared the hell out of me. With that razor-sharp tongue of hers, she could shred a man to pieces. Besides, she behaves like a dictator."

Actually, Dillon thought, fighting the urge to strangle his brother, Virginia's tongue was soft and tentative and inquisitive. At least when a man took the time to kiss her properly. He had the impression not many men had, and that caused him to feel a certain degree of possessiveness toward her, when he had no right to feel anything at all.

"So what are you going to do now, Dillon?"

"I'm going to wait. She said she'd make a decision this week sometime."

"Kelsey is going to be so disappointed if I don't get this settled soon. She's anxious to move out of the house, to get away from Cliff. She's been biding her time with school and volunteer organizations, but she's miserable."

Dillon shook his head. He'd met Kelsey several times at the company and because of Wade's infatuation he'd paid attention. In Dillon's opinion the woman was a spoiled brat. From what he'd learned of her through subtle queries, both Virginia and Cliff doted on her and tried to protect her from the world. Being the youngest, she'd taken the deaths of her parents the hardest. She was the type of woman Dillon avoided, the type who expected to be coddled and catered to. She knew nothing about coping with real life.

But then, Wade wasn't exactly a model of maturity himself. "You sure this is what you want, Wade? We could still try to fight this in court."

Wade shook his head, frustration apparent in his every feature. "There's no way to get Cliff to drop the embezzlement charges. He's set me up for a reason, and he'll have no qualms about putting me away for good. I don't know what evidence he'll come up with, so there's no way I can fight it, but Kelsey said he's really confident, bragging about nailing me red-handed. So whatever it is, it'll be solid. He'll be sure of that."

Many times, Dillon had considered just beating the hell out of Cliff. It would give him no end of pleasure, yet it wouldn't solve the problem in the long run. Dillon needed to find out what trumped-up evidence Cliff planned to use against Wade. Short of that, he had to find a way to force Cliff to drop the supposed "investigation." If it hadn't been for Kelsey, Wade wouldn't have known of the setup until it was too late. Thankfully, Kelsey had learned of her brother's plan and told Wade.

As yet, no legal charges had been filed, but Wade had been discharged from his position without pay or benefits while Cliff gathered together his evidence. Once the officials got involved, it would be too late. Time was running out.

Cliff was a powerful man and diffusing this situation wouldn't be easy. Dillon had to pull off a tricky unauthorized private investigation. He had to go through files he had no right to see, search records that weren't his to search and still find a way to keep his own butt out of jail. To do it, he needed Virginia. He didn't want her hurt, but she'd have to be the sacrificial lamb; it couldn't be helped. There was no way to switch course now.

He'd ridden some tricky fences in his day, but this was turning out to be the worst.

Though he already knew the answer, Dillon couldn't stop himself from asking, "Are you sure Cliff wouldn't change his mind if he knew Kelsey was pregnant?"

"Ha! Are you kidding? He'd probably forget handling things 'legally' and just take out a contract on me. He thinks she's way too young to get married."

Dillon hesitated, then leaned forward, propping his elbows on his knees. "You know, Wade, he wouldn't be entirely wrong. Kelsey is only twenty-two, and you're not much older. Marriage isn't something to be rushed into."

Wade stiffened and his hands fisted. "She's pregnant, Dillon. Am I supposed to abandon her now? I know from experience that a woman raising a child alone doesn't have an easy time of it. The baby deserves a father, and Kelsey deserves a husband."

"There is that, I suppose." Actually, Dillon wished they'd both shown a little more responsibility and not gotten into the situation in the first place, but rehashing that issue wouldn't help now.

Wade began to pace. "It's not like Kelsey is a child. It's just that she's the only family Cliff has. He's very protective of her, and you know my background isn't something to excite a prospective brother-in-law. No man is good enough for Kelsey, but I want a chance to try."

Dillon made a sound of disgust. He hated hearing Wade harp on his unfortunate childhood. So he and their mother hadn't been rich. Dillon and his dad hadn't exactly lived a life of luxury, either. If anything, they'd lived a life of stealth.

None of that came out of his mouth, though. Instead, he heard himself say, "Cliff has Virginia, too."

Wade shook his head in dismissal. "They're not at all close. Virginia is too damn difficult. You know how she always bosses Cliff around. After their parents died, Virginia just took over. He despises her for it."

Dillon suspected that Virginia had taken charge because

no one else could. Cliff certainly wouldn't have had the smarts to keep things together. And Kelsey had been a mere teenager. Gritting his teeth, Dillon snarled, "If Virginia means so little to him, then why does he worry so much about who she sees?"

Wade shrugged. "I should think he'd be glad to be rid of her. Most men would be. I suppose Cliff worries about someone marrying Virginia for her money—and her shares in the company. From what I've heard, a few men have tried that tactic, but Cliff doesn't want to take any chances on losing the little control he has."

Dillon surged to his feet. This night wasn't improving with conversation and he needed time alone to put things in perspective. He couldn't allow himself to feel protective of Virginia; he needed the ruthlessness his father had taught him. He needed to be able to do the job, without emotional involvement. "Go home, Wade. I want to get some sleep, and it isn't safe for you to hang around here for long. If anyone finds out we're related, the whole plan is ruined."

"I know. And I'm sorry. But I just couldn't wait."

"You're going to have to wait from now on." He spoke sternly in the way he knew commanded attention. "Don't come here again. Do you understand?" He waited until Wade nodded, then he added, "I'll get in touch with you when I find out something."

Reluctantly, Wade turned away. "All right." He walked to the door and then paused. "You know how much I appreciate all this, don't you, Dillon? I didn't have anyone else to turn to. The one lawyer I spoke with was useless. He said the company probably wouldn't press charges because they'd most likely want to avoid the scandal and the possibility of being discredited in front of their shareholders. If it was anyone but Cliff, I'd agree. But he won't be happy just firing me. He wants to ruin me completely. Kelsey and I didn't know what to do. Against Cliff's money, I didn't stand a chance. He'll be sure to have the best lawyers around and they'll make mincemeat out of me. I'd already be in jail and Kelsey would have to raise our baby alone. Cliff would have given her a hard time over the scandal—"

"Enough already, Wade." Damn, but the rambling melodramatics were enough to make him sick. Wade had missed his calling. Instead of becoming an accountant, he should have joined the theater. Still, Wade was his brother, so Dillon forgave him his shortcomings, just as he hoped to be forgiven for his own. "I told you I'd take care of things and I will."

Wade nodded once more, sent his brother a shaky, endearingly familial smile, then left.

Dillon locked up the apartment and turned out the lights.

When he was finally alone with his thoughts, he wondered if he was doing the right thing. Maybe he should have tried to raise enough money to get good legal representation for Wade. Not the low-rate lawyer Wade had spoken with, but a sharpshooter who could match Cliff's. Dillon had property in Mexico he could have sold. That would have meant starting over, but then, he'd started over many times. He liked his home, but there were higher priorities to consider; he had to think about his father, too.

His dad lived with him now, and Dillon didn't want to

uproot him. His father wasn't a young man anymore, and he had a few health problems thanks to the hard life he'd led.

Besides, if Virginia had been a typical female, this whole thing would have been simple. But no, she had to be difficult and unique and a pain in the backside. He'd never known a woman like her.

Naked, he slid between the sheets and stacked his hands behind his head. It was dark and cold and snowflakes patterned his window, making the moonlight look like lace against the far wall. He wondered how Virginia would react when she realized his sole interest in her was her personal files. He wondered how she'd react to the news that her twenty-two-year-old pampered baby sister was pregnant and wanted to marry Wade, a man accused of embezzlement, a man with a less than sterling background. *A man related to him.*

Most of all, he wondered how Virginia would react when she found out he wasn't the wimp she assumed him to be. Would she cry with hurt? He closed his eyes at the vision and shuddered with reaction.

Whatever she did, it wouldn't be the expected. There wasn't another woman like her anywhere, and she had the knack of keeping him on his toes. She wouldn't make his job easy.

But he'd bet his last breath she'd make it interesting.

chapter 3

DILLON WAS IN Cliff's office when Virginia rushed in two days later. Lounged back on his spine in a casual sprawl, his legs wide, he made her forget why she'd wanted to see Cliff in the first place. Virginia noticed how the soft, worn material of his dark jeans cupped his heavy sex. His hands rested over a taut flat belly and his shoulders stretched the pressed material of his dress shirt. His hair hung to his shoulders, his collar was unbuttoned and his sleeves were rolled up. Her gaze traveled over him until she met his eyes. She shivered.

He looked totally relaxed, but his brown eyes were alert. She loved it when he acted so defiantly arrogant for her brother's sake. It made him look sexy and sinful and her heart immediately picked up rhythm.

She forced her gaze to where her brother sat behind a massive desk. One concern was replaced with another.

"What's he doing here, Cliff? Has there been some kind of trouble?" In the normal course of his job, Dillon didn't have much call to hang around Cliff's office.

Cliff glared at her—a look to which she was well accustomed to. "He's my head of security. Why shouldn't he be here?"

She strolled across the floor, trying not to react to the almost tactile sensation of Dillon's eyes on her as he tracked her every step. Propping her hip on the edge of Cliff's desk, she asked, "Are we considering making some kind of adjustment or improvement? Is that why he's here?"

Cliff slammed down the pen he'd been doodling with. "Damn it, Virginia, don't you have a diet class or something to go to?"

That hurt. Her weight had always been a problem, but it wasn't something she wanted to discuss in front of Dillon. Usually the clothes she wore were loose enough so as not to accent the more obvious trouble spots. Today, her simple wool tunic over matching slacks worked wonders—or so she'd thought. Now she was uncomfortably aware of the width of her hips, the weight of her breasts, the roundness of her belly and thighs. She wanted to escape both men's scrutiny.

She lifted her chin. Low blows were a specialty of Cliff's. She should have become immune to them by now.

She didn't dare glance at Dillon. She didn't want to know what he thought of her brother's comment or, at the moment, what he thought of her. "I'm a busy woman, Brother, but I think I can spare some time to see what you're screwing up now."

Cliff snarled, almost ready to explode. At the last second he pulled himself together and sent Dillon an exasperated look of shared male insight, as if to say, *Women.* Virginia stiffened. Fighting Cliff had become a way of life, both in business and in her personal pride. "You do remember, don't you, Cliff, that any decisions have to go through me first?"

"How could I forget with you forever shoving it in my face?"

"So?" She waited, and finally he turned a sheath of papers toward her.

She studied the new property sheets for a moment before commenting. "The Eastland project." She ignored Cliff's surprise. He should know by now that there was no facet of the business she wasn't fully aware of. The company was her life, the only thing she was truly good at. She wouldn't let anything slip by her.

She approved the idea of expansion by purchasing the retail property in Eastland. Once the new expressway was built, the mall would flourish. Time and invested money were all they needed, and Johnson's Sporting Goods had both. Their expansion would add new life to the floundering area, drawing in other retailers.

"Actually, it looks good. Send some copies to my office today and I'll let you know later exactly what I think."

Through gritted teeth, Cliff told her, "Everything has been worked out. The security upgrades have even been tested and approved. I planned to work out a deal today."

"No. Not until I've had more time to study the cost sheets. There's no rush. It takes time to—"

Cliff shoved back his chair and stood. Startled, Virginia glanced up. He was practically seething, his hands curled into fists at his sides.

"There'll come a point, Virginia, when you push me too

far!" He turned to Dillon and barked, "Be upstairs in the conference room in ten minutes."

He stormed out and Virginia was left there with her mouth hanging open and an uncomfortable silence disturbing the air. It wasn't like Cliff to put on such a display in front of employees.

Without really wanting to, she looked over at Dillon. He hadn't moved. He seemed unperturbed by Cliff's overreaction, but his dark eyes were cryptic. She tried a shaky smile. For some stupid reason she felt defensive. Having the world know her own brother reviled her had the same effect as being nicknamed "Chubby" in grade school.

"Well, I certainly pushed the wrong buttons this morning, didn't I?" she said, relying on flippancy to save her pride.

Dillon narrowed his eyes. "Or the right ones."

"What does that mean?"

"Why do you deliberately provoke him, Virginia?"

She pushed away from the desk and started for the door. Discussing family business with employees—regardless of how gorgeous they might be—wasn't done. Still, she couldn't resist one righteous parting shot. "I have as much right to know what's going on in this company as he does. Or more so!" When she turned, Dillon was right behind her. She gasped, took a step back and hit the door. She hadn't even heard him move.

He took another step closer, looming over her. His fingers touched her chin; his dark gaze touched everywhere else. In a rumble, he whispered, "There are gentler ways for a woman to get what she wants. Especially from her own brother."

For one instant she felt frozen by his touch. Her stomach curled and her nipples tightened into sensitive peaks. Then she shook her head. "So I should play meek and mild just to placate Cliff? I don't have a meek or mild bone in my body. I thought you understood that, Dillon."

He didn't smile. "Are you going to make time for me this weekend, Virginia?"

"Are you being pushy?" she asked automatically, still stinging from her brother's remarks.

To her disappointment, he backed down, both physically and mentally. For a single heartbeat, he looked frustrated, almost angry, but he took a safe step away from her and shook his head. "No, of course not. I'm just...anxious."

If he was really anxious, he'd insist she make a decision, she thought. But then, it wasn't fair of her to try to force her own dominant spirit on him. She went on tiptoe to kiss his chin. "I need to be here Friday for a meeting, but I can take off Thursday."

His gaze heated. "What time?"

"Whenever you like. You tell me."

Without hesitation, he said, "Early. We could spend the entire day together. The waiting is just about killing me."

After her brother's crack about her weight, Dillon's obvious desire was a welcome balm. She pressed closer to him for a kiss and felt his large hand cup her backside, gently squeezing. With her brother's comment still lingering fresh in her mind, she was uncomfortable with the touch and stepped away. His gaze searched her face, questioning, and she tried not to blush.

Other men who had come on to her had been discreet with their touches, never venturing so boldly in broad daylight as Dillon seemed prepared to do. In thirty years, she'd had two lovers, and they'd both made it a practice to have sex in the dark and under the covers, which suited her just fine. The entire experience had always been rather nice. Safe and predictable and uncomplicated. The sex itself hadn't been spectacular, but the sharing, the holding and touching had comforted her in a way nothing else could.

She hoped Dillon wouldn't prove too difficult about the arrangement. Surely he'd be satisfied with proper bedroom convention.

"This isn't exactly the best place, is it, Dillon?"

At first he didn't answer and her heart raced in both dread and anticipation. He shook his head. "No, it isn't. I'm sorry."

Virginia sighed. "Since I know you're worried about appearances, we'll meet in the mall parking lot by my home. That way no one will see us leaving."

"Can you be ready at six?"

"*That* early?"

His tone dropped to a husky rumble. "It'll give us more time together."

"All right, then." She smiled. "Where did you want to go?"

Dillon hesitated, then touched her cheek again. "Why don't you let me take care of that. It'll be a surprise."

"Hmm. A secret?"

He nodded. "What did you need to see Cliff about?"

She stared into his eyes, amazed by the mixed messages there. Hunger, but also…regret?

"Virginia?"

"What?"

He laughed, a low, rough sound that made her belly tingle. "You rushed in here to see Cliff, but got sidetracked. Was it important?"

"Oh." She paused. "Oh! Damn it, I needed to talk to him. Something's wrong with my car. I wanted to use his."

"That's not a problem." He dug in his pocket and pulled out a large key ring, then unhooked one gold key. "Here. You can use the company car. I left it in the garage, lower level, personnel entrance. But what's wrong with yours? Maybe I can help you with it."

"I'm not sure." Virginia accepted the key, feeling awkward with Dillon's concern. She wasn't used to anyone asking after her in such a solicitous way. For as long as she could remember, she'd taken care of herself. "Something's wrong with the brakes. I started out of the parking lot, then remembered some papers I needed on my desk. When I went to put on the brakes, they felt sluggish at first, not really catching, and when I pumped them, the pedal went all the way to the floor. I ran into a guardrail." She scowled, thinking of the damage that had been done to her bumper. "It's lucky I found out they weren't working before I tried to leave the garage. You know how the exit ramp slopes down right into the main road."

"And into heavy traffic," he added in an ominous whisper. Dillon's brows were lowered and a muscle ticked in his jaw. Suddenly, his arms surrounded her and he gave her a tight squeeze. With his mouth against her neck, he murmured, "You could have been killed."

Pushing herself away from his hard chest, Virginia laughed, trying to make light of his reaction. "Nonsense! It wasn't all that dramatic or life threatening, I promise. I'd barely gone three feet before I found out they weren't working. But I do intend to give my serviceman a piece of my mind. I had my oil changed not two weeks ago and he told me he'd topped off all the fluids."

Dillon bent to press his forehead to hers. "I'll take a look at it. You…might have had some damage to the brake lines."

Virginia shook her head. "Dillon, looking after my car isn't part of your job and not at all a necessary part of our relationship. Besides, I already called the tow truck. I can take care of myself, you know."

He looked as if he wanted to argue, but held his tongue. In this instance, Virginia appreciated his restraint. She liked her independence and wanted no infringements on it. She smiled her approval. "You know, it's too bad I have to check in here Friday morning." She smoothed her open palm over his wide chest and sighed. "I think I'd like a lot more time with you, truth be told."

His slight frown and the darkening of his eyes were confusing. He reached around her and opened the door, suddenly in a hurry to leave. On his way out, he muttered gruffly, "Save your wishes for something important, honey. You never know when you might need them."

She wondered what he meant, or if he'd meant anything at all. Dillon was an elusive man and most times she wasn't at all sure how to take him. But she did feel certain about one thing. She would definitely enjoy her fling with him.

"DON'T EVER SPEAK to me like a lackey again."

Cliff whirled around and stared. Dillon closed the door quietly behind him and stalked forward. He knew he wasn't precisely angry at Cliff, at least not over anything new. But he made a fine target. And right now, Dillon needed an outlet.

He hadn't reached Virginia's car before it was taken away, but he'd still had his suspicions confirmed. Someone had cut her brake lines. Reddish brake fluid made a large puddle where her car had been parked. This was no mere leak.

Cliff backed up two steps before he caught himself. "What are you talking about?"

Dillon flattened his palms on the highly polished table and leaned toward Cliff. "Don't give me orders. If you want to meet with me, say so, but don't get pissed off at your sister and then bark at me."

Cliff tried a show of umbrage. "Now, see here…"

"I'm a damn good employee, Cliff. I've upgraded your entire security system and saved you a bundle in the process. I've found glitches most men would never have noticed. That's my job and I do it well. But I don't need this job and I don't need to be talked down to. Understand?"

Dillon was pushing it, but Cliff seemed to gain more respect for him every time he asserted himself. Unlike Virginia. It made sense to Dillon. He'd be damned if he'd want some marshmallow in charge of protecting the interests of his company. Not only was Dillon in charge of securing the actual property against theft, both at the offices where Cliff and Virginia worked and at the retail outlets, but he evaluated the security potential and estimated costs of future retail sites. He also oversaw the personal security for employees, including the boss. Johnson's Sporting Goods wasn't a nickle and dime operation.

Dillon recognized his value to the Johnsons. He'd learned his trade from the best. His father had taught him how to secure, and how to breach, the legal and the illegal, which made him unique, and one of the best in the business.

Cliff needed him, especially with Virginia constantly breathing down his neck.

Besides, now that he believed Virginia was being threatened, he wasn't quite up to maintaining his pretense with Cliff. Virginia had finally agreed to some intimate time alone with him, and it was entirely possible he'd be able to settle things just by getting a few good leads from her. Surely Virginia would know what trumped-up evidence Cliff had manufactured. If she would talk.

God, he hoped it would work out that simply. He hated playing the dutiful employee. He preferred working for himself, hiring himself out on short-term jobs, spending his free time in Mexico with his father and his horses and his land.

Dillon figured that once he established a relationship with Virginia, he could quit the company. Virginia would undoubtedly find him more appealing as a free agent; there would be no reason for her to think she was being used.

Dillon shook his head. He didn't like the warmth that swelled over him when he considered pleasing her. It didn't matter what Virginia thought or would think. If her bright golden eyes were angry or aroused. None of it mattered. None of it *could* matter.

A heartfelt sigh from Cliff broke into Dillon's thoughts.

"You're right," Cliff said. "I do value you as an employee. It's just that Virginia can be so damn arrogant, and I've got enough on my mind right now without her harassment."

Very slowly, Dillon straightened. "Oh? Anything I can help with?" Little by little, Cliff opened up to him, making him a confidant, wanting him for a cohort in his grievances against his sister.

Cliff waved dismissively. "It's a matter that came up before you were hired. I have people already on the problem."

"What exactly is the problem?"

"A little matter of internal embezzlement. A former employee used his position to siphon funds from the company. The theft occurred mostly in insubstantial amounts, so it was hard to notice. I knew it was him, and I fired him on the spot, but of course I can't accuse him officially without solid evidence. Finding proof is taking some doing. You know how difficult it can be to trace numbers. However, I believe we finally have him nailed. We should be able to wrap things up any day now."

"What kind of evidence do you have?" Keeping his tone so mild, so bland, was more than difficult when he wanted to grab Cliff and slam his fist in his mouth. He wanted to force him to admit it was all a scam. Wade couldn't be guilty.

Except...Cliff didn't look as though he was scamming. He looked smugly confident. It shook Dillon.

"My lawyers have advised me not to discuss the case.

Suffice it to say, when we go to court, we won't lose." He pushed a button on the intercom, then requested that Laura bring in coffee. Cliff stacked some files and turned to face Dillon. "The others will be joining me soon, but I wanted to talk with you for a minute or two first. Virginia interrupted us downstairs. But now is as good a time as any."

This was curious. Dillon considered telling Cliff why Virginia had interrupted, about the cut brake lines, but decided against it. Cliff could be the very one who had tampered with Virginia's car. At the moment, he wasn't willing to put family loyalty to the test, especially not in Cliff's case.

Dillon hid his thoughts well as he gave Cliff his attention. "I didn't realize we were having a meeting. Is your sister invited to this one?"

"Hell no." Cliff chuckled. "I try to keep her as much out of the way as possible. You've seen firsthand how offensive she can be. No, the meeting is about expanding the downtown operation."

Not again, Dillon thought, tired of that tune and trying to explain to an idiot that opening an outlet downtown was a waste of funds. Unless the entire area was revamped, Cliff would be better off withdrawing and investing his money on renovations elsewhere. Though Virginia had told Cliff that countless times, it didn't take someone with her business sense to see it. Dillon had backed up her reasoning, on a security level. Cliff wasn't listening.

"You know how I feel about that, Cliff. I can upgrade all the systems there, hire good people to work in shifts, but it won't do you any good. Even without the petty theft, which is rampant and you know it, that store is a money hog. There's not enough business to warrant the effort."

Cliff gestured with his hand, looking distracted and annoyed. "That's not what I want to speak to you about. No, I want to talk to you about my sister."

Dillon turned his back to look out the third-story windows. Below him was human congestion, smog and noise. The sides of the street were piled high with blackened snow and sludge. Traffic flowed, the same traffic Virginia had almost encountered, without brakes. He shuddered.

He hated being here in Delaport City on this ridiculous ruse. He wanted to be home again, listening to his father grumbling and recounting all his old adventures. This didn't feel like an adventure. This felt like one huge mistake. "You want to talk about your sister? What about her?"

"I, ah, know from your file that your expertise includes surveillance."

"My *expertise* covers a lot of activities that aren't exactly part of a legitimate job résumé, especially not for the position you hired me for. I only gave you a few facts because I figured you'd need something to recommend me." The information was accurate, just in case Cliff had the sense to look, which Dillon wasn't certain of. But Virginia would have checked, of that he had no doubt. So he'd supplied the names of the few companies he'd ever worked for. Like his father, he could ferret out trouble—or cause it. With equal success, according to who was paying the most. It wasn't a trait he felt any particular pride over. Just a way of survival.

"Virginia insisted on checking into your employment background. She was impressed, which says a lot, even though your lack of consistency with any one job concerned her. Has she ever spoken to you about it?"

Dillon still faced the window. He was afraid if he looked at Cliff, all his anger would show. "No. Other than a few casual exchanges, we've never spoken."

"Excellent! Then she'll never suspect you."

"Suspect me of what?" He did turn to Cliff now. "What is it you want me to do?"

"I want you to spy on her, of course. She's up to something, seeing someone. God only knows what that woman's capable of."

Dillon grunted. He knew she was capable of making grown men cower, of scaring off any advances, of isolating herself completely with her sharp tongue and smothering arrogance. She was also capable of making him burn red-hot.

Was she capable of making an enemy who would wish her harm?

Dillon shook his head, feeling his tension simmer once again. "What do you mean, she's seeing someone?"

"The other night at the party, I caught her sneaking back into the kitchen."

With a dry look, Dillon said, "I can't imagine Virginia *sneaking* anywhere. It's not in her nature."

"No, you're right. She strutted back into the house, bold as you please, when she'd been out there conspiring with someone against me."

Dillon pulled out a chair and straddled it. Cliff's stupidity

TAKEN! 51

never ceased to amaze him. "Conspiring? How do you know she wasn't with a lover?"

He grinned. "That's exactly what she said! How about that—you two share a similar sense of humor."

Dillon heard a noise and looked up. Laura Neil stood in the doorway, holding a tray with fresh coffee and two mugs. Dillon wondered how long she'd been standing there, but then decided it didn't matter. He was more interested in the way the woman watched Cliff, sheer adoration clouding her eyes.

Cliff nodded to her and she entered. She leaned close to him while she poured the coffee, and asked if they needed anything else. Every so often, her gaze darted to Dillon. He almost felt sorry for her. It was obvious she was infatuated with Cliff, and just as obvious that Cliff had used his position to take advantage of her. To Dillon's mind, it was one more reason to despise Virginia's brother.

Cliff dismissed Laura. Dillon sipped from his cup, waiting. He knew his silence would annoy Cliff, so therefore his patience was its own reward.

After only a few seconds, Cliff exploded. "Well? What do you say?"

Dillon glanced at him over his mug. "To what? You haven't asked me anything yet."

"Oh, for... Will you check into it? Find out what Virginia is up to and who she's involved with?"

"What's in it for me?"

"A five-hundred-dollar bonus. Twice that if you come up with something concrete."

The irony of it amused Dillon—that Cliff would be paying

Dillon to spy on himself. But the little bastard was also spying on his sister, and Dillon's suspicions were growing. He didn't trust Cliff, not at all.

Dillon let Cliff wait while he pretended to think things over. Of course he'd agree to do it. It made perfect sense. If *he* was checking into things, Cliff wouldn't be hiring someone else who would get in his way.

Dragging out the inevitable, and hoping for any tidbit of information that might help him, Dillon asked, "Any clues at all who it might be? Any leads?"

"Just the obvious. The guy must be someone who could benefit Virginia in some way, someone in the company who might be able to sway votes."

From what he'd heard, Virginia always won every vote, so that theory didn't make sense. He refrained from pointing that out to Cliff. "Anything else?"

Cliff shrugged. "The guy's most likely passive, ineffectual, a spineless sort. You know how Virginia is. She'd never be able to get a man like you to put up with her carping and demands for some scheme of hers. And Virginia insists on complete obedience. She wouldn't accept any defiance."

Dillon couldn't help himself; he grinned. "So I'm looking for a wimp?" The description was apt.

"Yes, but a wimp with connections. Someone who could do her some good."

"But you're a hundred percent positive she's not involved in a personal relationship she just doesn't want you to know about?"

Cliff was already shaking his head. "Not Virginia. Men are

interested in her for one reason—to use her. And I'd want to know about that, too. Even though she's sworn she'll never marry, I have to protect her from those sorts. She's too abrasive and too overweight to attract anyone with genuine feelings. She'd only end up hurt, or hurting the company."

Abruptly, Dillon came to his feet. One more second with the loving brother and he'd throw him out the damn window. "I'll check into things." He crossed to the door, then turned back. "By the way, Virginia had some brake trouble today." He watched Cliff closely, waiting.

"Oh?"

"She's all right, but her car's out of commission for a while. I gave her the company car to use."

Cliff waved a hand, already distracted, as he gathered together the notes for his meeting. "That's fine."

Dillon clenched his jaw. He hadn't been asking for permission, but rather watching for a reaction. He didn't get one.

He jerked the door open and started out, saying over his shoulder, "I'm taking the rest of the day off. I'll be in touch later."

Cliff didn't argue. He couldn't have anyway. Dillon had already slammed the door.

chapter 4

VIRGINIA HAD JUST hung up the phone when the rap sounded on her office door. She glanced up, frustrated by the way her day had gone. First the problems with her car, then her run-in with Cliff. And her meeting hadn't gone at all well. Today was not her day, and she was tired. A hot bath and a long night's sleep seemed just the cure.

"Come in."

Dillon stuck his head in the door. "You about ready to head home?"

As always, one glance into those sinfully dark eyes turned her insides warm and jittery. With every minute that passed, she anticipated her day alone with him more. "Mmm. I was just about to call a cab. What's up?"

She didn't particularly relish the idea of doing any more business tonight, but for Dillon, she'd make an exception. Spending time with him was seldom a hardship.

He stepped into her office and closed the door behind him. His features were etched in a frown. Virginia sighed, knowing why he'd come by. "If you're here to tell me about Cliff's plans to rework the downtown office, I've heard all about it."

Dillon stiffened. "It's not my job to tattle on your damn brother."

She lifted a brow at his tone as well as his words. "No? Your loyalty to a prospective lover doesn't go quite that far?" Virginia knew she was taunting him, but damn it, her day had been rotten, and just once, she wanted to see Dillon lose his temper, cut loose and prove to her what a powerful man he could be. But instead, he merely narrowed his eyes and waited.

Virginia took pity on him. "I'm sorry. I was just about to head home and I'm a little out of sorts. It hasn't been the best of days."

"That's why I'm here," he said. "To offer you a ride."

"Chauffeuring is part of your job description?"

"Why not?" He stepped closer, his expression inscrutable. "I'm in charge of security. It's my responsibility to see that you make it home safely."

She couldn't help but smile. "That's stretching it, Dillon."

"Not so." He looked at her intently, his gaze unwavering. "I think your brake lines might have been tampered with."

She waited for the punch line, and when it didn't come she got to her feet and crossed to the closet to retrieve her coat. Before she could slip it on, Dillon was behind her, holding her shoulders. "I'm serious, Virginia."

"That's ridiculous." She turned to face him. "So some vandal picked our parking lot to play around in. We'll just increase security."

"That's just it." He raised his hand to her cheek and

stroked it. "Maybe it wasn't a vandal. Maybe whoever did it targeted your car."

"So now I have an enemy?" She could see he was serious, but she couldn't feel the same way. It was entirely too far-fetched. "You've been working too hard, Dillon. I think you need a day off more than I do."

His jaw tightened and his hands slipped to her shoulders again. After a deep calming breath, he said, "All right, then just humor me, okay? Let me drive you home tonight."

"I'm a big girl, Dillon, all grown-up. I don't need a caretaker."

He smiled, a beautiful smile that made her toes curl. He kissed her and she forgot they were standing in the middle of her office and someone could walk in at any moment.

He pulled back only far enough to speak, but his breath was warm on her lips, his tone husky. "You don't have to convince me of that, honey. I know it all too well." He kissed her again, a quick, hard kiss, then stepped back. "What did your mechanic say?"

Virginia had trouble bringing herself back under control. Lord love him, the man was a temptation, and she was quickly growing tired of resisting him. She stared up at him and tried to find her aplomb.

"I haven't talked with my mechanic yet. He won't have a chance to look at the car until tomorrow."

"Then will you please—for my sake—be extra cautious until then?"

She thought about denying him, if for no other reason than reasserting her independence. She'd always had to fight so hard to prove herself, she sometimes didn't know when to quit fighting. But truth be told, she loved the idea of him taking her home. Maybe he'd come inside, maybe he'd stop being so skittish about appearances and make love to her this very night. The mere thought caused her body to heat. "All right."

Dillon stared down at her a moment longer before he nodded. He held her coat while she slipped into it, then led her out the door.

DILLON DIDN'T WANT to explore his satisfaction too deeply. Having Virginia accede to his wishes made him feel like a conqueror. It hadn't happened often, and he had a feeling it wouldn't happen again any time soon. Virginia wasn't a woman to let a man call the shots. Right now, she was quiet. Too quiet. And he wondered if maybe she was regretting her small show of weakness. He didn't consider caution a weakness, but he knew she would.

"Turn left up here."

Startled out of his thoughts, Dillon reminded himself that he wasn't supposed to know where she lived. He had to keep his mind on what he was doing, rather than trying to dissect Virginia's psyche. He'd already discovered many times over what a futile and frustrating effort that could be. He just couldn't seem to help himself; she fascinated him.

For the rest of the ride, he waited for her directions, even though he knew the way. Before getting hired on at Johnson's Sporting Goods, he'd done a complete check on her.

When they pulled into her driveway, Virginia started to

open her door. Dillon ignored that and walked around to her side of the car. She stood there, embraced by selective moonlight, on this dark, cloudy night. Her head was tilted back as she stared up at him, her eyes wide, and he wanted her.

He hated himself for it, but he wanted her. The iron control he'd always depended on seemed to evaporate where this woman was concerned, and it didn't make sense. He didn't even like her.

"Do you want to come in for a while?"

He hesitated. It didn't take a genius to see the direction of her thoughts and, seeing that, he become instantly, painfully, hard. But making love to Virginia, especially now, wasn't a wise thing to contemplate. He racked his brain for any excuse that would be believable, but before he could speak, a shadow caught his eye and he jerked toward the house. He could have sworn he saw a curtain move.

He shoved Virginia behind him as he stepped deeper into the shadows. "Do you have any pets, honey?"

"No. Dillon what are you—"

"Shh. Someone's in your house." His senses rioted, telling him all he needed to know.

"What?"

"Give me your key."

Thankfully, Virginia complied, but when he told her to get into his car and lock the doors, she refused. As he inched closer to the house, she followed, leaving him no choice but to stop. "Damn it, Virginia." His whispered voice was guttural, his temper on the edge. He grasped her shoulders. "You can't—"

"It's my house. I know my way around a lot better than you do."

He shook her. He hadn't meant to, but she was so obstinate, so annoying, he couldn't help himself. "This isn't a game, damn it! For once, will you—"

They both heard the back door slam, the sound carried easily on the cold, quiet night. Dillon squeezed her shoulders hard. "Stay put!"

He took off at a run. Even before he reached the backyard, he knew the chase was useless. Woods bordered her property on two sides, and he had no doubt the intruder would have long vanished into the black shadows. He cursed, then cursed again when Virginia touched his arm and he almost threw her to the ground in reaction. In the split second before he touched her, he realized who she was.

Without a word, knowing she wouldn't follow an order even if her life depended on it, he dragged her up the back steps and into the house, keeping to the side so he wouldn't destroy any footprints that might have been left behind. His temper was on the ragged edge, the ruthless aspects of his personality ruling him.

He found two light switches just inside the door. One illuminated the kitchen with blinding fluorescent light and the other flooded the backyard. Dillon scanned the yard, but there wasn't a single movement caught in the glare.

"Call the police," he whispered.

She answered in kind. "Why? Whoever it was is long gone now."

"Unless there was more than one guy. Just do it."

She bristled, but he didn't have time to cajole her. He waited only until he saw her lift the receiver, then cautiously made his way down the hall, turning on lights as he went. Quickly, methodically, he went through the downstairs rooms, then trotted silently up the carpeted stairway to the upper level. He had explored all the rooms before Virginia finished making the call.

"Dillon?"

"It's okay." He answered from her bedroom, the last room he'd found. Virginia joined him there.

She glanced around, looking uncomfortable. "The police are on their way. They said to stay in the kitchen, not to try to be a hero."

He grunted. "This is what I'm trained to do, Virginia."

"To be a hero?"

He knew she was teasing. He could see it her golden eyes, shining now from the excitement. He shook his head. "Your bedroom is a surprise."

That small observation removed the smile from her lips. She stiffened and drew her auburn brows together. "What's that supposed to mean?"

He left the room, Virginia hot on his heels. With a deliberate shrug, he said, "It's a little more feminine than I had expected, that's all. I mean, I hadn't pictured you having ruffled pillow shams or lace curtains."

She apparently didn't know what to say to that, so Dillon changed the subject. "How about some coffee?" He approached the back door, examining it closely. "I'm sure the cops would appreciate it on a cold night like this."

He'd no sooner said the words than the sirens could be heard. Sure enough, the police were more than willing to swill coffee as they gave the house another examination. To everyone's surprise except maybe Dillon's, nothing seemed to be missing.

Still, the police wrote up the incident as a simple break and enter.

One young officer held his hat in one hand while cradling his coffee in the other. "With a house like yours, in this neighborhood, a burglar would be in heaven."

Another policeman confirmed what Dillon already knew. "They came in through the kitchen door."

"But how?" Virginia didn't seem unsettled by the whole affair—she seemed furious. "My doors are always locked."

"They picked the lock somehow." The cop shrugged. "Leave your floodlights on tonight. In fact, you should get a timer to turn them on as soon as it gets dark. And put in an alarm system, as well. A woman living here alone—"

Disgusted, Dillon interrupted. "I'll see to it tomorrow."

Virginia frowned at him, but kept her peace. Dillon's position, his reason for being with her, had already been explained. Since then the cops had been giving him a wide berth.

The policeman nodded. "Yeah, well, we'll patrol through the neighborhood the rest of the night, ma'am. You should be safe enough. Very seldom does a perpetrator return once he knows he's been discovered."

Dillon didn't agree, and he told Virginia so as soon as the officers had left. "You shouldn't stay here."

"Now, don't start, Dillon. I'm tired and I want to go to bed. I'm not about to start uprooting myself tonight."

He paced, trying to think while she glared at him, looking her most imperious. "What is the matter with you? You've been entirely too high-handed this evening and I've about had enough!"

He should have known she'd get her back up and make this more difficult than it had to be. "Virginia, has it escaped your notice that you've been threatened twice in the same day?"

She rolled her eyes. "I've had car trouble and a simple break-in. That's doesn't exactly add up to a life-or-death situation."

He clenched his fists tight, fighting for control. It seemed he fought that particular battle more since meeting Virginia than he ever had in his entire life. "How do you think the guy got inside?"

She shrugged. "He picked the lock."

"There's no evidence of a forced entry. What if he had a key?"

Her eyes widened and she took a step back. "What exactly are you saying, Dillon? You think someone I know is trying to hurt me? Who?"

He should probably have admitted his suspicions that he thought Cliff might very well be the one harassing her. But something held him back. Despite all her bravado, all her indignation and affronted pride, she was still a woman, soft and vulnerable. From what he knew of her, Virginia had never had an easy life, and she'd never had anyone to love her. To find out now just how big a scoundrel her brother could be might well devastate her. He couldn't bear that.

To his shame, though, he had another reason for hesitating. The possibility that if he forced the issue, she might blame Wade for threatening her. To Virginia, Wade would be a much more likely suspect. Her brother had accused him of embezzlement, and he'd been fired. Didn't that give Wade motive enough, in her mind, to want revenge? If he convinced her the threats were real, would it backfire on Wade?

Wade could end up being accused not only as an embezzler, but an assailant as well. And then, if Virginia thought Wade was guilty, she would let her guard down. The real assailant would have a clear field. It was too risky. And if Virginia got hurt because he was preoccupied with his brother...

Impulsively, he put his arms around her and pulled her close in a careful hug. She resisted, holding herself stiff in his arms until he said, "I'm sorry. I know I've been on edge tonight. But Virginia, at least give me the right to worry about you a little, okay?"

She smiled up at him. "If you insist. But it isn't necessary. I'll be careful. I'm not an idiot."

"I know." He kissed her and didn't want to stop kissing her. Her lips were warm and soft and she tempted him. He opened his mouth over hers, gently moving, savoring her taste. She made a small sound deep in her throat when his tongue licked over her bottom lip.

Cursing inwardly, Dillon set her away from him and reached for his coat. "Will you be all right tonight?"

He could tell by her expression that she wanted to ask him to stay; pride would keep her from it, though. And this time, he was glad. In less than twenty-four hours, everything had changed. His plans thrown into turmoil, he had to adapt. False accusations of embezzlement were no longer the only issue, and took a back seat to Virginia's safety. This new threat was much more tangible, much more immediate.

He felt responsible for Virginia, whether she liked it or not, and he'd do his best to protect her, even while helping his brother. If he had to be ruthless to accomplish both goals, so be it. In all fairness, he gave her one last chance to do things the easy way. "Why don't you take a vacation? Disappear for a while until things calm down?"

"What things? You really are overreacting."

His hands fisted at his sides. "This wasn't a simple break-in, Virginia."

"Of course it was—"

"Nothing was taken, damn it! How do you explain that?"

She shrugged. "It's like the police said. We probably interrupted the burglar."

He grabbed her arms, his patience at an end. "What if you'd walked in here alone? What if I hadn't been with you? Do you think whoever it was would have run?"

She stared at him blankly, her lips parted in surprise at his vehemence. With an effort, he eased his tone.

"This is what I do, honey. I know what I'm talking about. To be safe, you should get out of here for a while. Go to a motel. I'll join you Thursday, just as we planned."

She rubbed his shoulder as if to soothe him. "I have responsibilities here, Dillon. And the police really don't seem to think there's anything to be alarmed about."

Dillon drew a deep breath and released her. "Surely the company can survive without you for a few days." Without having to worry about her being threatened and with free run of her office, he could not only get the information he needed to absolve Wade, but most likely nail the bastard who was harassing her as well. All he needed was a little time.

She began loading empty coffee cups into the dishwasher, and when she glanced at him, a gentleness had entered her eyes. "I like you, Dillon, and I want to spend time with you. But one long afternoon will have to be enough for now. Don't ask for more. My first priority will always be running the company—you know that."

Only, it wasn't her company, it was Cliff's. And Dillon had a feeling Cliff had gotten tired of sharing it with her.

Her stubbornness knew no bounds; she wouldn't relent. He closed his eyes a moment, accepting the inevitable, knowing what had to be done, knowing his options had just become severely limited. From the moment he'd involved himself in this mess, he'd felt equal parts protective and possessive of her. He wouldn't let anyone hurt her. He'd protect her despite herself. Never mind that she'd probably despise him for it. Her hate had been guaranteed from the first.

He had one more day, Wednesday, to watch over her, while at the same time rearranging his plans and making new ones. He had a lot to accomplish in the time left to him, including the installation of an alarm system at her house that would put a stop to intruders.

He sighed as the ramifications of his new plan sank in. Virginia would miss her meeting on Friday after all. But at least she'd be safe.

chapter 5

DILLON HEARD the ringing as if from far away. It pierced his subconsciousness, but wasn't enough to get him out of the dream. And he knew he was dreaming, knew it wasn't real, but he couldn't force himself awake.

The cell was dark and cold, and in his dream he accepted that he would spend many years there, yet strangely enough, that wasn't what bothered him most. No, it was Virginia, standing outside his cell, round with a late pregnancy. His child. He broke out in a sweat. Cliff was pointing and laughing from the background, and Virginia's eyes looked wounded—and accusing.

The ringing became more insistent, sounding like a small scream, and he jerked awake. His heart thundered and all his muscles felt too tight, straining. He had an erection.

Unbelievable. He ran a hand over his face, drew several deep breaths. His stomach slowly began to unknot.

The covers were tangled about his legs and he felt like he'd been in a furnace he was so hot. The dream, and his reaction to it, made no sense, and even if in some twisted way it did, he shied away from probing the reasons. He didn't want to know what it meant, didn't want to dwell on the strange things Virginia made him feel. Kelsey was the one who was pregnant, and Dillon planned to do only what he had to do. He would save his brother, protect Virginia, but he wouldn't touch her. So there was no chance of the dream coming true.

Still, he felt a drip of sweat slide down his brow.

The bedside alarm continued its shrill call, and feeling drugged, Dillon reached for it. He glanced at the face of the clock. It wasn't quite five a.m. and he had to meet Virginia at six. Today was the day.

His heart still thundered from the dream—which hadn't been a dream at all but rather a damned nightmare. Dillon ran a hand through his hair, shoving it away from his face.

Peddling his legs, he kicked the blankets to the end of the bed and let the cold winter morning air wash over his naked body. The sweat dried quickly and he chilled as he considered what was on his agenda.

He was going to kidnap Virginia Johnson.

Ever since the break-in he'd tried to think of another way to do things, another way to protect her *and* his brother. But he'd come up blank, without a single alternative. She refused to take the time away from the office, refused to listen to reason or take extra precautions. He'd come up with only one solution.

And his stomach had been in knots ever since.

Anyone who'd met Virginia for more than two minutes would know how she'd react to being held prisoner.

Everything in her would rebel. Hell, he'd had to fight her tooth and nail just to get the alarm installed at her home yesterday. He'd hired the very best agency, interviewed them himself, selected the alarm. Virginia had been outraged, only grudgingly giving over to his greater experience. Dillon had made sure the system was installed that very day, in case she changed her mind.

Virginia, on the best of days, was hard-nosed and contrary and independent to a fault. She wouldn't be an easy victim, and in the normal scheme of things, with a real kidnapping, her sarcasm and sharp tongue could get her hurt. Not that he would ever hurt her. He didn't hurt women, and the very idea of harming Virginia made him ache. She'd been hurt more than enough over her lifetime.

Poor Virginia. A brother who ridiculed her to employees and a spoiled little sister who thought only of herself. No wonder she'd become such a tough woman. She'd had to to survive the jackals, the people who would use her without regret.

And now he would be no better.

All his life he'd thought there were only two kinds of families. The type he and his father had, that existed on guts and strength and commitment. Their lives centered on survival, and they watched each other's backs, because they only had each other. Their bonds ran deep with the bare bones of necessity.

Then there was the other kind, the one filled with love and tenderness. Children playing, dogs barking, barbecues in the backyard and family outings to the amusement park.

Now he realized there were many kinds, because Virginia didn't fit into either group. She was as strong as an iron spike, but she didn't have the respect and dedication from her family that same trait would have earned for a man.

Neither did she have the love or tenderness. Maybe none of that even existed. Maybe it was just something he'd conjured in his brain when things had been hard and he'd foolishly tried to imagine the life he would have had with a mother. He was damn lucky his father had stuck by him, lucky the man had seen fit to teach him how to get by in the world.

Dillon glanced at the clock again. In one hour he'd be picking up Virginia. She would be expecting a day full of intimacy. He was going to give her the fright of her life. More than anything, he'd like to simply walk away, to forget Virginia and her damn dysfunctional family. The ridiculous dream that couldn't mean anything, no matter how it made his guts churn, was just that, a dream. He didn't, *wouldn't*, care for her, but for some damn reason, he wanted her. And he wanted to protect her. Chemistry, unaccountable and indisputable.

It wouldn't be easy, not with the complications growing every day, but he'd manage. Once Virginia was safely stowed away, he could concentrate on Wade.

He wondered if Cliff was using Virginia's distraction with the embezzlement to try to hurt her, to drive her away from the company. He hadn't heard Virginia mention the embezzlement, so she might not even be aware of Cliff's treachery. Or maybe she had gotten too close to discovering her brother's underhanded tactics. Virginia took her obligations to the company very seriously; she wouldn't put up with falsifying evidence. Was Cliff afraid of her finding out?

Either way, Dillon knew in his guts that Virginia was threatened. And he knew Cliff would be closing in on Wade very soon now. They couldn't have much time left. He had to get into the files and find the real embezzler before it was too late. Taking Virginia was the only option open to him, the only way to settle both problems at one time.

Virginia wouldn't like it, wouldn't understand his motives. But Wade would. He knew it had to be now or never. He had no choice. Just as his father had watched out for him, he now watched out for Wade, regardless of personal feelings or conflicts. That much, at least, he understood about family.

With cold resolution he climbed from the bed and headed for the shower.

VIRGINIA COULDN'T HELP but be excited. She'd arrived at the parking lot fifteen minutes early. It was dark and cold and everything was covered in ice. The world sparkled beneath street lamps and moonlight, looking new and clean and magical.

Headlights curved into the lot and then blinded her as they slowly crept her way. Her heartbeat picked up rhythm, and she closed her eyes, trying to calm herself. Somehow, she knew Dillon wouldn't be like the other men. He wouldn't be satisfied with half measures and fumbling in the dark. The thought shook her, but in a small part of herself that she'd kept hidden for so very long, she was excited by the notion. She felt sexy.

Absurd, a woman her age, with her weight problems and

practical outlook on life, but she couldn't help it. She'd even worn sexy underclothes. A silk teddy, garters and silk hose. Instead of twisting her hair into a tight knot, she'd left it looser, more like the romantic Gibson-girl style. Little curls fell around her ears. She'd felt silly when she looked in the mirror, but she didn't redo it.

She wore a long winter-white cashmere tunic and skirt, with ankle boots of the same creamy color. Even her thick cape was a matching off-white. Her red hair was the only color. And the blush on her cheeks.

The vehicle that pulled alongside her, facing the opposite direction, wasn't the same car Dillon had kissed her in the other night. No, this was a big, mean, ugly truck. She squinted through the driver's-side window and saw Dillon step out, holding on to the truck door because of the ice. He'd parked so close only a few feet separated them. He reached out and opened her door.

"Be careful. It's like a frozen pond out here. Nothing but ice."

She put her gloved hand in his and carefully stepped out. He held her securely, protectively. For a moment she allowed it, and then she realized what she was doing, how she was being treated, and she pulled back.

All day yesterday Dillon had hovered over her. He'd fretted, much like a mother hen, and she knew it was because he was worried. The break-in, though no big deal to Virginia, had upset him. Despite his capabilities, he was a mild-mannered man in most instances, and she supposed the circumstances might be unsettling to someone without her constitution.

In a way she thought it was sweet that he'd been so concerned for her welfare. But being independent had become second nature to her. It was her greatest protective instinct. "I'm fine. Just let me open my trunk and get my bag."

"Your bag?"

Flustered, she fiddled with her car door. "You can't expect me to spend the entire day with you and not have…other stuff with me. I didn't know if we'd go out for dinner, or if you'd just want to…stay in the room." Her voice trailed off. She'd packed things to refix her hair, anticipating that it might get rather mussed, and she'd brought something sexy to wear for him when they went to bed, as well as a cocktail dress. She'd never before planned a rendezvous and wasn't certain of the protocol. But she had no intention of explaining all that to him.

"It's not important, Dillon. Just let me—"

"No. I've got it." He took her arm and, still holding on to his own door, pulled her toward his truck. "Just slide in on this side. I wouldn't want you to fall and bruise anything."

"I might fall, but you wouldn't? Does being male give you better coordination?"

In the dim light, she saw him close his eyes, saw his breath puff out in a sigh. "Virginia, if I fall, I don't care. And I can guarantee I'd be landing on a lot more solid muscle than you would."

She didn't know if that was a slur or not, but she didn't ask him to clarify because she didn't really want to know. Handing him the keys, she looked away and mumbled, "Fine. Suit yourself."

He tugged her close as she tried to slide past him. His forehead dropped to hers. "Virginia."

This close, she could see the dark sweep of his lashes, feel the warmth of his breath. He smiled. "You have an incredibly sexy ass. You know that, don't you?"

Her heart tripped with the rough compliment. He sounded sincere, and she peeked up at him. He looked sincere—and as if he was waiting for her acknowledgment of the fact. "You have a wonderful way with words."

His beautiful mouth tipped in a crooked grin, and once again his lashes swept his cheeks. "Sorry. Was my language too…colorful? I hope you won't mind. I don't know a lot of pretty words. But I do know a pretty bottom when I see one." His firm palm went to that area and gently squeezed.

She was eternally grateful for the darkness hiding her blush. As it was, he probably felt the heat from her that seemed to pulse beneath her skin. Sex talk was new to her. And the raw, spontaneous way in which Dillon spoke was far from the practiced lines she usually heard.

She tightened her lips and tried not to laugh. "Thank you."

His gaze lingered over a curl trailing past her cheek. "I like your new hairdo, too. Did you wear it this way for me?" His hand moved back to her waist.

Ironically, he didn't look at all pleased by the notion. A more sophisticated man wouldn't have asked. He would have assumed, and maybe been flattered, but he wouldn't have embarrassed the woman by mentioning it. Virginia started to reply, but Dillon interrupted her.

His eyes were narrowed, and he looked reluctant to speak,

but the words emerged anyway, low and raw. "Do you let it loose when you make love?" His gloved fingertips slid over her cheek, then over the upsweep of her hair. His gaze followed the path of his hand. "How long is it?"

Oh my. How could she possibly regain control if his every word made her mute with anticipation? Dillon lowered his head and kissed her. His fingers tightened on her skull and the kiss gradually grew more intimate until his mouth ate at hers, voracious and invading. Her fingers wrapped over his wrists, not to pull him away, but to hang on. His passion made her almost dizzy. It wasn't what she was used to. He was too unrestrained, too natural, too much man. The thought made her heart jump.

He drew back slowly, in small degrees, his tongue licking her lips, his teeth nipping. Finally, his forehead rested against hers and she felt the cool, soft sweep of his long hair over her cheek. His sigh fogged the air between them. "Get in the car. I'll throw your bag in the back and we can get out of here."

Virginia glanced into the back of the battered truck and saw that the bed was covered by a tarp. "Whose truck is this?"

"Mine. It gets better traction in the snow." He opened the trunk of her car, pulled out a small overnight case and cautiously picked his way back across the ice. He stowed the bag beneath the tarp while Virginia watched, then he carefully checked to see that her car was locked up tight. She held out her hand for her keys, but he'd already shoved them deep into his jeans pocket.

"Dillon…"

"In you go, honey." Not giving her a chance to comment

on his high-handedness, he lifted her off her feet, then un-
ceremoniously dropped her into the truck.

He slid in beside her and locked the door.

Virginia fumed. "Don't you *ever* do anything like that again!"

He didn't answer, disconcerting her with his silence. In
fact, he seemed different; the very air seemed different.
Somehow charged. He put the truck in gear and began
pulling away. She heard ice and snow crunching beneath the
tires, even over the sound of the blowing heater.

She shifted in her seat, nervousness creeping in on her
by slow degrees. Speaking her mind always helped her
overcome her fears, helped her to reassert herself, to regain
control of any situation. She'd learned that trick while still
in high school, throwing student bullies who would pick on
her about her weight into a stupor with her blunt honesty
and virulent daring. She'd employed her skill throughout
college and in the family business after her parents' deaths.
So hitting people broadside with arrogant bravado earned
their dislike? It also earned their grudging obedience. And
that had been good enough for her, because through most
of her life, she'd needed every advantage she could gain.
Cliff was the oldest and the heir; Kelsey was the baby—the
sweet, *pretty one*.

Virginia filled the distressing spot of chubby middle child.

She huffed to herself and tightened her cape around her,
regretting the brief stroll down memory's bumpy lane. Such
thoughts always brought up her defensive feelings and the
feeling of loneliness. Only, she wasn't alone now, and what
always worked for her would work at this moment.

She turned in her seat to face Dillon and prepared to blast him with a few facts of life, namely that she was still the boss and as such, due all courtesies.

"Put on your seat belt."

Of all the nerve! Her spine went rigid and her nostrils flared. "If you don't stop ordering me around, we can just forget this little escapade altogether!"

Jaw clenched, he reached for the center floorboards of the truck, where a small thermos sat in a molded plastic car caddy so it wouldn't tip and spill. Two lidded cups, already filled, were beside it.

"Here." He handed her a cup. "I thought you might like something hot to keep you comfortable on the trip. I got you out of bed so early I wasn't sure if you'd have time for coffee at home."

He glanced at her, and she knew he was judging her mood, trying to decide if he'd managed to placate her. She still felt affronted, but accepted that he was trying. And in a small way, his take-charge attitude stimulated her. In a *very* small way.

"Thank you."

He smiled, looking dramatically relieved, then he made a teasing face. "If I ask nice, will you also put on your seat belt? These roads are like a skating rink, and I don't want to take any chances with you."

She rather liked his teasing, and his concern. She smiled as she buckled her belt. "There. Happy?"

"Yes." He reached over and, fingers spread wide, put his large hand on her thigh, gripping her in a familiar way. She held her breath and her stomach flipped sweetly. She waited to see what he would do next, but he seemed preoccupied by the deserted road, almost distracted. An occasional street lamp or passing car lit the interior of the truck cab and she saw his gloved hand looking wickedly dark and sinful against the pale material of her skirt. He didn't move, didn't speak. But that heavy hand remained on her leg, and she was incredibly aware of it, of him. She wondered if that hadn't been his intention all along.

She sipped her coffee, then cleared her throat. "Would you like your cup?"

"In a little while."

"Where exactly are we going?"

He flashed her a look she couldn't read, then his gaze dropped to the cup she held. "It's a surprise." He returned his attention to the road.

She didn't want to spoil the adventure, but his strange mood put her on edge. She'd survived a long time by trusting her hunches, and right now, it felt as if things weren't aligned quite properly. She never felt like this about men, and they never acted like this around her. Always, Dillon had gone out of his way to speak with her, to turn on the charm. But now he seemed so distant, sitting there in a manner that felt very *expectant*.

Did he want something of her? Was she supposed to be doing something? If so, she didn't know what. Dillon didn't behave like other men, which was both exciting and a bit unsettling.

She continued to sip her coffee, trying to push the mingled uneasiness and anticipation away.

After a moment, they turned onto a deserted southbound expressway, heading for Kentucky. Virginia hadn't gotten enough sleep, so the silence, combined with the easy driving and the early-morning darkness made her eyelids heavy. She closed her eyes and rested her head against the seat. "Where are we going, Dillon?"

His hand left her thigh to rub softly over her cheek, then around her ear. "You look like a snow bunny, you know that?"

His words were so soft. They drifted over her like his lazily moving fingers. With considerable effort, she forced her eyes open and turned her head in his direction. "I wanted to look nice for you," she whispered, then closed her eyes again, wondering where in hell that bit of confession had come from. She held tightly to her coffee and sipped. The mug was almost empty, but that was okay; she didn't want any more. She wanted to sleep.

She heard Dillon sigh. "I'm so sorry, Virginia. Remember that, okay?"

Something wasn't making sense. He sounded pained, but somehow determined. She frowned and forced her eyes open again. Everything was blurred and it took her precious seconds to focus again. Dillon kept glancing at her curiously, his brow furrowed, his gaze intent and diamond hard.

Suddenly, she knew. Her chest tightened in panic and she stared at him. Her breath came fast. "You bastard. *You poisoned me.*"

"Not poison," he said, but his voice was strained and there was a ringing in her ears. None of it made sense, at least, in no way she wanted to contemplate. She wouldn't let the fear take her, wouldn't let him take her. Hadn't he warned her himself that someone was threatening her? But he'd been with her when the intruder had been in her house. Unless they were working together...

She narrowed her eyes on him and saw his worried frown. They were moving quickly down the expressway, too quickly. Farther and farther from home. The roads were empty, the day still dark and cold. She felt weaker by the second, and she fought it. She'd have to use her wits before they deserted her. Later, when she was safe, she'd let the hurt consume her. But not until she was safe—and alone once again.

DILLON WISHED SHE'D say something, anything, rather than stare at him in that accusing way. It reminded him of the dream and his stomach cramped. She had to be frightened, and he hated doing this to her. Nevertheless, his body was tense, prepared for whatever she might try.

"What have you done to me?"

He felt cold inside. "I drugged you, just as you assumed. It's a sleeping drug. It won't hurt you. Even now, you're getting drowsy. You might as well stop fighting it, Virginia." More than anything, he wanted her to sleep so he wouldn't have to see the disgust and mistrust in her eyes.

She shook her head as if to clear it. "Where are we?"

"Nowhere yet." He pulled off the main highway and onto a less-traveled rural route, slowing the truck accordingly. It would take longer this way, but there wasn't likely to be any traffic at all. "We've got a while to go."

Her head lolled on the back of the seat, and she looked out the windows at the scrubby trees, the endless snow. Dillon knew what she saw; no one had cleared this area, and the road was almost invisible between the trees lining it.

It had turned bitterly cold, and the wind whistled around the truck. He saw Virginia shiver and rub her eyes and a strange tenderness welled up in his chest. "Honey, don't be afraid, okay?"

"Ha! I'm fine," she managed to snap in slurred tones. She held her shoulders stiff and her hands clenched in her lap. He knew she was fighting the drug and her fear with everything she had. But it was useless.

"As soon as we get to the cabin and you're awake, I'll explain what's going on. I don't want you to worry."

"I'm thirsty," she whispered, ignoring his speech. He supposed, given the circumstances, his assurances *were* bizarre.

"Sure. Here, there's a little coffee left." She glared at him and he added, "Mine. This isn't drugged. See?" He lifted the mug to this mouth to demonstrate, and that's when she hit him.

He should have seen it coming, but he hadn't realized she still had that much strength. Her doubled fists smacked into the cup, jamming it into his mouth, cutting his lip and clipping his nose. He cursed, dropping the cup and doing his best to steer the truck safely to the side of the road. He hit the brakes and shifted gears. They spun to a rocky stop after sliding several feet.

Already, Virginia was working on her door. He'd locked it, of course, and she fumbled, crying in frustration as she tried to find the way to unlock it. He'd put a large piece of electrical tape over the lock switch, just in case.

His hands closed on her shoulders and she turned on him, twisting in the seat and kicking wildly with her small boots. She hit him in the thigh and he grunted.

Subduing her without hurting her proved damn difficult. He finally just gave up and threw his entire weight on top of her. She gasped and cried and cursed as he captured both her hands and held them over her head. His chest pressed against her breasts, his thighs pinned hers.

"Virginia, shh. Baby, it's all right."

She looked up, and stark fear darkened her blurry eyes, cutting him deeply.

"Aw, damn." He closed his eyes, trying to gather his wits. "Honey, I swear, I'm not going to hurt you. Please believe me."

"Then why?" She began to struggle again, but she was weaker now, her eyelids only half-open. He lowered his chest, forcing her to gasp for air, to go completely still.

"I promise I'll explain everything at the cabin."

"What cabin?" she cried, the words slurred and raw.

"The cabin where I'm going to keep you for just a few days, until I'm sure it's safe. Now, can I let you go?"

She stared up at him, blinking slowly, still fighting. "Your lip is bleeding. And your nose is turning blue."

"I think you might have broken it." He tried a small grin, but with his lip numb, it might not have been too effective. "You pack a hell of a punch, especially for a drugged lady."

"I don't understand you. You're not the man I thought I knew."

"No, I don't suppose I am. But I won't hurt you. And in a few days, I'll take you home. Okay?"

Slowly, she nodded, and when he cautiously released her, she dropped her head back on the seat and took several deep breaths. After a moment, she pulled herself upright. It seemed to take a great deal of effort, but he didn't touch her. He didn't want her to slug him again, or possibly hurt herself jerking away.

Her gaze went to the door and the electrical tape. "I should have noticed."

"It was dark." He dabbed at his split lip with a hankie. Thankfully, his nose felt more bruised than broken, but it still hurt like hell.

"I have to use the bathroom."

That stymied him for just a moment. He lifted his hands. "There's nothing for miles, no gas station, no restaurants…"

"I need to go now. I can't wait."

He measured the wisdom of letting her out, but then he looked at her face. He wanted more than anything for her to trust him just a bit. He frowned at his own weakness. "All right. But stay right beside the truck. I'll turn my back."

She swallowed and her face flamed. To Dillon, she looked remarkably appealing and feminine. Her hair was half-undone, long strands tumbling around her shoulders, waving around her face. Her strange topaz eyes were slumberous, filled with a mixture of muted anger and anxiety. She breathed heavily, slowly, her lush breasts rising and falling. He hated her fear, hated being the cause of it. But he hadn't had a choice.

Icy wind and wet snow assaulted him as he opened the door and stepped out. He turned and reached in for Virginia. She swayed, then offered him her hand to allow him to help her out on the driver's side. That was his first clue. Virginia never admitted to needing help with anything or from anyone. She especially wouldn't do so now, while she felt so angry and betrayed.

The realization hit just before she did. This time her aim was for his groin, and her aim was true, though thankfully not as solid as it might have been, given her lethargic state.

Air left his lungs in a whoosh and he bent double, then dropped to his knees in the icy snow. He ground his teeth against the pain and cursed her—the stubborn, deceiving little cat. This time when he got his hands on her...

Virginia tried to run, but her legs weren't working right. She was clumsy, stumbling and falling again and again. She headed for the scraggly trees, even though they wouldn't offer a speck of concealment. Dillon forced himself to his feet, leaning on the truck as he watched her. She moved awkwardly, hampered by her fear, the drug and the thick snow. He took one more deep breath, which didn't do a damn thing for the lingering pain and nausea, and started off in a lope after her.

She must have heard his pursuit because she turned to stare wildly at him—and tripped. Dillon saw her go down, saw her land heavily on the ground and not get back up. His heart stopped, then began to thud against his ribs. Oh God.

"Virginia!" He forgot his own pain and charged to her. She lay limp, her face in the snow, and he fell to his knees beside her. She didn't move. He gently lifted her head and felt for a lump of any kind. There was nothing; the snow had cushioned her fall.

She opened her eyes the tiniest bit and glared at him. In a mere whisper, she said, "You're a miserable jerk, Dillon."

"I know, baby. I know." He smoothed the silky red hair away from her face while cradling her in his arms. "Easy, now. It's all right. How do you feel?"

"You've drugged me." Her head lolled, her words almost incoherent.

"It'll be all right, Virginia. I promise. I would never hurt you."

He heard a low, weak cry, and knew the sound came from Virginia. "Shh. It's all right. I swear it's all right." He listened to his ridiculous litany and wanted to curse himself. Nothing was all right, and he had the feeling it might never be again.

He cuddled her close to his chest, rocked her. "Just relax and go to sleep, sweetheart. I'll take care of everything. I'll take care of you. That's all I'm trying to do, you know."

Her eyes shut and her body went limp. But just before she gave in, before she let him have his way, she whispered, "You never really wanted me at all." She sighed. "You never wanted me. Damn you, Dillon...damn you, you never wanted..."

He listened to her breathing. She was asleep. Deeply asleep. Quickly, the cold slicing through him, he hefted her into his arms and started back for the truck. His groin ached and his nose throbbed, but that was nothing compared with how his heart hurt.

For Virginia's own safety, he wouldn't take any more

chances. She had proven to be a creative captive, and he knew she'd fight him tooth and nail if he gave her the opportunity. That meant taking certain precautions that she wasn't going to like.

For the second time that day, he lifted her into his truck. But as he strapped her in, as he looked around to make certain there were no witnesses, his brain played her words over and over again. *You never wanted me.*

SHE WAS SO WRONG, so damn wrong. He wanted her more than he'd ever wanted any woman. And it made no sense. He didn't like her family or her problems or the confusion she made him feel.

She'd passed out cursing him. Typical of Virginia to fade out while raising hell.

He smoothed his hand over her head, which lay in his lap, her cheek against his expanding fly. He knew it was only his imagination, but he thought he could feel the soft warmth of her breath there.

He was a sick bastard, kidnapping a woman and then getting aroused over her sleeping body. But he couldn't help himself. Everything about her excited him, and he was helpless against her. He wouldn't violate her, never that. But he had taken advantage. He was the one who'd pulled her so close. And even as he drove, trying his damnedest to distance himself from what he'd done, he was pulling the pins from her hair and smoothing it with his fingers. He'd told himself he only meant to make her more comfortable, but he knew it was a lie.

Her flaming hair now lay thick and full and shiny over his lap and his belly and his thighs. He shuddered, feeling in his mind and body how it would be if he and Virginia were naked. He tangled a fist in the sinfully sexy mass and pulled it carefully away from her face.

Thick brown lashes lay over her pale cheeks, her lips slightly parted, all arrogance and dominance washed away. She didn't look like a virago or a witch. She was simply an incredibly enticing woman. But he knew better, and he could only imagine how she'd react when she awoke. It would be a while yet. She'd been sleeping for only an hour. Still, he hadn't given her that much of the drug, just enough to make certain she couldn't figure out where they'd gone. He hadn't wanted her to know where they'd be staying.

The sun was trying to show itself on this hazy winter morning and they'd almost reached their destination when he felt her fingers move, clasping weakly at his thigh. She made a small moaning sound and he stilled. He wanted her to sleep just a little longer. There was one more thing he had to do—one more precaution to take—once they reached the cabin, and it would be easier for both of them if Virginia slept through it.

Because he knew without a single doubt, Virginia would never willingly give up her clothes.

He didn't plan to give her a choice.

chapter 6

VIRGINIA OPENED her eyes and accepted the feeling of dread that swirled around her. Cautiously, not sure what was wrong or why she felt so disoriented, she lay perfectly still and peered at her surroundings. Her head pounded as she took in the rough plank walls and bare floor. She was in a narrow bed piled high with quilts, cozy and warm, but the air on her face was cool. The cabin, or more like a shack, didn't appear to have modern conveniences, but the fireplace across the room blazed brightly, the flames licking high and casting an orange glow over the otherwise dark room.

Memories returned in bits and pieces, and with them came a deep ache in her heart. She closed her eyes and bit her lips as the emotional pain swelled.

That rotten, deceiving conniver. That miserable creep. He'd kidnapped her! He'd played her for a fool, pretending to want her, when in truth it had all been a game. She opened her eyes and willed away the tears that threatened. Virginia Johnson did not cry.

After taking several uncertain breaths, she worked up the

nerve to turn her head and look for Dillon. She didn't see him anywhere. The minuscule cabin had only one separate room, not much bigger than a closet. Through its open door she could see it was a bathroom, butting up next to the kitchen area. There was one narrow counter, a stove, small freezer and refrigerator situated around a metal sink. The cabin's one and only window, mostly blocked by snow on the outside, was situated over the sink.

There were two chairs, one a wooden rocker, the other a threadbare armchair, facing the fireplace. The bed she was lying in—a cot, really—hugged the back wall. Beside the cot was a small dresser that served as a nightstand, holding a clock and a tiny lamp with no shade. In the middle of the room was a badly scarred pine table and two matching chairs.

There was no sound other than the snapping and hissing of the fire. She swallowed, wondering if she might have a chance to escape.

Damn the cold and the snow and whatever distance they'd covered. She would not accept being a victim without choices. It didn't matter to her if she had to run all the way home.

But as she cautiously sat up in the bed and the quilts fell to her lap, she realized something that had escaped her notice thus far.

Dillon had taken all her clothes.

She stared, appalled, at her barely covered breasts. She had on her teddy, thank God, but other than that, she was as bare as the day she'd been born. Her nipples, stiff now with the washing of cold air, could be plainly seen through the material. Her nylons were even gone, but it didn't matter.

Mortification hit her first. He'd removed her clothes! He'd viewed her imperfect body, no doubt in minute detail. He'd looked at her at his leisure and found the evidence of her extra pounds—her rounded hips and thighs, the softness of her belly, the fullness of her breasts. She wondered if he'd chuckled as he stripped off her clothes; had he been amused by her attempt at seductiveness?

She felt queasy, sick with embarrassment. Her face flamed and her vision blurred. It was more than a woman could accept, more than she could bear.

Thankfully, outrage hit next, bringing with it a bloodcurdling scream of rage that erupted from her throat and resounded through the tiny cabin again and again.

The door crashed open and Dillon came charging in, his body strangely balanced as if for battle, his gaze alert as he made a quick, thorough survey of the room. He held himself in a fighter's stance, his black gaze steely and bright. Virginia could only stare.

Oh my. Closing her mouth slowly, she looked him over. He'd shed his civilized demeanor and hadn't left behind a single trace. His long hair, held off his face by a red bandanna rolled and tied around his forehead, gave him a pagan appearance. The bruise shadowing his nose and the corner of his mouth, discolored even through his sunbrowned skin, added to the impression of savagery. His jeans were faded and torn, displaying a part of one muscular thigh and two bare knees. The material over his fly was soft and white with age and cupped him lovingly. His heavy coat was gone, and his flannel shirt lay open at the throat, the sleeves rolled high over a gray thermal shirt. Incredibly, he seemed to be sweating.

His black eyes lit on her, then perused her body, lingering on her throbbing breasts and the shadowed juncture of her legs. Belatedly, Virginia grabbed the quilt and snatched it to her throat. Her insides seemed to curl up tight.

"What's wrong?" he demanded.

Virginia stared at him. His chest heaved from whatever activity had made him sweat, and possibly the fright she'd given him. She realized that he must have come charging in prepared to rescue her from some unknown threat. She wanted to laugh—after all, he was her only threat—but she couldn't manage it.

When she remained mute, he firmed his mouth into a grim line and headed back to close the door he'd left hanging open. "Stupid question, right? Do you always screech like a wet cat when you wake up?"

She was taken aback by his uncharacteristic sarcasm, and it took her a moment to gather the wit to speak. "Where the hell are my clothes?"

"Gone."

That flat answer caused her heart to skip in dread. "What do you mean, gone? Damn it, Dillon, what's going on here?"

He walked over and sat on the edge of the cot, prompting her to scurry back as far as she could. The wall felt cold against her shoulder blades, but the alternative would have been to touch him, and that was out of the question. She could already smell him—a cold, fresh-air scent mixed with raw masculinity and clean sweat. His dark eyes had never looked more intense as he took his time gazing at her features.

In a low, awe-filled voice, he asked, "How the hell did you manage to hide so much hair in that tight little knot you usually wear?" His gaze followed the length of one long curl as it rippled over her shoulder, almost to her lap. Words beyond her, Virginia squirmed under his scrutiny.

He reached out and twined a thick strand around his finger. "I've never seen hair like yours."

Virginia jerked, then winced at the tug on her hair. Dillon released her.

He chewed the side of his mouth, all the while studying her. "I was outside chopping wood. I meant to be in here when you woke up so you wouldn't be frightened. But as you can see, the only heat we're going to have here is from the fireplace and stove."

"Let me go."

"No." He pulled the bandanna off and used it to wipe his face. His long hair fell free and she caught another whiff of that enticing scent unique to him. "After I finish splitting the wood, I'll put on some soup or something and you can eat. I'll have you comfortable soon enough."

No longer was he the man she knew. He didn't act or move or speak like the old Dillon. There was no feigned deference, no show of politeness. He told her what he would do, and seemed to think she'd simply accept it.

But her mind shied away from that, from the ramifications of being stolen away by a man she didn't know—*this* man. So she skipped the questions clamoring uppermost in her mind and concentrated on another, more immediate one. "Where are my clothes, you bastard?"

He made a tsking sound, amusement bright in his eyes. "Such language, and from a lady of your standing."

Without thought, she swung at him, her burst of anger overshadowing her better judgment. When he caught her fist, he was grinning with genuine humor. "I can't tell you how relieved I am you're not wailing and crying and shivering in fear." He moved, flipping her down on the bed and catching her other fist, too, as she swung it. He leaned over her, his big body hot and hard, covering her own. In a whisper, he said, "Don't fight me, Virginia. You can't win."

His gaze bore into hers, and he was so close she felt his every breath. Then, suddenly, he sat up and moved away. The racing of her heart and the jumping of her stomach refused to subside. She didn't move, too intent on trying to calm herself from what felt like a tussle with a large male animal. Which wasn't far from the truth.

He caught a chair from the table and swung it around, straddling it so he could face her. "I took your clothes so you won't try running off again. I can't let you hurt yourself, and that's exactly what would happen if you tried to escape me."

Slowly, keeping a watchful eye on him, she sat back up and rearranged the quilt to cover her body. "What would you do to me if I tried?"

Deep dimples creased his sun-bronzed cheeks as he laughed. "I don't intend to do anything to you."

The words, combined with his misplaced humor, hurt more than she wanted to admit. Virginia lifted her chin. "Of course I realize now that you never wanted me, that pretending to want me was only a nasty little scam to fool me. That's not what I meant."

The humor left as quickly as it had appeared. "We're a long way from anything," he said, biting off the words. "There's nothing but ice and snow and freezing cold out there. If you tried to find your way home or find help, you'd never make it. The snow has gotten worse, burying all the roads. Taking your clothes was just a way to discourage you from even trying."

"I won't run, I promise. Just give me my clothes."

He eyed her, his gaze drifting lazily over her face. "I know you, Virginia. I know how your mind works. You'll try to run because sitting here doing nothing is the one thing you won't be able to abide."

"Yes, you know me so well," she sneered, wanting to hurt him the way he'd hurt her. But she couldn't because he didn't actually care about her. He never had. "You've been working on this plan for a long time, haven't you? When exactly did you come up with the idea?"

"To kidnap you? After the break-in at your house."

"Ha! Can't you be honest even now? Do you expect me to think you were *ever* sincere, that anything between us has *ever* been real?"

His gaze never faltered, but she saw his hands tighten into fists, saw the muscles of his shoulders bunch. "I got myself hired on at the company and talked you into coming away with me, all for a single purpose."

Knowing it and actually hearing it were two different things. She fought back the lump that formed in her throat and tried not to sound as wounded as she felt. "That's what I figured. What an idiot I've been."

He cursed and she jumped at the sound. "You're not an idiot, Virginia. I'm just very good at what I do."

"Lying, you mean?"

His look was quelling. "You know that's not what I meant."

"Then what?"

He shook his head and she knew the subject was closed. "Are you hungry? Or do you want something to drink?"

"And have you poison me again? No, thanks. Maybe next time you'll kill me."

He growled and came off his chair with a burst of energy. Pushing long fingers through his hair, he paced away from her, then jerked back around to face her, his expression fierce. "I'm not going to hurt you. Just the opposite, damn it. I'm trying to keep you safe."

"Oh?" She raised one eyebrow, deliberately egging him on. Somewhere, deep inside, she refused to be truly afraid of him. She'd spent better than two weeks getting to know him, and she couldn't believe her intuition had been so flawed. She refused to accept that she could have made such an enormous error. But she was hurt. Very hurt. And that made her almost blind with anger. "I suppose I should accept the word of a kidnapper? A pervert?"

He propped his hands on lean hips and his jaw worked. "I am not a pervert."

"You stole my clothes while I was unconscious!" She still couldn't bear the thought of it. "You...you looked at me! That's the lowest, most despicable..."

He stalked closer and bent low until he was nose to nose with her. "I'll take the rest of your damn clothes with you wide-awake if you don't stop trying to provoke me!"

Again, she cowered, wondering why she'd ever wanted a man who would stand up to her. Right now, she'd gladly trade Dillon for a man who would do her bidding.

The look on his face and the set of his body told her there'd be no swaying him. She swallowed and wisely decided against saying anything that might agitate him further.

Dillon shook his head in disgust. He straightened and took a small step away from the cot. "Damn it, I don't want to yell at you. I don't want to frighten you."

"Could've fooled me," she muttered, forgetting herself again while still keeping watch on him.

His head dropped forward and he laughed. "Ah, Virginia, you just don't know when to quit, do you?" He scrubbed both hands over his face, then raised his gaze to her again. He no longer laughed, but his smile lingered. He shook his head when he saw how he'd confused her. "You're a unique woman, you know that?"

The softly spoken words wiggled down deep into her heart, and she almost choked on her bitterness. She would *not* play the fool again. "Are you forgetting, Dillon, that the game is over? There's no reason for you to continue to flatter me with your nonsense. I've already been duped. Your plan succeeded."

He sat back in his chair with a deep sigh. "Would you like to know what the plan actually is, or are you happier to sit there and bitch?"

Virginia felt the words like a slap and she scowled. "How dare you?"

"What? Are you going to fire me?" He laughed again. "Grow up, Virginia. We're on new ground now. You'll find I can dare to do whatever I choose."

Her pulse fluttered in dread, but Dillon just made a sound of disgust. "Now don't go rounding those big gold eyes at me. I'm not going to hurt you. I've already told you that."

"You're threatening me," she said indignantly.

"Not at all. Just trying to explain to you what I have in mind."

Virginia tightened her hold on the quilt and glared at him. "Well, you can save your breath, because I already figured it out."

"Is that so?" He waved an encouraging hand at her. "So tell me, Virginia. What have you deduced in that quick little mind of yours?"

"You want money. But that's plain stupid, and I hadn't figured you for stupid." She looked him over with as much contempt as she could muster, then added, "A criminal, maybe, but not a stupid one. Surely you realize there's no love lost between me and Cliff. In fact, he detests me. I won't be surprised if he refuses to pay you a single penny. He'll probably be glad to be rid of me."

"That's part of what had me so worried, truth to tell," he admitted, his words sharp and filled with anger.

"Ah, that bothers you, doesn't it? You're stuck with me and there's no way to collect. Now what'll you do?"

Very deliberately, he stood and put his chair back at the table. As he retied the bandanna around his forehead, she watched the flexing of his biceps and the bunching muscles of his forearms and thick wrists.

"Virginia?"

Her gaze shot back to his glaring face and she reddened, knowing he'd caught her staring.

"I think I'll save the conversation for later. If I stay in here and listen to you go on, I might be tempted to violence."

"Ha! You said you wouldn't hurt me. Are you a liar as well as a kidnapper and a pervert?" She silently cursed the words once they'd left her mouth, but right now, words were all she had. She felt defenseless and vulnerable and emotionally wounded. She hated it. She almost hated him.

Dillon headed for the door. "No, I'm not a liar. And I won't hurt you. At least, not the way you're implying. But if I hear you putting yourself down like that again, I will turn you over my knee. And trust me, you won't enjoy the experience." As he opened the door he looked at her over his shoulder, and his black gaze lingered on her hips. "Although, considering what you've put me through these past weeks, I think *I'd* probably enjoy every second of it."

The door slammed closed behind him and Virginia let out her breath. Good grief, she felt scorched by that look and the words that had accompanied it. Put herself down? Was that what she'd been doing? And why should he care anyway?

Dillon wasn't the man she'd believed him to be. He definitely wasn't the meek, considerate lover she expected. No, Dillon would never accept half measures in the dark; she had a feeling that when he made love, he did so with the same intensity he'd just shown her. He wouldn't be *nice* about it; he'd be demanding, taking everything a woman had and giving her back just as much of himself.

Virginia shivered at the thought of making love to this new Dillon. He was hard and commanding—but for some reason, she still, ultimately, felt safe with him. At times his expression seemed foreboding, but she never feared any real harm or she wouldn't have given her mouth so much freedom. Dillon would not hurt her.

His contradictions—the way he used his strength and power with such devastating gentleness—thrilled her to the center of her feminine core. Every time he looked at her, her heart knocked against her ribs and her stomach tightened with desire.

She still wanted him, probably more than ever. But to him she was only a means to an end. For that, she would never forgive him.

She closed her eyes on a silent groan. She had to be the biggest fool alive because she wanted him anyway. Until now, she hadn't known such a need could exist. If she didn't get away from Dillon soon, she'd probably end up begging him to take her.

She couldn't let that happen.

chapter 7

CHOPPING WOOD PROVED to be cathartic. Dillon could release his tension, both sexual and emotional.

Seeing her sitting there, her thick mass of hair loose and silky, her heavy breasts with the large dark nipples barely restrained by her sheer lingerie, had cost him. When he'd undressed her, he'd tried to be detached. He hadn't looked any more than he had to, and he'd detested himself because he got aroused anyway.

With Virginia wide-awake and spitting venom at him, he hadn't *not* been able to look. He wanted her. He wanted her so bad he couldn't stop thinking about it. He lingered on the memory of those rounded breasts in his palms, and he wanted, at this moment, to know the taste of her nipples, to suck her and lick her and hear her moan for him.

He should have explained it all to her. That would have put her at ease, at least on one level. But she'd have been devastated to know the lengths Cliff had gone to to get rid of her. He wanted to demolish Cliff, and before this was over, he probably would.

Virginia might not believe him if he told her all his suspi-cions right now. She'd admitted to knowing how little Cliff cared for her, but Dillon knew she didn't think he was really capable of hurting her. She disdained Cliff, she didn't fear him.

Still, Dillon should have explained about Wade. Then maybe she wouldn't consider him a mercenary bastard driven by monetary rewards. She would have known, too, the absurdity of her charge that he didn't want her. He wanted her too damn much.

But putting some distance between them had been the most immediate necessity. He'd kidnapped her, and once this was over, he'd leave. That was an irrefutable fact. He wouldn't complicate things by giving in to his need. Throwing in the threat of a paddling had been sheer self-defense. He had to find a way to get her to stop baiting him, so he could find a way to keep his distance and do what he knew to be right. But with every word out of her mouth, she tempted him in a way no other woman had. He wanted to kiss her quiet, to prove his dominance over her, to be male to her female.

Not that he would ever raise a hand to her. His father had taught him that hurting anyone smaller or weaker than himself was a sign of true cowardice. Even worse was to hurt a woman. Females were to be protected, looked after. Just as you protected your family. Only, Virginia didn't want or need anyone to protect her. Disregarding physical strength, she was the most capable woman he'd ever met. Which meant he had no place in her life at all. What he had to give, she didn't need. And when all was said and done, she wouldn't want him around anyway.

But he wasn't going to explain his feelings to Virginia. If she feared him just a little, maybe she'd keep her insults behind her teeth and give him some peace. He enjoyed her show of defiance, but right now he needed to enjoy her a little less so he could maintain some control.

His arms loaded with firewood, he kicked the front door open. He automatically looked toward the bed, and Virginia, but she wasn't there. Only sheer instinct caused him to drop the wood and roll away a split second before a heavy frying pan came swishing past his head.

He cursed, then grabbed her bare ankles and jerked. She went down hard on her bottom, screeching curses so hot it was a wonder they didn't melt the snow. He snatched the frying pan out of her hand when she tried again to heft the damn thing toward his skull.

"Goddammit!" It was like wrestling with a wild woman. He did his best not to hurt her when he slammed down on top of her, using his knee to spread her bare thighs so she couldn't kick him and holding both her wrists in one tight fist. "Keep still, Virginia, before you hurt yourself!"

"You're the one hurting me, you cretin! Let me go." She thrashed and her hair whipped around her face, slapping against him.

"No." Dillon dropped his forehead to her shoulder, then quickly flinched away when she tried to sink her teeth into his neck. Clasping her chin with his free hand, he growled, "Maybe I should give you that paddling now."

"Try it and I'll emasculate you!"

So much for empty threats, he thought.

She wiggled and he felt the softness of her, the giving of her feminine body cradling his own. He clenched his jaw even as his muscles hardened and his penis followed suit. From one breath to the next he was as hard as a stone, pressing into her soft belly. "You already tried emasculating me, remember? I may never father children."

The low, husky sound of his voice gave away his dilemma, and Virginia stilled, her eyes wide on his face. In a whisper, she asked, "Criminals don't want to father children, do they?"

The absurdity of it hit him. How could this woman, whom—he kept reminding himself—he did *not* like, keep making him lose his head? It defied reason.

"Forget I said that." He pushed up, coming to his knees between her spread thighs. She gasped and struggled, but he held her wrists.

Staring hard into her eyes, he asked, "Why did you attack me?"

"Because I can't let you use me."

Despite his best intentions, Dillon gazed over her body. Her legs were sprawled around him, the teddy pulled tight to her frame, showing every curve and hollow. Damn but she was lush and rounded and generously built, the way a woman was supposed to be built. She would cushion a man with her feminine curves. He felt all that giving softness beneath him, and the feeling tempted him. Damn but it tempted him.

Forcing himself to look away from the outline of her feminine cleft, the hint of soft curls, he raised his gaze to her face. He saw her flushed cheeks and the wariness in her eyes. He understood. He himself could barely breathe. "Virginia, I have no intention of forcing myself on you. You don't have to be worried about rape."

Her mouth fell open before she narrowed her eyes and hissed, "I wasn't talking about that, you ass! I was talking about your using me in some moneymaking scheme."

She strained against his grip, and he struggled to subdue her. "In that, you have no choice." He touched her shoulder where an angry red welt had risen against her white skin. "Did I hurt you when I yanked you down?"

"This is insane!" Her voice now sounded shaky and he continued to soothe the small injury with strokes of his fingertips. "First you kidnap me and now you're concerned about giving me a bruise or two?"

"You have other bruises?"

The flush spread to her breasts and she looked away. "No, I just..."

"Show me, Virginia."

Her chest heaved and she briefly closed her eyes. "Get off me, you oaf."

When she looked at him again, he could see her embarrassment in the way she squirmed. He tilted his head, then surveyed her lush hips, remembering how hard she'd hit the floor. "Your bottom? Did I hurt you when I pulled you down?"

He could feel her trembling. "Dillon, *please,* this is ridiculous."

He released her and stood, then caught her upper arms and pulled her to her feet. He didn't like hearing her beg, didn't like seeing her fear of him. Holding her a moment longer than was necessary, he studied her downcast face, the way her hair fell like a curtain, hiding her expression and a good portion of her body. He dropped his hands and took a step away. "Get in the bed before you catch pneumonia. This floor is like ice."

Her back stiffened. "Why don't you just give me back my boots then?"

No matter how he tried, he couldn't put the thought of other bruises from his mind. He studied her, his gaze lingering again on her hips.

"Dillon?"

He shook his head. "No. I like you better just the way you are, honey."

Her beautiful eyes narrowed and she hissed a vicious curse at him.

He couldn't help but laugh, then he chucked her chin. "Face it, Virginia. Like this, you're more manageable. Now get in the bed before I put you there."

He picked up the frying pan and stepped over scattered logs as he went into the kitchen, not bothering to see if she obeyed. A moment later, he heard the cot squeak, and when he looked, Virginia was again buried beneath the quilts. She stared toward him, her expression stony.

After washing his hands, he opened the refrigerator and found a small roast. He put it on a battered old cutting board. "Clift is charging my younger brother, Wade, with embezzlement."

Using a sharp knife—one he vowed to remember to hide after he finished his chore—Dillon cut the meat into small chunks and put them in a stew pot. "I know you had no idea Wade Sanders is my brother. Actually, we're half brothers, so our last names are different and we don't look a hell of a lot alike. We share the same mother, though I never knew the woman." He glanced at Virginia to see how she took his explanation. She watched him, blessedly silent for a change.

"Wade is innocent, of course, but since I don't know what trumped-up evidence your brother has on him, I couldn't defend him. We obviously don't have the money your family has. Taking this to court would be ludicrous. Your brother's high-priced lawyers would crucify Wade. I had to think of another plan."

He added water to the pot and lit the stove. After throwing in a chopped onion and putting on the lid, he went to the fireplace and piled on more logs. Sparks leaped out at him, then landed harmlessly on the dusty wooden floor, where they faded away.

Personally, he thought the room was already too warm, but then, he was fully clothed. And damn near fully aroused.

He glanced at Virginia. Her entire body was rigid. "This may come as a surprise, but Wade and your sister, Kelsey, are in love."

He heard her gasp and their eyes connected. He felt touched by her anxiety, but forced himself to ignore it. It was past time she got things straight.

Small logs were scattered all over the floor from where he'd dropped them when she'd attacked. He began gathering them up, more to give himself something to do than for the sake of neatness. "On top of all that, and regardless of what you think, someone is trying to hurt you. I don't know for sure who it is yet, but I have my suspicions." He wouldn't come right out and name her brother. That would serve no purpose, at least not yet.

"You're the one trying to hurt me, Dillon."

He stilled in the process of stacking the wood by the fireplace, unable to ignore her sneering tone. Without looking at her, he said, "Never. I didn't lie about that, Virginia. When this is all over, I'll take you back and then disappear. You don't have to be afraid about that."

"After you've collected your money?"

"I'm not asking for any money. I need to clear Wade. But I couldn't do that, not while I was distracted worrying about you."

She appeared to chew that over. "You said you'd leave when this is done. Where will you go?"

He shook his head. He couldn't tell her he'd be flying to Mexico, back to his home. The less she knew about him, the better. "With you out of your office, I should be able to go through some files, do some checking."

"You kidnapped me to get me out of my office? You drugged me and dragged me to this dirty little cabin in the middle of nowhere, stripped me and scared me half to death, just so you could access my files?"

She sounded appalled by such logic. She also seemed to have forgotten the fact of her own threatened circumstances. But he wouldn't remind her of that again. "Cliff hates Wade, and he's trying to railroad him. All I need is a little time to prove it."

"You could be wrong."

"No. I'm good at reading people."

"I used to think the same thing," she said with a great deal of disgust.

He went on as if she hadn't interrupted. "I've gotten to know your brother pretty well. He's a petty bastard who wants things his own way whether that's the right way or not. He objects to your involvement because it injures his pride, not because he thinks it isn't necessary. And he's accusing Wade of embezzlement because he doesn't want him involved with Kelsey, not because Wade is guilty. Cliff is insecure, and he deals with his problems in an underhanded way."

She didn't respond and Dillon cleared his throat. He didn't have it in him to force the issue of Cliff's violent tendencies right now. "Anyway, Wade and Kelsey will be married."

"No!" Virginia shot forward on the bed, her expression and tone frantic. "Kelsey is too young and—"

"And Wade isn't good enough?"

"That's not what I was going to say!" she nervously smoothed her hands over the quilt and licked her lips. "Kelsey doesn't know what she's doing. She's only twenty-two."

"Almost twenty-three, and she'd disagree with you. She thinks she knows exactly what she's doing. She claims she loves Wade. And I know he worships her. He'll take good care of her, Virginia."

"No, Dillon, please. You have to let me talk to her, reason with her. Please."

Dillon walked to her, holding her gaze as he approached. There was no fear, only anxiety. He caught her chin between his fingers. "Don't ever beg for anything, Virginia. It doesn't sit well on your shoulders."

"Damn you!" She reached out one small fist and thumped his thigh. "This isn't a joke."

Her eyes plainly showed every emotion she felt. He shut his heart against her turmoil. "I'm sorry. But Kelsey is pregnant, with Wade's baby. Do you know, he wasn't as worried about going to jail as he was concerned with leaving Kelsey alone as a single mother. Wade is determined to take his responsibilities seriously."

Tension vibrated through her body. She bunched the quilt in her lap and held it tight. "If that was so, he wouldn't have gotten her pregnant in the first place."

Dillon lifted his brows. "I suppose that's true enough. But it's spilled milk now. Or rather, spilled—"

"Don't say it!"

He couldn't help it. He chuckled. "You know, Wade didn't exactly act alone. They both played and they both got caught."

"There are alternatives to marriage."

He didn't want to hear her make any suggestions, didn't want her to consider giving the baby away or disposing of it. Narrowing his eyes, he tried to deny the tightening of his gut. "Such as?"

"I could help Kelsey raise it. Women these days don't need a man around to take care of things. Single mothers survive every day. And I could more than provide for them both. She's my sister. The baby would be my niece or nephew."

He relaxed, enough to be distracted by her incredible hair again. He ran his fingertips down a long red curl that reflected the firelight with hints of gold. His fascination with her hair didn't seem to be dwindling as he got used to looking at it. Just the opposite.

And this time Virginia didn't move away. "You're saying Wade would be denied his child? Is that your ingenious plan, Virginia?"

"No… I don't know. I need time to think about it."

"There is no time. Decisions have to be made now. Wade and Kelsey *will* marry. Wade being a member of the family ought to protect him from Cliff in the future. It wouldn't do to have one's brother-in-law in prison, now would it?"

"How do you know Wade didn't do it?" Virginia licked her lips and refused to meet his gaze. "From what I remember, there was pretty strong evidence against him."

His fingers trailed over the curl, then tucked it behind her ear before tilting up her chin. "Do you know what the evidence is?"

A mulish expression came over her face. "You think I'd tell you? In case you're missing something, you're the bad guy in this scenario. I'm the victim. I certainly can't make it easy for you."

He grinned, thinking just how *hard* she made things. "No, I don't suppose you can. Fair enough. You don't give me any details, and I won't give you any more."

Slowly, her brows drew down in a suspicious frown. "Now, wait a minute. That's not fair. I need to know what's going on."

"You need to know only what I tell you."

"That is *not* acceptable!"

"We're not at the office, Virginia. You can't give me

orders, because I won't obey them. I don't work for you," he enunciated clearly. "From here on, I'm the one in charge. I know it'll be a new experience for you, but you might as well get used to it."

She practically hummed with anger. "If that's the way you want it, *fine*. But don't expect me to miss the next time I come at you with a frying pan!"

He sat on the edge of the cot. Virginia held the quilt up to cover her breasts, and her rich titian hair hung almost to her elbows. She shook it back. This time, she didn't cower from him when he leaned close, caging her in. Instead, she squared her shoulders and thrust her chin toward him in a silent challenge.

She looked so enticing, which shouldn't have mattered. And it didn't, not in the big picture. But here, closed in the cabin with her, he could feel her presence, could smell the light womanly fragrance of her. He loved how women smelled, and Virginia seemed especially inviting. He braced one hand on the bed beside her hip and used the other to cup her chin, making certain he had her mutinous attention.

"So you deliberately missed the first time, but you won't be so considerate again? I appreciate the warning, sweetheart. Now I can take necessary precautions."

"What…what do you mean?" Some of her defiance faltered.

"Did you notice that this is the only bed in the room, Virginia?"

Her lips parted and she surveyed the bed as if seeing it for the first time. "It isn't exactly a bed," she sputtered. "It's a narrow little cot that's barely big enough for a single body."

"Then I suppose we'll have to scrunch up real close, won't we? Maybe lay spoon fashion."

She shook her head while color rushed into her cheeks. "You are not getting into this bed with me, Dillon, so forget it."

He grinned, but decided to let her statement pass. "Since you were generous enough to warn me of your intent to lay me low, I guess I should warn you, too. Tonight, I'm going to have to tie you up."

"No!"

"I'd like to wake in the morning with my brains intact. That means," he said, flicking the end of her nose, "I have to restrain you and your more violent tendencies."

"Dillon…"

"Why don't you rest for now, honey? We'll have lunch in a couple of hours."

He walked back into the kitchen, grinning, knowing he'd just set himself up. Virginia would go out of her way to keep from being tied up. But he could handle her. And he'd rather deal with her anger any day than her hurt or fear. Even now, she was probably planning his demise.

He only wished he weren't looking forward to her efforts.

chapter 8

HE WAS A GOOD COOK—she'd give him that. But with him watching every bite she took, she felt obliged to skimp. She knew she was overweight, and she didn't want him thinking of her as a glutton. Vanity had no place on a victim's shoulders, but then, she refused to think of herself as a victim. Somehow she'd find a way out of this mess. This wasn't the time to deal with her insecurity about her figure. Besides, she'd already spent years trying.

"Is that all you're going to eat?"

He'd been quiet for so long and her thoughts had been so personal Virginia gave a guilty start. She had to make a grab for the quilt as it started to slide down her body. Dillon watched the path it took and the way she then clutched at it. His gaze locked with hers and remained there.

Awkwardly, she tucked and tugged until the quilt shielded as much of her body as possible. She knew she looked ridiculous with the thing wrapped around her like a sarong, but Dillon flatly refused to return her clothes to her, and she refused to continue cowering in the bed. It was a clash of wills that she fully expected to win. "I, ah, I'm not that hungry."

He made a small sound—a male snort of acknowledgment, then looked away. "You need to eat to keep up your strength. You can't very well give me hell if you're lying in bed too weak to argue, now can you? And I know you haven't eaten all day, so you have to be starved. Come on, finish up."

"No, thank you."

Her stomach muscles tightened, then fluttered, at the searing look he sent her way. "I never thought of you as the fainthearted type, willing to wilt away like a martyr. I thought you were made of sterner stuff." Soft sandy brown hair fell over his brow as he shook his head in mock regret. "You've disappointed me, Virginia."

She thinned her mouth and glared at him. "I have to watch my weight."

Speaking around a large spoonful of meat-filled soup, Dillon asked, "Why?"

He looked genuinely puzzled and she wanted to hit him right between his gorgeous eyes. But he wasn't obtuse, and she assumed he was toying with her. Automatically, her chin lifted. "Because I'm ten pounds overweight, that's why."

"More like twenty." Again, his gaze slid over her, and she felt the touch of it everywhere. "But it looks good on you. Damn good. Makes you nice and round. Skinny women are too pointy. Pointy bones, pointy breasts, pointy hips. Most men prefer a woman with a little meat on her." His gaze lingered on her breasts and her nipples pulled tight in reaction. "Provides a nice cushion."

In her entire life, Virginia had never heard anything so crudely put, or so ridiculous. How dare he speak to her that way, correcting, insulting and complimenting all in the same breath! Flustered and confused, she went for a show of umbrage. "Well, thank you, Mr. Dillon Oaks, for your masculine insight, but…"

He laughed. "Dillon Oaks *Jr.* to be exact. I carry my father's name."

Halted in midtirade, she stared at him. "You're a junior?"

Dillon finished his soup and then carried his bowl to the sink. "That's right, though I don't share that fact with just anyone. My father is rather…infamous in this country. If the connection was ever made, it could lead to a lot of questions I don't usually want to answer."

Virginia couldn't begin to fathom a Dillon Oaks Sr. One man of Dillon's caliber, of his appeal and arrogance, was more than the female populace should have to contend with. "Don't tell me your father is a kidnapper, also?"

Dillon glanced at her over his hard shoulder, then began running water in the sink to clean the dishes. Virginia thought he seemed to be much more domestically inclined than she was.

"Eat the rest of your soup and I'll tell you."

Obligingly, she ate. What the hell—she was hungry, and as Dillon had pointed out, he already knew she was overweight, although he didn't seem to mind. Starving herself for spite didn't make a bit of sense. Plus he was a wonderful cook. All he'd done was add canned vegetables and a few spices to meat, but it tasted better than good. Virginia always ate more when she was excited or upset; right now, she felt equal parts of both.

Nodding in satisfaction as Virginia dipped her spoon into the bowl, Dillon launched into his first story.

"My father was close to forty and set in his ways when I was born. The military had become his life, and my mother pretty much took him by surprise when she caught him in the States on leave and dumped his newborn infant in his lap. He says it was the biggest shock of his life." Dillon grinned, twin dimples flashing in his darkly tanned cheeks.

"My mother made it clear she didn't want any part of me, and Dad said he could tell by looking at me that I was his kid. Even as a newborn, I had the same dark eyes and light brown hair, and our features are the same, even to this day. Looking at Dad is like looking forty years into the future."

Virginia tried to imagine Dillon as an older, less powerful man, but she couldn't manage it. Somehow she thought Dillon would have a raw strength about him regardless of what exalted age he reached.

He chuckled now, a low rich sound that danced down her spine and sank into her bones. "When my mother started to hand me to Dad, I spit up on her. That was exactly what he wanted to do, but rudeness to a lady went against his grain. Since I'd done it for him, he gladly accepted me. Gradually, he left the military to take on the dubious role of parent."

The image of a man just like Dillon caring for an infant squeezed something in Virginia's heart, leaving her breathless and captivated.

Dillon tidied the kitchen efficiently, cleaning off the stove and scrubbing the pans. He didn't look as if he needed, wanted or expected her help, which was just as well, because she would have refused. The kidnappee did not help the kidnapper tidy his prison.

Dillon glanced at her, a half smile still hovering around his mouth. "Now, leaving the military might not sound like much to you, but you have to realize my father was an old war dog. He was in active duty in World War II, the Korean War, even the early stages of Vietnam. He had the military haircut, the tattoos and the salty language testifying to his past. He had no idea how to be a civilian, but he did know that without a wife, he couldn't very well raise a child and stay in the army."

Pulling her legs up onto the chair and bracing her heels on the edge, Virginia settled herself more comfortably. She made sure the quilt covered all her vital parts, then wrapped her arms around her knees. The cabin was now cozy and warm, except for the cold air drifting over the hard floor. She leaned her chin on her knees and regarded him. "Did your father ever consider putting you up for adoption?"

He made a rude grunting sound of disbelief. "Not my dad. He admits he didn't know much about parenting, and there were some real rough times, but he'd always believed in taking care of his own. Blood is blood. And you never, for any reason, turn your back on family."

Virginia supposed that accounted for Dillon going to such lengths to rescue Wade. Not that she forgave him just because he had a reason. "So what did your father do then?"

Dillon shrugged. "He tried off and on through the years

to get a regular job. But Dad is the original renegade. Ordinary life doesn't suit him. He's not...domestic enough. He doesn't fit in with society, and society is scared to death of him. There's a rough, almost dangerous edge to him that people pick up on within seconds of meeting him." He sent her a mischievous grin. "It scares the hell out of most men, and excites most women."

It sounded as if there was a lot of his father in Dillon, she thought, letting her gaze stray over his hard body, taking in the broad muscled back, the tattered jeans over solid thighs and tight, narrow hips. He had a natural arrogance that set him apart from other men, a self-confidence that went beyond being big and handsome and capable.

There was an aura of danger about him—something about the intensity of his eyes—that was very appealing. She could easily believe he shared that trait with his father. Curiosity got the better of her and she asked quietly, "Were you ever afraid of him?"

Dillon turned to face her, leaning back on the counter and crossing his arms over his broad chest. "No. I was afraid for him a lot, though. There were times when he'd be out of the country for long stretches—a month or more. I'd get antsy and nervous, but he always came back."

"Who watched you then? Who raised you?"

Dillon chewed the side of his mouth, his gaze on a far wall. "Dad always had one woman or another hanging around. They swarmed to him. When he had to leave, he'd give one of them money to make certain I made it to school and ate regular."

Virginia couldn't imagine such an existence. Knowing her words to be cruel, but unable to help herself, she said, "Maybe you would have been better off adopted. At least you would have had a parent who spent time with you!"

He gave her a pitying look and shook his head. "Dad spent more time with me than most kids ever hope to get. He taught me everything he knew—how to protect myself, how to get what I need, how to stay ahead and take care of those people who depend on me. He taught me morals and values and personal ethics and self-worth." His gaze was hard, almost accusing. "He taught me about the world."

She shouldn't ask. Knowing about Dillon's life and his family would only get her more involved. But the words couldn't be held back. She *wanted* to know everything about him, even more than she wanted to be free. "If he was such a great father, why did he leave you?"

When Dillon turned back to the dishes, Virginia wondered if she'd pushed too far, if maybe he wouldn't answer her at all. Then his voice, soft and low, came to her. "Dad became a mercenary. He continued to do the things he knew how to do best, but he did them on his own time...and for a lot more money."

For some reason, she wanted to go to him, to hold him. She shook her head. Touching him would be a very dangerous thing. To her heart.

"Your father was a hired killer?"

"You make him sound like an assassin." He cast her a glance. "He didn't exactly run around slitting innocent throats. His job was generally to apprehend and hold. And more often than not, it was the government who hired him for assignments they couldn't get sanctioned through the regular channels. Not always, though. He worked for other agencies, too. And he came through for them every time."

"You sound proud." If her parents had taken part in illegal activities, she would have died from shame. But Dillon actually seemed pleased by his father's sordid accomplishments.

He flattened his palms on the edge of the sink and looked out the window. "I don't know that 'proud' is the right word. But I know my dad did whatever had to be done so he could keep me. He made certain I understood how much he cared about me, that I was the first priority in his life. I've always known that no matter what, he's there for me. It doesn't matter if I'm right or wrong, if I'm in danger, he'll back me up." Dillon was silent a moment, then added, "That's what family's about. Unqualified support."

She'd never thought about her family in those particular terms. Sure her parents had loved her, even though she hadn't been their favorite. But Dillon spoke as if life was a war, filled with risks and hazards and deviousness. She supposed, given his upbringing, that might have been the only world he'd known.

She felt that tightening in her chest again and had to take several breaths. She would *not* feel sorry for him. What he'd done was unforgivable. She didn't for a minute believe that nonsense about taking her to protect her. He planned to ransack her office and defend his brother. If Cliff caught him at it, Dillon would go to jail. She had to find a way to reason with him. He had to let her go.

Dillon carried a dishrag to the table and began to wipe the surface. "I'm proficient with every weapon there is, but I'm especially good with my hands. Dad started teaching me self-defense when I was about six, after he got home from a mission to find out his girlfriend had taken off and left me alone. He wanted to be sure that if it ever happened again, I'd know how to take care of myself. He taught me all about security, how to create it, how to break it." He grinned. "That information is what got me hired by your company."

Hesitating for only a second, she asked, "Have you followed in your father's footsteps? Do you hire yourself out as a mercenary?"

"No." His black eyes flashed, and he smiled. "Kidnapping you is the only time I've walked on the wrong side of the law. I own a horse ranch, and Dad lives with me now. For the most part, that keeps me plenty busy enough. Over the years, before Dad mellowed and settled down, I bailed him out of a few situations that hadn't gone quite as planned. And I went with him on a few jobs. But they were legit, and I learned a lot. And I have to admit, my skills have come in handy recently."

Virginia sighed theatrically. "Wonderful. I get to be your guinea pig?"

He leaned his hip against the table and considered her. "Yeah. But I swear I think storming an enemy platoon would have been easier than taking you." He touched the swollen bruise on the bridge of his nose. "Do you plan to keep abusing me?"

"Not if you plan to turn me loose anytime soon," she replied sweetly.

Dillon chuckled again. His mood seemed to have improved quite a bit. In fact, she couldn't remember him ever being so relaxed. She wasn't sure she liked it; it made him appear less dangerous—and more appealing than ever.

As if he'd read her thoughts, he laughed and then tapped her chin. "Want to play cards?"

The quick switch threw her and she stared at him. "You're kidding, right?"

"We're stuck here for a while, Virginia. There's no television, certainly no outdoor activities. I can see that active mind of yours churning, but I won't be letting you go, so relax. Why make us both miserable?"

"Because you deserve to be miserable?"

"But you don't. So why not loosen up. We still have a few hours before bedtime."

Thinking of bedtime made her shiver and she looked away; beneath the quilt, her body turned warm, too warm. Nothing in her life had prepared her for this man. She had no idea how to deal with him. At the moment, sarcasm seemed her only option, the only way to keep the distance between them. "Do you plan to leave me here alone while you ransack my office?"

"Yes, tomorrow morning. But you don't need to worry. You'll be safe enough."

"Safe? What if something happens? I mean, there's no phone anywhere around here for me to call for help. And I assume we have no close neighbors."

He went to a cabinet and pulled out a battered deck of cards. "No. There's no phone nearby, no one to hear you scream. When I leave to check things out, you'll be on your own. But as you keep telling me, you can take care of yourself. It'll only be a few hours."

She struggled not to reveal her reaction to his words. If he left her alone, she'd finally have a chance to escape. Surely the truck would leave tracks, and she could follow them to the main road. There would have to be traffic of some kind, and she'd hitch a ride—

Damn, she needed her clothes! She couldn't very well go outside in what she wore now. Not only would she freeze, but no one would pick her up. They'd all think she was a lunatic.

Realizing that, she glared at Dillon. "I'm cold. Why don't you at least give me back my sweater." She'd work on the other clothes as she went along, slowly earning his trust and gaining back her whole outfit, especially her boots. They weren't exactly designed for treks in this kind of weather, but they'd have to suffice.

Dillon laid out a game of solitaire. Without looking at her, he said, "You're not an idiot, Virginia. You should know better than to underestimate me." He glanced up, and there was regret in his eyes, but determination, as well. "There is absolutely no way for you to leave this cabin. We're miles from everything, and the snow is piling up. By morning, it'll be a couple of feet deep."

She lifted her chin. "You plan to leave."

"The truck is four-wheel drive. You're not. If you tried to leave here by foot, you'd freeze to death—even with your clothes. If you're not worried about your own hide, think of the company. Under Cliff's sole guidance, it wouldn't last long. We both know it."

Frustration nearly smothered her. "Bastard."

He seemed unruffled by her insult. "I can make you a deal, you know."

Oh, the way he said that, with his voice husky and low and suggestive. Her thighs tightened reflexively, and she searched his face for a clue to his mood, but his expression was inscrutable. Cautiously, she asked, "What kind of deal?" Her voice broke, and she had to clear her throat. Even with his head down, she saw Dillon smile.

"Virginia, Virginia," he chided. "What are you thinking? Here I am, offering you a legitimate exchange, but you insist on laying evil deeds at my door."

Her feet hit the floor hard and she put both palms on the table. His teasing made her feel like a fool. "Let's see. Beyond kidnapping, drugging and stealing a woman's clothes, what else might you be capable of? I'd say the possibilities are endless!"

His humor vanished, and his tone turned gentle. "I told you I wouldn't hurt you."

"You also told me you—" Appalled, she stopped herself. Had she really been about to berate him for not wanting her sexually? The truth of that hurt, but damned if she wanted to let him know it. She crossed her arms tightly over her chest and slouched back in her chair.

A strained silence fell between them. She could feel his gaze, but she refused to meet it. Instead, she stared at the fireplace until her vision blurred and she could breathe normally again.

Somehow Dillon seemed to know the moment she

regained control. He returned his attention to his cards as if nothing had happened. "You give me the evidence Cliff has on Wade, give me a chance to prove it's false, and I'll take you back that much sooner. Maybe you could even help me figure out who the embezzler is. I know you're a woman who likes control, who needs to be kept informed. You might enjoy the challenge."

He never looked at her, just continued to play the game, moving and adjusting the cards at his leisure. His attitude infuriated her, but she didn't think she could stand not knowing. Her pride had forbade her to ask again, but now he had offered.

And what would it matter if he knew the evidence? If anything, it might convince him to get his brother out of the country, instead of involving Kelsey in his ridiculous scheme. One thing was certain, though. Never would she tell him it was she who had found the evidence of missing funds, not Cliff. Dillon's reaction to that news wasn't something she wanted to experience while she remained his captive.

She drew a deep breath, considering. Dillon laid the ace of spades at the top of his line of cards.

"Will it make things easier on you if I tell you what evidence Cliff has?"

"It might hurry things along a little. But the outcome will be the same either way." Now he did look up, and the hardness in his expression chilled her. She shivered and wrapped her arms around her knees.

"Regardless of what you do or don't tell me, I'm not

letting my brother go to jail to satisfy Cliff's warped sense of obligation to his sister."

Virginia couldn't look away. "That's what you think all this is about? You think Cliff got upset because Kelsey was seeing your brother, so he concocted this whole scheme just to get Wade out of the picture?"

"That's how a coward fights. Backhanded, through lies and deception."

"Coming from you, that doesn't say much!"

"I give as good as I get." He flipped another card. "Kelsey knew how Cliff would react. It's my opinion that's why she started chasing Wade in the first place. At the time, he was involved with Laura Neil and wouldn't even have noticed Kelsey. But she knew you two would have a conniption if she got involved with the hired help."

"But we didn't know!"

"Cliff found out. And not long after that, he decided Wade had been embezzling."

God, had she inadvertently handed Cliff the perfect tool for revenge? When she'd given him the faulty accounts, she'd known immediately that his satisfaction, in balance with his rage, had been too keen. At the time, she hadn't suspected anyone, she'd only wanted the matter looked into. She was even running her own private investigation. But Cliff had jumped on it, and it hadn't taken him long at all to blame Wade Sanders.

She leaned forward and rested her elbows on the table, but that drew Dillon's gaze to her breasts, and she quickly sat back again. Frowning, she tried to understand his reasoning, to sort it all out in her mind. Blaming Wade may have been convenient, knowing how Cliff felt about Kelsey. He considered her his only ally, his family, in a way Virginia had ceased to be soon after their parents' deaths. Cliff wasn't beyond doing something so reprehensible if it suited his purposes. She just didn't think he was quick-witted enough to concoct such a scheme.

There were also a lot of facts to deal with, beyond the emotional issues. Virginia felt as if too much was hitting her at one time. She couldn't quite sort it all out. "You're telling me Cliff's known for some time that Kelsey and your brother were seeing each other, but he never mentioned it to me?"

"I think he expected to take care of it on his own, without your interference." He flipped over another card, only briefly scanning the deck before returning his gaze to her face. "You treat Cliff like a little boy. It's no wonder he sneaks around trying to do something, anything, on his own."

"You're defending him!"

"Don't get me wrong. I think he's a fool—" his gaze narrowed on her face "—for letting you dictate to him. A real man would have taken charge long ago."

Virginia forgot her precarious position as victim; she forgot that she needed to trade information and sort out facts. She forgot everything except her pride. Running the company was all she had, the only truly wonderful thing she'd ever accomplished. It defined her life, her integrity, her strength, her independence. And now Dillon would strip that from her with a few callous words. She'd worked hard to get that modicum of business respect; she wouldn't let him or anyone else take it from her.

She came to her feet so fast her chair tipped over, landing with a crash in the silent cabin. She whirled to storm away, only to come up short when Dillon grabbed the back of the quilt. Like a dog running out of leash, she jerked to a stop. Staring straight ahead, she saw nothing but the walls, a tiny enclosure with no place to go, no place to run. She nearly choked on her bitterness, and then Dillon began tugging on the quilt, reeling her in.

She would have released it, but then he had her arm in an unbreakable grip, and it took only one small yank for her to fall solidly into his lap. Without any real effort on his part, he subdued her struggles. To her mortification, tears threatened. She'd never felt so vulnerable or helpless. Or hurt. She didn't like it. Lifting one fist, she thudded it against his shoulder, which felt like hitting a boulder.

Dillon didn't so much as flinch. "Don't you want to know how I would have taken control, Virginia?"

She shook her head, or at least she tried. Dillon had curled her so close her cheek pressed into the solid wall of his chest. Beyond all her anger and frustration, she felt an awareness of him, of the hardness of his body, his incredible scent, the gentleness of his hands as one coasted over her back and the other tangled in her hair. Effortlessly, he had surrounded and invaded her.

"I'm going to tell you anyway."

She felt the light touch of his mouth against her hair, and everything inside her seemed to shift and swell. Her body pulsed with awareness. She didn't know what that small kiss meant, or what she should do about it.

"Virginia, I would have made you a visible partner. I would have used your obvious strengths for the benefit of the company. Anyone who meets you knows you have an air of command, that you can aptly take charge of any situation. Cliff's biggest mistake is in trying to steal from you what you do best, instead of using it to his and the company's advantage. By giving you the credit you deserve, he would have gained a portion of that control."

The praise stunned her. Carefully, she tipped her head back to see his face. His mouth was only a few inches from her own, his expression implacable and hard. At the moment, there seemed to be no tenderness about him, but she knew better. "You're only trying to soften me up."

"No, baby. You're soft enough as it is."

Her eyes narrowed, but before she could speak, his fingers tightened in her hair like a rough caress and he kissed her temple. "You know what I say is true, Virginia. Cliff could only make himself look better with you at his side. He's a fool for keeping you in the shadows."

"So I've told him."

Dillon grinned and those dimples, so seldom seen, charmed her, adding to the heat that kept gathering beneath her skin, weakening her muscles. "I know you have. Repeatedly and with a great deal of vehemence. It's the way you tell him that makes him dig in his heels. You need to learn a little about compromise."

Virginia couldn't help but grin, too. "Lectured by a kidnapper. What's the world coming to?"

Dillon cupped her head, his fingers thrusting deep into her hair. "Tell me what evidence he has, Virginia."

She sighed. There was really no harm in telling him, even if his motives hadn't been firmly established. And for some reason, she felt more generous now than she had a few minutes ago. "All right."

She straightened, prepared to leave the warmth and comfort of Dillon's lap, but his hands tightened and she knew she couldn't move unless he let her. It didn't seem worth the struggle, so she relented. She really didn't want to move anyway.

She had to pick her words carefully, to give him only the bare bones of it, leaving out her own involvement. "As you probably already know, Wade Sanders was fired. I wanted to give him an indefinite leave of absence, but Cliff wouldn't hear of it. I believe he gave Sanders some vague excuse about too many errors at first, not wanting to tip anyone off." That had actually been her suggestion, the only one Cliff had listened to. Though Cliff had been adamant about firing Wade, Virginia hadn't wanted to take the chance that they might fire the wrong man. Wade had been with them for several years and never caused any problems.

Why wouldn't Cliff listen to her? Now look at the trouble they were in.

Of course, she hadn't known Kelsey was seeing Wade. Which wasn't surprising. Other than organizing the donations made by the company to various charities, Kelsey never involved herself in business. She and Kelsey and Cliff all led separate lives, with different priorities. Virginia made the business her life, while Kelsey chose to keep herself apart, both emotionally and physically. Lately, the two sisters seldom talked.

The gentle movement of Dillon's fingers on her scalp lulled her, and she went on with a sigh. "It was all done quietly, with no suspicions being announced. That way, if Wade wasn't the one embezzling the funds, the embezzlement would have continued and they could have trapped the person responsible. But since Wade was fired, no more money has been taken."

She looked at Dillon, at the concentrated frown on his brow, the dark eyes intense with thought. She wanted to soothe him, to comfort him, because in her heart she believed his brother to be guilty. And she knew it was going to come as a terrible blow to him.

He had some antiquated notion of family honor that wouldn't allow him to believe his brother capable of embezzlement. The contradictions in him amazed and intrigued her. He was by far the most dangerous man she'd ever met, but at the moment, bizarre as it seemed, she trusted him implicitly. The same code that would force him to risk his own life for his brother would keep him from ever deliberately hurting her. When he said he only wanted to save his brother, she believed him.

"Dillon, since the day Wade was relieved of his position, no more money has been taken," she repeated. "The investigation has been very quiet. Other than the two professionals Cliff hired to find proof that it was embezzlement and not accounting errors, no one knew except Cliff, Wade and me."

Idly, Dillon traced his fingers up and down her bare arm while he stared toward the fire. His light brown hair shone with highlights from the flames and his dark, dark eyes seemed almost fathomless. More contrasts, Virginia thought, and not only his coloring. He seemed contemplative and regretful, but beneath it all, the internal conviction of his brother's innocence was still there.

"Dillon? Don't you see? No one else knew except Wade. Not knowing the theft had been discovered, the embezzler probably would have continued to steal. But it didn't happen. The fact that the embezzlement ended the day Wade left the company almost proves his guilt." Almost, though Virginia wanted solid proof, and that's why she'd set up her own investigation.

Dillon finally looked at her. His large rough hand rose to cup her cheek, his thumb stroking over her temple. Slowly, inexhoribly, he urged her closer, and his mouth began to lower.

Virginia didn't know what to think, what to do. A whispering roared in her ears, and she accepted the fact that she wanted his kiss more than was wise. Pride, determination, common sense, seemed to evaporate. All she could concentrate on was the scent of Dillon, the hard comfort of his body, the way her own body reacted to him.

When his mouth touched hers, without passion but with tenderness and concern, she wanted to snuggle closer and stay safe, with him, in this cabin.

The thought appalled her, but before she could pull away,

he lifted his head and then set her on her feet. "It's almost bedtime, honey. Why don't you go take a shower or do whatever it is women do to get ready for bed."

Stupified, Virginia stared down at him. She swayed before catching herself and locking her knees against the weakness he caused. "Didn't you hear what I said? Didn't you understand? Wade is guilty."

Dillon gathered up the cards and stacked them neatly in his palm. "Go on, Virginia. There are clean towels in the bathroom, and I unpacked your shampoo and cleanser and all that other feminine stuff you had in that tiny bag."

He stood and Virginia reached out to clutch at his shirt. Dillon stared down at her, his expression veiled. She wanted to shake him, to make him understand that this would never work, that he was trying to save his brother against all odds.

"Dillon, you can't go through with this! You'll only implicate yourself in Wade's actions."

He pried her fingers loose from his shirt and then held her hand close to his chest. "You're wrong, honey. You say Wade is the only one who knew, but don't you wonder how I knew it was embezzlement he was suspected of, before any charges could be made? Don't you wonder how Wade contacted me so quickly that I was able to set this whole damn thing up *before* Cliff even began his investigation?"

"I...I hadn't really thought about it." She felt a stirring of dread, of sick premonition.

Dillon turned her toward the bathroom and gave her a light push. "It's easy, Virginia. Someone else knew. If Cliff didn't make it up or take the money himself, and if there really is money missing and Wade doesn't have it, someone else is guilty. Maybe the same person who's trying to hurt you. Maybe even the person who warned Wade in the first place."

"Why would anyone do that?"

"For the same reason you tried to keep it quiet. If the embezzlement stopped, Wade would look guilty. And who could look more innocent than the person trying to save him?"

She held on to the bathroom doorknob and looked back at Dillon. She felt both hope and dread that it might be all over. "If Wade didn't do it and you think you know who did, then the problem is solved. We can forget this little charade and go home. I promise you I'll do all I can to settle this."

But Dillon shook his head. "Are you forgetting the threats against you? And don't shake your pretty head at me, damn it. Someone cut your brake lines. And someone came into your house, using a key. If I hadn't been with you, I don't know what might have happened. But I do know I don't like the idea of anyone hurting you. I won't let it happen."

He took a step toward her, before stopping himself. "I'm sorry, Virginia. But the *problem* is far from solved. In fact, things just got a whole hell of a lot more complicated. Because I happen to think the two problems are related. And that narrows our suspect list down considerably."

chapter 9

SHE WANTED HIM to explain, but Dillon couldn't find the heart to tell her the truth. Not yet. Not until he had more information. Explaining to Wade was going to be tough enough, something he already dreaded.

He'd gotten used to the idea of blaming Cliff, and it felt good to blame him. But Cliff couldn't have been working alone because he wasn't savvy enough to pull off such a stunt. He should have realized that sooner.

Dillon believed the embezzlement charge and the threat to Virginia were related. That meant Cliff was the one tampering with her car and hiding out in her house or he'd hired someone else to do it. Either way, Dillon intended to destroy them all. He only hoped Virginia wouldn't be destroyed in the process.

Facing the fireplace, he listened to the sound of the shower and knew Virginia was only yards away, naked and wet and worried. Lord, he wanted her, wanted to hold her and comfort her and protect her from her damn deranged family and their deadly manipulations. Kissing her earlier had been so sweet, an odd feeling he'd never experienced before. There had been no passion, at least not on the surface where she would detect it. He'd simply been holding her on his lap, aware of her turmoil, sensing her insecurity. And he'd kissed her as a sign of comfort and understanding.

It was the first time he could recall sharing such a thing with a woman. Usually, if he kissed a woman, it was a foregone conclusion that they'd end up in bed. He didn't have the time or the interest for romantic relationships, so he settled for sexual ones. He'd always been discreet, and very careful with his health and the issue of responsibility, but he'd never claimed to be a monk. He enjoyed women, and in return he made sure they enjoyed him.

Yet he'd kissed Virginia, knowing he couldn't make love to her, knowing she was the one woman off-limits to him. And it had been so incredibly tender he'd wanted to go on holding and kissing her all night.

Of course, that hadn't been the only feeling storming him at that moment. Having her on his lap caused his body to surge in awareness. The firm pressure of her behind had been incredibly arousing and had stirred up visions of how they could mate, leaving his brain muddled with erotic images of her naked and warm and wet.

Not only did he want to comfort and gentle her, he wanted to claim her, to make love to her while she sat on his lap in just that way, her breasts vulnerable to his hands and mouth, her legs draped over his flanks. He wanted to break down her rigid defenses and force her to be a woman, his woman. He wanted to hear her whisper his name while he manipulated her to a blinding climax again and again. He would bury himself so deep inside her lush body she'd forget everything and everyone else. But that was impossible, as well as unconscionable. He wouldn't take advantage of her, no matter how severe his own need became.

So he'd settled for that one chaste kiss of comfort, and strangely, he'd reveled in it.

The shower finally shut off and Dillon closed his eyes, imagining her drying her body, the soft towel moving over her generous curves, around her full breasts, between her plump thighs.... His erection was almost painful, but he couldn't control the reaction of his body. He stood, then paced to the window over the sink. The snow fell continuously, burying everything, serving his purpose nicely. The deeper it got, the less he had to worry about Virginia trying to run off when he left her in the morning. Travel would be difficult enough for him, even with the truck. He'd have to adjust his time frame to accommodate the extra hours it would take to maneuver the icy roads.

The bathroom door opened and he turned to see Virginia peeking out.

"I need something clean to put on."

He sighed, ruthlessly bringing himself back under control. "We've been over this already, Virginia. I'm not taking any chances, which means the less you wear, the safer you'll be."

Her lips firmed and her slim auburn brows drew down in a frown. The severe look was a familiar one to him, but mixed with the incongruity of her cowering body behind the door, it almost made him smile.

"Fine. I understand that. But don't expect me to put on the same thing I've been wearing all day. Give me something else."

He considered that for a moment, then nodded. "I'll be right back."

As he headed for the door, she said, "Dillon!" and he heard the alarm. It made his insides twist with regret, because he was solely responsible for making her so uncertain, for stealing away her cockiness and arrogance. "I'm not leaving, honey. I'm just going out to the truck to fetch one of my shirts."

He saw every thought that flashed through her quick mind, and he laughed. "Don't get any ideas about bashing me over the head and stealing my clothes or my truck. I've disconnected a few things on the engine, and it won't run again until I reconnect them—easy enough for me, but unless you know a lot about mechanics, you won't get the thing started. And my suitcase only has a few shirts and clean skivvies anyway. Except for trying to strip my jeans off me, you'd have to leave here bare assed."

Her response was to slam the bathroom door in his face.

As Dillon dashed through the snow to the truck, he realized he wore a sappy grin on his face. Damn, but the woman amused him with her flash temper and biting wit. Now that he was no longer constrained to keep his natural responses to himself, he actually enjoyed her sharp tongue. They played a game of dominance, and even though he knew he'd come out ahead, that in the end he could conquer her if that was his wish, the game still thrilled him. Virginia proved a worthy adversary and she kept him on his toes.

When he returned to the cabin with a spare white T-shirt

for her and a few things for himself, he did so cautiously. He didn't doubt her ability to take him by surprise; she'd already done so numerous times. But Virginia was still in the bathroom, and when he knocked, she merely stuck her hand out through the narrowly opened door.

After she'd snatched the shirt from him, he heard a muttered, "Thank you." He went back to sitting by the fire.

He didn't know quite how to handle her now, but he had decided to give her options. He'd found in the past that it was easier for people to accept the idea of having choices than being totally dominated. Not that he was looking forward to his next move. Hell, it would likely be much harder on him than it would be on her. At the moment, she pretty much detested him—rightfully so—while his feelings came no-where close to such a negative emotion. But he didn't want her fighting him, either, and possibly hurting herself. He had to find a way to gain her compliance so she could get some badly needed sleep and he could relax his guard.

Turning as the bathroom door opened again, he watched Virginia creep across the floor with the quilt thrown over her shoulders and held close to her breasts by a tight fist. It dragged behind her like a queen's robe and suited her haughty stature better than she could know.

She wore his shirt. He could see the hem of the white T-shirt brushing her dimpled knees as she walked, and the sight filled him with a primitive satisfaction. The shirt signified a claim, a stake he couldn't make but wanted all the same.

Ignoring her wary gaze, Dillon came to his feet and braced himself for the newest confrontation. "Into the bed, Virginia."

She faltered and her beautiful eyes widened, looking more amber than gold in the dim room. They seemed to dominate her face, a face scrubbed clean of makeup, pink and fresh and young. He knew she was thirty years old, but at the moment, she barely looked nineteen. As usual, her chin went into the air and her shoulders squared.

"What are you going to do?"

He picked up the rope he'd laid on the mantel. Gently, he said, "I told you I'd have to tie you, remember?"

"No!"

"I can't take a chance on you doing anything foolish."

"You're not going to tie me, Dillon."

The warning was there, but the trembling in her tone belied the vehemence of her words. He felt like an animal, and he hated himself, hated what he had to do. He clenched his hands into fists, tightened his abdomen and said, "There's only one other choice."

Hope shone in her eyes, mixed with the caution she tried so hard to hide. "What choice?"

"I'll have to sleep with you." She took a quick step back, and he said, "It's one way or the other, Virginia. I'm a light sleeper, and if I'm right beside you, I'll know if you try anything. But if you hate the thought of having me so close, I can sleep in a chair. It wouldn't be the first time." He stared at her, refusing to back down from the accusation on her face, refusing to acknowledge the stirring of lust that twisted his gut and tightened his groin. "But then I'll have to tie you. Those are your choices."

"Which leaves me no choice at all."

The rope slid through his fingers as he wound and rewound it. "Don't be bitter, honey. Accept what has to be. We both need some sleep."

With her gaze on the rope, she chewed her lip and squirmed, and it was so unlike her, this indecisiveness, that he almost relented. Hell, he could go another night without sleep. He could easily sit by the fire and watch her all night as she rested; it would be an apt punishment for involving her in all this, for using her.

"All right."

Taken by surprise, Dillon stared at her, wanting no mistakes, no illusions. "All right what?"

"You can sleep with me."

She tried to scoff, shrugging her rounded shoulders and shifting her feet nervously. She wouldn't meet his gaze, no matter how he willed her to.

"I mean, what's the big deal? You've already made it clear you don't want me. Right?"

He didn't—couldn't—answer. Surely the woman wasn't blind to his lust; at thirty years of age she'd had lovers, or so he'd understood. Virginia was in no way a naive spinster who wouldn't recognize the signs.

The material of his worn jeans was straining he was so hard. He felt huge, hot and throbbing, and it wouldn't take much more than a single touch from her to make him come. The thought caused a shudder to skip down his rigid spine. He held his breath in reaction.

Even an inexperienced woman would notice such an obvious arousal. He wasn't a small man, not in any way. But then, Virginia tried not to look at him, and he'd never seen her this distracted, this...*shy*. His heart twisted.

When he remained silent, she went on, determined to brazen it out. "We'll be separated by a quilt and we could use the shared warmth tonight when the fire dies down."

"Fine." Dillon put the rope back up on the mantel and snatched up his own change of clothes as he headed for the bathroom. Right now, he needed a cold shower, and given the size of the hot water tank, that was likely all that was left. "Get into bed. I'll be there in just a few minutes."

He didn't wait to see Virginia's reaction to his curt order. He didn't want to be tempted further by the sight of her, by the length of her gorgeous, sexy hair, her bare feet or wide-eyed gaze.

He didn't want to think about lying close to her warm soft body but not touching her in all the ways that tempted him most.

In the bathroom, he leaned back against the door, then opened his eyes and met the sight of her pale silk teddy draped over the towel bar. She'd rinsed the thing out, but the material was so sheer it already looked dry in places.

Like a sleepwalker, he stepped over and raised it in his hand. Cool, smooth. Damp. He lifted the material to his nose and drank in her woman-soft, musky scent, knowing the delicious smell would be so much stronger on her body, her heated skin. His pulse throbbed and he rubbed the slippery material over his cheek. Finally, disgusted with his self-torture and the expected results, he draped the teddy back on the towel bar and turned on the water.

It took him only minutes to realize the cold shower wasn't cold enough. His skin prickled with the chill, but still he felt hot and aroused, his loins full and heavy, his muscles drawn too tight. He couldn't go to her this way, on the very edge of exploding. Not only would he frighten her, he'd be testing his control beyond dangerous limits. Since no woman had ever had this effect on him, he felt angry and helpless at his inability to deal with it. With a curse, he made up his mind.

The shower was barely wide enough for his shoulders, but he braced his back against the icy tile wall and closed his eyes. The freezing water sprayed his face and chest and groin like sharp needles and he allowed that feeling, allowed it to grow and torment him until he couldn't breathe. Then he relieved the pressure.

It didn't take much, not with the way he'd been aroused all day. When his climax hit, he clenched his teeth and growled, pressing his shoulders hard against the cold wall. The feelings went on and on and finally he slumped on a ragged groan, his body slowly relaxing.

With his lust diminished but far from gone, he left the shower. His thighs still trembled, his breathing still uneven. Shivering, he briskly dried himself, then pulled on his underwear and shoved his legs back into his jeans. Normally, he slept in the nude, but lying beside Virginia without the protection of sturdy denim would be disastrous, even after his release. He wasn't a fool, and he knew his own limitations. After finger-combing his hair and brushing his teeth, he quietly left the bathroom.

The cabin seemed too silent, and he wondered for a brief instant if Virginia would launch another attack; he wasn't at all up to fending her off. But then he saw her in the bed, curled on her side, the quilt tucked tightly around her, her hands beneath her cheek. The fireplace cast a dancing golden glow over everything, but especially on her hair, which fanned out behind her and covered a good portion of the bed, including the part where he would lie.

She kept her eyes tightly closed, even though he knew she wasn't asleep.

Shadows in the darkest parts of the cabin seemed to insulate them from any intrusion. The fire hissed and the air smelled pleasantly of winter and wood smoke and Virginia.

The bed dipped as he put one knee beside her hip. She clutched at the edge of the mattress to keep from rolling toward him. He watched her eyes squeeze a little tighter, her shoulders hunch, and he wanted to yell, to shout out his frustration like a madman. Ill equipped to handle sleeping chastely with a woman who turned him on, he felt angry, at himself and her. He remained poised beside her for several heartbeats while he took deep breaths and resigned himself to the inevitable.

"I'll have to curl around you to fit on the bed."

She didn't respond. Cautiously, he stretched out full length beside her, pulling the spare quilt over his body, then flipping the extra over her so that she was covered by both quilts. The room would get chillier as the night wore on and the fire burned down. Virginia never moved a muscle.

Reaching over, he caught her waist and pulled her snugly

against his body. She made a small sound, then went perfectly still again. His body hummed with tension. "Try to relax, honey. I never bite a woman unless she asks me to."

Her elbow came back with surprising force. He grunted even as he grinned, then tightened his arm in a quick hug. "That's better. I thought maybe you were concentrating on playing possum."

"Actually, I was concentrating on pretending you don't exist."

He chuckled at her continued sarcasm, able to see the irony now that she wasn't so frozen beside him. "You know that's not going to work. Not with us both so cozy in this bed." Feeling her bottom tucked snug against his groin worked wonders to revive his libido; his earlier release might never have happened.

"It could work if you'd shut up and let me get to sleep."

He hugged her again, pressing his nose to the back of her neck and breathing in the sweet fragrance of her hair. It felt soft on his face, and he wondered how soft it would feel on the rest of his body. Just as quickly, he chased the stirring thought away, sensing disaster. "Good night, Virginia."

Several minutes passed, and she remained motionless. Dillon thought she had dozed off until she whispered, "Dillon?"

"Hmm?"

Again she was silent, before finally asking, "What would you do if Wade was guilty?"

He nuzzled her ear, unable to help himself, and was rewarded with her slight shiver. He decided masochistic tendencies must be part of his genetic makeup. "First, I suppose I'd beat the hell out of him."

Virginia half turned to see him and they nearly bumped noses. Her face showed astonishment as she searched his gaze for sincerity. "Your own brother?"

Firelight licked over her cheekbones, turning her eyelashes to gold and making her skin glisten. Dillon tucked a loose curl behind her ear, that damn tenderness tightening his chest again, mixing with the lust to confuse and agitate him. "Especially my brother. I couldn't let him go to jail, but I'd definitely want him to understand that what he'd done was wrong, and there's always a price to be paid. We'd eventually talk about it, I suppose, and hopefully I could make him understand so the situation never occurred again."

Virginia considered his words, then turned back to her pillow. "I think it's really nice that you care so much. Not many families are that way."

"What about you, Virginia?" he asked tentatively, trying to find the right words. "What would you do if you found out Cliff or Kelsey had broken the law? What if Cliff resorted to blackmail…or Kelsey put herself at risk for money? What would you do?"

She shook her head. "I don't know. Things aren't as clear-cut for me as they are for you."

"You love your brother and sister."

"Yes. But we don't usually see eye to eye. We don't have the rapport that you evidently have with Wade and your father."

He smoothed his hand up and over her shoulder, then back to her elbow. "You could have, if you'd be willing to work for it." He wanted to stop touching her, but he couldn't seem to help himself and his fingers lingered on her soft white skin.

"It might be too late now. If you get your way, and Kelsey marries Wade, nothing will ever be the same again. Our family will be more divided than ever."

"You can't know that. Problems have a way of either destroying a family or bringing it together. If you'd give Wade half a chance, and trust my judgment just a bit, you might find things are in better shape than ever."

"Ha!" Again she twisted to see him and her cheeks were flushed with righteous indignation. "Not only do you kidnap me, but now you refuse to tell me who you suspect of setting this whole thing up. How can I possibly trust you?"

"Give me a little time." He splayed his fingers over her belly and heard her audible gasp. Her soft stomach quivered before he felt her muscles tighten. "Give me a chance to check things out, to get my facts straight, and then I'll tell you what I know."

"When?"

"Tomorrow when I get back."

"I could leave while you're gone, you know."

"But you won't." Dillon was painfully aware of their present situation, their lying together in intimate surroundings, the night dark and the fire warm, talking in bed like an old married couple. Virginia seemed to have put her uneasiness aside for the moment. That alone proved some measure of trust. "You're not afraid of me, for yourself or your family. There's no reason for you to run."

"You can't know what I'm feeling!"

"But I do. You trust me not to hurt you. Trust me enough to find out what I can tomorrow, then we'll decide together what to do."

She chewed her lip in indecision. "You'll tell me everything? All your suspicions? Anything you find out?"

"I promise."

Her sigh was long and dramatic. "It's a sorry day when I take the word of a kidnapper, but I suppose I have no choice." She dropped her head back to her pillow and wiggled to get more comfortable. It was Dillon's turn to suck in his breath. Virginia seemed to have difficulty getting settled, and finally she punched her pillow. "Cliff is going to give me hell for this whole mess."

Dillon grabbed her hips to still her movements before he forgot his good intentions and shoved her T-shirt high and threw the quilts off the bed. He wanted to feel her bare buttocks moving against him. "I have no doubt you'll give as good as you get. Cliff doesn't stand a chance."

"Good night, Dillon."

He let his body ease against hers, moving his arm around her waist, the other under her pillow, supporting her head. *He* wasn't comfortable; he was too alert for comfort. But he thought he might eventually sleep. Tomorrow would be horrendous, filled with confrontations, and he'd need a little sleep if he was to deal with the difficulties in the best way.

About a half hour later, he heard Virginia's breathing taper into sleep and her body sighed into his, warm and feminine and soft, fitting against him perfectly. He stared into the fire and thought about all the problems and all the players involved, while his fingertips continued to smooth over her skin. With only a few words, everything had gotten more complicated. And there was no way he could protect Virginia from what would come. He realized he didn't want her hurt, not in any way. Somehow, someway, he'd begun to really care about her. He could no longer attempt to convince himself that he didn't like her, because he liked her far too much.

Admitting what was in his heart, even to himself, scared the hell out of him, but it was too big to deny.

The odds of getting away from this damn scheme unscathed had drastically diminished.

THE HEAT DISTURBED HER, covering her in thick, pulsing waves, mixing vividly with the dream. She moaned, trying to force herself awake and away from the tormenting heat. As she stirred, she curled her fingers, and felt them dig into solid muscle. She panted for breath, for recognition.

The scent of hot, excited male filled her nostrils as she sucked in a long breath. Stunned and disoriented, unable to move with any speed, she lifted her eyelids.

Her nose twitched, tickled by the dark hair of Dillon's chest, close to one flat brown nipple. Her heart skipped a beat, and she couldn't seem to get her thoughts organized other than to realize her face was pressed to Dillon's bare chest and her pelvis was perfectly aligned with his. The solid length of his erection burned against her bare belly, even through his jeans. A sweet, insistent pressure between her thighs made her shudder. Confused, she raised her head just a bit. Dillon's diamond-hard gaze immediately snared her.

Lazily, he murmured, "You're awake."

The husky rumble of his voice rubbed over her and she moaned. That was when she realized his thigh pressed against her in the most sensitive of places. Her legs straddled him and one large calloused hand anchored her naked bottom in place, his fingers pressing into her flesh, roughly caressing. Somehow the quilts were pushed low on the cot and her T-shirt had gotten shoved to her waist. His fingers dipped, sliding between her buttocks, moving down toward her mound, and she jerked in startled, excited embarrassment. *"Dillon?"*

His smile was gentle, even as those fingers slid lower, coasting over her, probing, seeking. "I like waking up with you hot and wet for me, Virginia. I like it a lot." He closed his eyes as one finger circled her, briefly pressing into her body. "Do you feel how wet you are, babe? How hot?"

A slight trembling started deep inside her. "I don't understand."

"You crawled right on top of me." As he spoke, his gaze moved over her face, lingering on her lips, then her throat, where she knew her pulse raced. He lowered his thick lashes, hiding his eyes.

She swallowed, wanting to deny his statement, but how could she when she made no effort to move away from him? She didn't want to move. She'd gone to sleep excited, wanting him so much, more than she'd ever thought it was possible to want anyone or anything. The things he did to her now, the bold way he touched her had to be forbidden. But he continued, and she didn't try to stop him.

Dillon had a strength she'd never imagined, but there was also a gentleness about him, the careful way he wielded his strength. His power was a sexy, vital part of him and she wanted him.

Unable to help herself, she squirmed. Dillon pulled his hand away, then raised his thigh a bit more, pressing hard against her while her body moved of its own volition to a rhythm she hadn't known until he showed her with a guiding hand. She gasped at the acuteness of the sensation, closing her eyes and pressing her head back.

She felt his fingers tangle in the length of her hair, moving it over his chest and shoulders. "You are so sexy."

She couldn't stand it. She shook her head, knowing it wasn't true, knowing she behaved shamefully, practically attacking Dillon in his sleep. He palmed her breast, weighing it, his fingertips rubbing roughly over her aching nipple. It pebbled hard and he lightly pinched the very tip, tormenting her. Her body become more sensitive, more alive with each small movement. She cried out.

"Do you have any idea what you do to me, Virginia?" His whispered words added to the quickening building beneath her skin. "I couldn't sleep, not with you so near at hand. And then you crawled over me, cuddling close, and you touched me, just my chest, but I felt it to my very bones."

His leg thrust higher, forcing her forward and she cried out again, arching her back to add to the delicious pressure. "Dillon…" The embarrassment was there; she'd never done anything like this before, certainly not with a man watching her so closely. And she'd never felt this way, scattered and fractured and ready to explode, *wanting* to explode. She could feel her own wetness, her heat, and she kept moving against him, seeking the sharp pleasure that kept expanding but seemed just out of reach.

Dillon lifted her breast higher and bit her nipple lightly through the cotton shirt. "I want to taste your nipples, Virginia. Hell, I want to taste all of you."

She opened her eyes, staring at him, uncomprehending. He smiled and touched her face with a trembling hand. "Let me help you, honey. You need me right now, don't you?"

"I don't know." But she did know. She wanted Dillon inside her, she wanted to know what it was to be loved by this man, even if the lovemaking was a sham. He'd lied about wanting her, lied about being attracted to her, but he wanted her now. She could feel his body moving in subtle shifts, his huge erection grinding against her belly.

"Trust me, Virginia?"

He made it a question, not an order, and she groaned, hardly able to think with his hands teasing her and showing her how to move, urging her harder against him, faster. "I do."

In the next second, Dillon flipped her onto her back, shoving her T-shirt up and over her breasts. His slim hips planted firmly between her widely spread thighs. Virginia clutched at him, stunned and excited and a little scared by the way he made her feel so out of control, so uncaring about everything in the world but the pleasure of him and the ache inside her.

Then his mouth was on her nipple while his hand held her breast high, like a sacrifice. He sucked and licked and Virginia didn't know if she could stand it, it was so exciting. She bit her lips to keep from begging, to stop herself from crying out like a wild thing. But she couldn't hold still and she writhed under him, holding his head, feeling the hollows of his cheeks as he sucked her hard, mercilessly.

The torture went on and on. He switched from one breast to the other, never quite satisfied, and she did cry, only it didn't deter him from his course. He seemed intent on driving her out of her mind, his mouth and hot tongue first light and teasing, then frightening her with sharp little nips of his teeth and rough kisses. She thrust her mound against him, rubbing and seeking, anxious to gain her own pleasure. But whenever she got close to that mystical realm of satisfaction, he would hold her hips and force her to be still, even while he continued to taste her and whisper hot, forbidden words to her.

"Damn you, Dillon." Her gasping breaths made it difficult to speak. Her words sounded high and weak.

"I want you to remember this, honey, to remember me." Now he used both hands to lightly pinch her nipples, tugging and rolling, keeping her poised, her back arched while he watched her respond with satisfaction. "I want to give you something you've never had before."

"I can't stand it…."

"Shh." He bent to lave her nipple with the very tip of his raspy tongue. "I'm not giving you a choice. Not this time."

The words sent an erotic thrill of warning down her spine. "Make love to me, damn you!"

One hand left her breast to trail down her side, then over her belly. "Not a good idea, Virginia. You want me now, but when this is all over, you're liable to hate me."

"No." She moaned as his hand slid over her, separating her slick folds, teasing her further. When she cried out, he pushed two fingers deep inside her, high and hard. Instinctively, she tried to twist away. Dillon wouldn't let her.

"Don't hide from me, Virginia. Give over to me. *Trust me.*"

How could she trust him when it seemed he only wanted to make her crazy? If he wouldn't make love to her, then why torture her so thoroughly? But she couldn't think, couldn't find a rational thought, not with his fingers stroking her, stretching her.

"Open your legs wide for me, baby. Wider...." He groaned. "That's it."

He kissed the sensitive underside of her breasts, then her ribs, counting each one. When she felt his mouth low on her belly, she held her breath, wanting to protest, but unable to speak or even think past the heightened sensation and acute painful need.

He sat back on his heels and looked at her. Using his thumbs, he spread her open, slicked up and down, sometimes dipping, then rubbing over her.

"No," she moaned, pushing his hands away and trying to cover herself. But he caught her hands and pinned them to her sides. Their gazes met and she shuddered at the hot, determined look in his eyes. "I like to see a woman touch herself, Virginia, to watch her play with her own body. But not now, not yet. Right now, I'm playing."

"Bastard." But the word was only a whisper and she didn't fight him anymore.

He released her hand and said, "Do you want me to stop?"

She trembled, then shook her head. "No."

"Then don't move. Do you understand me, Virginia?"

She didn't think she could move even if she'd wanted to. Meek compliance went against every fiber of who she was. But she knew she'd die if he stopped now, so he left her no choice. She swallowed, then turned her face away and whispered, "Yes."

"Look at me."

Again she seemed to have no choice but to obey. Her heart pounded so hard it hurt.

He trailed his fingers down her ribs, watching as she trembled from the tickling sensation that only added to her raw nerves, making her body more frenzied. Both hands stopped at the top of her thighs and he pushed, spreading her even wider.

"You look beautiful like this."

She knotted her hands in the sheets and tried to concentrate on the sight of him, his hard body, the way every muscle seemed drawn tight right now. His jaw was rigid, his eyes were burning. He traced her femininity with one rough finger, then tweaked her curls, smiling and saying, "So pretty." As he toyed with her, he asked, "Hasn't any man ever really looked at you, honey?"

She shook her head, unwilling to voice the words. Caught in a maelstrom of embarrassment and overwhelming need, she didn't dare speak for fear of what she might admit.

"Fools. I could look at you forever."

Just as he had done with her nipples, he caught her swollen bud between the very tips of his fingers and thumb. Her body bowed, lifted high, and he held her like that, lightly abrading her, stroking, pulling. If she started to close her thighs, he'd stop and rearrange her again before returning to his torment. She bit her lips and sobbed and then he bent low and she felt his breath.

Carefully now, he slid his fingers back inside her, adding a rough friction while his hot mouth closed over her, drawing gently. Everything in her tightened, the sensations all rushing to that one spot, then radiating out again in rolling waves. His lips nibbled over delicate, throbbing flesh and suckled gently while his fingers continued to fill her, and she exploded, her climax taking her by surprise as her legs tightened and her vision went blank and her body screamed in a rush of unbelievable pleasure. The power of it was so devastating, like an attack to her every nerve ending, that she honestly wondered if she'd survive—and didn't really care.

The sensation went on and on, stealing all thoughts. She wasn't even sure what it was now that Dillon did with her body and it didn't matter, as long as he continued to do it. He murmured to her, encouraged her and praised her, until she trembled and her body went utterly limp. She tugged weakly at his hair, unable to bear it a second more, hardly able to breathe.

Dillon released her with one last, leisurely lick, and she collapsed back against the bed, her skin damp with sweat, her heart pounding against her ribs, her body tingling yet almost numb. She waited for him to enter her, to gain his own pleasure. But instead she felt a gentle kiss, as soft as a breeze, over her belly, then on each breast. She was so sensitized to his touch she groaned.

Forcing her eyelids open, she saw Dillon looking down at her, his cheekbones flushed darkly, his eyes bright and burning, his lips parted and wet. He leaned over and kissed her nose, her mouth. She could taste herself and she could feel the heat of him, the repressed energy as it seemed to sizzle between their bodies. "Go to sleep, Virginia."

She blinked, barely able to keep him in focus. The firelight worked like a hypnotic drug, lulling her. "Don't you want to…?"

One side of his mouth quirked. "Oh yeah, I want to. Now, go to sleep."

When she started to speak again, he covered her mouth with his fingertips. They were still damp and scented by her body. She shuddered. "Sleep."

Though she fought it, her eyes did shut, and the last thing she remembered was Dillon gathering her close again, half pulling her over his body and covering them both with a single quilt.

Cozy and comfortable and for the first time in her life totally, completely sexually satisfied, she must have slept like the dead. She couldn't recall stirring a single time the rest of the night, even though she'd never actually slept with a man before.

When she awoke late in the morning, her head felt muzzy and full of cotton, as if she'd drunk too much. She shifted and her body complained, sensitive in places she'd never thought about before. She winced, remembering what she'd done, what she'd let Dillon do.

How could she face him now? What would he say?

Cautiously, her eyes darting around the room, she sat up in the bed. The quiet penetrated and she gasped. No, surely he hadn't left without waking her! Not after last night. She crawled out of the bed, untangling herself from the quilts, and rushed to the door. Before she opened it she saw the note on the center of the table.

Dillon was gone.

chapter 10

THE COLD, HAZY blue-gray day could have accounted for Dillon's mood, except he knew the real reason, and it didn't sit right with him. He wasn't the sort of man who normally suffered extremes of temperament. And he wasn't the sort of man who normally felt the need to dominate a woman so completely.

Much as he missed Virginia already, he didn't look forward to facing her again. He'd slunk out of the cabin like a coward, and felt perverse satisfaction at the way she slept on undisturbed, too replete, too sated, to wake.

Last night had been the most incredible sexual experience of his life, and he hadn't even taken her.

He scratched at his rough-whiskered jaw as he pulled the truck into the parking lot of his apartment building. When he opened the door, wind whooshed past him, flapping his coat and sapping his heat. Even though the truck's heater was adequate, he felt frozen through and he worried about Virginia, wondered if he had brought in enough wood to keep her comfortable until his return. He wanted to get his business over with quickly.

He glanced at his watch as he bounded up the apartment stairs, and saw that he had less than an hour to get to Cliff's office. He wanted to be there, to go through Virginia's files before anyone else arrived. Once it became known she wasn't going to show up, the uproar would begin, and stealing information would be even more difficult. Already his head ached, both from wanting Virginia and because he needed to leave before he got any more wrapped up in this emotional mess.

He rushed into his apartment, prodded by more than time limits. He needed to get back to Virginia, to make sure she was okay after last night. He'd pushed her, and the reward had been sweet. But would she understand?

This time, Dillon needed a hot shower to relax his stiff muscles and clear his head. With any luck at all, it would also wash away the insistent ache of unrequited lust, and the more disturbing element of overwhelming tenderness.

CLIFF WAS SITTING BEHIND his desk, poring over a stack of mail. Dillon walked in unannounced and sprawled in a plush padded chair. He waited impatiently for Cliff to finish reading. He was anxious to get this over with.

Owing to his position within the company, he had keys to every office, and as early as he'd arrived, Virginia's secretary hadn't yet been at her desk. He'd entered the inner office with no problem. He'd expected to have to weed through endless files to find any information, but he'd been surprised by a thick envelope lying in Virginia's In box. The package was without an address, blank on the outside, but tightly sealed. Without remorse, he'd opened it, and found two computer discs, along with a brief note. He'd taken the discs, together with Virginia's laptop computer, out to his car. He'd drive home, grab his truck and head back to the cabin to confront her. Anger still simmered just below the surface, where he hid it from Cliff.

He shouldn't have been surprised to discover Virginia was running her own investigation. In fact, he should have anticipated it. She took charge of everything, so why would this situation be any different? But he felt oddly nettled. She hadn't trusted him enough to confide in him. She obviously had her own suspicions about the embezzlement, but she'd kept quiet. Was it because she, too, wanted to pin the charge on Wade?

His hand fisted. He now had more than one reason to see the conniving little witch again. And he wasn't feeling overly patient.

All he needed was for Cliff to become aware of Virginia's absence, which should be any minute now. The calendar on her desk had her marked for an early meeting. But Miss Virginia Johnson was at present mostly naked and stranded in a deserted cabin. When he'd left, she was sleeping, exhausted from the pleasure he'd given her. Just the way he wanted her.

His muscles twitched in impatience. Dillon knew Cliff, knew his habits, and going through mail like a little boy hoping for a Christmas card was one of them. Sometimes it seemed as if Cliff could only believe he was really the head of the company by opening mail addressed to him as "President."

"So." Cliff looked up after laying aside the paperwork. "Have you found out anything?"

"I assume you're inquiring about your sister?"

"You're damn right. I have to know what she's up to. Do you realize she wasn't here at all yesterday? Didn't show up for work. She told her secretary she was taking the day off, but didn't say where she was going."

"Yes, I know. I went through her date book, but she didn't have anything personal written down for yesterday."

Cliff looked stunned, then very pleased by the idea. "Her date book. I never would have considered that. But maybe I should look at it, too. I mean, it's possible something that looked harmless to you could have been a meeting with a conspirator."

Dillon shook his head. He felt he had to protect Virginia's right to privacy from Cliff, even though he himself had invaded it only minutes earlier. "No. I recognized all the appointments. They were legitimate."

"Damn."

"I'm not surprised I didn't find any suspicious names there. Virginia isn't stupid or careless. If she's doing something behind your back, she certainly wouldn't make a note of it."

"Oh. I suppose that's true."

Cliff appeared to make the admission grudgingly. It probably felt too similar to a compliment for his tastes. He seemed struck by another thought. "If you knew you wouldn't find anything, why the hell look there in the first place?"

"I didn't say I wouldn't find anything. I said I wouldn't find anything concrete. What I was checking for was unaccountable time. Virginia is very organized and she strikes me as a woman who marks down all her appointments religiously. If there had been an hour or two left free, with nothing penned in—"

A knock on the door interrupted Dillon's well-rehearsed speech. Laura Neil breezed in with fresh coffee and an expression of concern. Predictably, Laura hovered near Cliff, who ignored her. He took the coffee without even a polite platitude. Dillon waited, his body in its usual negligent sprawl, but his muscles tightened in expectation. Finally, when Laura didn't leave, he saw the frown gather on Cliff's forehead.

"What is it, Ms. Neil?"

She stiffened at his tone, but otherwise showed no emotion. "Ms. Johnson's secretary says she hasn't arrived yet."

Cliff's brows rose. "Virginia's late?"

"Yes, sir. She had an appointment thirty minutes ago. Mr. Wilson from financing is downstairs waiting. He said the meeting was very important."

Without a word to Dillon, Cliff picked up his phone and punched in a number. "Damn irritant. Not like her to oversleep. What is she thinking," he muttered. Dillon, very aware of Laura listening, wanted to drive his fist into Cliff's face. He forced himself to sit still, to wait. After a moment, Cliff slammed down the phone. "She didn't answer at home, either. She's probably on her way in."

To Laura he said, "Call downstairs. Have Mr. Wilson escorted up here. And have Virginia's secretary bring me his file, right now."

Laura hesitated. "Ms. Johnson could get here any minute…."

"And I don't want to wait! Do what you're told."

Dillon heard Laura's gasp, but his biggest concern was conserving Virginia's business relations. The office door closed with a quiet click and Dillon stood. "Maybe you should think about this for a minute."

Cliff's face darkened and seconds later he flew out of his seat, cursing and pacing around the desk. He looked to be at loose ends, not quite sure what he should or shouldn't do. Dillon decided to give him a nudge in the right direction.

"For the sake of the company's reputation, why not just tell Mr. Wilson that Virginia is ill. There's a nasty flu going around. I'm sure Mr. Wilson would be willing to reschedule. No matter how important the meeting is, it can surely wait a day or two."

"You don't think I can handle things?"

The tone of Cliff's voice showed mingled concern and anger. "I think it will look bad for the company if anyone gets wind of the fact Virginia didn't show."

"Where the hell could she be?"

Surprised, Dillon narrowed his eyes and studied Cliff. "You sound almost worried."

The phone rang and Cliff, still pacing, pushed a button so that the call came over a speaker. Virginia's secretary responded to Cliff's curt hello, saying she didn't have the keys to Virginia's desk or file cabinet and that she couldn't access the files without them. Cliff swallowed. "What's on her agenda today?"

"Three meetings here at the office and a business lunch."

"Keep trying her home number. Let me know if you reach her, or when she shows up."

"Yes, sir."

Cliff disconnected the call. After a long hesitation, he started to reach for the phone again, then cursed instead and pressed his fist against his forehead. "Yesterday and today. Something isn't right."

This wasn't quite the reaction Dillon had expected. He leaned forward on his seat. "What is it?"

Cliff drew several breaths, then dropped his hands to his sides. "Something must have happened. In all the years she's been part of this company, Virginia has never, *not once,* missed an appointment."

Dillon slowly got to his feet. This show of brotherly concern, of near panic, was rewarding in its own way, reassuring him that Virginia wasn't totally despised by her family. But it also made him wonder about his own conclusions on things. If Cliff was guilty of sabotaging Virginia's car, why would he now look so worried about her welfare?

Every time Dillon turned around, things got more complicated. "What do you think could have happened?"

"How the hell should I know? Maybe Virginia screwed up. Maybe whoever she was working with turned on her. She was involved with someone, and I knew—*I knew*—it wouldn't turn out good. She ought to understand by now that no man pretending to be interested in her would be sincere. She should know better than to trust anyone like that."

Dillon's shoulders ached from strain. He wanted, needed,

violence. The urge to hit someone or something almost overwhelmed him. "You have to give her credit for having some common sense. She wouldn't put herself at risk."

"Ha!" Cliff stabbed Dillon with an incredulous look. "She's too damn pigheaded to be cautious. She storms through life as if she alone owns it, and everyone will bow to her wishes."

Dillon thought of the way she'd writhed beneath him, pleading, crying in need, then screaming with an explosive orgasm. She hadn't been bossy then; she'd been more than eager to follow his commands.

"Damn her! What has she gotten herself into?"

Cliff's outburst cut through Dillon's heated memories. He was through playing. He needed to get back to Virginia, the sooner the better. Once they had this all wrapped up, she could deal with her brother however she wished. It wouldn't be his problem.

Summoning his most authoritative tone, the one he knew Cliff would automatically listen to, he said, "Tell Mr. Wilson that Virginia took ill. Tell him she'll have to reschedule when she's feeling up to it. The last thing you want right now is panic running through the building. I'll go check out her house, make certain everything is secure there. I'll talk to a few people, find out who saw her last."

Cliff stepped back to lean against his desk as if he needed the support. "You think something's wrong, too, don't you?"

His face was white, and for the first time, Dillon wavered in his hatred of the man. "I have no idea. But to be on the safe side, I'll look into it." He started toward the door. "I'll get in touch with you later. Don't worry. And don't spread the news around, whatever you do."

Just as his hand closed on the doorknob, a knock sounded. He opened the door and there stood Laura with Mr. Wilson. Dillon stepped back. Cliff reached out his hand to shake Mr. Wilson's. After rapid introductions, where Dillon greeted the older man, Cliff said, "I'm sorry for the inconvenience, but Virginia is home sick today. She got taken by surprise with a case of the flu. I was hoping I could reschedule for her."

Dillon relaxed, seeing that Cliff could handle things. But as he pulled the door shut behind him, he caught the surprise on Laura's face. She stood near her desk, watching him with a worried frown. So she, too, had wondered about Virginia's well-being? Dillon nodded to her, but she caught his arm as he passed by. "She's truly okay?"

Laura was a nice woman, if a bit standoffish; it was a damn shame she wasted herself on Cliff. Dillon patted her hand. "She's fine. Just under the weather."

"You're certain?"

His own gaze sharpened. "I'm certain. Don't give it another thought."

She didn't look convinced, but she forced a smile. "Good. I was…concerned."

Dillon stood watching her a moment longer as she seated herself behind her desk. "Ms. Johnson will appreciate your concern."

"Will you give her my regards, tell her I hope she'll be feeling better soon?"

One brow lifted. "You'll likely be seeing her before I will, Ms. Neil." Crossing his arms over his chest, he waited. He didn't like it that the secretarial pool was speculating on his relationship with Virginia. And that's what it was. Laura's concern now seemed more like curiosity.

"Oh. Of course. What was I thinking?"

"I'm sure I have no idea." With that, he left, feeling ridiculous for getting huffy with a secretary. Before much longer, everything would be settled, and when he left, all gossip would be put to rest.

His chest tightened at the thought. He knew Virginia was the type of woman he could have easily had a relationship with. She was headstrong, capable of standing up to him and anyone else. Her intelligence was appealing and her wit sharp. She was also the most sensually responsive woman he'd ever made love to, even though the lovemaking hadn't included total consummation. He knew having Virginia Johnson beneath him, open to his gaze, her soft flesh touching his, her taste on his tongue, was an experience he'd never forget. When he left her, he'd leave a part of his heart behind.

He figured he'd owe her at least that much.

HE HEARD THE SCREECH when he pulled up in front of the cabin. Given the howling of the wind and the fact that the cabin's only window and door were closed, it must have been a mighty loud screech. His blood seemed to freeze in his veins, and then his instincts kicked in.

Dillon had the door open and his body braced for any

TAKEN!   169

number of threats in less than a heartbeat. What he saw was Virginia, wearing nothing but his white T-shirt, frantically wielding a ratty broom and racing around the floor. "Virginia?"

Her wide, panicked eyes swung around to him, then she threw the broom and flew into his arms. An unexpected rush of emotion gripped him and he held her to him, cradling her close. But Virginia had other plans. She practically climbed his body, still yelping and babbling. He had little choice but to lift her as her frantic urgency sank in, and in the process, the T-shirt ripped. Her gaze searched the room, and Dillon, holding her secure, did the same. Then she pointed and began struggling against him again.

A big black spider, looking totally harassed by all the commotion, scuttled around the dusty floor, going first one way, then the other.

"Kill it!"

He couldn't help laughing. In the next instant, his head was ringing from the blow to his ear.

"Damn you, it's not funny. *Kill it!*"

She screamed suddenly as the spider made a haphazard, indirect line toward them. The sound caused his ears to ring yet again. He nearly dropped her when she launched into a renewed frenzy. Tightening his arms, he stepped toward the spider and, with the side of his boot, swept it out the open door. Virginia hid her face against his neck, her arms so tight around him she nearly choked him. Which was good, because it helped to keep his chuckles muffled.

Once the spider was dispatched, Dillon kicked the door

closed. His earlier anger with her seemed to have evaporated as he relished the feel of her warm weight against his
chest. "It's all right now, Virginia. The bug is gone."

She kept her face hidden and her grip didn't loosen at
all. "It wasn't just a bug. It was a huge hairy spider and it…it
chased me."

His lips twitched, but he sounded calm when he said,
"Spiders don't have hair and they're more afraid of you
than you are of them."

"Not that one. I was going through the wood, to add to
the fire, and it jumped out of the pile and looked right at
me. Before I could even run, it came after me. I kept
pushing it away with the broom…." She shuddered and
pressed her face closer, her warm breath feeling like a caress.
"It wouldn't go away."

"How do you know it was looking at you?" he murmured,
rubbing his cheek against the softness of her hair. "Could
you see the evil glint in its eyes?"

"Yes, damn you, I could!"

He laughed, and this time she didn't hit him. He kissed
her cheek, her temple. "It's all right now. I'm sorry you were
afraid. I got back as quick as I could."

She sighed, pressing even closer, not lifting her face a
single inch. "I feel like an idiot, you know."

"Is that why you're still hiding?"

She nodded. "I really truly have no liking for insects."

"Really truly, huh?" Dillon glanced toward the door,
smiling slightly. "I'm sure that one isn't particularly fond of
you, either. It's damn cold outside."

She leaned her upper body away from him, and her cheeks were bright red. Dillon was more than a little aware of her soft thighs resting on his forearm. Beneath the T-shirt, she was naked, and his body was slowly coming alive to her scent, the feel of her in his arms.

She drew a trembling breath and his gaze dropped to her breasts, then stayed there. The neckline of the T-shirt had ripped and one soft nipple was partially visible, taunting him, making his body shudder with a violent rush of hot lust. He closed his eyes, and then Virginia's voice, strained and quavery, sounded in his ear.

"Put me down. Right now."

chapter 11

VIRGINIA FELT LIKE crying, and that infuriated her. This morning she'd been first so angry she could barely see, then so filled with remorse that she felt hollow inside. The realization that she loved Dillon had come slowly, but the thrill of it had invaded her body and soul. She knew when he left her, she'd be empty. She also knew he wouldn't, *couldn't* stay. He hadn't lied to her, hadn't led her on. He'd only made her love him, only showed her what she could have if things were just a bit different, if she were a different woman, and the knowing almost killed her.

All she could hope for now was to seduce him, to make him give her physical love, since there was no hope for emotional love. She wanted that desperately, wanted to make him feel the same things she'd felt last night. She wanted memories and awareness so that when he was gone, she'd still have a part of him. She knew her life, knew what goals she could reach and those that would never be. There would never be another man for her. Never.

So she'd intended to greet Dillon while lying on the bed,

to play up to him, to be soft and feminine until he gave up and gave in. Instead, she'd raced into his arms like a lunatic, hysterical over a damn spider. Shame bit into her pride. She'd more or less forced him to hold her, when she knew she was no lightweight; she could feel his arms tremble with the strain. Never had she felt so unappealing.

"Put me down, Dillon."

He didn't answer, except that his arms tightened. Virginia peered at him and saw where he was looking. She looked down, too, and heat washed over her. Her breast was bared to his view, pushed up by the position of his arm, one nipple exposed. "Oh."

She started to reach for the shirt, to readjust it, but Dillon said, "Don't," and she went still. His eyes had turned black, filled with heat. It seemed an effortless endeavor for him to lift her even higher, enough so that his mouth could close over her nipple, and Virginia gasped. Her fingers tangled in his silky soft hair, cool from being outside, and she moaned.

He took his time, licking, sucking, rocking her slightly in his arms. He seemed in no hurry to relinquish her weight. She drew an unsteady breath. "Dillon... Put me down. I'm too heavy for you."

In answer, he raised his face and his mouth came down on hers, voracious, hungry. He bent her head back over his arm while he ate at her, thrusting his tongue possessively into her mouth, sucking her tongue into his. She felt him moving, but didn't know what was happening until her back came into contact with the cool quilts on the cot. Dillon followed her down, still kissing her, his hands busy shoving the T-shirt up. "You're not heavy, Virginia. You're perfect."

He placed biting, open-mouth kisses on her throat, her shoulder. He shoved the T-shirt out of his way and again drew on her sensitive nipples, a little roughly, shocking her, thrilling her. He moved down her ribs and belly.

"No!" Virginia caught at his hair, certain where this would lead, when what she wanted was so much more.

He lifted his face to look at her. He was so sexy, so gorgeous, she caught her breath. "No, Dillon."

His chest heaved and he leaned back to look at her, first her face, but his gaze quickly moved over her naked body. His nostrils flared, his jaw locked tight. "I want to give you pleasure, sweetheart."

The endearment touched her soul, made her feel vulnerable. She lifted her chin. "Make love to me, then."

He was shaking his head before she'd finished her request. "I can't, Virginia. You know that."

Brazenly, she cupped his heavy erection in her hand, then shuddered at the size of him. In a husky whisper not at all feigned, she taunted him, wanting to break his control. "Surely you're up to the task, Dillon."

His eyes closed and he groaned. "That's not what I mean and you know it."

"I don't care what you mean. I want you to make love to me, damn it."

"Contrary to what you believe, Virginia, you can't always have what you want."

He was set on refusing her, and she almost hated him—

wished she *could* hate him. "Then leave me alone. I want everything or nothing."

"You want too much."

Disappointment choked her and she shoved him away, scrambling to her feet. She flipped her long hair over her shoulders and stalked to the kitchen, where she leaned against the counter and tried to collect herself. She would not let him know how he'd hurt her. She couldn't.

She heard the bed squeak and turned to find Dillon sprawled on his back, one forearm over his eyes. Never had she seen such an appealing sight. He'd thrown off his coat and his shirt was pulled tight over bulky, solid chest muscles and broad shoulders. His throat was tanned and she wanted to lick him there, to taste his skin. His worn jeans hugged lean hips and a tight abdomen, and his thighs, half-off the bed so that his feet rested flat on the floor, were thick and hard. In his reclining position, the tight jeans clearly defined his erection, and his size and thickness took her breath away. He was an impressive male, in every way possible.

She swallowed audibly, a little afraid of so much masculinity, but drawn to him just the same. On silent feet, she approached him, and without warning, her palm smoothed over him. He jerked, dropping his arm and eyeing her cautiously.

She straddled his lap and heard him growl. "All right, Dillon," she lied. "If you won't give me everything, then at least be fair and let me take from you what you took from me."

She felt him jerk, felt his erection move against her buttocks. His mouth opened and he sucked in air. "Virginia…"

"Shh." She caught his hands as he reached for her, and mimicking him from the previous night, she pressed them down at his sides. "Don't move."

His eyes narrowed at her familiar arrogant tone, and his smile twisted. "You haven't got the nerve."

She caught his flannel shirt in two fists and, staring him in the eye, gave a vicious jerk. Buttons flew across the room, pinging off the wall, rolling across the hardwood floor. Dillon watched her, not saying a word, but as her palms smoothed over his bare flesh, her fingers tangling in his chest hair, his eyes closed and he groaned. She shoved the shirt off his shoulders and down his arms until it caught at his elbows, where he'd tightly rolled the sleeves. She left it like that, trapping his arms, tangled above his head. His biceps bulged; his shoulders strained. She shifted, scooting on his lap, and he growled, lifting his hips.

Virginia leaned forward and lightly bit his nipple. He cursed and went still again. She licked the small wound, touching him everywhere on his upper body. His chest hair was dark, like his eyebrows and eyelashes, contrasting sharply with the sandy-colored hair on his head. She traced the bulges of muscles on his chest and shoulders, felt the silky softness of the hair in the hollows of his arms, then counted down the rippling muscles in his abdomen. She dipped her tongue into his navel and heard his harsh breathing.

"Virginia…"

"Don't you like this, Dillon?"

His words were low and guttural. "I don't think I've ever been so turned on."

She smiled and said, "Good," then nipped his erection through his jeans.

His hips lifted sharply, almost unseating her.

She nibbled on him, thrilled by his response. One hand crept lower, cradling him where he was softer, and his moans grew harsh.

In a rush, Virginia sat up and unsnapped his jeans. When she started on the zipper, he jerked his hips to the side. "Easy, baby. Slow."

Feeling how tight the material was around him, she understood the need for caution. Carefully, she eased the zipper downward, and his erection pushed free of the restriction. Heat enveloped her. His dark briefs weren't sufficient to contain him, and Virginia stood, turning her back to him and straddling one leg to tug off his boot and sock. She knew Dillon had propped himself on his elbows, that he watched her with hot eyes and a small smile. She didn't care.

Stumbling forward as the first boot came free, she steadied herself, then dropped the boot and straddled his other leg.

Dillon made a sound of approval. "I do love the view, honey."

She jerked hard and his boot slipped off. She dropped it, too, and turned to him, dusting off her hands. "Good. I love your whole body."

Fisting her hands in his jeans, she pulled them down. Dillon lifted his hips to help her. "I've never had a woman molest me before."

"I've never been kidnapped before."

His underwear came off next, and once she tossed the briefs with his jeans, he pulled his arms free of the shirt.

Virginia would have reprimanded him for that, except she was too busy ogling his body. He was all hard bone and muscle and overwhelming masculinity. He lay there on the bed, propped on his elbows, watching her at his leisure.

"You going to chicken out?"

She shook her head, but couldn't find adequate words.

"It's all right, Virginia. I won't hurt you."

She didn't quite believe him. She'd had only two lovers in her life, and neither of them had been built like him. How could he not hurt her?

"It doesn't matter." She sat on the side of the bed and wrapped one small hand around him. She couldn't circle him completely, and that fact made her heart race with mingled fear and excitement. He felt heavy and hot and incredibly hard.

He breathed heavily. "Take off your shirt, honey. If we're going to do this, let's do it right."

Virginia shook her head, then leaned forward. Her hair fanned out over his belly and thighs. Dillon groaned, his hands tangling tight in the quilt, his body rigid. When her lips slid over him, he shuddered and curled forward, one hand sliding down to her bottom, the other cupping the back of her head, guiding her. He pulled her shirt up so his hand could touch naked flesh, and when she sucked him, opening her mouth wide to fit him in, his fingers bit into her flesh.

"That's it." Dillon caught her up and tossed her backward on the bed. "I can't take it, Virginia. I've wanted you too long."

"You did it to me."

Despite his arousal, he grinned. "It's just a little different."

Tears welled in her eyes, no matter how she tried to hold them back. "Don't leave me, Dillon. Make love to me. Please."

Their eyes locked for a long instant in time. Dillon cursed low. "I have your laptop in my truck. I have discs from your personal investigator, along with a note that claims unwavering evidence. It'll end today, Virginia, one way or another. And then I'll have to go. Do you understand? I can't stay here. I…"

She opened her arms to him. "Then make love to me now, before it's too late. Let me have what time I can. Everything else will wait."

He hesitated only a moment more, then jerked her legs open and positioned himself between them. His mouth was everywhere at once, urgent and hot. He helped her get out of the shirt, then whispered, "Promise me you won't hate me."

"Never."

"Don't be afraid of me, either."

"I'm not." Virginia found it difficult to talk with his naked body covering hers, moving over her. She clutched at his hard shoulders, relishing the feel of him, his heat and his enticing scent that made her heady with need.

Dillon's mouth touched her cheek, and he spoke against her skin. "You'll take me, Virginia. It'll be a snug fit, so snug I'm liable to lose my mind, but I'll make sure you enjoy it."

She shuddered, lifting her hips into the rhythmic pressure of his; neither of them seemed capable of holding still. She didn't see how it would be possible, but she wanted to feel him inside her, all of him. "Do it now."

"Oh no. You're not ready. And no way in hell am I going to rush this." His hands were at her breasts, his thumbs teasing her nipples. "I have only one condom with me."

"I have a whole box." She spoke before she thought about it, and heard Dillon's laugh.

"A whole box, huh? You really did have some high expectations for me, didn't you?"

Her body ached. Her stomach quivered, and he found the wit to joke? She pounded on his shoulders. "Dillon…"

"All right, baby." He snagged his jeans off the floor and retrieved the condom from his pocket. It was only late morning, but the cabin was still dim due to the cloudy day and the lack of windows. The firelight was mellow and golden, not bright. As Dillon opened the foil packet with his teeth, Virginia took the opportunity to touch him, to familiarize herself with his body. When she again leaned down to kiss him, mesmerized by his response to her mouth, he groaned and pushed her back on the bed.

"You're going to be the death of me, woman."

He slipped the condom on and came down over her. "Wrap your legs around me."

Nervously, anxiously, Virginia did as directed. Dillon kept his gaze glued to hers and hooked his arms beneath her legs, lifting them even higher. She felt open and vulnerable, and in a small part of her mind, she admitted she liked it. As he started to push into her, she winced, automatically tightening her body.

He crooned to her, keeping up the subtle pressure, the slow steady rocking of his hips. "Relax, sweetheart. Don't fight me."

She tipped her face back, not wanting him to see her discomfort. Her teeth sank into her bottom lip.

Dillon released one of her legs and reached down between their bodies. With the rough pad of his thumb, he stroked her. She jumped, startled. The feeling was too acute and she tried to shy away from it.

"Shh. I'll help you, honey. Just relax." He continued plying her most sensitive flesh, determined. "Lift your breast for me."

Virginia whimpered, already in an agony of sensation.

"Do it."

With shaking hands, she cupped one breast and offered it high. His mouth clamped onto her nipple and he drew gently. "Umm."

"I can't stand it," she said, her voice high and tight.

He licked, circled her nipple. "Yes, you can."

She felt him sink a little deeper into her body. The intrusion burned, but at the same time soothed. Her body seemed to be demanding conflicting things. There was an emptiness that she wanted him to fill, and the aching pressure of him doing just that. She wanted to pull back, but she also wanted to draw him nearer.

"Dillon…"

"Just a little more. Come on, Virginia. Open up for me. You can take all of me." His thumb pressed and manipulated and she cried out. "That's it. A little more."

Her heart raced, urged on by the gentle friction of his thumb, and she gave a broken moan, lifting herself to him, hearing him groan in return, and then he thrust hard and filled her.

She recoiled, shocked, but he held her hips, keeping her still, keeping himself buried deep inside her. His chest heaved against her.

It was too much; she felt stretched too tightly, felt him much too deeply. She hadn't imagined anything like this, lovemaking out of her control, both physically and mentally. She couldn't seem to draw a breath, couldn't move because he held her so close, pinned by his body.

Slowly, she became aware of other things, of the furious gallop of Dillon's heartbeat, the strain of his muscled body over her as he struggled to remain still, his harsh, deep breathing. God she loved him, and he was hurting as much as she.

Virginia smoothed her hands down his back and kissed his shoulder. After a shaky breath, she said, "I'm okay."

He laughed, a strained sound. "I know it. But I'll admit I'm glad you realize it. I don't know how much longer I could've waited."

When he began to thrust, slow and smooth, it both hurt and tantalized. He filled her, and each deep push dragged against her sensitive flesh as surely as his thumb had. She kept her arms around his neck, her legs tight around his hips, and held on, half-afraid to let go. Dillon tangled a hand in her hair and turned her face up to his, kissing her deeply, fusing their mouths as well as their bodies. Virginia felt the first stirrings of a climax gaining quickly on her, the sizzling heat began to swirl low in her belly. *"Dillon."*

He lifted her hips in his large hands and pulled her more snugly to his body, touching her so deeply she screamed. "Yes," he groaned. "Now, baby, please, now."

He shouted, his head thrown back, every muscle in his body taut and delineated, showing his incredible strength and the wonderful way he tempered it.

Virginia watched him through a haze of pleasure and tears, loving him, missing him already. As Dillon slowly lowered himself over her, she held him close, and their heartbeats mingled. Whatever else happened, she would never regret meeting this man. And she'd never love this way again.

HE WISHED SHE'D put on some clothes. Making love to Virginia three times in as many hours hadn't satisfied his need. He felt desperate to tie her to him, to take all of her that he could while he could. Fighting his growing need for her, biting back the words he wanted so badly to say, was keeping him on edge.

But Virginia, now that she'd decided they should be lovers, held nothing back. She kept touching him, tenderly, *lovingly*, in ways he'd never been touched before, and that would set him off. Even a simple touch to his back or shoulders held special meaning when her golden eyes were smiling at him. Especially since she still wore only his shirt, even forsaking the damn quilt. She'd look at him and her lips would tremble and he'd get a hard-on every time. He wanted to drown in her scent, and had tried to do just that until she'd cried and begged and threatened to kill him if he didn't take her. He'd placed one last kiss on the warm, sweet heat of her body and then thrust into her, giving her the release she needed.

Even in bed, she was a demanding, bossy woman. She

pleased him more than any woman he'd ever known or could have imagined. Leaving her would be the hardest thing he'd ever done, but he had no choice.

After a hasty lunch of sandwiches, he'd set up all her computer equipment on the rickety table and she was in the process of reading the discs. Dillon couldn't have read them at work because he didn't have the necessary password to find the files, but he was looming over her shoulder, not willing to trust her a single inch. She typed in the words *You got it.*

"That's the password?"

She laughed. "Yeah. Every time I ask Troy to do something almost impossible with computers, he says—"

"You got it."

"Right." As she spoke, she sorted through files. "Troy is my inside guy. He helped me set up some stuff on the company's computer system."

"Stuff your brother knows nothing about."

Virginia grinned at him. "Yep. You see, each computer terminal is coded. So not only does the person using the computer have a user ID, but we can track who used which computer. According to Troy's note, it got complicated tracking the embezzler because— Ah, here we go."

She read a moment, Dillon peering over her shoulder, then suddenly she stiffened. Dillon read on a moment more before he began to snicker. "Ms. Johnson," he said with mock severity. "So you were the culprit all along."

Virginia didn't think it was funny. She turned to glare at Dillon. "That bastard used my ID!"

He kissed her mouth, then didn't want to stop kissing her.

She clutched at his shirt. When he pulled back, she asked, "You don't really think—"

He kissed her again, quick and hard. "Of course not." He took her hand. "Honey, did you see which terminal was used?"

Virginia glanced back at the screen. "No, I…"

Dillon waited. "It's your brother, Virginia."

"Ridiculous. Cliff would have no inkling how to do anything this elaborate." She scanned the typed words, then frowned.

"But he would surely know your user ID and all the passwords. And it was the computer in his office."

Without responding, Virginia hit a button on the keyboard and backed up several pages. "Ha! That transaction took place during a week when Cliff was out of town."

Dillon stared thoughtfully at the screen. "You're certain?"

"I think I know what's going on in the company, thank you."

"Okay, so that only means he's working with someone, which is what I suspected all along. I had hoped, for your sake, that he wasn't involved, but it's the only thing that makes sense."

"And who would he work with?" As she spoke, she turned to face him, swiveling sideways in her chair. Seeing her naked legs and the shadow of her nipples through the T-shirt made reasoning very difficult.

Dillon knelt in front of her. "Honey, you have to realize you've collected a few enemies along the way."

"The employees respect me."

"I know that. But a lot of the management, especially the men, resent you. Don't you think it would be easy for Cliff to find a cohort if he chose to?"

"I suppose." Then she narrowed her eyes and crossed her arms under her breasts. "You told me yesterday you suspected someone. Cliff was it?"

Dillon chewed on the side of his mouth, debating what he should say to her, how he should say it. Virginia slapped a hand on the table. "Stop it! You promised to tell me everything, but now I can see you calculating! Just for once, be truthful with me."

He didn't like her tone or her attitude. Slowly, he straightened, glaring down at her. She glared right back. He didn't want to hurt her, but she did deserve the truth. Virginia, more than any woman he knew, could handle the truth. "I think it's possible Kelsey could be involved."

She sat frozen a moment, then chuckled. "Oh, Dillon, really. Kelsey is a child."

"A child having a child? She's pregnant, she's a little desperate and from what Wade tells me she resents the constant animosity in the family."

"And you're telling me she blames me alone? Cliff's as much at fault as I am."

"Unless Cliff has convinced her otherwise. Kelsey isn't like you, babe. She's wants to be a wife and mother, not a corporate leader."

Virginia turned her face away. "I want those things, too." She shrugged, looking suddenly small and defensive, and Dillon wanted to hold her, to carry her back to bed and try to keep the world at bay. But he knew he couldn't.

"I haven't been given a lot of choices in what I want to do with my life, Dillon. The company is all I've had."

He shoved his hands deep into his jeans pockets. "Are you saying you'd give it up? That you'd walk away from it to be a wife, to have babies?"

He watched her hands curl into fists on the table, watched her shoulders stiffen. "Why couldn't a woman have both? This is a new era. A huge percentage of women work and have families."

Dillon felt the last of a small dream die away. Virginia would never leave her family's company, and he had to take care of his father in Mexico. There was no future for them, and never had been. He'd known that from the first. He'd warned himself time and again that touching her would be a mistake. It had been nothing but foolish romanticism making him wonder if whatever she felt for him could ever be more.

Dillon pulled out the chair opposite her and straddled it. Virginia wouldn't quite meet his gaze. "I see no reason you couldn't have both, honey. If any woman could pull it off, you could. I wish you all the best, you know."

Virginia sighed. Her eyes were shiny with tears, but he pretended not to see, knowing how badly she'd hate the sign of vulnerability. She propped her head on her hand and sent him a small, shaky smile.

"I wish you the same."

They stared at each other until Dillon cleared his throat. "Well, unfortunately, the embezzlement is only part of our problem. There really was a physical threat to you. Someone got into your house using a key, and since I was with you, we'll never know what might have happened. But someone also tampered with your brake lines, and that intent can't be misconstrued. They knew what you'd be driving into, that you could have been killed. Think about it. Who would gain if you got hurt or lost your standing in the company, other than Cliff. And Lord knows that man resents your intrusion."

"I'm not intruding! I have every bit as much right to be involved as he does."

"I believe you, but does Kelsey? Does she think you might be stepping on some toes, angering her brother and in effect causing family problems?"

"You're suggesting that my family—*my brother and sister*—would deliberately do me harm."

He hated the way she looked, that obstinate set of her shoulders that told him how much he'd wounded her. He took her hand and held tight when she would have pulled away. "I just don't know, Virginia. Before today, I would have said yes, that Cliff was more than capable of such a thing."

"What happened today? Did Cliff suddenly grow a halo?"

"No. When Laura told Cliff you hadn't shown up for work, he all but panicked. He looked more concerned than I've ever seen him. In fact, I'm supposed to be looking for you right now."

"Is that right? Working a side job for Cliff?"

He started to tell her about his side job, that Cliff had hired him to keep tabs on her, but saw no point in it. She was hurting enough. "As soon as we finish reading through the results of your investigation, I can take you back, and Cliff will no doubt welcome you with open arms."

She made a face. "Don't push the bounds of reality, Dillon. If Cliff wants me kept safe, it's because he knows he can't run the company without me, regardless of the fuss he makes sometimes. That in itself proves he couldn't be the embezzler. But I suddenly have an idea who it might be."

Dillon waited, but Virginia only shook her head. "Let's finish seeing what Troy turned up, and then we'll know."

They pulled their chairs together and continued reading the data entered in an organized way. Each case of missing money was noted, and which terminal had been used, plus the user's ID. Several of the initial thefts had been done using Wade's password. After that, things got sketchy. Small amounts were removed using Cliff's ID, Virginia's and several others. They were all taken from the same terminal. Dillon narrowed his eyes as he came to the same conclusion as Virginia.

"The necessary info could have been stolen from Cliff. Only the people with highest security clearance would have had access to all those codes."

Virginia nodded. "I keep my important files locked up, but Cliff isn't nearly as responsible. It's possible that someone with access to his office could have found the codes, without knowing that the terminals were also monitored."

"Laura Neil." Dillon stared at Virginia as so many things started to take shape in his mind. "It makes sense. The original thefts were blamed on Wade, and he used to be involved with her before he met Kelsey."

"And Cliff got her on the rebound. I hate to say it, but he hasn't treated her well. She knows that we argued about her, that I tried to convince Cliff to have her transferred if he was going to become involved with her. But he refused and I let it go. Now it appears their affair is over, but she's in the awkward position of still being his secretary."

Dillon leaned back in the chair and rubbed his eyes. "I felt sorry for her today, Cliff was so indifferent to her. She acts like she's still very hung up on him."

"'Acts' being the operative word. It wouldn't do for her to show she despised him. If that happened, she might get fired, and that would put an end to her skimming money."

"Damn, I can't believe I overlooked her. She just seemed so...pathetic."

Virginia made a rude sound. "Face it. You overlooked her because she's female and you wanted to blame Cliff."

With a raised brow, Dillon admitted, "That, too."

"We have to get out of here. I need a phone so I can call Troy. He can put a personal audit on Laura. We should be able to figure out if the money has shown up in her accounts. Plus he knows her. Any fancy new cars or expensive vacations might prove interesting."

"Troy can access her accounts?"

"He's a top-notch hacker, which is the main reason I keep him around and pay him a damn good wage. I want him working for me, not against me."

Virginia stood, then looked at Dillon expectantly. "I'll need my clothes."

Once again, his gaze skimmed her body; he relished the sight of her, the lush curves and feminine roundness. "Not yet. I have a cellular in the truck. Let me get it and you can call Troy from here."

"Why not just go back to my place and call?"

With his hands on her shoulders, Dillon bent low to give her a direct look. "Because someone wanted to hurt you, which you seem to keep forgetting. I'm not taking any chances with your safety. Once I find out if it really was Laura, then we can contact the police and go from there."

He could tell Virginia wanted to argue, but he ignored her protests and went out to the truck. She could make her calls, but there was no way he would let her put herself at risk. He might not always be around to protect her, to cushion her from the world and her own prickly pride, but he was here now, and he wanted her to know how important she was to him. He couldn't tell her, but he could try to show her.

VIRGINIA HUNG UP the phone. It was nearing six o'clock and Troy had been diligently applying his computer expertise for the past several hours. She turned to Dillon, feeling equally relieved and sad. They had the information they needed, and that was a relief, but it also meant their time alone was over. Dillon would take her from the cabin and the real world would intrude. She felt the loss like a physical blow.

"What did he find out?"

Virginia had been jotting down all Troy said, and now she flipped the piece of paper toward Dillon. "Laura had enough of the deposits in her accounts, in the same amounts as the missing funds, to prove her guilt. Stupid, really, but I suppose she thought the amounts were small enough not to matter. I mean, a couple of hundred here and there is really not all that noticeable when taken from so many different sources. Troy said she also has her house for sale."

"The amounts might have been small, but they really added up." Dillon stood and stretched his shoulders. "I guess that cinches it."

"If it's okay with you, I'd like to go by the office and get all the files on this together. We can notify the police in the morning from my house."

She watched him, hoping he wouldn't argue. They should probably move tonight, but she was so tired, and she hoped to have one more night alone with Dillon. His sad smile showed he had the same thought. Though they'd made love for hours while waiting for news, it hadn't been enough. Virginia didn't think a lifetime would be enough, but every day was precious.

"Tomorrow is fine," he told her softly.

He stepped close and kissed her, holding her face between his large warm hands and lingering until she thought she might beg him to stay at the cabin with her. But she knew that couldn't be. According to Dillon, Cliff was worried, and she could only imagine how relieved Wade would be to know he was in the clear. Those people deserved to be told as soon as possible.

Dillon brought Virginia's clothes in from the truck and laid them by the fire to warm while she showered. A half hour later, they were on the way home.

chapter 12

DILLON KNEW SOMETHING was wrong the second the elevator opened onto the floor. He couldn't exactly explain his unease to Virginia, because it wasn't anything concrete, just a gut reaction that told him she was in danger.

She'd been holding his hand since they left the truck. No woman had ever held his hand, not even when he was a kid. He never had a mother, and the endless string of women his father had brought around weren't interested in a little boy. The gesture now seemed sweet and almost protective. He didn't want her to let go. But he had to keep her safe.

"I want you to wait downstairs with the night-shift guard."

Virginia raised her brows. "Why? Cliff is surely gone for the night, so you won't get a chance to confront him, if that was your thought."

She was too astute for own damn good. "I would have done that. In fact, I'd like to break his damn nose. But right now I have other concerns." He hesitated a moment, then admitted, "Something doesn't feel right."

Smiling, Virginia tugged on his hand and started him down the hallway to Cliff's office. "Let me guess. You expect to find Laura Neil brandishing a bazooka and threatening the masses?"

Dillon pulled her up short and shoved her behind him, staring down the dim hallway. "Now who's underestimating a woman?" He nodded toward Cliff's office and they both saw that a light was on, shining dully through the etched window in the door. The entire floor should have been shut down and locked for the night.

Virginia stared. "Well, hell. What is that brother of mine up to now?"

"Shh. Not another word out of you or I'll lock you in a closet." When she started to protest, he said, "I mean it, Virginia. I have the keys in my pocket, so don't test me."

Luckily for his peace of mind, she didn't argue. Dillon pressed her down on the floor, in the shadows of a large decorative plant. "Stay here. I'm going to see what's going on." He narrowed his gaze on her. "Don't move."

Glaring, Virginia gave him a mock salute. He answered by kissing her. "I couldn't stand it if anything happened to you, honey." As he crept away, he could feel Virginia's eyes on his back.

The door to Cliff's outer office opened silently. Dillon peered in, saw the inner office was the one brightly lit and slid through the doorway. As he moved along the wall, nearing the inside door, he could hear the muffled tones of people speaking. Rather than burst in, he took his time, listening and assessing the situation.

It didn't take long to figure out that Laura had already guessed her game was over. Cliff feebly tried to claim he loved her, gaining even more of Dillon's disdain, but Laura only laughed. Her voice overrode Cliff's panicked one.

"You always were a sniveling bastard, Cliff. You deserve anything I do to you."

"I thought you cared about me."

Her words took on a hard edge. "Yes, maybe at first. When Wade dropped me, I was content to set him up, to make him pay. You'd fired him, and that was enough punishment. But your sister insisted on investigating everything. She wanted to ruin all my plans, including my plans for you."

"Virginia had nothing to do with me and you."

"You're so naive, Cliff. You pretended to care about me, and I stupidly thought you'd marry me. I knew the only hindrance would be Virginia. She'd go to any lengths to protect this damn company, and that means she'd keep digging about the missing money until she finally caught up to me."

"You did something to her?"

There was indifference in Laura's tone. "I didn't really intend to hurt her, just distract her from the investigation. I figured if she had to worry about her own life, she wouldn't have time to stick her nose into the business."

Dillon heard Cliff clear his throat. He could almost taste the man's fear and assumed Laura had a gun trained on him. Cliff's voice shook when he spoke.

"But then I lost interest in you, so that changed everything?"

"Not really. I'd already realized that even if you married me, it wouldn't have mattered. Eventually Virginia would have succeeded in totally discrediting you. She's the ruling factor in this company, not you. So I decided to take one more hefty sum and get out. It was stupid of you to show up here tonight, Cliff."

"I was worried about my sister, damn you."

"Hmm. And that surprises me. I thought the two of you hated each other. Or were you worried because you know without Virginia, you'd fail completely?"

For the first time, Cliff sounded angry. "*Bitch.* She's my sister, and regardless of our differences, I love her. This damn company has nothing to do with it."

Dillon sensed Virginia's presence even before she touched his arm. He turned. She stood in the darkness right behind him, tears glimmering in her eyes. He wanted to curse, wanted to throttle her and lock her away someplace safe, but he couldn't do a damn thing. Any noise at all would distract Laura, and after Cliff's melodramatic confession, he really didn't want to see the man shot.

Dillon raised a finger to his lips as Laura again spoke.

"I do wonder where your errant sister is."

"If you've hurt her, Laura, I'll kill you."

That caused a burst of hilarity. "I'm the one with the gun, Cliff. And believe me, I wouldn't mind putting a bullet through your cold heart. But first, finish transferring the funds as I told you. We've done enough talking."

There was the almost silent pecking of the keyboard, and then Cliff said wearily, "It's done."

"Excellent. Now, stand up and come over here."

"You can't shoot me in the office, Laura. The night guards

would hear. And you know, since hiring the new security manager, the men working are more than capable."

"Shut up while I think."

"You know why I grew tired of you so quickly, Laura?"

"Shut up."

"Probably the same reason Sanders did. You play the role of lapdog to perfection. You can complain about my sister all you like, but at least she's an intelligent woman. She provides conversation and wit, not just babbling."

"Shut up, damn you!"

"All I got from you was blind adoration, and at times it almost made me sick."

Laura lost her temper, screeching in rage, and that's when Dillon threw open the door. Laura whirled, getting off a wild shot that missed Dillon as he rolled across the floor. Cliff ran to the outer office, almost knocking Virginia down as she stuck her head in the doorway. Dillon effectively tackled Laura, gripping her wrist and squeezing until she dropped the gun. Virginia, much to his dismay, ran in and picked up the weapon. Laura still fought him, scratching his neck and the side of his face, kicking her long legs wildly.

When Virginia realized Dillon planned to do no more than hold her, regardless of how she injured him, she knelt by Laura's head and whispered, "Put one more mark on him, and you'll have me to deal with."

There was enough venom in her tone to make Laura go completely still. Dillon grinned at Virginia, then came to his feet, holding Laura's wrists in one hand.

Security guards rushed in, guns drawn, and they took

control of Laura. Dillon removed the automatic weapon from Virginia's hand, giving her a chiding glance. "You were supposed to stay in the hall, safe."

Before she could answer, Cliff began a hysterical recitation of the events. Dillon listened with half an ear, most of his attention on Virginia, who looked pale. The guards handcuffed Laura and led her to the outer office. The police had been called and would arrive shortly.

"It's really over, isn't it?"

Huge tears welled in her eyes and Dillon had difficulty swallowing. "Don't do this, baby. You're killing me."

"I love you, you know."

He closed his eyes, drawing a shuddering breath. "I have to leave now. My father's waiting for me in Mexico. Nothing will change that."

Cliff sidled up to them and clamped a hand on Virginia's arm. "Oh, this is rich. I'm here, almost getting shot, and you've obviously been off whooping it up with an employee!"

Dillon gave Virginia an apologetic look, his eyes never leaving her face, and with his left hand, socked Cliff right in the nose. The smaller man went down like a stone.

His hand, no longer fisted, cupped her face. "If you ever need me, honey, just let me know."

Her expression changed, became almost desperate. "No, you can't leave now. I won't allow it."

Her panic twisted his insides. "It's better if I don't get tangled up with the police. You can handle things."

Cliff writhed on the floor next to them, holding his bloody nose and cursing.

"Dillon—"

He leaned forward and kissed her, a kiss of tenderness and regret. "I love you, Virginia." The tears spilled over and he groaned in genuine agony. "Shh. God, don't cry, Virginia. If I could change things, I swear I would."

Her chin lifted. "I'm glad you kidnapped me."

He managed a smile at her false bravado. "I have a feeling it'll always be my fondest memory." He touched her cheek one more time, then turned to go. As he passed through the outer doorway, he heard Virginia bark, "Oh, come on, Cliff, get up. We have to take care of this mess."

Dillon smiled. She would be okay. She didn't need him. The truth was, he needed her. She'd filled him up, made him whole and gave credence to his beliefs about life and love and reality. His gut cramped painfully, more so with every step he took, and he decided he might as well get used to the feeling. Because he knew that for the rest of his life, he would feel empty.

He figured it was no more than he deserved.

A month later—

"WADE SAYS HE GOT a hefty promotion, along with a bonus."

Dill Sr. laughed. "A little retribution to ease the guilt?"

"I suppose. Virginia was responsible for the promotion. Cliff, believe it or not, provided the bonus as a wedding present, and from what Wade said, it was a large one."

"Good for him. Doesn't hurt to start off a marriage financially sound. True love will take you only so far."

Dillon stared at his coffee for long moments, lost in

thought, then finally tipped the cup to his mouth and took a large gulp. The bitter taste suited him just fine on this hot, dusty morning. He put Wade's letter aside.

Staring at his father, seeing a glimmer of amusement in the dark eyes so like his own, he said, "Virginia is handing over a lot of the control to Cliff. According to Wade, Cliff's learned his lesson."

"So why the long face, then? You know, I'm getting damn tired of watching you brood."

His father grinned when he said it, had been grinning since the moment Dillon walked back in from his week-long buying trip a few hours earlier. "I'm not brooding. There's just something I don't understand." He ignored the toast his father pushed toward him and concentrated on his coffee, instead. "According to Wade, resolving the problems in the company has brought Virginia and her family closer together. Virginia even offered to sell out to Cliff, but he wouldn't take her offer. He says he needs her guidance and input until he learns how to run things on his own. Kelsey has gotten involved, too, along with Wade, so they're lending a helping hand."

"Sounds like a real family-run organization."

"I suppose. But I can't see Virginia offering to sell out. That company means too much to her. It's her whole life. I'm afraid something's not right."

"You're just afraid you made a damn fool mistake, that's all. I keep telling you, you should go back for her. You find a woman like that, you don't just let her go."

Dillon had heard it endless times. For weeks, his father

had picked his brain for every detail. Dillon hadn't admitted to loving Virginia, fearing his father would suffer guilt, rightfully assuming that Dillon stayed only because his father needed him.

"Tell me again what she looks like."

"Dad…" Talking about Virginia, remembering, hurt like hell.

"Long red hair, right? Round in all the right places."

"Yeah." Dillon grinned despite himself. "And soft and sexy, but so mule-headed she scares most men away."

"Humph. Not my son."

Dillon grunted at his father's misplaced pride. "She's strong. And a fighter."

"A woman like that'd make a damn good wife and mother."

Thinking of Virginia that way tormented Dillon. He could so easily see her with a baby in her arms and a corporate report on her desk. She'd make beautiful babies, with tempers as fiery as her own. And between the two of them, their children would never feel alone or afraid.

But it wouldn't happen. Dillon had told her that if she ever needed him to let him know. She could easily have gotten his address from Wade, but he hadn't heard from her. She'd gotten on with her life, just as he'd told her to do, but the reminder of what he'd lost ate at him day in and day out.

He finished off his coffee and shoved back his chair. "I have a fence to repair today and the vet's coming to check over the new mares I bought. I gotta get out of here."

As Dillon started to stand, his head swam. He sank back into his seat, cursing. His father grinned.

Dillon couldn't get sick now, because that would give him too much free time to think about Virginia. Since returning to the ranch, he'd filled his days with the hardest physical labor, working from sunrise to sundown. His nights were the worst; he filled them with endless paperwork and expansion plans. None of it helped. Virginia was never far from his thoughts.

He looked at his father, but his face wouldn't come into focus. "What the hell is going on?"

He heard a door open and Virginia stepped into the kitchen. Dillon blinked, not sure he was seeing right, wondering if he'd only imagined her because he missed her so damn bad. He lifted a heavy hand toward her and she dropped to her knees by his chair. "I love you, Dillon."

"God." He must be dreaming. "You can't be here."

"Oh, I'm here all right. It's payback time. You told me to let you know if I needed you. Well, I do. But I need you forever, not just for a little while. You didn't come to me, so I'm taking you."

He could feel himself fading. "What did you do?"

"I drugged your coffee."

And his father, through his chuckles said, "Damn, but she learned from a master, didn't she?"

As Dillon started to slump, Dill Sr. called out, "Come and give the lady a hand, boys. My son is no lightweight."

Virginia, a touch of worry in her tone, said, "Thank you, sir, I wouldn't want him to get hurt."

"Call me Dad. We're going to be related, after all."

And Dillon smiled groggily.

DILLON AWOKE NAKED. He opened his eyes slowly, looking around. He felt silk sheets beneath him, nothing over him. At least he'd had the decency to leave Virginia in her lingerie, providing her a bit of modesty. He'd even covered her with a quilt. Of course, Virginia wouldn't show such consideration, the witch. He chuckled.

This...*palace* was nothing compared with the cabin he'd taken her to. There was champagne chilling in a bucket of ice beside the bed and a gas fireplace blazed brightly. He started to sit up, and that's when he realized his hands were tied. He looked over his shoulder. A soft, woven velvet rope was knotted around his wrists and then looped through a scrolled newel post on the back of the bed. His body stirred, his loins tightened.

Virginia opened a door and walked in, her bare feet sinking into the thick carpet. "You're awake!"

He tugged on the ropes, working up a believable frown. He didn't want to spoil her fun. "Was this necessary?"

Perching on the side of the bed by his hip, she surveyed his naked body. Her gaze lingering on his erection. "What have you been thinking about, Dillon?"

"About making love to you right now."

Her eyes brightened and her cheeks flushed. "Yes, well... I do believe we have a few things to get straight first."

"Take off your robe."

She made an exasperated face at him. "Really, Dillon. I'm the one in charge right now. That's why you're tied down. You have a tendency to run roughshod over me."

"You like it. Now, take off the robe."

She hesitated a moment, then shrugged. "Suit yourself." The gold satin robe slid down her shoulders to pool at her hips. She stood, then pushed it aside. Dillon stared at her lush body. "I missed you something terrible, baby."

She lay down beside him, one hand resting on his taut stomach, her head on his chest. "Not as bad as I missed you. Every day, I wanted to call you, to insist you come back to me. But you were so final when you left, and it…it hurt too much to think you might turn me away again."

"I never did that, honey."

"I know. Wade told me that you'd never leave your father. He said he thought you wanted to be with me, but that your loyalty would keep you in Mexico."

Dillon kissed the top of her head, carefully testing the strength of his restraints. He didn't know how much longer he'd be able to wait and let her lead the way. "I knew you wouldn't leave the company, and I couldn't leave Dad. I'm all he has, Virginia."

"I understand. But the company doesn't mean that much to me. I thought it did, because it was all I had. But then I had you, and I knew nothing else mattered as much."

"You offered to sell your share of the company to Cliff so you could come back to Mexico with me."

She surprised him by leaning up and shaking her head. "No. I can't see me living in Mexico *and*," she said when he started to object, her expression stern, "you will let me finish. I'm not good at roughing it, Dillon."

He glanced around at his surroundings. "So I can see."

"Well, I'm sorry, but being chased by huge nasty spiders and having my feet freeze aren't memorable moments."

He narrowed his eyes. "And what about the rest of it?"

"The stuff women dream of."

He grinned.

"Kelsey will give birth in a few months, and Cliff still needs me to guide him, at least until he catches on a little better. I'm going to be a consultant for him."

"I see."

"Living in Mexico would really complicate things, put me too far out of reach."

Dillon fought back his rising anger. "You're not leaving me again, Virginia, so you can forget it."

She kissed him, long and deep, her body moving over his, her hands exploring. Finally she lifted her head, and Dillon felt sharp frustration.

"Your father and I have it all worked out."

He groaned. "You've been plotting with my father?"

"We talked quite a bit while you were out of town. He wants to live with his housekeeper."

"With Maria?" Dillon couldn't quite take it in. Maria was a wonderful person, ten years younger than his father, and not at all his type.

Virginia laughed. "They're in love. They want to get a small house and take care of each other. I thought we'd hire someone to check up on them twice weekly, just to make certain they're doing okay." Her brows drew together in a frown. "As big and powerful as your father seems, he's still old enough to need a little help, I think."

Dillon chuckled. His father was six feet two inches tall, weighed almost as much as Dillon and still had a commanding air about him. "Lately he's had a few health problems, but he doesn't like to admit it. Come to think of it, Maria is the only one he lets pamper him. Now I know why."

Virginia toyed with the hair on Dillon's chest, not quite meeting his eyes. "Don't get mad, okay?"

He stilled. "What did you do?"

"I bought a ranch." She spoke quickly, giving away her uncharacteristic nervousness. "It's a little bigger than the one you have in Mexico— Damn it, Dillon, stop shaking your head at me! It's not like it's a bribe or anything. Once you sell your ranch, you can pay me half on it, okay?"

"No, it's not okay." He tugged at his restraints, but stilled when she huffed out a curse.

She sat up, her legs astride his hips, her arms crossed under her bare breasts. "This is why I tied you down! You're so damn stubborn!"

He choked on that, distracted from the enticing view of her body. "Me? You think *I'm* stubborn?"

"Yes! I love you. I want us to be together. I'm willing to let Cliff run the company now, but I can't let him ruin it, and I can't just sit idle. So I'm starting my own business. The ranch and the business property I just bought are in the States, not that far from your father, but closer to my family so I can check up on Cliff and we can visit with Wade and Kelsey and the baby when it gets here."

"Virginia—"

"You'll love the area, Dillon, I promise. It's in New

Mexico, due north of Albuquerque, and the ranch house is huge and the land is beautiful and the people who owned it raised horses but then they had to sell and...well, it's perfect...for us."

Dillon dropped his head back and laughed. She could make him nuts with her take-charge attitude, but he'd missed her so much. "All right. I'll look at the ranch. But I'm paying you back for all of it. I'm not going to live off your money, Virginia." He didn't want her ever to wonder at his motives, not when so many men had tried to use her.

She snorted. "Then I won't live off yours, so if you won't let me pay half for the ranch, I can't live there. I guess that leaves us at an impasse."

Quietly, he studied her rigid posture and mutinous expression. He knew she felt free to be so bossy, given that he was tied down. He decided to put an end to that before things got out of hand. They might as well start things off right. "Honey, move for a minute."

She looked hurt first, then angry, as she scuttled off his abdomen to stand beside the bed. Dillon laced his fingers together tightly, flexed his arms and broke the small spindle off the back of the bed. Virginia stood there, her eyes wide, and gaped at him as he loosened the rope and tossed it aside. He turned to her with a narrowed gaze. "Now."

She launched herself at him, knocking him back on the bed and sprawling over him. Her hands tangled in his hair and she held his face still while she kissed him all over, his nose, his chin, his eyes. "I love you, Dillon. Please, say you'll marry me. Let's have babies and a home and grow old together."

He locked his arms around her and rolled her beneath him. She was so beautiful to him, so determined and gutsy and proud. Her hair fanned out over the pillows, wild and tangled and as fiery as the hot temper he adored. Her cheeks were flushed, but her golden eyes seemed filled with doubt, and he wouldn't allow it. He didn't like her being humble, not when she had arrogance and bravado down to a fine art. "I love you," he growled, tightening his hold. "One way or another, I'm never letting you go, so you might as well get used to it."

She grinned as he kissed her, tears seeping from her eyes. When Dillon lifted his head, he said, "Everything will work out, Virginia. I really do love you."

"I love you, too." She spoke softly, almost shyly, peeking up at him. "And I adore your father. He made me promise we'd have some babies right off." Her gaze flicked up to his face, then away again.

Dillon kissed her nose. "I'm willing."

"I told him if he got rid of that horrid tattoo of a naked lady on his arm, he could be a surrogate grandfather to Kelsey's baby, too."

Astonished and momentarily distracted from his need, Dillon croaked, "You're kidding, right?" When she just blinked up at him, he said, "You tried telling my father what to do?"

She snorted. "I didn't try. I told him. He can't possibly be around children with that…*thing* on his arm. It's obscene." She shuddered. "Do you know where he got that? He told me the most outrageous story—"

Dillon kissed her quiet, the love inside him almost more

than he could bear. She was incredible. No wonder his father was so anxious to see him married to Virginia. He couldn't think of another woman who'd ever dared to try to boss his father. More than anything, Dill Sr. respected courage, and Virginia had that in spades.

He'd also loved being a father, despite his claims of incompetence. Dillon had no doubt his father would make an excellent grandpa, but he was pleased to let his dad begin with Wade's baby. He could start all over again with the lectures on family bonds and loyalty, and this time, he'd have Dillon and Virginia to help him.

Dillon decided he'd make a show of sizing up the ranch, just to keep Virginia from getting the upper hand. But in truth, he didn't care two cents for where he lived, as long as she lived there with him. Having her for a wife, having children with her, sounded as close to perfection as he was ever likely to get.

Then Virginia moaned softly for him, accepting him as he slowly joined his body to hers, and he knew he'd already reached perfection. She was a bossy little woman, but she was his, and it couldn't get any better than that.

* * * * *

SAY YES

chapter 1

IT WAS THE LOUD, SHRILL scream of rage that drew Gavin Blake's attention, along with the frantic shrieks that followed. Gavin stared down the middle of the narrow street, blinking hard to make certain he wasn't hallucinating. But no. There was his usually calm, very friendly neighbor Sara Simmons, her dark curly hair bouncing out behind her as she ran hell-bent after Karen, his used-to-be girlfriend. He hadn't seen Karen in months, not since their breakup, and the sight of her now wasn't what fascinated him. No, it was gentle, sweet, *passive* Sara—who at the moment held a rake which she wielded with all the force and efficiency of a massive war club. And each time she swung it, punctuating her efforts with low, threatening growls, Karen wailed in fear.

A disbelieving smile twitched on his mouth as he heard Sara issue a rather lurid, improbable threat. So far as Gavin could tell, Sara hadn't even touched Karen yet, but it was a close thing. Karen's shirt was open, but her efforts were all centered on escaping the woman bent on retribution, not on covering her half-naked chest. As they neared the entrance to the garage where Gavin stood, he tried to get himself out of the way. But Karen made eye contact, and evidently, even though they were no longer involved, she decided he might be her savior.

Hah! Sara behaved very much like a woman scorned—or a woman who had caught her fiancé intimately involved with another woman. And knowing Karen as he did, that assumption wasn't unrealistic. He'd learned some time ago that Karen would never be a faithful, devoted, loving partner. Which was why he'd ended the relationship and sent her on her way months ago.

But as the two women ran straight for him and he saw the fury—and the hurt—in Sara's eyes, Gavin knew for a certainty Karen had been up to her old tricks. He decided to stay out of the matter and let Sara do her worst, knowing she wouldn't actually hurt Karen. But the women had other ideas.

They tried to use him as a maypole.

He dropped the file he'd been holding and saw the approved plans for another subdivision scatter across the garage floor. He struggled to maintain his balance with Karen trying to shield herself behind him and Sara trying to go straight through him. He bent to retrieve a floor plan being mangled under furious feminine feet and was promptly shoved away and onto his backside. Having just come from the office, he was unfortunately wearing dress pants. He started to grumble, but then Karen made a dive for the house, and Sara followed, climbing right over the top of him.

There was another loud screech, and Gavin couldn't help but grin. He'd known since first meeting Sara that she was a passionate little thing, filled with energy and an abundance of emotion. But this was the first time he'd seen that emotion really set free. The jerk she'd planned to marry would never have made her happy. Gavin supposed, in a way, he owed Karen his thanks for showing Sara just how big a jerk Ted really was.

Then he heard the sound of breaking glass and decided he'd have to intervene after all. Knowing Sara, and he'd come to know her very well since she'd moved into one of the houses he built, she'd hate her loss of control once she calmed down.

He wondered briefly if she'd allow him to console her.

Coming up behind Sara, he was just in time to duck the rake as she took another swipe at the cowered, screeching Karen. Gavin snatched it out of her hands, and when she rounded on him, he pulled her close in a careful bear hug. "Just calm down, honey."

He tried to keep the satisfaction and good humor out of his tone. Little by little, the enormity of the situation was sinking in, and he was starting to feel damn good. He'd now see the end of Sara's fiancé—and without a guilty conscience. He'd held back, keeping his personal interest to himself, unwilling to involve himself in a set relationship, even though he knew the relationship was doomed. Sara was much too good for Ted, she just hadn't seemed to realize it.

But with these new crimes against him, Sara would surely send Ted packing. Finally they would both be free of ties, and he'd be able to pursue her the way he wanted to.

Sara growled, and he had to admit, the menacing sound was very effective. "Let me go, Gavin."

No way. She felt damn good in his arms, too good. He looked down at her rigid expression, her bright eyes, and had to fight to keep from kissing her. This was the first time he'd ever been able to actually hold her, and he liked it—a lot. She growled again and he saw that slightly crooked front tooth, the one that always taunted him, made him want to touch it with his tongue. He tightened his hold just a bit more, relishing the feel of her small body tucked up against his, and breathed in her gentle fragrance. Sara always smelled of sunshine and softness and woman. He lowered his mouth to her ear.

"I think you've made your point, honey. Karen understands the error of her ways."

She struggled in his arms. "You don't know what they... They were in my *house,* in my bed!"

He did know. The house meant everything to Sara, but very little to Ted. In fact, Sara had bought the place herself, no small feat for a woman alone with a moderate income. And not a day went by that she didn't tell him what a wonderful job he'd done building that house. She made him feel as if he'd given her the moon.

"It won't happen again, Sara. I promise."

He had a hell of a time controlling his elation. And when Sara peeked up at him with energy and emotion blazing in her blue eyes, he couldn't help himself. He smiled.

Very slowly she looked around. A lamp lay broken on the floor and Gavin saw her wince. When her gaze landed on the shattered picture, she closed her eyes as if in pain. Color flooded her smooth cheeks.

Behind him, he heard the sounds of Karen slinking away.

No doubt she planned to make a strategic retreat. Gavin ignored her. In the three months she'd been gone, he hadn't missed her once. "Sara? Are you okay now?"

"Let—me—go."

Cautiously, making certain she wouldn't bolt after Karen again, Gavin lowered his arms. She stood there, her eyes still closed, her cheeks pulsing with heat. She said in a strangled whisper, "I'm sorry."

Gavin touched her cheek, swamped with tenderness and a real healthy dose of desire. "Hey, don't worry about it. After a boring day in the office, I needed a little excitement."

She drew in a long, slow breath, then opened her eyes, but didn't look at him. Instead she surveyed the damage. "I didn't mean to break anything."

"Karen would probably disagree."

Her gaze shot to his face and her hands curled into fists. "I don't want her anywhere near me ever again."

She was such a ferocious, impassioned little thing when duly provoked. "Don't worry. I think Karen has learned her lesson. Besides, I wasn't the one who invited her here."

She scowled. "No. Ted apparently did."

"What will you do?" He was very curious, but he held no sympathy for Ted. In fact, he wanted to rub his hands in glee over Ted's folly. The idiot.

Sara lifted her chin, then slowly stepped around the broken glass on the floor. "I'll take care of Ted." Gavin watched her stiff posture as she walked away, and he wondered if he should accompany her home so she wouldn't have to face Ted alone. Then he thought better of it.

Ted didn't stand a chance.

Besides, Sara was private, with a streak of dignity and pride a mile wide. She wouldn't want an audience when she gave Ted the boot. He knew Sara—not as well as he'd like to, but probably better than Ted would ever know her. At least he knew enough to realize how important old-fashioned values were to her. Possibly because they were important to him as well.

She'd talk to Ted, listen to his lame excuses, then toss him out on his miserable can. She'd be hurt for a while, but she'd get over it, just as she'd get over Ted. Gavin was willing to give her some time.

And then it was finally going to be his turn.

HOUSE FOR SALE BY OWNER.

Stunned, Gavin slowed his truck until he came to a complete stop. Sara had been avoiding him. The friendly talks in the yard had ceased, as had her spontaneous visits to the construction sites. It used to be that Sara couldn't keep away when she saw the crew working on another house on her street. She loved the process of seeing a house built, of everything coming together to make a home, almost as much as he did.

But lately, her pride and embarrassment had caused a wall he was damn tired of beating his head against.

And now she wanted to sell? Like hell.

Cursing to himself, he put the truck in Park and climbed out. He glared at the stormy, cloud-filled skies, then glared even harder at the For Sale sign. Stomping over to her yard, he ripped up the sign and threw it into the back of his truck, then brushed his hands off in a show of satisfaction. Try to sell, would she? Without a single word, without giving him the chance he'd been waiting for? Ha!

He'd been patient too long, that was the problem. He had a plan, and it was time he put it into motion. He wanted Sara, had wanted her for a long time. And starting right now, he was done with waiting.

SARA WAS NAKED, she was wet, and she was frustrated.

She was also alone.

Water sloshed over the sides of the large Jacuzzi tub when she jerked awake. The vivid fantasy she'd conjured in her mind evaporated. She realized it was the loud clapping of thunder that had startled her from the luxury of her bath—and the man she'd been dreaming of.

Disgusted, she shook her head. She'd made a point of avoiding Gavin since that awful, fateful day. She shouldn't be dreaming about him, either. She was tired, that's all, too much overtime at work wearing her down. She'd counted on a leisurely soak in her Jacuzzi tub to ease away her weariness and her aches and pains. But since Gavin had built the house and installed the tub, it was no wonder her thoughts had chased after him again. Now the storm was here, and her fantasy gone, so she supposed her bathtime was over.

Water dripped onto the ceramic tile floor as she threw a worn towel around her body. Sheesh. Even in her imagination, she couldn't indulge a satisfactory romantic interlude. Maybe she should give up on dream men, just as she'd given up on the real thing. Romances, even the imaginary kind, evidently weren't meant for her. Besides, dogs were much more reliable. Unfortunately, like the house, dogs required upkeep. And as much as she wanted one, she wasn't home enough to keep a dog company— or vice versa.

Still dripping, she stomped off to close the windows. Without the cooling breeze, the interior would soon become unbearable, but she couldn't afford air conditioning any more than she could afford a dog.

The evening had turned very dark, and she remembered her front door was open, with only the screen door latched. As she went to close it, she saw the threatening sky, felt a spattering of the rain as it blew in over her porch. She thought again how nice a pet would be, another living thing to keep her company on a dreary night like this. Granted, a dog wouldn't provide quite the same company as a man, but then, a dog required much less maintenance. Dogs weren't as messy as men. They were more loyal and friendly. Dogs never made promises they couldn't keep...

Suddenly she noticed her For Sale sign was missing. She'd only just put the thing in the yard that day!

Distracted from her daydreams by the possibility of vandalism, she clicked open the lock on the screen door and stuck her head outside, automatically breathing in the churning, moist night air.

"You planning to dance buck-naked in the rain?"

Squealing, she lurched backward and slipped off her wet feet before the familiarity of that deep, masculine voice could penetrate. She would have fallen if her backside hadn't smacked up against the gaping front door.

It took her a moment to regain her dignity—what was left of it—before she cautiously stuck her head outside again. A burst of white light splintered through the night, and she saw her one and only neighbor, Gavin Blake, standing to the side of her door. He was in the shadows, but she would recognize his body, his voice, his *presence*, anywhere. She shivered. *Boy, could she recognize him!*

But Gavin would forever be relegated to the role of her fantasy man. Nothing more was possible. Not after the incident.

She continued to stare, then blinked in surprise as her eyes adjusted. Soaked completely through by the storm, Gavin stood there in a soggy T-shirt and shorts, with a bottle of wine in one large hand.

Good grief! He was too darn gorgeous, too big and imposing and male. He was also the last person she ever wanted to see, other than in her dreams.

But…but there he stood.

Her stomach took a free fall and her heart shot into her throat. She squeezed her eyes shut, but when she opened them again, he was still there, still watching her. "A pet. I most definitely need a pet."

Gavin raised his brows, his dark eyes glinting in the shadows, his tone amicable. "Hey, I hadn't planned on anything so forward, at least not this soon, but petting's good. I'm into petting if that's what you really—"

"No!" Sara dodged his outstretched hand and ground

her teeth together, feeling foolish. "I meant a pet, as in a dog that might have barked and let me know someone was here."

His gaze slid from her face to her towel-wrapped body. "Then I'm glad you don't have a dog."

With a gasp, she ducked into the house and shielded herself behind the front door. After a long, silent moment, she began to realize he wouldn't just go away, and that she'd once again made herself look ridiculous. She poked her head around the door.

Gavin chuckled. "I'm getting soaked standing here, babe. You going to ask me in or what?"

"Ah… No. Not a good idea." She knew her tone lacked conviction. She'd wanted him, *really* wanted him, for the longest time, but not now, not at this precise moment.

Not dressed only in a towel.

He looked down at his feet, as if considering the situation, then pulled the screen open and stepped inside. "Sara." His tone was chiding. "I've given you plenty of time. I hoped you'd be willing to talk to me now."

She couldn't hold his direct gaze, so she glanced at the bottle of wine in his hand. "What do you want, Gavin?"

"You."

Oh wow. Heat washed over her in undulating waves, and she took a hasty, nervous step back, bumping into the wall. She couldn't, wouldn't, look at him. Gavin cupped her cheek with a rough palm and lifted her face. His smile gentle, his voice low, he murmured with a good dose of sincerity, "I like you, Sara. I always have. From the very first day you looked at this house and proclaimed me a master planner and the best builder you'd ever come across, I knew we were destined to be very good…friends."

Teasing, she thought. *Only teasing.* But he *was* a talented builder, putting that little extra into a house to make it special. Gavin Blake was, at only thirty-three years of age, an extremely successful man.

Sara could still remember the first time she'd laid eyes on him. He'd shown her around the house himself because he'd been inside, adding some touches to the existing kitchen. He'd been enthusiastic, speaking about his work with the intensity of an artist, while looking every inch the rugged male in his ragged jeans and work boots. There had been a healthy sweat dampening his T-shirt, and he'd smelled *so* good. The cocky way he walked kept grabbing her attention. He was confident of his abilities, and with good reason. What he did was exceptional; he expected the same of the men who worked for him. He'd shown her all the perks his housing offered, all the ways he'd improved on the average plans to make his creations special.

And she'd fallen instantly in love…with the house. But she'd also felt a very real attraction for the man. Gavin had the sensitive hands of an artist, and her fertile mind had imagined those hands everywhere they shouldn't be.

Though she'd been engaged then, and he'd had a relationship of his own, it hadn't taken her long to realize she was planning to marry the wrong man.

But once she'd become free of Ted—the cheating slime— it had been too late. Gavin had witnessed the worst of her, and she was too embarrassed to see him again. And too realistic to keep trying for a romantic future that would only elude her.

But now Gavin was here, in the flesh.

"You used to come and talk to me while I worked." He leaned closer, his gaze drifting over her face. "I've missed you, Sara."

His suggestive tone shook her. She shifted from one bare foot to the other, her naked knees pressed together as she remembered their easy camaraderie, the swell of excitement she always felt whenever he was near.

Gavin watched her, his gaze straying over her shoulders and across the tops of her breasts. She knew her blush had spread, and that it was visible even in the dim light. Then his hand lifted from her cheek and he slid a rough fingertip over her lips. Her breath caught somewhere in the bottom of her lungs, making her dizzy.

"You never used to blush so much."

She thought she should move, but she didn't. She swallowed, then stated the obvious. "I never had good reason before."

"Ah." He turned to look outside, his hands propped on his lean hips, the wine bottle still held securely. "I assume we're talking about the...incident?"

Sara swallowed. It had been a fiasco and the most humiliating moment of her life. It wouldn't have been quite so horrendous, catching Ted with Karen, if she'd handled the situation with a modicum of grace, a little poise. But no. She'd had to go and do her impression of a berserk gardener, grabbing the closest weapon, which happened to be a plastic rake, and chasing a near-naked woman up the middle of the street!

Catching her bottom lip in her teeth, she groaned. The memory was not a humorous one for her, and now here she was, cowering behind a door, making a total fool of herself once again. She would have straightened her shoulders if it wouldn't have caused her towel to slip. "Just why are you here, Gavin?"

He stared at her, or more precisely her mouth, watching as her teeth worried her bottom lip. He was so tall—over six feet, making her five foot five seem very diminutive. And his wet T-shirt had turned transparent, clinging to his wide shoulders, taunting her with what it both hid and revealed. She could see the dark hair on his chest, appearing so very soft in stark contrast to his hard body.

She knew she didn't want to see what the rain had done to his cutoffs. She felt flustered enough as it was.

His tone was gentle, insistent. "It's been six weeks, Sara. I figured that was plenty of time for you to get over whatever ails you and get friendly again. You've been snubbing me ever since that day."

Her brow puckered at the misunderstanding. "I wasn't snubbing you. I...I wasn't at all sure, after the damage I did, if you'd want to talk to me again." That was a partial truth, because she'd sent him a note of apology and asked for the amount of the damages. She'd found the note stuck inside her screen door, with the message, Paid In Full, scrawled across it. It was sheer embarrassment that kept her away now.

He sighed, then shook his head. "Why don't we sit down and talk? I'm going to set you straight on a few things."

Without waiting for her agreement, he kicked off his wet tennis shoes and headed for her kitchen, giving her the perfect opportunity to make a fast break for the bedroom. She did, back-stepping the whole way just in case he turned. And with every foot that separated them, she pondered the possibilities of why he was here. A tiny flare of excitement stirred, but she ruthlessly snuffed it out. Gavin wasn't for her, and he never would be.

chapter 2

WHEN SARA ENTERED the kitchen a few minutes later, wearing a loose sundress that fell to her knees, she found Gavin leaning against the counter. He gave her a slow, thorough once-over, his gaze intent, his mouth tipped in a slight smile. Then he plucked at his wet T-shirt, pulling it away from his body. His voice was pitched low and deep when he spoke. "The storm took me by surprise. Do you mind if I take this off so I can get comfortable, too?"

Her mouth went dry. She tamped down the natural inclination to lick her lips, and shook her head instead. Heaven only knew what she might do if presented with such temptation. "I'm not sure if that's a good idea. There's not much for us to talk about."

"Of course there is." He peeled off the shirt with no thought for modesty or her overly rapt attention. She stared, anxious to catch every riveting detail of exposed male flesh.

She laced her fingers tightly together and held herself still as he shook out his shirt and laid it over the back of a chair to dry. Facing her, he adopted a no-nonsense expression, a stern warning that she was to pay close attention.

The man was half-naked—he had her attention.

"I didn't care about the lamp, Sara. Or the picture." There was a pause, then he added, "I didn't even care about—"

Wincing, she cut him short. "I didn't realize I'd broken more than the lamp and the picture."

"You didn't." He sprawled into the chair, stretching out his long bare legs. He was muscled everywhere, the physical labors of his job keeping him in excellent shape.

She remained standing, too nervous to relax. It was a mixed reaction from the electric charge of the storm, sheer exhaustion, and Gavin's presence. The man had always affected her in one way or another, but since the incident, she'd done her best to repress her more emotional feelings.

Now they were swamping back in force.

Gavin cleared his throat, waiting until she met his gaze before continuing. "I was going to say I didn't mind that you'd chased after Karen."

She sucked in a breath, her shoulders going rigid. "Well, I should hope not! She was...was..." Sara searched for a more delicate word than those coming to mind. There weren't many. She finally settled on, "Unfaithful."

He smirked, one brow raised. "She was that. But then, unlike you, I wasn't engaged. In fact, if you'll remember correctly, Karen and I had broken up months before. She wasn't here because of me, Sara, she was only here to visit Ted."

Sara made a grimace, knowing what he said was true. She certainly couldn't blame him for Karen's presence, not that she would have anyway. Blame had nothing to do with her avoidance of him. Humiliation did. "Karen and Ted were the only ones responsible. I know that."

He nodded. "Good. Then there's no reason why we can't remain...friends. Is there?"

Put like that, what choice did he give her? "No. I guess not."

"By the way, whatever happened to lover-boy? I assume you sent him on his way?"

With a sound of disgust, she shook her head. "I didn't have to. When I got back Ted was already more or less dressed and anxious to go. I found him peeking out the door, watching for you I suppose. He crawled out to his car, then slithered inside. He left skid marks in my driveway he was in such a hurry to escape. I think he was afraid you'd come after him."

"More likely he was afraid of you." Gavin slanted her a look, his smile once again in place, though this time it looked more tender than humorous. "You swing a mean rake, lady."

Another wave of heat inched along the back of her neck, but she refused to look away from his probing gaze.

"Besides," he continued, "I wasn't angry at Ted. I'd long since given up my claim on Karen, and in a way, he did me a favor. If he'd hung around, I might have even thanked him."

Sara stared. "You've got to be kidding me."

"Nope." With no sign of amusement now, he leaned forward in his seat and reached for her hand. "Ted hung himself. He made certain you'd never be able to forgive him, to take him back. I wanted him gone, Sara, because I knew he wasn't right for you. He'd never have been able to make you happy."

She had to agree with him there. Ted was not the man she wanted to be tied to for life, and in a way, she almost felt grateful, too, because his lack of morals had freed her before it was too late.

Feeling hesitant and uncertain, she asked, "It didn't bother you—not even a little—that he'd been having an affair with Karen?"

"It made me mad as hell that they hurt you. But for myself? No. Karen is free to do as she pleases, not that she ever felt any restrictions to begin with."

He hadn't loved Karen. Sara was both relieved, and depressed. If tall, beautiful, outgoing Karen hadn't been able to gain his affections, a woman like herself wouldn't stand a chance.

But then, she'd always known that.

She pulled her hand away and tried to fill the silence. "I applaud your control. I'm afraid I was a little more sensitive about the whole thing."

"I know." He gave her a teasing look. "I remember."

Dropping into her own chair, Sara propped her elbows on the table and covered her face with her hands. It all seemed so ridiculous now, but at the time... "I still can't believe I barged through your house, swinging a rake and raving like a lunatic. It was so unlike me. I've never before indulged in such a fit, no matter what the provocation."

She heard a low choked sound, and peeked from between her fingers to see Gavin trying to contain his humor. "What?"

He shrugged, then mumbled around his chuckles, "I was

just thinking of the strain you must have been under, keeping all that explosive emotion bottled up."

"I'm not an emotional person."

He sputtered, then lost the fight to keep from laughing. Dropping her hands, she scowled at him, but that only served to make him laugh all the more. At her. She felt renewed humiliation and jerked to her feet, her eyes narrowed on his face. "Go home, Gavin!"

He caught her wrist and tugged her close despite her resistance, trying to rid himself of his smile, and failing. "Ah, Sara. If you could have seen your face that day! It was damn impressive. Outrage and indignation and a good dose of evil intent… Hell, for a second there, you terrified even me. I thought about running for cover along with Karen! But with you shouting accusations and threats so horrid my ears rang, it didn't take me long to realize what had happened, and—"

"And you were amused."

He sobered instantly. "No." Squeezing her fingers, he held her hand close to his side. "I was relieved. You were too good for that jerk and I was glad you realized it before you married him and ruined everything."

Feeling perverse, partly because she didn't understand him, and partly because he was still smiling, she said, "You hardly knew Ted."

"Wrong. I'd spoken with him several times, though not nearly as much as you and I talked. He was a worm. Believe me, Sara, you're better off without him."

She scowled, thinking of Ted's empty promises, and her

empty house. Her own gullibility. She'd wanted to be wanted so badly, she'd been willing to be duped by Ted.

Now she merely felt like a fool. "He worked hard to convince me to marry him."

Gavin tilted his head, his eyes intent. "Whatever he told you was probably lies."

She knew that now. Ted hadn't really cared about her at all. Big surprise. "He said we'd make the perfect couple, that love was something that came over time. We were too old to be frivolous, to wait for the kind of relationship you see in movies and read about in books. He said he was as alone and lonely as me, and he convinced me he wanted the same things. A secure home, a lasting relationship. So we approached this wedding business in a logical, no-nonsense fashion. We discussed up-front who would be responsible for various things, and what was expected of each of us. We had the future all mapped out."

Gavin was attentive, staring at her, seemingly fascinated.

She tried to ignore his hold on her wrist, the warmth of his palm and the way his scent made her toes curl. "Ted broke nearly every promise he made. I still wonder why he wanted to marry me in the first place."

"What promises?"

Trying to act indifferent, she shrugged. "You mean apart from the promises to be faithful and act honorably and to stick around through thick and thin?"

Gavin watched her with compassion, and she hated it. She knew she sounded like a woman scorned, but a part of her still felt betrayed, not by Ted, because he didn't really matter, not anymore. But by her own foolish hopes for things that either didn't exist, or else weren't meant for her.

She sucked in a slow, calming breath. "Part of the deal was that I'd buy the house, and he'd furnish it." She lifted her free hand to indicate her almost barren kitchen. A small, aged Formica table and two chairs sat in the middle of the floor. They were ugly and looked totally out of place in the exquisite kitchen Gavin had constructed. The rest of the house was the same, the rooms either near-empty or "furnished" with used, mismatched pieces.

"As you can see, Ted left before furnishing anything. Even the backyard is barren, and I'd really wanted a porch swing and a pet and a picnic table." She sighed. "I'd thought this could be a real home. Instead it's just an empty shell."

Gavin leaned back, one dark brow raised high. "Let me get this straight. You were willing to hook up for life with a bastard like Ted just for some lawn furniture?"

Sara blinked. Put that way, it did sound rather foolish. Not that he understood it all. She had planned to be a good wife, to do whatever it took to make the marriage work. She'd wanted kids and Christmas, family budgets and a family car. She'd even wanted the struggles that came with maintaining family unity.

She'd gotten nothing but a severe dent to her pride.

She hadn't loved Ted, but she had liked him, and she'd been willing to put every effort into making a solid marriage.

But how could she explain all that to Gavin? He was a man who never wanted for companionship, a man who had his pick of women ready to stand by his side. He would never consider accepting a woman he didn't really want, just for something as base as companionship.

"So everything wasn't perfect," she allowed, "I thought we could manage. We would have grown closer with time. We could have made it work." She took a deep breath and mumbled, "I still think the least Ted could have done was furnish a room or two before he ruined everything."

Gavin shook his head. "You can get what you need later, without his help. Be glad you didn't marry him. It would have been a disaster."

He seemed so vehement. But then, that was one of the things that had drawn her to him, his self-assurance and confidence. "You don't understand, Gavin. You've never had any desire to be married."

"Why do you say that?"

Trying to refrain from making another scene, she wiggled her wrist free of his hold and sat down. She wished she'd kept her mouth shut, but now he was waiting for an explanation.

No way did she want Gavin to know just how fascinated she was with him, or the extent of her emotions. She'd suffered such enormous guilt when her feelings toward him had turned…lecherous. She'd never suffered sexual frustration in her life, but when it hit, it *really* hit. Like a tsunami.

It was doubly difficult because her feelings for Gavin had begun as respect and friendship. More than anyone else, more than Ted or any other man she'd known, even more than her parents, Gavin made her feel accepted and liked. She was comfortable around him. She supposed it was only natural that her fertile mind had started to meander into forbidden topics. So she'd felt guilty.

Right up until she came home and found Ted in bed with Gavin's girlfriend. *Ex-girlfriend,* she reminded herself. And then all hell had broken loose. Or, to be more accurate, she'd broken loose, reacting like a demented ogress.

Gavin was watching her, and she had to tell him something. Trying to pick her words carefully, she said, "Karen told me once, when I'd first moved in, that you weren't the marrying kind. She claimed you liked a lot of—" she cleared her throat "—*variety*. She was bragging, because you supposedly cared enough about her to ask her to move in. She said you wanted only the best."

Gavin didn't react the way she expected over the invasion of privacy. He seemed intrigued, and his cocky grin spread wide over his face. "You discussed me with Karen?" At her noncommittal shrug, he propped his elbows on the table, laced his fingers together, and leaned toward her. "What else did she say to you?"

"Oh, this and that." Actually, thanks to Karen, she knew things about Gavin she shouldn't have known, intimate details that made it more than difficult to be around him, and twice as tough to control her imagination.

At least she didn't have to worry about guilt anymore, since she was now free. And alone. She didn't even miss Ted, which was almost sad since she'd once been engaged to him. But long before she'd caught him with Karen, she'd had doubts about marrying him. He didn't have the same respect for marriage, didn't have the same commitment that she did. To her, marriage meant a lifetime, not until the convenience wore off. Few people seemed able to suffer that small stipulation. Her parents hadn't understood. Neither had Ted.

So along with shedding Ted, she'd rid herself of the idea of marriage. She'd simply given up. Obviously there was something about her that made a long-term commitment impossible. She'd come to the conclusion she needed something shorter term.

Like a blazing, red-hot affair.

She glanced up at Gavin, afraid he might be able to read her mind. But no, he just looked thoughtful. She sighed. Such a gorgeous man, so proud and confident, sometimes arrogant, always fair. But Gavin was more a fantasy man, the perfect male to manifest in a dream, with the reality a million miles away.

Yet…they *were* both single now, and he was sitting right there in her kitchen chair, wearing nothing more than damp jean shorts and a healthy dose of male charisma, insisting they should be friends, which could possibly mean…what? Sara blinked, realizing she'd been quiet too long while contemplating short-term, sizzling, erotic plans.

His wicked grin had turned smug. "So you talked about this and that, meaning…?"

The best defense was a good offense, and she was tired of acting like a ninny. "Gavin, are you actually fishing for compliments?"

"Would you give me any?"

"No." She grinned at his feigned hurt, feeling some of the

old camaraderie return. "You certainly don't need me to bolster your ego. You surely know how attractive you are."

He went perfectly still, and his voice turned husky and suggestive. "You really think so?"

She pulled a wry face. "I'm not blind, Gavin. And you don't wear humility worth a darn."

"You never acted the least bit interested. Whenever we talked, it was about the house, or what you intended to do to the yard." He lowered his brows over his dark brown eyes. "Or about your upcoming wedding." He said the last in a disgusted tone, as if the very idea turned his stomach.

"I was engaged! Did you expect me to flirt with you?" Besides, she thought, even after she'd gotten rid of Ted, she knew she wasn't in Gavin's league, not by a long shot. Where he was tall, dark, gorgeous—basically perfect—she was basically plain. Her dark curly hair was always unruly, her eyes a medium shade of blue. There was nothing remarkable about her, other than her slightly crooked front tooth, which certainly didn't fall under the category of sexually appealing traits. She was a very ordinary woman, and he was an extraordinary man.

So why was he here?

Gavin came to his feet, pacing away from her, then back again. He seemed unsettled and she didn't know what to expect. Then he stopped before her.

Crossing his arms over his bare chest and staring down at her, he said, "So we're both available now, right?"

"Uh…"

"And you've already admitted you like me."

Had she actually come right out and said that? She didn't think so. It wasn't likely she'd take another chance on rejection. "I've always liked you, Gavin. You're a nice guy, and you're unbelievably talented…"

"There, you see." He nodded, apparently more than satisfied with her comments.

"But—"

"No buts." He shocked the rest of her thoughts right out of her head when he gripped either side of her chair and leaned down until their noses almost touched. His voice emerged whisper soft, his eyes staring into hers. "I like you, too, Sara. And I want to see you."

Completely frozen, Sara simply stared back. What he said, how he said it, seemed unbelievably seductive. She told herself not to be foolish, not to misunderstand, but she felt her stomach curl up and squeeze tight. For a moment, she thought she might swoon in excitement. Or maybe throw up in sheer nervousness. It was a definite toss-up.

His gaze dropped to her mouth, lingering for a long moment, but to her extreme disappointment, he moved away. "I came today to celebrate. And to convince you to stop hiding from me."

After sucking in two huge gulps of air, she managed to speak without croaking. "Uh, celebrate what?"

"Your freedom. We can start with a toast. I'll pour the wine." He went to the cabinets, and before she could stop him he opened the top drawer, then the next, looking for a corkscrew.

Sara groaned, knowing what he would find, knowing she

would be mortified; she resigned herself to the inevitable. She was almost getting used to it.

There was a moment of stunned silence before Gavin turned to face her, a pair of her pale bikini panties dangling from one long finger. He wore an expression of mixed chagrin and incredulous disbelief. "Do you always keep your underwear in the kitchen drawers?"

She would definitely throw up.

There wasn't anyplace adequate for her to hide, though she did consider crawling beneath the table. Of course, he'd still be able to see her, and she'd still have to come out sometime. She didn't think he would just go away.

She dropped her face to the table and covered her head with her arms. "I told you I don't have much furniture." It sounded like an accusation. "The only drawers in the house are the ones here in the kitchen."

Her words were muffled, but she assumed by Gavin's rough chuckles he'd understood her. When she heard him opening and closing other drawers she jumped out of her seat to stop him. He had a silk camisole in one hand, a garter belt in the other and a look of profound masculine interest on his face. The feminine garments looked very fragile and soft in his big hands. Sara snatched them away, glaring at him despite her embarrassment.

He made an obvious, rather measly effort to hide his reaction. "Damn, I'm glad I came today. I'm learning all kinds of things about you." He reached out and stroked the garter belt with a knuckle, his tone dropping to an intimate level. "I had no idea you wore such racy lingerie."

Her face felt so hot, her vision blurred. "Don't you dare laugh at me again, you big—"

The sky exploded with a splintered streak of neon light and the house shook with the accompanying thunder. They both jumped, and in the next instant were left in complete darkness. Sara held her breath, stunned into silence.

Gavin reached out and felt for her, his fingers landing first on her throat, then skimming across her collarbone before curling over her shoulder. "Sara?"

"Lightning must have hit a power line." Her voice lowered to a whisper in deference to the fury of the storm.

"Probably."

They stood there in the dark, and Sara could hear him breathing, could feel the heat of his body as he slowly, relentlessly pulled her closer. She could smell his wonderful, delicious, toe-curling scent. Her heart knocked against her ribs and she cleared her throat. "Well. So much for drinking wine. What do we do now?"

It was a loaded question, unintentional of course. But Sara saw the amused flash of Gavin's white teeth. "It just occurred to me," he whispered. "If your underthings are all in here, and you changed in the bedroom, what are you wearing beneath that dress?"

She managed a horrified gasp just before he lowered his head. She knew he was going to kiss her, and she didn't voice a single complaint.

She may have even met him halfway.

chapter 3

HE WAS RUSHING IT.

Gavin knew he should pull back, give her time to adjust to his intentions, but he couldn't quite get his body to agree with his mind. She was so soft, so sweet against him. And it seemed as if he'd wanted her forever. Hell, it had been forever. A lifetime, in fact.

She was breathing in quick, gasping pants. Touching her mouth with his own, he stifled the small, arousing sounds and gently kissed her. It took all his control to keep the contact light. The feel of her full breasts pressed to his chest tested his resolve.

So many times in the past he'd brushed against her, or shaken her hand, or patted her shoulder. Casual touches that left him wanting so much more. He'd teased himself by visiting with her so often, especially whenever she spoke about Ted. Even if the man hadn't turned out to be a jerk, Gavin would have hated him because he had Sara.

He smiled to himself, thinking what a challenge she was,

how complex and complicated her personality could be. She'd surprised him more times than he could count.

When she suddenly opened her mouth on his, then grabbed his ears in both hands and kissed him with an intensity he hadn't expected, he wasn't only surprised, he was stunned. And thrilled.

He slid his arms around her narrow waist, marveling at how feminine she was, how perfect she felt to him and with him. Her mouth was hot and damp and clinging to his. When he slipped his tongue just inside her mouth, she groaned. The small sound made him shake. He could have kissed her forever.

But the idea of her underwear continued to plague him, and without even meaning to, he allowed his hands to wander until he cupped her lush backside and discovered for a fact she was naked beneath the dress.

He shuddered again and his body reacted. He pressed her forward against his groin, his hands kneading, rocking her into his hips. His control slipped, but she didn't seem to mind. Things were happening fast, but that suited him. Giving her time, waiting for her to get over her embarrassment, had nearly used up all his patience.

Just remembering all the lonely, frustrated, lust-filled nights he'd suffered through recently filled him with renewed purpose, and he slanted his mouth over hers until she accepted his tongue completely. He explored her with a leisurely thoroughness, fascinated by that small crooked tooth, touching it with his tongue. And then…

She pushed him away. Gavin tried to reorient himself, but

the room was dark, and all he could see of Sara was her outline and the gleam of her wide eyes, watching him. He could hear her breathing, as harsh as his own, and knew, even without the benefit of light, she was surely blushing again.

"I want you, Sara."

She started to step back, but he reached out and caught her. His hand landed first against a plump breast, but he quickly altered his hold to her upper arm. They both breathed hard.

Sara trembled, and even that excited him. He'd never known a woman like her, with her honest reactions and sincere emotions. She couldn't hide her feelings, even when she tried. There wasn't an ounce of guile in her entire being. That alone made her unique.

"Why?"

Her tone dripped with suspicion. Because it was dark and she couldn't see him, he gave in to the urge to grin. He was happy, dammit. After allowing her six long weeks to recover from her embarrassment and any lingering feelings she might have had for her damn philandering fiancé, he was finally with her.

He'd wanted her from the day she'd walked into his house and proclaimed him a genius. It was the first time a woman had noted anything about him other than a physical attribute. He was proud of the houses he built, and so was his family. But no other female had taken the time to realize the extent of his natural talent when it came to his work.

It hadn't merely been the compliment that had done the trick, though. It had been her exuberance, her expressive nature. She was aware of life and the world around her in a way he'd never considered before. She took pleasure in such simple things, in the house he'd built, in her yard work. And he'd watched while she made plans to turn that house into a home with a family...*for another man.*

God, it had eaten him alive, kept him awake at night, and generally filled him with a morbid kind of desperation. She was meant for him, he knew that. And it wasn't just her enthusiasm for him and his work. It was everything she did. Sara was the type of woman children would instinctively trust. Men would gravitate toward her because she was secure and comforting. She drew him with her honesty and her optimism and her generosity...and that lush little body of hers that constantly tempted him to touch. He couldn't discount the body.

He looked at Sara and thought of home and hearth, Christmas and...rumpled sheets on a rainy night. Sara, naked and warm. He groaned. It was an eclectic mix of emotions she stirred, volatile in their power. But knowing he couldn't overwhelm her with his full plans or feelings yet, he said simply, "You're beautiful."

There was no reply, just a telling silence. He sighed, knowing well enough she didn't believe him. "It's true, Sara. Ted probably didn't tell you often enough, bastard that he was, but you're very easy on the eyes."

She cleared her throat, and he waited with a half smile, anxious to see what she would say.

"I'm short."

Ignoring her resistance, he pulled her close for a quick

hug, his chuckles rumbling in the quiet of the kitchen. Her head tucked neatly under his chin, his arms looped at the small of her back, he pretended to measure her against him, then nodded. "You're perfect."

"Gavin…"

He knotted his hand in her curling hair and tugged until she tilted her face up. Between small, nipping kisses that she greedily accepted, he said, "You're also very sweet and sexy. It's been hell staying away from you."

"I had no idea—"

He didn't let her finish, kissing her again until her hands came to his bare chest and smoothed over his skin. Her touch was shy and curious and he knew he'd lose control again if he didn't put some space between them. Damn, now *he* was trembling like a virgin on prom night.

She'd been hurt by Ted, and he didn't want her on the rebound. He didn't want her doing anything she might regret later. And he didn't want her only for an affair.

When he made love to Sara, it had to be because she wanted him as much he wanted her, which was one hell of a lot. Her confidence was a bit low now, and she was obviously gun-shy about getting involved with anyone again. But he could be patient. Being with Sara would be worth the extra effort.

Whispering, because she was still pressed close, her lips nearly touching his, he asked, "Where do you keep the candles and matches?"

"In the cookie jar."

"Ah. Of course. Where else would they be?"

Sara straightened away from him, and he could imagine her fussing with her uncontrollable hair, her nervous hands busy. She moved toward the counter and he heard the *clink* of a glass jar. "I keep them here because the drawers are all full and... Well, I know it doesn't make any sense, but I just couldn't quite bring myself to put my panties in the cookie jar."

"I do understand."

She went still, then asked with a touch of renewed suspicion, "Are you laughing at me again, Gavin?"

He tried to make himself sound appalled. "I've never laughed at you."

"Hah!"

He ignored that. It was obvious he'd have his work cut out for him. "Find a corkscrew, too, and we can take the wine to the other room and get comfortable." He felt her hesitation before she began opening cabinets and rustling through drawers. Very cautiously, she handed him two glasses in the dark, then took his arm to lead the way. It was an unnecessary measure on her part. He knew this house as well as she did, knew exactly where the family room was. And the master bedroom. But he would never refuse her touch, no matter how platonic.

He hadn't been inside much since she'd moved in, though, and he had no concept of the placement of furniture, what little there was. She led him to a couch, then sat beside him.

"I'm sorry I can't offer you a better seat, but the sofa is it." She struck a match, then held it to the candle.

Gavin looked around the room. There was a portable

television sitting on a crate, the sofa arranged against the back wall, and one end table next to it with a lamp. The oak moldings along the floor took on a soft sheen in the candlelight. So did Sara.

She turned toward him, her mouth open to speak, and caught him staring. There was a moment of complete stillness, their gazes locked, and then she jerked to her feet, flustered. "I forgot to get anything to put the candle in. I'll be right back."

"Oh, no, you don't." He wrapped his fingers around her narrow wrist and tugged her back into her seat. "We can use one of the glasses, and share the other."

"But it'd be just as easy—"

"I've already kissed you, Sara, very thoroughly." He kept his tone soft and quiet, his gaze holding hers. "Your tongue was in my mouth. Surely sharing a glass can't bother you that much."

Her eyes were huge, locked with his. "It…it's not that."

"Good." He didn't give her time to form more excuses, and he didn't want her alone in the kitchen, building up her defenses. He opened the wine and filled the glass, then handed it to her. "Here's to your narrow miss at unhappiness, and my escape from monotony."

Quiet and still, she searched his face, her brow drawn in concentration. After a few cautious sips of the wine, she handed the glass back to him. "You really aren't at all upset with me for attacking your house?"

The question overflowed with uncertainty, and Gavin took her hand in his again, rubbing his thumb over her knuckles. "Seeing the look on Karen's face was worth it. You surely did impress upon her the hazards of poaching."

She'd been a stunning sight that day, a virago with a rake, female fury at its finest. He smiled. All he really remembered feeling that day was relief, because he knew Sara would never tolerate infidelity. Ted and Karen, with their lack of morals, had provided him an unhindered chance to attain something he'd wanted very badly.

He honestly couldn't say he regretted the incident, but it prodded him like a sore tooth that Sara had been hurt. The thought of her mooning over another man filled him with territorial and possessive urges that would shock a liberated woman.

Deliberately he took a large swallow of the wine, then handed the glass back to her. She needed to relax just a bit, to take down a few of those walls that kept her so rigid. He wanted Sara to be as he first remembered her—filled with unrestrained excitement and bubbling enthusiasm.

With his arm along the back of the couch, Gavin made himself comfortable, stretching out his legs and making certain his thigh pressed close to Sara's. She was familiar with him as a friend and neighbor. He wanted her familiar with him as a man. *As a lover.*

She didn't move away. When she looked at him again, he dropped his hand to her shoulder in the natural way of offering comfort.

"Quit fretting, honey. You've got plenty of time to find the right man for you, someone who better suits you, someone who'll appreciate you, someone who…"

She shook her head, denying him long before he finished praising her. "No way. I went that route and it was a far cry from matrimonial nirvana. I've given up on the idea of marriage forever. It's nothing but a hoax, anyway. I've decided to stay blessedly single. I'd rather have a pet instead of a troublesome man."

Gavin's heart and breath both froze. He wheezed out, "Excuse me?"

"You know. A little friendly furry pet to keep me company."

"Ah…somehow I don't think it's quite the same."

"Yeah, well. It's a sure bet an animal would be more fun than a husband. More loyal. Steadfast. As long as you're good to an animal, they won't ever leave you."

That was *not* what he wanted to hear. He chewed his upper lip, contemplating her stubborn expression. He hadn't calculated on quite this attitude. For as long as he'd known her, Sara had talked about getting married and settling into domestic bliss. "I can see where you might be a little more reserved now, but it'd be ridiculous to judge every man by Ted."

"I wouldn't do that! I'm not dumb." Then she said in disgust, "But it's not just Ted. I've never seen one really successful marriage. I'm not sure there is such a thing. But I do know I don't intend to waste my life looking for a husband. Ha! No sir. Not anymore. Pets are less mess, and they're guaranteed to be more trustworthy." She punctuated that statement with another long drink, finishing the glass and promptly refilling it. "It was past time for me to reevaluate and alter my thinking. I did, and I decided marriage is a waste. At least it seems to be for me."

Now *he* needed the drink.

But Sara had become vehement in her speech, and in-between stating her newly revised plans, which from what he could tell meant avoiding any kind of human commit-ment, she practically guzzled the wine. Her cheeks were flushed and her eyelids were getting heavy. Bemused, Gavin sat back to watch her.

She made a face with each drink she took, until finally the glass was empty again. She obviously wasn't used to drinking and didn't care for the taste. He didn't want her flat-out drunk, only relaxed. So he snatched up the bottle before she could take it, then pried the empty glass from her hands.

"I understand why you're bitter, Sara, but good mar-riages do exist."

Flopping back against the couch, she rolled her eyes, then directed her gaze at him. She was sprawled against his side, effectively caught in the curve of his arm. She crossed her legs and swung one small foot. Her words were low and cynical. "Sure they do. Maybe one out of every hundred. And even those aren't really happy, they're just making do. I don't like the odds. Now, a cute little puppy—I could handle that. You make certain they have food and water, clean paper to piddle on, and you can cuddle with them all you want. Done. There's nothing else to it. You love them and they love you. Unconditionally."

It was such a change in attitude for her, he was tempo-rarily thwarted. He wanted to get married, dammit, wanted to settle down for the first time in his life, and now the woman he wanted was dead set against marriage. After all the empty relationships he'd had, he didn't intend to get involved in another. He'd just have to find a way to put Sara back on the straight and narrow.

A good example couldn't hurt. "My parents have been happily married for forty years."

A strange look crossed her face, and her smile wobbled.

"What?" Gavin felt a little uncomfortable with her intense study. She seemed to be contemplating the wonders of the world. "Sara?"

She shook her head, and one lock of curly dark hair fell across her eyes. "Nothing. I just hadn't thought of you that way."

He smoothed the hair back behind her ear, enjoying the intimate contact, the tender touching. It beat the hell out of a handshake any day.

He coasted his fingertips over her fine, soft skin, then continued to cup her cheek. He liked the feel of her, warm and soft and so damn feminine. He liked having her so close and comfortable with him. He could build on that. Friendship was a great start to deeper things. "What way, Sara?"

"You know. With a family."

"Oh?" He touched her ear and the curve of her chin, the sensitive skin beneath it. "You thought I was found under a rock?"

She smiled. "No."

"So how did you think of me?"

She gave his simple question a great deal of consideration before answering. "The eligible bachelor. A playboy, maybe. But definitely not a family guy." She frowned, then snuggled against his palm. "Do you have any brothers or sisters?"

She looked very content, curled up by his side. He wanted to kiss her again, but held himself back. He wanted her to know about his family. He wanted her to *meet* his family. "No brothers. Three sisters. All older than me."

She giggled, something he'd never heard her do before. Usually her laughs were deep and throaty and full, not teasing. "You were the *baby?*"

He tried to look indignant and failed. "That's right. And it was pure hell fighting for any rights in that house. Do you have any idea how much time three teenage girls can spend in a bathroom?"

"No." She looked away, then reached up to cover his hand with her own. "I was an only child."

"Hey." The way Sara pouted was more enticing than a hot kiss. Damn, he hurt with lust. He looked away from that tempting mouth and stared at her ear instead. It was a cute ear, but it didn't send him into a frenzy of lust. "I'll gladly give you my siblings. All three of them." He forced a laugh. "Actually they'd love you. So would my mother."

"I don't know, Gavin. My own mom isn't all that fond of me."

He felt something freeze inside him at the sincerity in her eyes. Lust was forgotten. "That can't be true."

She nodded her head in sharp response. "Yes, it is. She and my dad fought all the time. They were divorced, with joint custody, but they both had busy lives and I…well, I guess I just interfered."

Frowning, Gavin asked, "So you got shuffled between the two of them?"

"Yeah. Dad kept me more than Mom, but even then, it was

never for more than a few months. But at least he tried. Once, he even bought me a puppy, to keep me company while he was gone to work, he said. But then a few weeks later, I had to leave because he got a new girlfriend, and Mom had a fit about the dog and…and Dad gave it to a guy who owned a farm. The pup had plenty of room to run around and play, he said."

Oh God. Gavin could feel her pain, could see it in her eyes. He couldn't begin to imagine how a small child, especially one as tenderhearted and sweet as Sara, might have reacted to such a blow. She must have been crushed.

So many things were starting to make sense. He said very quietly, his eyes on her face, "You really cared about the dog, didn't you?"

She wouldn't look at him. "Of course I did. He was a cute little thing, always running by my side, sleeping in my bed at night. We'd take long walks together, and play together down by the stream. I loved him. But what was really awful was that he loved me, too. He thought I'd always be there for him, but there wasn't anything I could do when Dad took him away. I begged, but Mom only offered to let me get a fish." She peered up at him. "Fish aren't nearly as messy, you know. But they are pretty hard to cuddle."

He'd never guessed Sara might have had a less than perfect upbringing. She was always so filled with optimism. He'd just assumed, with her so determined to marry, that she'd come from a background similar to his. But he realized now her need for a marriage, a home, even a pet, wasn't because she'd seen the wonderful side of that life, but because she hadn't. Ever. She'd been shuffled around and she wanted now to find some stability.

He supposed it made sense, the way she'd reacted to her upbringing. His parents had shown him the better side to marriage, his sisters, too. But still, when they'd all wanted to see him happily settled, he'd rebelled. They wanted him to do one thing, so he fought to do another. It was a response borne more of stubbornness than logic, but being the only son in a family of females had bred that stubbornness. Fighting for your independence in the midst of a gaggle of coddlers was a hard habit to break.

"Is that why you were so anxious to get married? You wanted a home of your own?"

Without his encouragement, she raised her small hand and smoothed it over his chest, tangling her fingers in his body hair. The wine had helped to lower her inhibitions, and she seemed very intent on exploring the different textures of his body. She apparently enjoyed touching him, feeling him. And heaven knew, he wouldn't discourage her from it. But now her gestures had new significance. He wondered how often, if ever, she'd been coddled and held.

Her gaze came up to meet with his, and he caught his breath. Damn, she was so sexy, and she didn't seem at all aware of it.

"I think I wanted to prove to my parents how easy it could have been if they'd only tried. Neither of them spent near the energy on their relationship that they gave to their jobs."

They evidently hadn't spent much energy on their daughter, either. Gavin leaned down and kissed her forehead, wanting to crush her close, but also wanting her to continue talking. "Sara... I understand how you must have felt. But trying to prove a point to your parents isn't a good reason to marry the wrong person."

"I know. Ted was *nothing* like a pet. Well, maybe a whiskery little rat." Her brow puckered as she considered that, then qualified, "One with mange."

She said it so seriously, and he agreed so completely, Gavin couldn't stop himself from kissing her again. He meant it as a tender touch, a form of teasing comfort, but Sara didn't cooperate. She cupped his face in her hands and licked over his lips, making small, soft sounds deep in her throat that drove him crazy.

He loved her enthusiasm, but he wanted so much more. "Sara..."

"You taste so good, Gavin. I knew you would."

Oh Lord, he'd put himself in a hell of a position.

He knew it was the wine and her own vulnerability making her speak so boldly. Sara was generally rather reserved and circumspect in her behavior. But then, she'd been engaged, and he knew she would never have betrayed a commitment.

He'd never understood why the house meant so much to her. Now he did. It symbolized all the things she hadn't had as a child. And he had built it for her. His chest puffed up and he felt like crowing. Surely that had to count for something in her eyes.

Her soft hands moved across his shoulders, his chest...his belly. He caught his breath and heard her laugh. Then he caught her hands. Much more of that and he'd forget his good intentions.

"You're awfully hairy," she whispered. "Probably not as hairy as a puppy, though. And you smell much better than a dog would."

"Thank you."

She smiled at him, their noses only half an inch apart, and her eyes nearly crossed. He shook his head, thoroughly exasperated with her, but mostly with himself. He'd had such grand plans, self-centered plans, and now he'd have to alter them a bit to give her the time she needed. He felt the weight of responsibility, and knew he'd never do anything to hurt her.

As he came to a few decisions, he watched her sway in her seat. She seemed to be trying to keep him in focus. "You're awfully serious, Gavin."

"And you're awfully drunk. You sure as hell can't hold your liquor."

"I know." She didn't sound sorry, only accepting. "Ted used to say I was too prissy. It irritated him that I wouldn't drink with him. But I knew if I did, he'd take advantage of me."

He wished Ted was here now. He wished he'd gone to see him six weeks ago, when he'd first cheated on Sara and hurt her. He hadn't then because he didn't want it to seem as though he'd coerced her final decision in any way. If she left Ted, it had to be because she chose to, not because he made her feel she should.

Pushing her back enough so he could catch his breath, Gavin asked, "Aren't you worried I'll take advantage of you?"

"No. Unfortunately," she said, in a mournful voice, "you're too honorable for that." Then she gave him a slow, exaggerated wink. "But maybe if you drink enough, I could take advantage of you?"

She swayed again as she said it, and nearly fell off the couch. Gavin caught her, then held her upright. "You'd like that, would you?"

"Oh, yes." She pushed his hands away and curled close again, snuggling the side of her face against his chest. "I probably shouldn't tell you this, but I've fantasized about you."

The air squeezed out of his lungs. He gasped and choked before he could manage to say, "Come again?"

Either she didn't notice his shock, or she chose to ignore it. "I think about what it would be like with you." She peeked up at him. "You know. *Intimately.* I was thinking about you just before the storm hit and made me leave my bath. They were *very* nice thoughts, Gavin."

"Ah, Sara..." He sounded like he might strangle on his own tongue.

She sighed. "Karen would tell me all sorts of private things, boasting, you know, and I'd want to smack her because she was living my fantasies."

Damn, he was hard. Really, really hard. It seemed every time he got his libido under control, she'd say something, or do something, or smile—Lord, he loved her smile—and then his body would react. He stayed semierect around her, though she was naive enough not to notice. But Karen had. He wondered if that was why she'd shared intimate details with Sara, to stake a claim of sorts. He shook his head. None of that mattered now, but the small woman curled against him deserved his better judgment, not his lust, which meant he couldn't do a damn thing about the opportunity presenting itself.

He muttered a curse and she heard him. Peering up to see his face, she traced his mouth with her finger and he swallowed hard. She looked so...*ready*. Damn, did she look ready.

And physically she might be. But emotionally, he figured Sara had a long way to go before she would really trust him and accept his feelings for her. Right now, she didn't seem to feel ready for anything more than a house pet. Damn, damn, double damn.

"Sara..."

"Don't you want to know what my fantasies are?"

"No!" She was trying to seduce him, and succeeding admirably. If sex was all he'd wanted, he'd be the luckiest man alive. But he wanted so much more with her. And allowing her to do something she'd regret tomorrow wouldn't aid his case. It'd make him damn happy for one night, there was no question about that, but in the long run, he'd lose out.

He held her at arm's length, trying to convince himself of his own thoughts. "Sara, why don't we talk about something else?"

She pushed against his rigid arms, trying to get closer again. "But—"

Her stomach growled, giving him the excuse to interrupt. "Are you hungry? What time did you eat dinner?" She continued to stare at him a moment, as if the change in topic had thrown her. Then she shrugged.

"I haven't eaten yet. I was too tired when I got home, and I just wanted to soak in the wonderful Jacuzzi tub you installed in my bathroom. But then the storm hit, and I knew I had to close the windows. And then you were here, so…"

Images of her lounging in the spacious, tiled tub—naked and thinking of him—played havoc with his better intentions. A man could only take so much. He cleared his throat and tried to calm his racing heart. "Why were you so tired? A hard day?"

"All my days have been hard lately. I've been working twelve-hour shifts during the week, then volunteering my weekends to the animal adoption center."

Gavin stared at her a moment before dropping his head into his hands. *Wonderful. He'd been pouring wine down an exhausted, hungry woman.* Then part of what she said really hit him. Twelve-hour shifts? He frowned at her, tilting her face up so he could better understand. "You've been putting in a lot of overtime?" She nodded, her eyelids drooping, and he asked, "Why?"

A look of sadness came over her face, and she seemed ready to cry. Gavin vowed then and there never to let her drink again. He'd always turned to mush around weeping women, and with Sara, he felt particularly susceptible.

"I love my house, Gavin."

She said it in a near wail, startling him. "Calm down, babe, and tell me what the problem is."

She threw her arms out, nearly slugging him in the eye. He ducked, then watched her cautiously in case she started to go off the couch again. "I can't afford to stay here. I have to sell my beautiful house."

"What?" He tried to sound surprised because he wasn't ready yet to admit to stealing her sign.

She went on in a rush, making broad gestures with her hands. "I used most of my savings on the down payment. Ted was supposed to buy the furniture, and then pay half on all the monthly bills. The utilities, the groceries, the taxes, the insurance, the…"

"I understand." He rubbed his forehead, frustrated. The house was rather expensive for a single person. His was only slightly larger and he knew how expensive maintenance could be.

He'd come to think of this house as Sara's. Long before she'd actually moved in, he'd made it special for her, added little things, put in extras. He'd known she would love the tiled tub, and she had. He'd thought of her reaction as he installed the beveled glass mirrors. Everything in it, from the time she'd chosen the plans, had been picked specifically for her. The idea of anyone else living in it just didn't feel right. It was almost…sacrilege. "There must be another solution besides selling."

"I've been trying to find one." Sara twisted around in her seat until she faced him. Her sundress had hiked up to her thighs, and one strap hung loose down her pale, smooth shoulder. Her hair, always a little unruly, drooped over one eye. Gavin hid his grin. She looked ready to fall asleep on him, but first, she needed something to eat.

"Come on, Sara." He hauled her to her feet, supporting her when she would have slumped back down again. "Let's go scrounge you up some food."

The candle had formed a small pool of wax in the bottom of the wineglass, and Gavin picked that up to guide them through the darkened house. The air had gotten hot and muggy; his skin felt damp with sweat. Sara snatched up the wine bottle before they left the room.

He led the way into the kitchen, hearing her hum beside him. "Am I going to find any other surprises in your kitchen cabinets?"

She dropped to a kitchen chair, then shrugged. "Who knows? I can't even remember where I've put everything."

"While I'm hunting up some food, why don't you tell me just how short you are on making ends meet." It was a personal question, but Sara didn't seem to mind. She propped her head up with one fist and regarded him as he searched through the refrigerator.

"It gets a little worse each month. I figure I can make it through the summer, then *pffftt*, I'm out of luck."

Gavin raised one brow. *"Pffftt?"*

"Yeah. I'll be flat broke."

"What about your family? They won't help at all?"

"Hah!"

No. Her family didn't sound like the type to pitch in. And Sara wasn't the type to ask for help. She was an independent little thing. Several times when she'd been doing things to or for the house, he'd had to force her to let him help her. Ted hadn't been anywhere around then, but he seldom was when work needed to be done and Gavin had enjoyed stepping in to fill the slot.

He remembered when he'd gotten his first apartment.

His parents and his sisters had all come over with donations, things ranging from furniture to food to cash. And
they'd all helped to paint and arrange furniture and prepare
the apartment for him to move in. But Sara had no one. He
couldn't imagine being so totally... *alone.*

He looked at Sara. Her eyes were closed, and she appeared
so serene, so accepting, he wanted to protect her, he wanted
to declare himself. But it was too soon. He had to get her used
to having him around more, had to give her time to adjust
and get over her ridiculous prejudice against marriage.

He found some lunch meat, cheese and pickles and set
them on the table for sandwiches. He also poured two large
glasses of milk. When he sat in the chair opposite her and
began stacking meat and cheese on the bread, her eyes
opened. She gave him that killer smile, the tip of her
crooked tooth just barely visible. He faltered, then shoved
the loaded sandwich at her.

Rather than starting on the food, she continued to watch
him, and Gavin knew he had to divert her attention or he'd
never make it through the meal. "I could give you a loan."

She bolted upright, nearly throwing herself off the chair.
Outrage shone clearly in her expression. "Absolutely not!"

He'd known that would be her answer, but he wanted to
help her. "Now, Sara—"

"Don't be ridiculous, Gavin. For Pete's sake, we're only
acquaintances, despite my rather lurid fantasies. And I have
to face facts. If I can't afford this place now, a loan isn't going
to help. I'd only end up in the same situation, but then I'd
owe you, too."

He stared, that part about "lurid fantasies" still singing through his brain.

"Gavin?"

She was right, but he wouldn't accept her moving. He could alter his plans a bit, but he wouldn't have them completely ruined. He wouldn't give up. He'd spent months mapping out his strategy, and he wouldn't let a little thing like finances get in his way. "Maybe…"

She held up a hand to stop him. "It's not your problem. Besides, I've been working on it, and though I'd rather not, I think I may have come up with a solution."

Thank goodness. Gavin nudged the sandwich toward her again, wanting her to eat. "What are you going to do?"

"I'm going to look for a roommate."

It was a viable solution, he supposed, but… "Do you really want another woman living here?"

"Heck no. Women tend to run a household, to be territorial about where they live. They want to add their own little touches, leave their mark. This is my house, and I don't intend to let someone else take it over. I'd rather go ahead and sell it first."

She gave him a drunken leer, then explained with a flourish, "I was talking about a *man*."

chapter 4

GAVIN STARED, feeling as if someone had just sucker-punched him in the gut. Was she trying to kill him? Sara with yet another man? *Hell no!* He'd only just gotten rid of Ted-the-despicable. He had no intention of going through that personal hell again.

She gave him a sleepy smile, unaware of how tense he'd become or the agony she caused. He watched as she folded her arms on the table, then rested her head there. She continued to watch him, and she continued to smile. She looked...adoring, and that made him uneasy. After a deep sigh, she said, "I've always thought you were the most beautiful man."

Ridiculously he felt a blush inching up his neck. Thank God it was too dark for her to see, even though her gaze was direct and very intent. "Eat your sandwich, Sara."

She chuckled at his brusque tone. "I'm not all that hungry."

He took a vicious bite of his own ham and cheese. The room was so silent, he could hear himself chew. He also heard her small, dreamy sighs. "Where, exactly, do you intend to find this *person* who will live with you?" He couldn't quite bring himself to specify a male.

"I'm not sure yet." She gave an elaborate shrug. "I suppose I'd want someone willing to pitch in, not just expect me to do all the work. And he'd absolutely have to be fun. I can't stand a sourpuss. And he'd have to like pets. I really do want a pet. Maybe a cute little floppy-eared puppy. There's always plenty of them at the shelter that need homes. Too many, in fact. We're nearly full now, and still, every day, someone drops off a litter and..."

"Sara?" He couldn't bear it if she started crying again.

"Hmm?"

"You're digressing. Where do you intend to find this paragon who'll live with you?"

"I suppose I could ask around at the office on Monday. Or maybe I could run one of those ads."

"No! No ads." Her eyes widened at his tone, and he shook his head, then paced away from the table. "You don't know what kind of crazy might show up with an open ad."

He couldn't exactly picture her questioning the men at her office, either. She worked as a secretary for a large corporate firm, and the people there were very stuffy. He knew, because he'd done some contracting for them. How Sara could thrive in that environment, he didn't know. All those suits and exacting regulations would have driven him batty. But for Sara, who always smiled and carried a cheerful disposition, it would be doubly difficult. He supposed it was just one more example of her ability to overcome the obstacles in her life. She'd evidently learned to adapt with her parents, and with her work. But there was only so much adapting a gentle, honest woman like her could do.

And that was why she wanted a dog.

Did she really think having a pet would fill her life? Did she think a dog could act as a buffer against the outside world? He was certainly no psychologist, but it seemed obvious to him Sara wanted to be loved, despite her new resolve not to marry. And since she'd given up on finding a man to fulfill that important task, she was willing to give the duty to a pet.

He snorted. She'd just have to settle for him, and that was that.

But how to convince her? He chewed his lip a moment, undecided, but he knew in his heart what he would do. He stared at the window and tried to keep his body inattentive to his plans. He cleared his throat. "I suppose there's only one solution."

He waited for Sara to ask him to explain, and when she didn't, he turned to frown at her. "Sara?"

His only response was a soft, snuffling snore.

Amused, he smiled at the picture she made. Her mouth was open, one cheek smooshed up by her arm, and even when he smoothed a hand over her hair, she didn't stir.

Well now. It was Friday. She didn't have to be at work tomorrow, and neither did he. All kinds of possibilities presented themselves, and this time he'd throw nobility out the door. All's fair in love and war, and with Sara, he had a feeling it would be a balancing act of each.

Unfortunately he'd have to start with the war.

THE SUN WAS BRIGHT when Sara opened her eyes. She stretched, then winced at the pain in her head. She felt lethargic and didn't particularly want to get up, which was unusual because she usually woke easily.

She swung her legs over the side of the bed, noticed she wore a badly rumpled sundress instead of her nightgown and then she remembered.

She'd gotten drunk last night.

She'd gotten drunk and hit on Gavin.

Mortified, she pressed a hand to her chest to contain her racing heart, trying to remember everything she'd said to Gavin. Though her head pounded from her overindulgence, it unfortunately didn't obliterate her memory. She recalled several damning tidbits of conversation that had slid silkily off her muddled tongue, and she knew for a fact she'd simply curl and die if she ever had to face him again.

He sauntered through her bedroom door carrying coffee and wearing a wide smile. "Good morning, sweetheart. Did you sleep well?"

She quickly closed her eyes. Death had to be imminent. Any second now.

If she just waited…

"Sara?"

No such luck. Sara peeked one eye open and saw that Gavin loomed over her, his brow lifted in question. She blinked, caught her breath and her stomach began flip-flopping.

Gavin was still wearing his cutoffs, but now they were unsnapped and only partially zipped.

Partially was enough to make her eyes buggy.

In the full light of morning, he was simply breathtaking. And with a dark beard-shadow covering his lean jaw and his hair sleep-mussed, he looked good enough to be breakfast. He was also waiting for an answer to his question. "I, ah…"

"I slept great," he said. "Your bed is a little short for me, and it was hotter than hell with both of us snuggled in there, but then—" he gave her a wink "—I could overlook the little discomforts."

Everything in her jerked to a shuddering standstill. Her heart stopped beating, oxygen snagged in her lungs. She was frozen, staring, mouth agape.

He had to be teasing.

Oh God, please let him be teasing.

There was no way he'd slept with her. Surely, even through a drunken haze, she would have remembered such a momentous occasion. She looked directly at him, refusing to flinch, prepared to dispute him and call him on his bluff. She opened her mouth, cleared her throat, and out came something that sounded vaguely like, *"Hmgarph?"*

Gavin set the coffee mugs on the nightstand, then plumped the pillows behind Sara. "Here, lean back and get comfortable. I thought we'd have our coffee in bed."

"Hmgarph," she said again, because his warm hands had closed around her calves as he swung her legs onto the mattress, settling her despite her stiff resistance.

How many times had she imagined something like this? Something like this…after something much more significant of a sexual nature. She'd dreamed such things, but she'd certainly never considered them actually happening.

After all, Gavin was…well, he was Gavin. And she wasn't his type, not at all. She'd even been stretching the boundaries of fiction to imagine it in her dreams.

Yet here he was, and here she was, and all she could do was make nonsensical garbled sounds. If she could only understand why he was here, maybe she wouldn't be so nervous. It couldn't be for the most apparent reasons. Gavin couldn't be interested in her. After all, even Ted had found her so lacking, he'd quickly wandered. Her own parents hadn't deemed her interesting enough to want to have around. There was simply something about her that made people keep their distance. So surely Gavin wouldn't…

He scooted in with her, quite at his ease, his big luscious body taking up a lot of room. He casually handed her a mug of steaming coffee. His smile now was one of satisfaction and contentment. "Now, isn't this better?"

Better than what? she wondered, and drank half the cup in one gulp. Despite the heat of the drink, she shivered. It hit her suddenly how cool the room was. Before she could ask, Gavin offered an explanation.

"The electricity came back on about five this morning. It had gotten damn steamy in here, so I turned on your air."

That got her tongue temporarily unglued. "I can't afford to run the air conditioner."

What an inane comment to make, she thought, given the fact she was lying in bed with a mostly naked, utterly devastating man, who surely wasn't there for the usual reasons a man put himself in a woman's bed yet she didn't know why he was really there and couldn't seem to find the wits to ask him.

But her mind simply refused to focus on the real issues. It was too much to take in, and with her heart doing wild leaps around her chest, and her eyes busy exploring every inch of Gavin's hard body, her concentration was nil. Her brain kept screaming, *What happened?* but her heart kept whispering, *I'll bet it was good!*

Gavin took a long sip of his coffee before turning to her. "You can afford to be comfortable, Sara. Remember, you've got a roommate now to split the bills, so there's no need to suffer this heat wave."

Roommate? She remembered mentioning the half-baked idea to him, but she never claimed to have found anyone. She wasn't even looking, not since she'd decided she had no choice but to sell. She bit her lip, frowning.

Gavin reached up and rubbed his thumb across the edge of her teeth, freeing her bottom lip and halting her heartbeat in erratic midpump. "I love how you do that." His voice was a rough whisper, deep and compelling. "It makes me hot."

Sara felt like a zombie. A wide-eyed, speechless, sleep-rumpled zombie who could do no more than stare. She swallowed hard to remove the choking disbelief from her throat. "How I do...what?"

"The way you chew on your lip." His big thumb continued to caress her mouth, his eyes watching as she struggled to breathe. "It's so damn sexy. Especially with that little crooked tooth. When I kissed you last night, I felt that tooth with my tongue."

He thought her crooked tooth was sexy? Sara laughed, comprehension dawning. Of course. It was all a dream! She was probably still in the damn tub, and she'd drown herself before she actually woke up. It would be poetic justice.

"What's funny?" Gavin still looked at her lips when he asked that question, and Sara had to fight not to smile. She didn't want him to think she was deliberately flaunting her sexy tooth.

She laughed again, covering her mouth with a hand. How ridiculous that sounded, even in a dream. She shook her head. "I just realized I must still be asleep, that's all."

Gavin looked up to meet Sara's eyes. *Hot.* His gaze was so hot, Sara hoped she never woke up. She liked having him look at her like that, as if he cared for her, as if maybe he loved her a little. It was a foolish notion, but if dreaming made it seem real, she'd willingly stay asleep.

"When I was younger, the schoolkids used to make fun of my teeth. Mom said she couldn't afford cosmetic dentistry, and Dad kept forgetting. Now that I'm older, it really just doesn't matter anymore."

Gavin's eyes narrowed just the tiniest bit, as if someone had just pinched him, then his gaze dropped to her mouth. "You have a beautiful smile, and the one tooth is only slightly turned, certainly nothing for kids to tease about. I'm glad you didn't fix it."

She chuckled again, finding his answer as bizarre as everything else that happened. She said, "A crooked tooth is a crooked tooth."

Very slowly, Gavin leaned across her and took her coffee

cup, setting it on the nightstand with his. As he moved, his broad, hard chest crowded her back and she inhaled his sleep-musky intoxicating scent. She had only a moment to contemplate his motives, and then he kissed her.

Just as he'd said, his tongue pressed between her lips, warm and soft and damp, then probed along the edge of her teeth. *This was no dream.* Sara made that acknowledgment the same instant she decided she didn't care. It was too exciting, the way he teased her with his tongue. She opened her mouth wider, her hands moving against the firm contours of his chest. The hair there was crisp, but soft, tickling her palms and curling between her fingers. And the heat—there was so much heat.

He gave a low groan and urged her closer, then tilted her into the bed until he was lying on top of her.

"Sara," he whispered, his lips moving over her cheek, her forehead, her mouth again. He lifted himself onto his elbows, caging her between his muscled arms. With one hand, he smoothed her wildly rambunctious hair away from her forehead, then gave her a tender smile. "You're not drunk anymore."

Sara blinked at the change of subject. Her mind was still back there with that kiss, with the damp heat and his talented tongue and… She shuddered. "No."

"Hungover?"

Since she'd never been hungover before, she wasn't sure. But it sounded vulgar, so despite her pounding head she rejected the idea. "Just tired. And a bit of a headache."

With a slow thrust of his hips, he reminded her of all the

places they touched, how intimately they were entwined. "Good. That's good." His gaze lifted to lock with hers. "Now tell me about these fantasies."

Her eyes widened.

With the lightest touch, his mouth brushed over hers. "Last night, you said you fantasized about me. You even offered to tell me what those fantasies were."

Even the air conditioning couldn't counteract the flustered heat she generated, and she hadn't even made it out of bed yet. "I…ah, I was drunk."

His tender smile curled her toes and made her thigh muscles tingle. "I know. But you didn't make it up, did you? Tell me now."

"I should never have said anything."

"I'm glad you did."

"I feel so ridiculous."

"I think you feel very soft and warm and sweet." He pressed against her to emphasize his words, and groaned deeply. "Oh, yeah. Very sweet."

His tone of voice, rumbling and deep, could be lethal. "Gavin…"

"Sara…" He mimicked her, then gave her another light, taunting, tell-me-all kiss. It was almost as if he couldn't stop himself. Sara was considering that possibility, her eyes still wide, when he said, "When do you want me to move in?"

She reeled. True, she was lying flat on her back, and Gavin's weight kept her securely stationed against the bed but still she reeled, at least mentally. Did he intend to keep her off balance all morning? "Uh…what are you talking about?"

His low sigh fanned her warm cheeks, her lips. "I can tell you're not a morning person." His kiss this time lingered, and left her bemused. "That might be a problem, babe, because I definitely am."

"Am what?" In truth, she *was* a morning person. But then, she'd never awakened before with a gorgeous man looming around, endearments tripping off his oh-so-suave tongue, while flaunting his too tempting, mostly bare, exquisite body. So she understood her vast confusion even if he didn't. It had very little to do with her sleeping habits. "Gavin, will you make sense?"

"All right." He kissed her once more, short and sweet, then said, "I'm your new roommate. You do remember asking me to move in last night, don't you?"

When she only continued to stare, waiting for the punch line, he added, "You were very convincing, shooting down all my arguments, even threatening me with that damn rake once. I had no choice. No choice at all. You insisted I see things your way. And of course, I did. Who could resist a begging woman?"

She narrowed her eyes, knowing she would never beg, not even in a drunken stupor. The rake attack…well, they both knew that was possible. But not begging. "I haven't begged for anything since…well, since I was kid."

His expression softened, the teasing gone to be replaced with tender understanding. "When you begged to keep your puppy?"

She didn't want to talk about that, not now, not when her emotions already felt so raw and exposed. "You're only playing with me, aren't you?"

He gave a sigh of long-suffering affront. "I've been a perfect gentleman, despite your provocation." Then he glanced down at their layered bodies. "Though I'll admit playing with you has entered my mind several times."

Good, she thought. Let's play, and you can quit trying to confuse me with things I can't accept. She thought it, but she hoped her silent encouragement wasn't too obvious.

He sat up, then pulled her up, too. She swallowed her disappointment as he moved to her side, trying to concentrate on what he had to say.

"It's all settled. I can get most of my stuff moved in over this weekend, if that's okay with you. Actually I was really relieved when you asked. I was only kidding about you having to beg me. This will work out perfect. It's been a real pain letting people through the house with me living there. I'm not a slob or anything, but I hated having to worry about every little thing I left out of place. And people have no respect for your privacy. They snoop through drawers and cabinets as if they already own the place. This way, with me living here, I'll still be close enough to supervise things, which is why I moved into the model home in the first place, but my privacy will be protected." He raised a brow in her direction. "That is, as long as you don't suffer a penchant for prying."

Her back stiffened. "I do not pry."

"You said you asked Karen personal questions about me."

"I didn't have to ask," she sputtered indignantly. "She gloated on and on about what a phenomenal stud you are. She practically shoved the information down my throat. I tried not to listen—"

"But she was insistent? How annoying for you." His smug grin set her teeth on edge and set her head to pounding. Now that he no longer touched her, she was beginning to see the situation with just a tad more clarity. Still, there was too much she couldn't remember.

"I have no recollection of asking you to move in. In fact, I never once considered such a thing." *Not seriously, anyway.*

"Well, why not? We've always gotten along well. Are you telling me you made promises while you were drunk that you've no intention of keeping?"

That was the rub. She wanted to grab this opportunity and take complete advantage of it and him. He was the most compelling man she'd ever met, with a strength and gentleness that formed a potent mix. This could prove to be a page right out of her fantasies. She thought of Gavin's skilled hands, his confidence and capability, and her stomach leaped in encouragement. *Say yes, say yes,* her body screamed.

But she'd made a vow to herself after her breakup with Ted. Never again would she leave herself open and vulnerable to humiliation. A woman should only have to suffer one such incident in her lifetime, and she'd had her quota. She would have to stay in control of any situation, especially those involving men. Right now, with Gavin, she certainly wasn't feeling any sense of real control; she was mired three feet under in deep, dark confusion. He seemed to want her, yet he kept pulling away. Not far away, especially given that he wanted to move in, but just enough to make her want him more, when she already wanted him plenty! It wasn't fair. It wasn't the behavior she was used to from men. Not that she'd been a highly sought after female, but the men she had known had made their intentions plain. Gavin was evidently willing to keep her guessing. But why?

When she remained quiet, Gavin prompted her with a slight nudge to her shoulder. "Well?"

Feeling trapped, she asked with a degree of obvious caution, "Did I make very many promises last night?"

His look was suggestive. "A few."

Her teeth sank into her bottom lip, and she saw his gaze drop to follow the action, the intensity of that gaze palpable. She immediately hid her teeth behind her lips, but not before their thoughts collided. They were each remembering last night, and the fact he thought she was sexy.

She had to give herself a few minutes to collect her composure, without his disturbing influence, before she made any decisions. Gavin had the power to hurt her much more than Ted ever could have. Ted had been a solution, but Gavin was a desire, a need, a dark craving. To have him, for whatever reason, and then lose him, could be devastating. "Why don't you meet me in the kitchen after I shower and change and we can…discuss all this."

"Hell of an idea." He was already on his feet, moving with an air of triumph. "I'll throw together some breakfast."

Her nervousness was enough to choke a cow, and her stomach rebelled at the mere thought of food. "I don't think…"

"Don't worry. I promise to go light." He was halfway out of the room before he added, "I'm an excellent cook, Sara, and I don't mind pitching in. I've even been accused of being fun on occasion, so you shouldn't have any complaints at all."

Gorgeous *and* an excellent cook? But what was all that nonsense about him being fun?

Sara heaved a sigh. She had no idea what was going on. One thing was certain, he had her interest. It was almost too good to be true, though she wanted it to be.

God, how she wanted it to be.

It was terribly risky, especially since she knew deep down that if she accepted Gavin, on whatever silly terms he spoke of, she might end up totally devastated.

Then again, since she was no longer looking for husband material, knowing exactly how futile that endeavor would be, Gavin might very well be the perfect roommate. She couldn't expect a man like him to commit himself to one woman. Commitment was no longer a requirement. Right? She nodded her head at her own question, but still wasn't convinced. As long as she had her fair share of his time...

Ground rules, that's what they needed. He should be hers exclusively for at least a while. She could glut herself on his masculine charms, then move on to newer game. Men did it all the time.

The thought of newer game actually sickened her. Lately all men had seemed a big turnoff, at least romantically. But not Gavin. Maybe that was because he was such a good friend, too.

She saved the uninteresting, disturbing thoughts of greener pastures for later and concentrated on the glutting part while she prepared for her shower. Now *that* was enough to get a woman wide-eyed and bushy-tailed in the morning. Everyone deserved a little fantasy time, and it looked like this might be hers.

Maybe this would all work out after all.

GAVIN'S PLAN WAS MOVING along rather smoothly. All he needed now were a few ground rules. He had to get Sara to commit, somehow, even if for a short while. He'd work on extending that time as they went along, teaching her to trust him, to trust her own feelings again, and eventually, she would be his. Only his.

It would have to be a unique role reversal, but he planned to hold out on her. She wanted him, that much was obvious. Not as much as he wanted her, which was impossible given his constant state of arousal. But he was more determined, and therefore it stood to reason he could control his reactions better. At least, he hoped he could. He prayed he could. Damn, could he?

It wouldn't be easy. It would be his greatest challenge. More so than building an expansive house, more than doing a renovation, more than...

He grinned, thinking he had likened himself to a superhero, ready to leap tall buildings to rescue his lady-fair—by withholding sex. Actually, leaping a building might be easier than holding out on Sara.

She wasn't a woman who inspired higher levels of celibacy. Not when she went all soft and warm and willing every time he touched her.

But he wouldn't let her use him.

He chuckled out loud, pondering his course of action. He'd force her to be a *gentlewoman* and do the honorable thing, namely marriage. Teasing her would be fun, and a type of stratospheric sensual torture, because teasing her meant teasing himself and he was already on the ragged edge of lust. But with the promise of success, he could take it.

Hopefully Sara couldn't.

He had breakfast ready when she wandered in, looking refreshed and in control. Her cutoffs matched his own, but she wore a pastel T-shirt, where he opted to remain shirtless. He hadn't missed her fascination with his chest, and while he'd always been aware of the attention from other women, it hadn't mattered to him nearly as much as Sara's appreciation. He knew if she hadn't liked him as a man, she wouldn't have given his body more than a single, cursory glance. But she *did* like him, and she did a lot of gawking, not just glancing. So if flaunting his body would help capture Sara, he'd flaunt away without an ounce of remorse.

"Feeling better now?"

She gave him a wary look, then nodded. He was pleased to see she was still uncertain how to deal with him. As long as he kept her off center his odds of success were improved. She didn't want marriage, so he was going to have to sneak it in on her.

"Breakfast smells good."

"Then your appetite has returned. I'm glad. You never did eat your sandwich last night."

When she looked puzzled, he decided to be benevolent and explain. "You fell asleep. I carried you to bed."

Her eyes widened. "Then…?"

"Nothing happened, Sara. Is that what you're wondering about?" He tried for a look of masculine affront. "I told you I behaved myself, though I swear it wasn't easy."

He loved how she blushed. Looking down to avoid his gaze, she pushed her hair behind her ears and fidgeted. Gavin waited, fighting to keep his amusement hidden.

"Last night is…something of a blur. At least parts of it are. Some things I remember clear as a bell, but others…" She hesitated, then forged on. "I have no memory of asking you to move in. None at all."

Guilt swamped him. She looked too confused, vulnerable, too. He considered confessing, maybe giving her some partial truths that would reassure her, when she shook her head.

"It doesn't matter. I'll be glad to have you."

Gavin felt his lips twitch, along with his heart and other numerous, masculine parts of his body. "Have me?"

Her eyes flared, and she stammered, "That is, I mean, I'll be glad to have you *here*."

He raised one brow, his skeptical gaze going to the kitchen tabletop.

"I don't mean *have you*, have you, I mean… You could come here…"

He opened his mouth but she quickly cut him off.

"No! I don't mean…" Slapping a hand to her forehead, she said, "I'd…I'd like you to move in."

He never said a word, giving her the chance to state her intentions outright. She had to make the ultimate decisions of what and who she wanted.

"It will have to be a complete partnership. I'll continue with the house payment myself. The rest of the bills we'll divide down the middle, even the groceries. And we'll have to share all the chores." Then she seemed to consider that. "Although, if you really do know how to cook, maybe we could work out a deal. I wouldn't mind doing the grocery shopping and cleaning up the kitchen if you'd fix the meals. It's the truth, I'm an awful cook."

"No problem. When I can't cook, we'll order in or dine out. What do you say?"

She looked suspicious again, so he tried a very sincere smile, which only deepened her frown. "That's fine, I guess, but there are a few more things we need to iron out."

She seemed entirely too serious, so Gavin handed her a plate of food, hoping to distract her from her thoughts. "Here, eat while we talk. You need some nutrition after your raucous night of drunken revelry."

She accepted the plate, then breathed deep of the combined scents of scrambled eggs, toasted English muffins and fresh fruit. "It really does smell delicious. I hadn't realized I was so hungry."

Gavin watched her taste everything, then nod approval. He said, "My mom and sisters didn't want to turn me loose when I moved out. It seemed one or the other of them showed up twice a week with homemade meals. I either had to learn to cook for myself, so they wouldn't worry, or be forever indebted to them. I chose to learn to cook."

Sara smiled around a mouthful of warm muffin. "They sound like very nice people."

"Yeah, and I'm spoiled rotten." He waited until she had another mouthful of eggs, then added, "You'll get to meet them next Saturday. They're coming to visit."

She sputtered and choked and coughed while he patted her back. "Are you all right?"

She wheezed a deep breath. "The damn muffin went up my nose."

Gavin bent down to look in her face. "No kidding?"

She took several more gasping breaths, a large drink of juice, then demanded, "What do you mean they're coming to visit?"

With a deliberate shrug of indifference, he said, "Mom always calls on Saturday morning. I knew she'd be worried if she couldn't reach me, so I phoned and gave her this number. One explanation led to another and now she wants to meet you. And whenever my mom interferes, my sisters are close on her heels."

"But...but...I can't meet your family!"

"Why not?"

He watched her search frantically for an answer, and finally come up with, "Because!"

"Because?"

She made an elaborate show of exasperation. "You know why, Gavin. What will they think?"

That I've finally met the woman I intend to marry. He didn't tell her that, of course. If he had, she'd have put a stop to his folks visiting real fast. She was so damn skittish about marriage and family and commitment now. But his family was the better part of him, a real selling tool to a woman like

Sara. She wouldn't be able to resist any of them, and they wouldn't be able to resist her. He was certain of that.

Hoping to distract her once more so she wouldn't put up too much fuss, he leaned forward until his mouth was only a hairbreadth away from her lips. "You've got a whole week to get used to the idea."

Her eyelids fluttered, then closed as he kissed her. It was a very light kiss, soft and void of sexual intent.

For about three seconds.

Her soft moan shot his good intentions all to hell. When her tongue touched his lips, Gavin stumbled out of his chair and pulled Sara from hers, all without breaking the kiss. With only two steps he had her backed to the counter, trapped there with his body. She was so soft and sweet from her shower, so warm, he couldn't resist touching her.

Tangling his fingers in her dark, curly hair, he tipped her face to the side so his mouth could explore her throat. She hummed a small sound of pleasure, her hands gripping his bare shoulders, urging him closer. He felt the slight sting of her nails.

The distraction worked. In fact, he forgot why he was distracting her.

He kissed her again, wet and hot, his tongue sliding in, imitating what he wanted. What *she* evidently wanted, too, a truth that his carnal side relished. She wasn't drunk this morning, and she knew what she was doing. That thought kept pounding through his brain, driving him.

She groaned and arched into him. It was too much, and he lost control. He was hard, urgent, and he pressed his erection against her soft belly, hearing her groan again and feeling her cuddle him closer. One hand moved to cup her breast, and her nipple was stiff, ready. He started shoving her T-shirt up. He wanted to taste her, to have her nipple in his mouth, sucking, licking…

"Gavin?"

"Hmm?"

Breathless, she whispered, "Are we going to do a lot of…this, when you move in?"

His brain shut down for a single heartbeat. "Aw, hell." Reminded of his plan, he shoved himself away from her, jamming both hands into his hair. Immense frustration rode him, along with total disgust. He'd never get her to marry him if he was so easy. How did that saying go? Something about not buying the cow if the milk was free? Not that he liked comparing himself to a cow. A bull, maybe, but still…

He forced himself to take several deep breaths and face her. She looked aroused. Her lips were a little puffy, her shirt half untucked, her cheeks flushed.

But it was her eyes that grabbed and held his attention. They were bright and clear and filled with hot anticipation.

"Don't do that." His tone was cautious, and he backed up a step. Sara slowly followed. Her gaze remained glued to his, and as he watched, wary, she licked her lips. He felt like a meal set before a starving person.

It wasn't an altogether unpleasant feeling. "Sara…" he warned.

"I wasn't complaining, Gavin, when I asked if—"

"I know." He held up a hand to ward her off, both physically and verbally. If she said much more, if she touched him again, if she licked her lips just one more time, he was a goner. Thankfully she stopped. He wondered how to begin, what exactly to say. He needed her to know how much he wanted her. That was an important fact she had to understand with unwavering certainty. But he also had to make her understand he wouldn't allow her to toy with his affections. There would be no simple fling. If she wanted the beef, she had to buy the bull. Period.

"What is it, Gavin?"

Trying to look stern, he folded his arms behind his back and paced. "You're just coming out of a bad relationship, Sara. People tend to react on the rebound whenever they've been hurt, and—"

"How do you know?" Then her eyes narrowed. "You're talking about your breakup with Karen, aren't you? You said she had stopped being important to you long ago."

Her tone was accusing, and he flinched at his poor choice of wording. "True. Karen didn't mean that much to me. But it was another example of a failed relationship, and I'm getting too old to keep involving myself in dead-end situations. Do you understand?"

She nodded, the movement slow and thoughtful. "But I didn't think you were looking for involvement anyway. And I've already learned all I need to know about these things. If you're afraid I'll get clingy, I promise I won't. I'm not looking for happily ever after. Not anymore."

So. That hadn't just been the drink talking. Having her reiterate her intentions so plainly pricked his temper. He didn't like the idea that she planned to use him for mere sex. For mere, mind-blowing, torrid, delicious sex. God, he was an idiot. A determined idiot.

Glaring, he said, "That's just it. We're both looking for different things now. And that means we should move slowly."

Her gaze skittered away, and she nodded. "I see."

Exasperated, he said, "No, you don't. I want you, Sara. A lot. That much should be plain."

Lifting her shoulders in a shrug, she said, "I suppose."

"Dammit! You're deliberately provoking me. No, don't try to look innocent." He saw her lips quirk in a small smile, then she frowned again. "Sara." He said her name as a chastisement. "We'll have to get together on this if it's going to work. Do you at least agree to that much?"

"If what will work?"

"Me staying here. We'll need some rules."

"Such as?"

"Such as…" He gestured with his hands, indicating the two of them. "We'll have to work on maintaining some decorum."

"You don't want to kiss me anymore?"

"Oh, yeah," he drawled, letting his gaze linger on her mouth. "I want to kiss you. But it'll have to stop there. We need time to get used to each other. Time to form some sort of understanding, without the past getting in the way."

She raised one brow, waiting for him to elaborate.

"You're going to have to stop making it so easy on me."

"Me? What about you? You're the one who started the kissing."

He smiled to himself, preparing his trap. Give and take,

that's what was needed. "Yeah. But you didn't have to go all soft and hungry on me."

"Hungry! I wasn't…"

"Yes, you were. And you made those sexy little sounds." He stepped closer again, one finger touching her warm cheek. "I've kissed other women and not lost my head like that. So it must be you." He had to bite his lip to keep from laughing, she'd gone so rigid, her frown so fierce.

"I'm not going to let you blame me for this, Gavin! Why, you're the one who climbed into bed with me when I was drunk!"

"But I'm not the one who tried to crawl on top of you in the middle of the night."

She sucked in so much air, she choked. "I would never…!"

Nodding, he said, "Yes, you would. *You did.*" Then he added in a low voice before she could get too worked up, "But I didn't mind. Not at all."

"Gavin…"

"Are you going to help me move a few of my things here today?" He threw that in just to change the subject before she could get angry enough to toss him out on his ear. Not that he'd let her toss him out, but accomplishing his goals would be easier if she didn't want to wring his neck.

After blinking several times, she glanced at the clock, then accepted the new topic with a vague show of relief. "I suppose I could help a little. But I have to go to the shelter this afternoon. I'm sorry, but they're counting on me. If I'd known everything that would happen, maybe…"

"No, that's okay. I can manage on my own." And without

her help, there was no way he could haul his mattress and box springs down the street. Leaving the sleeping arrangements as they were suited him just fine, at least for the time being.

"If you're sure?"

It was obvious to Gavin she wanted some time alone, time to sort through all he'd thrown at her over the past twelve hours. "Positive." Then he nudged her plate at her to get her to finish eating. "It seems to me you're a damn picky eater. That won't do. I like to cook and I'll expect you to be properly appreciative of my efforts."

Sara lifted her chin. "I think that's one rule I won't have a problem abiding by."

"Good." He waited until she finished eating, then went to the side of her chair. Time for the next step. He could hardly wait for her reaction. Damn, but he was a genius.

She glanced up at him, her expression alert.

He tried to look serious. "Now, I was thinking, Sara. Maybe you ought to pick out that pet you want today. I know it's kind of soon, but since we'll both be living here, it shouldn't be a big problem or an expense to keep up with one cute little animal. I'll be glad to help out some, to look after it when you're not around, to take it for walks every now and then. What do you think?"

Her eyes widened, and the look of naked excitement that came over her features was worth any amount of nuisance. Gavin didn't look forward to a puppy's accidents, or the chore of housebreaking, but he had thought it an excellent way to start stepping in the right direction. Once she saw how supportive he could be of her pet, she'd realize he wasn't the least bit similar to Ted. And he'd been right.

She leaped from her seat, wrapped her arms around him and gave him a strangling hug. She talked nonstop about whether or not she wanted a large or small pet, male or female. Gavin silently congratulated himself when she rushed out the door, anxious to reach the shelter.

He rubbed his hands together. Things were moving along just as he planned. And as Sara had once told him, he was a master planner.

chapter 5

SARA GLANCED AT THE HOUSE, but saw no sign of Gavin. She didn't want him to witness her approach. Stealth wasn't her forte, but she felt certain if she could only initiate the idea of this particular animal slowly, everything would go better. No way would she give up her pet now that she had chosen. It had loved her on sight, and the feeling had been mutual. This animal was now hers. But that didn't mean she wanted to fight about it, either.

Her mind whirled with everything the day had brought her way. Throughout her stint at the shelter, her feet had barely touched the ground. She was truly happy. More than that, she was excited. First Gavin, and now her very own pet. And not just any old pet, she thought with satisfaction.

Lugging the heavy box from the back seat, Sara murmured soft soothing phrases to the animal within. Jess and Lou, the couple who owned the shelter, were thrilled when she made her choice. They were also endlessly amused.

That was nothing new, because Jess and his wife had a bizarre sense of humor, a humor that often escaped Sara.

But in this instance she hadn't been nearly as obtuse as they'd assumed. And she hadn't minded their good-natured teasing, either, not when they'd supplied all the shots and a thorough checkup on the newly arrived animal for free.

It had been imperative that she take the pet, because if she hadn't, it was a certainty no one else would have.

She'd barely gotten through her front door, huffing with the effort to carry the large box and the weight within, when she heard Gavin approaching. The second she saw his face, she set the box on the floor and stepped in front of it, plastering a bright smile on her lips. "I'm back."

Gavin looked her over from head to toe as if he'd missed the sight of her. "So I see."

His voice was soft, and Sara only blinked when he leaned close and gave her a sweet, welcoming kiss. As he started to pull away, she tilted into him and the kiss intensified.

He seemed determined to keep her at a physical distance. She was determined to make him relent.

He was in her house. He was available. She figured the least she should do, as an enterprising, healthy woman, was take advantage of the opportunity presented to her.

It was amazing the effect he had on her, she thought, deliberately wrapping herself closer. She hadn't known feelings like these existed until Gavin decided to move in. And since, she'd suffered constant frustration. If he didn't give in soon, she'd go crazy from unrequited lust. Damn his ridiculous ethics.

His hand had just started down her back, encouraged no doubt by her soft moan, when a loud, rumbling growl erupted from the cardboard box.

Gavin froze, his mouth still touching hers, but his eyes wide-open. "What the hell was that?"

Uh-oh. Teatime. She winced just a bit, then whispered, "My pet?"

His eyes flared even more and he took her shoulders, moving her aside and staring down at the box. "What did you get? A mountain lion?"

"Well, actually…" That was as far as Sara got before the box seemed to explode and a massive streak of mangy yellow fur shot out, like a marmalade cannon blast. The huge alley cat surveyed its surroundings in a single derisive glance, swishing its badly bent tail then giving a vicious shake of its monstrous, square head. A small, lopsided pink bow hung precariously over a damaged ear, an ear that was only half there.

Gavin's mouth hung open. "My God."

The cat gave him a look filled with disdain, then strutted past, sniffing the carpet and, for the most part, ignoring the humans.

"What the hell is that?"

Sara forced a cheerful expression, hoping to brazen it out, but her words were too quick and nervous to hide her concern. "My pet, of course. Isn't she beautiful? The man who dropped her off today said she was expecting."

"Expecting…what?"

"Kittens!" Sara glanced at the cat, who stared back without a single blink of its large pea-green eyes. Perhaps if Gavin believed the ruse, he'd be more inclined to accept the shabby monster. Surely no compassionate person could turn away an expectant mother. "Her name is Satin."

Gavin sent her a skeptical, slightly horrified look, and Sara rushed on. "She's had a few…mishaps, and being as old as she is, the shelter didn't really hold any great hope of finding her a home. I couldn't leave her there indefinitely, without hope, without prospects. I just couldn't."

The cat chose that moment to give them both its back, walking away with a hunter's stride and sticking its bent tail high into the air. Again, Gavin's mouth fell open, then quickly tightened in chagrin. "Ah, Sara? That cat's about as pregnant as I am."

She already knew that, but she wasn't ready for Gavin to realize it. It was her best excuse for bringing the beast home.

She swiveled her gaze back to him, her brows lowered in stern regard. "If you've gotten yourself into trouble, Gavin, don't look at me. You said our night together was innocent enough."

His smirk proved he wasn't fooled, or diverted. Walking to the cat, he said, "Come here, fella. Let's get that hideous bow off your head."

To Sara's amazement, the aloof cat halted his exit and waited in regal patience while Gavin knelt down and worked the bow free. He ignored Sara as he spoke with the cat. "Satin, is it? More like Satan, I'd say, given the looks of you. You've raised some hell in your days, haven't you, boy?"

The cat's purr was more of a scratchy growl, and the first Sara had heard. It was clear to her the animal hadn't led a pampered life. She'd taken one look at the poor creature and every nurturing instinct she owned had kicked in. The farmer who'd brought the cat in had hoped to escape the shelter's costs by claiming it to be a future mother. He'd dropped off the box and left again all within a matter of moments. But the second the cat had been cautiously lifted free of the cardboard confines, it was obvious he was a tom.

That hadn't deterred Sara. And while she'd pretended to believe the farmer's story, she had put up with her friends' amusement. What the heck? It had gotten the cat some pretty special treatment, and the truth was, she was almost embarrassed to admit she wanted the cat simply because he was alone and unwanted, a feeling she understood all too well.

She felt a strong affinity to a rather homely, bedraggled animal. And that wasn't something she wanted to explain, even to her friends.

Gavin stood again and faced her. "Have you had this animal checked? He looks like he could be carrying any number of diseases."

The cat rolled on the carpet, stretching and luxuriating in his freedom from the bow. Everywhere his big body touched, a patch of dull yellow cat hair remained. He desperately needed a good brushing.

"Jess is a vet, and he checked her...ah him, over. Other than a few scrapes—"

"And missing body parts."

Sara nodded. "Yes. Other than the missing ear, he's healthy. His tail is bent for good and his voice box is damaged, I'm afraid. There's nothing we can do about that. But I have vitamins for him, and a good cat food that should put some shine back in his fur and—"

Sara was cut off as the cat decided he wanted more of

Gavin's attention and made a sudden, smooth lunge into his arms. Gavin had no choice but to catch the weight, which was considerable, Sara knew. He staggered, cursed, then reluctantly held the beast. There was a look of distaste on Gavin's face, but still, he scratched the cat's head with his free hand.

Amazed at the cat's show of affection, Sara laughed. "Oh, Gavin, isn't that sweet? He likes you."

"Yeah. Sweet." Gavin grimaced as the cat began to purr again, all but drowning out any attempt at normal conversation.

Satisfaction filled her, and Sara nodded in approval of Gavin's attempt to treat the animal with kindness. "I think he feels indebted because you knew he was a male."

"Uh-huh. Right."

"Don't look at me like I'm screwy. It was obvious he didn't like that pink bow."

"We men feel strongly about that sort of thing."

"Wearing bows?"

"No. Having our masculinity questioned."

"Ah."

"Sara? Did you really believe this beast to be a…"

Before he could finish his question, she had the front door open and headed out. "I have a lot of stuff in the car yet. A litter box, a bed, the food. Will you keep an eye on Satin while I bring everything in?"

"Satin, hell. At least forget that name, will you?"

Chancing a glance at his face, Sara saw Gavin was resigned. She sighed in relief. "What should we call him?"

Looking at the cat as he considered her question, Gavin

finally said, "With that vicious purr, Satan suits him well enough."

"He does look like the very devil."

To Sara's surprise, Gavin became defensive of the cat. "Just because he's not some prissy feline shouldn't matter. He's a good mouser, I bet." Then he added, "I had a cat like him when I was a kid. He'd go out every so often and either come home the strutting victor of a romantic rendezvous, or a bedraggled soldier from battle. Either way, there was always a female involved somehow." The cat rubbed his large head against Gavin's chest in agreement, leaving a blotch of fur behind.

"Well," Sara said on her way to the car, "his nights on the town will soon be curtailed. I'm going to have him neutered."

The cat gave a loud hiss and Sara looked back to see him racing down the hall. Gavin scowled at her, then went after the cat, calling in soft sympathy, "Here, kitty, kitty, kitty…"

Everything was working out, Sara thought. Only two days ago, she was alone, without a single soul who cared. Now she had Gavin—no matter how temporary that arrangement might be—and she had a wonderful new pet. Not only that, the two males had bonded already.

Now, she thought, feeling lighthearted and happy and half-silly, the only thing missing in her life was lawn furniture, and it no longer seemed so important.

GAVIN LOOKED DOWN at the cat twined around his bare ankles. "At least you enjoyed my dinner." He knew today had to make an impact; it was the first day of their "relationship." So he'd made, in his humble opinion, a stupendous dinner, topped by a killer dessert. Sara had eaten a fair portion, had even complimented him on his efforts, but other than that, her attention wasn't where he wanted it to be—on him.

Handing the cat another scrap of meat, Gavin considered his next step. Sara hadn't as yet asked how his moving in had gone. She'd been much too busy settling Satan and enjoying being a pet owner to concern herself with anything as mundane as the new man in her life.

Pushing back from the table, Gavin left his seat and walked to where Sara stood rinsing dishes in the sink. "Are you sure you don't want any help?"

"We had a deal, Gavin. You cooked, so I'll clean."

"I wouldn't mind helping…"

"You've done enough today." She turned, giving him a fat smile. "The meal was fabulous."

Without giving himself a chance to think about it, he leaned down and skimmed her cheek with his mouth. She smelled so damn good, even after working in an animal shelter all day. He nuzzled her hair, her ear. The catch in her breath was audible, and he leaned closer, caging her between his body and the counter.

Water dripped down his neck when her wet hands settled in his hair, holding him still so she could kiss him. But he darted away. Seeing the disappointment in her eyes, he hid his smile, and his own frustration. But he'd just decided what to do next. "I think I'll go take a shower, then, if you're sure you don't need any help."

"Fine. Go." She returned her hands to the sudsy water, her stiff back showing her disgruntlement.

With a hidden grin, Gavin turned, and nearly tripped over the cat. Satan seemed to want to stay right on his heels, no matter where he went or what he did. He said to the cat, "Sorry, no shower for you. Stay here and visit with your new master."

The cat answered with a grouchy, rusty roar, but he did stay.

Whistling, Gavin went into the bathroom and stripped down. Even with the door closed, he could hear Sara banging the pots and pans around, venting her own frustration no doubt. But that was fine with him. He wanted her so frustrated she wouldn't be able to resist him when he suggested making their relationship more permanent. He wanted her on the edge, willing to overlook her reservations on marriage in order to get her sexual needs fulfilled.

And to that end, he'd do what he had to do.

After quickly showering, he reached for a towel. Leaving the water running, he pulled the door open and yelled, "Hey, Sara?"

There was a moment of silence, then she stuck her head around the hall. She stared at him, her gaze dropping quickly from his face to his wet chest and then down his belly. She stared at the loosely draped towel wrapped low around his hips and mumbled a crackly, "Hmm?"

"I left my shampoo in a box by the front door." His smile was innocence personified. "Would you bring it to me, please?"

He watched her swallow, then drag her eyes back to his face. "Shampoo?" she asked, as if in a fog.

"Yeah. I've got a preference for my own, if you don't mind."

"No. No, I don't mind."

As he watched her hurry away, the cat slipped through the

door and wove itself around and between his ankles, leaving his damp legs with clinging yellow fur. Gavin pushed the door wider and tried to nudge the cat out. Satan refused to budge.

"Go on, scat."

The cat hunched back, preparing to leap into Gavin's arms again.

"No!" Gavin backed away, holding the towel with one hand and shooing the cat with the other. He took three steps into the hall, hoping Satan would follow.

"Here you go."

The sound of Sara's breathless voice brought him back around. She held out the bottle of shampoo while staring at his legs. Gavin deliberately widened his stance, letting the towel part just a bit, then saw her eyes flare.

He saluted her with the bottle. "I appreciate it, honey. Thanks."

"Uh…you're welcome."

It was dirty pool to use her attraction for his body against her, but he would do it all the same. He started to stretch, raising one arm over his head and feeling much like a determined exhibitionist. He was just getting into the game, appreciating Sara's attentiveness, when he felt Satan's front paws land solidly against his backside, throwing him off balance. Gavin jerked forward, almost stumbling into Sara, then turned with a yelp when Satan began contracting his claws in his butt.

The problem, the way Gavin figured it, wasn't that the cat had inadvertently scratched him. It was that as he'd turned, Satan hadn't released his hold and as a result the cat's claws were now snagged in the towel, leaving Gavin bare-assed, with only the top corner of the towel preserving his frontal modesty. What was that about best laid plans?

Sara was no help at all; she was too busy ogling.

Gavin thought about abandoning the towel in favor of maintaining his consequence. Being hunched over with your backside exposed while you fought with an alley cat over possession of a towel wasn't a very dignified position, certainly not one to impress the woman of his choice.

A quick peek at Sara showed she wasn't impressed so much as stunned. "Dammit, Sara, get the cat."

She seemed to shake out of her speechless stupor, and then leaned against the wall, folding her arms over her breasts. "Why?"

"So I can get the towel."

She waved a negligent hand, her gaze glued to his backside. "Just let him have it. That would be easier than untangling you both."

Her words were careless, but when she glanced up, the look in her eyes was pure dare. Now that his options had been severely limited and his plans had gone awry, Gavin knew he had little to lose. Unfortunately he felt embarrassed, which was stupid considering he'd been blatantly flaunting himself anyway. Not that he'd planned to flaunt to the degree of total nudity, but it was too late now.

He couldn't let her have the upper hand, not tonight. He needed to get things moving; the sooner the better. So he stiffened his resolve, gave her a narrow look to warn her of his intentions and released the towel.

To his relief, Sara gave up the game and fled. He'd barely straightened before she rounded the corner of the hall, her wild hair flying out behind her, her startled gasp still filling the air. He frowned down at the cat, who only blinked back. "Any more stunts like that and I'll put the damn bow back on you myself."

The cat quickly followed in Sara's footsteps. Gavin shook his head. "Onward to Plan B. And let's hope it's just a little more successful."

SARA MANAGED TO AVOID any prolonged time with Gavin for the rest of the evening. She took an extended walk with Satan, leading the cat off a thick leash. Then she took her own leisurely bath, soaking for a long time in the Jacuzzi tub until her toes were wrinkled and her muscles finally relaxed.

Still, her mind churned in chaos, playing the same scene over and over again. The picture of Gavin totally nude wasn't something she would ever willingly erase from her mind. The memory of it was enough to send a warmth of anticipation swelling through her body. So it was her own reaction that had her taking long walks and hiding in her tub.

She had literally run! It wasn't to be borne. What had overcome her, she didn't know, but part of it had been self-preservation, she was certain. If she'd stayed, she wouldn't have only looked. Oh, no. Even now, her fingers tingled with the need to touch. The man was too fine for words, too much temptation to resist. She probably would have attacked him. He'd been naked, so therefore unable to offer much defense.

She had no idea what he had hoped to accomplish with his striptease act, but she had no doubt it had been deliberate, though maybe not the part where he actually lost the towel. After all, there was no way he could have prompted Satan to interfere. But the man was up to something. The question was: What?

After she'd finished drying and brushing out her impossible hair, she put on the gown she'd bought herself last Christmas. It was pretty, definitely the prettiest gown she owned, but it wasn't very comfortable. Not that comfort mattered right now. Pretty mattered; comfort ran an insignificant second.

She needed the fortitude of knowing she looked her best before she faced Gavin again. They needed to talk, to clear the air, and she had no wish to wait until morning, giving herself the long night to fret over her cowardly race down the hall. And besides, he might want to kiss her again...or more. She voted for more, not that he'd asked her opinion.

She tried to gather her thoughts and organize them into some semblance of sanity, but they jumped here and there, filled with anticipation and hope and frustration. And as she entered her bedroom from the master bath, her hands busy smoothing the starched fabric of her gown, she stopped in midstride. The sight of Gavin's large, masculine body sprawled across *her* bed in nothing more than leisure shorts with a magazine in his work-worn hands, swept her mind clean of even her insane notions.

He planned to sleep with her again?

She was at first shocked, then immeasurably optimistic. All day, even while picking out her pet, she had nurtured a small hope that Gavin would forget his reticence and let his basic instincts take over. She didn't understand why he kept hesitating. They knew each other well enough, better than many married couples, she thought, considering how much they'd always talked, and six weeks had already passed since her breakup with Ted, assuring she wouldn't react on the rebound, as he'd claimed.

Determined, she sidled toward the bed, waiting for him to acknowledge her presence. The epitome of nonchalance, he held one finger in the air to indicate he needed a moment more to finish the article he was reading.

Irritation was a nasty element to add to an already confused female brain.

"Excuse me." When he looked up, one brow raised at her waspish tone, she added, "What are you doing?"

"Reading."

He plainly thought she should have figured that one out on her own. Irritation turned to a tinge of anger. "Okay. Why are you reading in my bed?"

"Oh." He set the magazine down and scooted higher against the headboard. "I wasn't able to move my bed on my own—it's a king-size, you know. All I got transferred today were my clothes and personal items. By the way, I took the closet in the guest room. And since your stuff is in this bathroom, I thought I'd use the one in the hall."

"So…you're sleeping here tonight?"

"Where else?" He crossed his arms and tilted his head, his dark eyes sincere. "Your sofa is much too small. And I'll tell you, the thought of the floor isn't the least bit appealing."

"So why not just sleep in your own house tonight?"

"Because all my clothes and personal items are here. Remember?"

He sounded so reasonable. She wasn't buying it for a minute. He was up to something. Only she didn't know what it was he wanted to achieve, and this time she knew better than to try to outmaneuver him.

Then it hit her. The man was in her bed—exactly where she wanted him to be. She didn't *want* to outmaneuver him.

Trying not to look as anxious as she felt, Sara pulled back the covers and slid into bed. She felt as stiff as the lace collar on her nightgown, and just as ridiculous. The touch of Gavin's gaze was a tangible thing, and very unsettling.

Without looking, she knew he would be smiling. He would be amused by her nervousness, maybe even a little smug at the effect he had on her. She didn't want to add to his confidence, but she didn't know what to do or how to act. Having anyone close, especially a man, wasn't a feeling she'd experienced much in her lifetime. And this man seemed to genuinely care for her to some degree. The feelings he evoked, those of lust and a craving for tenderness, would be visible in her eyes. She kept her gaze on the sheets, not wanting him to see just how confused she really felt. Then she couldn't help herself and looked at him anyway.

He wasn't smiling; there was nothing of a humorous nature in the way he watched her. Sara started to turn away again, but he captured her chin on the edge of his hand. "You're beautiful."

Staring, her chest tight with emotion, Sara bit her bottom

lip. His eyes flickered, then narrowed on her mouth. With a harsh groan he turned away. "Lord, Sara, you make it so damn hard."

Her eyes widened and her mouth opened.

"Not…" He shook his head, laughing a little, groaning again. His eyes met hers, chagrined and filled with the tenderness she craved. "This is damn difficult. You're making me crazy."

"Gavin…"

"No. Don't you dare say it."

"Say what?"

"I don't know. But it's for certain whatever it is will push me right over the edge. Now give me a kiss good-night and let's get some sleep."

Only her eyes moved, searching his expression, hoping to see some sign that he was jesting. "Just like that? Go to sleep?"

Gavin reached past her to turn off the bedside lamp, then settled his upper body over her, his large hands holding her face. "No," he whispered, his mouth feathering her lips, his breath warm and soft. "The kiss first, then we sleep."

And what a kiss it was. Sara clung to him, feeling the wet touch of his tongue, the rough caress of his fingertips as he tunneled his hands into her hair. It was a kiss meant to prepare her, but not for sleep.

When it ended, she wanted to wail in frustration. But then Gavin pulled her against his side, settling her close and covering them both. His hand smoothed over her arm, and her cheek rested on his chest, the uneven tempo of his heart sounding in her ear.

She hadn't gotten the lust she wanted, but the tenderness was there, enough to wallow in, and for the time being, she decided it was more than enough.

chapter 6

WAKING WITH A WARM, SOFT body curled close had its advantages. And its disadvantages.

Gavin peered down at Sara's face and felt every masculine instinct he possessed surge to the surface. He wanted her, and his body reacted, painfully so. It was a wonder the sexual pulsing in his lower body didn't rock the entire damn bed. If Sara awoke, there would be no way for him to hide his desire.

But it also felt remarkably right to have her here with him, to breathe her unique scent first thing in the morning, to feel the comfort of her nearness. She slept like the dead. He had hardly slept at all.

The radio alarm buzzed, then loud music kicked on. Turning his head to see the clock, Gavin realized it was almost ten. He needed to rise, to begin a new day of plans. This morning, he intended to overwhelm Sara with his culinary expertise.

A wise person somewhere once claimed the way to a man's heart was through his stomach. Couldn't the same apply to a woman? He would prove to Sara how indispensable he could be, and when she softened toward him, and the attitude of marriage, he'd be ready.

The music hadn't disturbed Sara's sleep. Gavin turned to look at her again, feeling overwhelmed with compassion at her obvious exhaustion. Her cheeks were flushed with the warmth of sleep and there was a darkness around her eyes that showed the level of her fatigue.

She'd been trying so hard to keep it all together—the house, the job, the humiliation from the incident. He wished now he hadn't waited so long to approach her. All he'd done was give her time to chastise herself and build up her defenses. When he thought of her past, he knew she would have a difficult time taking another chance on love.

His thoughts were interrupted by a loud, rasping roar. Gavin looked down at the floor and saw Satan. The cat gave him a blank-eyed stare, then prepared to heave his heavily muscled body into the bed. Since Gavin didn't want Sara awakened yet, he forestalled the cat with a hand and carefully slipped his arm from under her head. She made a slight sound of protest and curled into his pillow.

It was a sunny day and Gavin felt enthusiastic about his chances of making headway. Satan followed him as he pulled on jeans and walked through the door, closing it quietly behind him.

The cat also followed him into the bathroom and wound around his feet, making his morning ablutions more difficult than usual. Satan had the uncanny ability of being right where Gavin wanted to step, each time he wanted to step. Walking had never seemed so difficult before.

He grumbled at the cat, stumbling along down the hall, but the sight that met him in the living room stopped him in his tracks.

There was so much cat fur floating around, the damn cat should have been bald. Gavin looked down, but no, Satan was as shaggy as ever. "Did you have to rub against everything?"

Satan showed his sharp, pointed teeth in what Gavin chose to believe was a feline grin, not a threat. "Okay, so you're telling me you need to be brushed? I'll have to brush the damn house first."

He let Satan out the back door, then checked to see if he had the ingredients for omelets. He'd been known to make a really mean omelet. One bite, and Sara would have to accept her good fortune in having him as a roommate.

Unfortunately, thirty minutes later when he had everything set on the table, the rich aroma of coffee in the air, steam rising from the egg dish, Sara refused to get up.

Gavin shook her shoulder again. "Come on, sleepyhead. I've got breakfast ready for you."

She snared a pillow and pulled it over her head. "Go away."

"Babe, I know you're tired." Gavin did his best not to sound impatient. She'd been in bed for over nine hours, and he knew for a fact she'd slept soundly because he'd laid awake, torturing himself all night by listening to her soft breathing. "I've cooked you breakfast. You don't want it to get cold."

She started to snore.

Gavin lifted the pillow in disbelief. Her eyes were closed, her features relaxed, and her lips slightly parted. A soft, very feminine snore escaped those lips.

Then Gavin saw that her nightgown had slipped down one shoulder and the slope of her breast was exposed. He swallowed hard. Last night, he'd felt that plump breast pressed against his side once Sara had decided to relax. In fact, it hadn't taken her long at all to decide she liked being held close to him, even lying half on top of him.

She'd stayed that way throughout the night, tormenting him, and reveling in the comfort of it. It had been so apparent that she'd never had such comfort before, Gavin hadn't minded staying awake. He'd do it again if she wanted him to. He had intentions of holding her every night from now on.

He gave up on trying to wake her when she rolled onto her stomach in the middle of the bed and sprawled wide enough to cover the whole mattress. He gave one gentle pat to her cute rounded backside and left the room.

This wasn't turning out to be the idyllic morning he'd planned. How could he woo the woman if she wouldn't wake up?

Satan came back in to keep him company while he ate his own omelet. He lingered over the meal, still hoping Sara would awaken. Every so often, he made an especially loud noise, scraping a chair across a floor, banging a plate on the table, but she slept on. Finally, when the eggs were cold, he gave Sara's share to Satan, who sniffed it repeatedly before concluding it might actually be edible. After cleaning the dishes, he located a brush and carried Satan outside.

The cat began purring even before he'd put the brush to his hide.

Another half hour passed before he realized there was no end in sight. Satan looked sleek and well groomed, his large head appearing more square without the benefit of excess fur to soften the effect, and his tail looked more bent for the same reason. But there were still hairs falling loose. His coat was so thick, that no matter how much Gavin brushed, he couldn't remove all the excess. Every time Satan stepped, he shed.

Several old scars were now visible through the smooth coat, however, and Gavin eyed the cat with respect. "You're a regular warrior, aren't you, boy?"

Satan stretched, arching his body high and spreading his considerable claws wide. His mouth opened in a yawn that displayed an impressive array of sharp teeth. All around the yard, hanging from the trees and clinging to the flowers, were clumps of yellow fur, some drifting loose to float in the air like dandelion fluff, rolling across the lawn with the sultry breeze. A small cloud hovered around the porch, the air filled with cat hair as if it were a fine morning mist. Gavin did his own stretching, being careful not to inhale the hair, then turned at a sound from the house.

Sara stood in the doorway, now dressed in loose shorts and a pullover top, a slight smile on her face. "You've been brushing the cat."

Gavin stood and looked down at the cat hairs now clinging to his own body. He had to fan the air so that he could see her clearly. "However did you guess?"

He knew he sounded sarcastic, but he was now a grubby mess, breakfast was over and there she stood, looking so damn desirable he wanted to carry her right back to bed.

The lengths he was forced to go to just to win her over. And she hadn't even had the decency to get out of bed.

"Satan looks very handsome."

"Handsome is not a word that will ever be applied to that monster, but I suppose he looks much better." Gavin studied her closely. She still appeared a little wiped out, as if she'd only just opened her eyes. "You okay?"

She flushed, then quickly nodded. "Yeah, fine. I'm sorry I slept so late. I don't suppose there's anything to eat?"

A sleepless night took its toll on his patience. "I had omelets and muffins and fresh coffee, but you refused to get up."

Sara bit her lip, then looked up at the sunny sky. "What time is it?"

"Almost noon."

That startled her. "Good grief. I'm sorry."

"It's my day off. I had hoped we could spend some time together."

"Oh."

She sounded less than enthusiastic. Then he saw her put her hand to her stomach. "Are you sick?"

"No, of course not." And she flushed again.

"What finally encouraged you to get out of bed?"

"The phone rang. It was...Jess. He wanted to know if I could come out to the shelter."

"Why? Isn't Sunday *your* day off, too?"

"Usually. But I...well, I already told him I'd stop by."

Gavin tightened his jaw. The day rapidly dwindled into a dismal failure. "For how long?"

"I don't know. But I told him I'd be there in about an hour."

"Dammit, Sara. Why today? Why can't it wait?"

She flinched, then lifted her chin. "You have no right to curse at me. This is one of the ground rules we should have covered. You don't tell me what to do, and I won't tell you what to do."

Gavin knew he'd lost his edge, knew he was pushing too hard, but he couldn't seem to stop himself. He'd been sexually deprived too long, dammit, especially considering all the provocation he'd suffered. He was a man on the verge of exploding, and he figured when it happened, his hormones would cover more ground than Satan's hair.

Trying for a moderate tone while his body screamed in frustration wasn't easy. He cleared his throat. Twice. "I really wish I'd known beforehand." *There*. That had sounded calm enough.

She frowned. "Are you getting a cold? Your voice is all raw and scratchy."

He stared at her, seeing the concern now in her eyes. If he wasn't so horny, the entire situation might have been humorous. Gavin drew a deep breath, and choked on a cat hair. "I'm fine," he wheezed, when she started forward. Then he waved her off. "Go on. I've got plenty to occupy me for the day, I guess. Satan shed all over the house. I'll stay here and clean it up. What time will you be home?"

"It's not your job to clean up my cat's mess."

He stared at her hard. "I'm the one that suggested you get a pet."

"Still…"

It was annoying the way she constantly looked at him as

if waiting for him to turn on her. Did she think just because the cat had obliged him to do a little vacuuming, he'd get angry and walk out? After how hard he'd worked to walk in? He snorted.

But then she nibbled on her bottom lip, and he saw that sexy crooked tooth, and forgave her for doubting him. He cursed, then locked his jaw against the unbearable provocation she presented. "I asked you what time you'd be home."

She suddenly exploded. "I'll be home when I'm darn good and ready."

Gavin was stunned by her outburst, but evidently not as stunned as Sara. She gasped, stiffened up like a lightning rod, then turned and ran back into the house. Gavin stood there, wondering what in hell had brought that on.

When he heard her car driving away, he cursed again, this time rather viciously. Satan wrapped around his leg and roared his approval.

Well, hell.

Obviously he wasn't handling things right. He supposed, given his frustration from the night before, Sara might be under the same stress. He'd always thought it rather arrogant of men to assume women didn't suffer the same sexual discomforts as men. Frustration was frustration, whether you were male or female. *And she had wanted him.*

A slow smile spread over his face. Maybe he'd been looking at this all wrong. It was possible making love to her would reach her far better than anything else. It would prove how much he wanted her, and that was certainly important since Sara didn't seem to have a clue about her own desirability.

It would also offer that special closeness that always occurred between two people who really cared about each other. He was convinced Sara did care about him. She was merely being stubbornly cautious.

He'd have to be careful to maintain control, but he could do it. It wouldn't do to let her think their lovemaking was *only* sex. He couldn't let her use him without reaching for the commitment. He wasn't easy. No sir. Gavin Blake was not a man to be trifled with.

And he'd be certain to say all the right words, to treat her tenderly, to show his love.

With that determination, he decided not to wait for the night. As soon as Sara returned home, he would allow her to seduce him. He rubbed his hands together and grinned in heated anticipation. Satan, being a perceptive cat, grinned with him.

SARA DREADED SEEING GAVIN again. She was never her best at times like these, and having an extra person in the house had only complicated matters. As long as he didn't push her, she could probably maintain control. But if he insisted on cutting up at her, or trying to second-guess her, she might very well explode.

And speaking of exploding…the constant yapping from the back seat had become very wearying. The tiny dog, a mixed miniature breed of some sort, was the noisiest, most rambunctious little creature she had ever seen. And how one little minuscule animal could move so fast on only three legs she didn't know. But boy, this one could.

She was glad Jess had given her the excuse to escape the house, and she was even grateful that they'd given her the chance to look over the tiny dog. But dragging in another animal for Gavin's approval, especially when he'd been annoyed when she left...

The second she pulled into the driveway, she saw his truck was still there. Everything inside her started to relax; though she dreaded another confrontation with him, she also drew comfort from knowing she wasn't alone, from knowing Gavin was inside. But then he stepped onto the porch, and his disconcerting gaze settled on her face.

Renewed heat rose in her like a tide.

He looked wonderful and strong and handsome; she looked like hell. Mother Nature had a hand in that and there was little she could do about her puffy features and tired eyes. But he didn't know that. Yet.

And she was certain he could hear the constant, annoying yapping from the back seat. She tightened her hands on the steering wheel.

Strolling down the sidewalk, Gavin flicked his glance from her face to the back of the car several times. Then he stepped around and opened her door when she didn't show any indication of doing it herself.

For the moment he seemed inclined to ignore the dog. "You weren't gone very long."

"Nope. Not long at all." Sara tried a smile, but it felt more like a grimace.

"Long enough to pick up another pet?"

"Well...you see, it's like this. The dog sorta looked at me, and…well, we bonded." Sara rushed on, wanting him to understand. "She's had an accident and lost a leg. But she's still plenty scrappy, and she gets around fine. She just needs some TLC. As busy as the shelter is, they can't possibly give her the attention she deserves."

"But you can?"

His tone seemed mild enough, only curious, though he had to raise it to be heard over the racket the dog made. Sara wasn't at all certain of his mood. And she knew her own mood was precarious at best.

She stepped around Gavin and started to lift the cage from the seat. He pulled her aside to do it himself.

She drew a deep breath. "I suppose this is one of those times when you think I should have consulted you first. But you see, there really wasn't any point. I couldn't very well leave the dog there."

Gavin ignored her and started up the walk, holding the cage away from his body and wincing at the continued grating sound. "It's not very big."

"No. She's very fragile."

He said with a touch of sarcasm, "She doesn't sound fragile. Does it ever shut up?"

"Well…no. Not so far." Then she hastened to say, "But I'm certain once she settles down, she'll get quiet."

Gavin sent her a doubting look as he carried the dog through the house. "You didn't bother to wonder what I would think, but did you stop to wonder how Satan might react to the dog? She wouldn't make much more than a snack for him. He might just mistake the dog for a squirrel or some other rodent. And in case you didn't know, Satan is real fond of catching rodents."

Sara's eyes widened. "No, I hadn't considered that."

"Make certain the front door is closed tight."

Sara started to ask why, then saw that Gavin was about to open the cage, and the little dog was running in circles as if winding itself up for the event. She checked the door, and just as he released the dog, Satan strolled into the room to investigate. The dog shot out as if propelled by force and skittered to a frenzied halt directly in front of Satan.

Then the yapping began again.

Satan endured it with nothing more than a mild look of disgust before he turned away. When the dog made a grab for his tail, Satan turned, punishing the animal with a quick swipe of one paw, then sat back to judge the results.

The dog went instantly mute.

Keeping a wary, worried gaze on Satan, the dog began slinking very slowly over to Sara, its gait awkward due to the missing leg. Satan blinked once in dismissal and curled up in the center of the floor to sleep.

Sara picked up the dog and smiled. "There, you see. They get along fine."

Gavin seemed to be considering her. He watched her for so long, she began to squirm, and finally her temper ignited. "Will you stop it?"

He lifted one brow. "Stop what?"

"Stop trying to dissect me. I brought home a dog. This is still my home, Gavin. I can do as I please."

It sounded like a challenge, a rather nasty one at that,

even to her own ears. She was immediately contrite, but it put her on edge having him study her that way.

Gavin dropped his gaze to the floor and his hands went to his hips. She could see his chest rising and falling and knew he struggled to control his own temper. She almost wished the dog would start barking again. It was too damn quiet.

And then Gavin started toward her. She backed up two steps before she caught herself. He took the dog from her arms and set it on the floor. It wandered cautiously, creeping on its three legs, over to where Satan slept.

Gavin tugged her close to his chest. "I don't want to fight with you today, babe."

His voice had been so low, so husky, Sara blinked in confusion. What was he up to now?

He nuzzled her neck and she felt her annoyance melt like a chocolate bar in July. Her heart started galloping. He was such a sexy man, and it was so unfair of him to keep teasing her like this. When his hands settled on her back, then coasted down to her bottom, she sucked in a quick breath and shivered. "Gavin…"

"Shh. You're so tense, honey. Relax, will you?"

Relax? She couldn't possibly relax. Not when he was touching her. At the best of times he could arouse her with only a look, but touching, too? She tried to step away, but Gavin tightened his arms.

"I want you, Sara."

Her mouth fell open, then she leaned back to see his face. "What?"

"I want you. Now."

She continued to stare at him, disbelieving, her anger building to the boiling point, then suddenly detonating. "Of all the rotten, mean, underhanded…" She shoved him away, seeing his face go blank in surprise. "Have you looked at me, today? Well, have you? Do I look the least bit attractive?"

Both Gavin's brows shot up. "Well…yes, you do. You always look nice."

She leaned forward, jutting out her chin. "I'm *bloated*," she growled in a near demonic tone, as intimidating as Satan ever hoped to be.

"Uh…"

"And at the moment," she continued, "I'm feeling especially mean."

Just as the dog had reacted to Satan, Gavin backed up, keeping a wary eye on Sara. "I…ah…"

"I wanted you yesterday, Gavin, but *noooo*. You wouldn't give in." She began stalking toward him, and he continued to back up. "I also wanted you last night. Jeez, I practically begged you. But you couldn't relent then, could you? Oh, no. But now today, oh sure, *now* you want to!"

Gavin stared at her as if she'd lost her mind. "Sara, what in the world is the matter with you?"

"I can't *today*, you ass."

Ignoring her insult, he asked carefully, "What do you mean, you can't?"

Her face felt hot already, but she didn't care. What a dirty trick. Offering himself when she couldn't accept. Lord, men could be so obtuse. "Think about it, Gavin. It'll come to you."

Her tone had been laced with so much sarcasm, he

shouted in return. "Think about what? You're not making any sense. You said you wanted me, well, I want you, too. So what's the problem?"

"I wanted you last night. I'll want you again in a few days. But not until then."

Gavin went still, his frown clearing as understanding dawned, and then slowly, he began to grin. "You're on your period? That's what this is all about?"

Sara punched him in the shoulder. It hurt, like smacking her knuckles against a rock. "Don't you dare laugh at me!"

"Honey—" He reached out for her but she dodged away.

"And don't try to placate me. I'm not in my best of moods at this time of the month."

He bit his lip. "Yeah? I'd already guessed as much."

"Oh, this is so unfair!" she wailed, and the little dog jumped up and chimed in, throwing her head back and howling in a high-pitched, excited whine. Satan decided he'd had enough of all of them, and lifting his massive head, he let loose with a loud, commanding roar.

That was evidently all it took, because Gavin started laughing, and then he couldn't stop. He looked at Sara between his bursts of hilarity, met her outraged gaze, and fell against the wall, holding his sides, roaring every bit as loud as Satan.

Disgusted, Sara stomped from the room. If he was enjoying himself so much, he could just do it without her. She heard him struggling to control himself as she neared her bedroom, and right before she slammed her door shut, he said to the animals, "Now look what we've done. You guys better start thinking of a way to apologize, or we'll all be sleeping outside tonight."

Sara thought that wasn't a bad idea at all.

GAVIN GAVE HER FIFTEEN minutes to calm down. No more, because he was afraid she'd go to sleep again. And no less, because after all, he wasn't a complete fool, despite his recent conduct.

He opened the door without knocking, very cautiously peeked inside and saw Sara curled up on the mattress, holding her middle.

Gavin walked quietly into the room. "I fixed you some warm tea and a sandwich. The tea always helped my sisters."

Very slowly, Sara turned on the mattress to face him. "Needless to say, I feel like a fool again."

"Nope, not this time. It's my turn." After setting the food on the nightstand, he reached out and touched her cheek. "I am sorry, babe. Here I was making grand plans for a day together, and you weren't feeling at all well. I should have realized."

She narrowed her eyes and stared at him. "Grand plans?"

"Never mind. How do you feel now?"

"Men aren't supposed to be understanding about this sort of thing, Gavin."

"Are you kidding? I've got three sisters, and believe me, they forced understanding down my throat until I choked on it. I had no choice at all."

Sara moaned and turned her face away. "This is too embarrassing."

"Don't be ridiculous." Gavin caught her shoulders and

hauled her upright, plumping the pillows behind her. "Here, drink your tea." Gavin watched her sip carefully. She still blushed, but of course, she had no way of knowing how he enjoyed taking part in her womanliness.

He regretted like hell that they wouldn't be making love after all. He'd damn near worked himself into a frenzy just thinking about it. Then she'd showed up with that silly dog and he'd almost forgot what he wanted.

But maybe this would work out better.

He wanted to break through all her defenses, and this was a surefire way to get to sleep with her, without becoming sexually intimate. They could talk, and he could hold her, and he could show her how much she meant to him, how special she was.

She watched him over the rim of the teacup, and he smiled. "The animals seemed to be getting along. They actually started playing a little. That is, if you can call Satan chasing that little squirt playing. The dog didn't seemed frightened, though, even if Satan did sound a bit annoyed."

Sara picked up the plate with her sandwich on it and broke off a piece of the crust. "About the dog, Gavin…"

"Does she have a name?"

"I don't know. When Jess and Lou found her, she didn't have a collar."

"Maybe you should name her, then."

Sara hesitated, then bit her lip. He could see her mentally girding herself, and he anxiously waited to see what argument she would present.

"Gavin, I know I said a lot about this being my house, and

I could do what I want, but I didn't mean to say I wouldn't take your feelings into consideration. I want you to be comfortable here."

He couldn't help smiling inside. This was the closest she'd come to admitting she wanted him to stick around.

"After I left today, I regretted losing my temper. I sort of thought you might decide it wasn't worth the convenience and be gone when I got home."

"I'm not going anywhere, babe."

She looked dubious. "It's not like me to be so emotional, but—" She stopped when he started grinning again. "Despite what you think, Gavin, I am not an emotional woman. At least, not in the normal course of things."

"I wasn't exactly a prince this morning, myself. I had planned to finesse you with my great cooking ability, but I couldn't get you out of bed. I ended up feeding your very excellent omelet to the damn cat. Then Satan needed brushing, and it turned into a much bigger chore than I'd intended."

Sara looked very chagrined. "You fixed me a special breakfast?"

He leaned forward and kissed her. "Don't worry about it. Satan showed appropriate appreciation of my efforts."

"I'm sure it was delicious." She peeked up at him, then sighed. "No man has ever cooked me breakfast before."

He'd be willing to bet no man had ever played hard to get with her before, either! He merely smiled.

A few minutes later she had finished the sandwich and was once again yawning. Gavin removed the plate from her lap and stretched out beside her. She sent him a horrified look.

"Come here. I'll make you feel better."

"A man of many talents?" She looked uncertain, but she did lay down beside him. Gavin moved her around until she was situated against his body, spoon fashion. He laid his large palm over her abdomen and began to gently rub her. Sara groaned.

"Feel good?"

"Mmm."

She nestled closer and Gavin had to bite back his own groan as her rounded buttocks rubbed against his groin. He kissed her on the side of her neck, then whispered, "Now that I'm here, you'll be able to rest more." It wasn't a very subtle hint, but it was true. She'd realize her good fortune if he had to point it out to her every damn day.

"I don't want to take advantage of you, Gavin."

Her voice edged toward sleep. Gavin kissed her again, hugged her a little tighter. "You can't use someone who's willing, honey. I want to be here, with you."

"And with the pets?"

"Yeah. Even with the damn pets."

Her sigh was soft and dreamy and a bit hopeful, then she said, "I've never known anyone like you, Gavin."

He was counting on that being the case, because he knew, even if she didn't, he had been a goddamn *saint!*

chapter 7

HE HAD MADE REMARKABLE headway reestablishing their friendship in only a week.

But still, Sara blanched at the idea of meeting his family. They were due to arrive this morning, and while he felt they still had plenty of time, he couldn't go back to sleep.

He'd come to the conclusion, sometime around the middle of the week, that he was most assuredly a man of steel. Only a superhero could have withstood the magnitude of denial he'd forced on his body.

He'd slept, in painful celibacy, with Sara every night.

In some ways it had been unbelievably erotic, holding her, whispering in the dark of the night, discussing the past and the present. He hadn't yet been able to get her to talk about a future. And the more he learned of her childhood, the more he understood.

That was why, even though Mother Nature no longer conspired against him, he hadn't taken that small step beyond holding her to making love to her. Their relationship became more concrete by the day, but it was still a delicate thing.

Several times Sara had tried taking the initiative, but he always managed to put her off. He wanted to hold out for a declaration of her feelings. He wanted marriage and commitment. He wanted her to buy the cow...er, bull.

But with every day, it got tougher to cling to his high convictions.

And though Sara certainly seemed to like and trust him more now, she was no closer to declaring herself than she had been when he first moved in.

Instead he continually suffered the agonies of unrequited lust, and he honestly didn't know how much more he could take.

Hopefully his family, with all their loyalty and unity and open friendliness, would have an impact on her. He glanced at the clock again, and decided he might as well shower and get dressed. But he was loathe to leave the bed, to leave Sara. The effect she had on him was alarming and confusing and so damn sweet. No other woman could stir all his senses the way she did. She left him aching with lust and hurting with tenderness.

He heard a small sigh and glanced back at Sara. He caught her staring.

Trying for a cavalier facade to hide his emotions, he gave her a cocky grin and a wink. "Morning, sweetheart."

Dropping her gaze to his mouth, she reached up and touched one finger to his lips. "Gavin?"

Those slumberous eyes, that gentle touch, were his undoing. Gavin groaned, then accepted her kiss when she leaned up and pressed herself anxiously to him. Her body was sleep-warm and womanly soft. The encouraging sounds she made were low and lazy, still ruled by her slow wakening. When she slipped one bare thigh over his legs he discovered her gown had gotten twisted up high during their sleep.

The week of sleeping together had taken a toll on both of them, so rather than pause to think about what he was doing, Gavin helped to settle her hips over his. Her arms wrapped around his head, her mouth ate at his, kissing him in a way that crumbled rational thought and any resistance. Though what she did was enough to drive any man crazy, there was an awkwardness to her movements that told him she hadn't taken the lead very often. He reveled in that fact.

"Sara, honey…"

"Gavin, please! I don't want to wait anymore."

She kissed his mouth again, seducing him, holding him still for her assault. She was brazen, voracious, and he loved it.

His hands smoothed down her spine to her backside, lush and firm. Growling, he pushed the tangled gown aside and cupped her, feeling the silkiness of her panties and the warmth of her flesh. His fingers probed.

Sara straightened her arms, her head thrown back, her hips pressed firmly into his. Even with her eyes closed, she appeared stunned, excited and so sexy he no longer thought of long-term plans or goals. She needed him now, and that was enough.

Switching their positions, Gavin pinned her beneath him then began his own seduction. He pulled the tiny buttons open on her gown, baring her breasts. Her nipples were taut and full, and he carefully closed his teeth around one, hearing her harsh groan, feeling the urgency of her hands as she sank her fingers into his hair.

He suckled and tugged, licked and teased. Sara moved beneath him, trying to wriggle out of the gown without breaking contact. She only managed to get it tangled around her belly, but her arms and legs were free. Gavin leaned back to look at her.

Flushed with need from her brows to the tips of her toes, she was a beautiful sight. Her small hands knotted in the sheets on either side of her hips, and her legs were slightly sprawled. He grasped a handful of the gown in each hand. "Raise your hips."

Within moments, she was naked, the gown and her panties tossed aside. Gavin wasn't given a chance to enjoy the sight before Sara had grabbed him again, tugging him back to her. He kissed her throat, the sensitive skin below her breasts, her belly. She arched into him, gasping.

Then he felt the cat leap onto the bed. Beside the bed, the dog began yapping, wanting to join the cat, but unable to manage it.

Gavin tried to nudge Satan away with his foot. The beast thought it was a fine game, and swatted at his big toe. The dog howled for attention.

"Scat, dammit."

Sara moaned softly. "What?"

It was ironic enough to be funny, but when Satan bit his toe, and the dog began her infernal yapping at top volume, his amusement vanished. Grumbling and cursing, Gavin got to his feet, then met Sara's confused gaze. "Sorry. I need to put the cat and dog out."

"Oh." She scrambled for the covers, but Gavin caught her hands.

"No. Don't move. I swear, I'll be right back." Sara hesitated, then relaxed into the bed, giving Gavin an uncertain smile. After one more long, sweeping look at her body, he hauled the reluctant cat into his arms and left the room, the dog following in his wake.

He refused to think about his decision. Sara was ready, he was sure of it. So what if she hadn't told him she loved him, or even hinted that such a thing was possible? The fact they couldn't resist each other had to count for something. It would be a good bargaining tool for marriage.

The cat kept giving him quizzical looks, and Gavin felt compelled to explain. "Don't take it personal, big guy. You two just happen to have rotten timing, that's all." He sat the cat down and opened the front door. After hooking the dog to her lightweight chain and watching her run out, he turned to the cat. Satan stared back, refusing to budge. Again, Gavin nudged him with his foot. Satan only blinked.

Narrowing his eyes, Gavin murmured, "Now where did Sara put that bow...?" With a disdainful snarl, Satan sauntered out. Chuckling, Gavin was just about to close the door when his mother and father pulled up to the curb. Behind them was another car, and then another.

It looked as though the whole Blake family had arrived. Nieces and nephews began tumbling out the open car doors, and one of his sisters waved. Closing his eyes, Gavin silently went through every curse he knew. It didn't help one iota. Talk about rotten timing.

It took his mother only a moment to reach him, and then he was smothered in a hug. He looked over her shoulder to the end of the sidewalk and saw Satan suffering a similar fate, only it was a group of four children who gathered around the cat. The dog was thrilled with her share of attention, and barked in canine elation. His father and brothers-in-law were slower in leaving their cars.

It was a regular family get-together—not quite what he'd planned, and certainly not how he'd planned it. He cleared his throat when he heard Sara singing along with the radio, then watched as his mother looked in that direction.

"Your new lady friend?"

"Ah, yeah. Mom…we weren't exactly up yet."

"Well, no problem." She patted his shoulder, her smile impish. "You two can go ahead and get ready while we unload a few things."

Gavin groaned. "Tell me you didn't."

"You know I can't come empty-handed, son. It wouldn't be right. Especially now that you've—"

Sara's voice, slightly outraged, interrupted. "Gavin! Don't you dare change your mind again. You started this, now come back here and finish it!"

Horrified, Gavin stared into his mother's wide eyes, then winced as Sara's voice rang down the hallway again. "You don't want to be accused of being a tease, now do you?"

His mother raised one brow, indicating where her son had gotten the habit, and Gavin could only be thankful the rest of the family hadn't heard. They were taking their time reaching the porch, stopping every so often to admire one of the newer houses being built on the street.

Gavin floundered. "She's, ah…"

"Impatient?" his mother supplied, deadpan.

He shook his head, then walked to the hallway. "Sara!" He had to shout to be heard over the radio. "My mother is here."

The radio snapped off, and after a moment of heavy stunned silence he heard the telltale sounds of Sara rushing around the room. She flew into the hall, wearing only a sheet.

"Sara!"

Running toward him, she yelled, "Don't let her in until I get a pair of panties out of the…" She came face-to-face with Gavin's mother. "Kitchen."

The rest of the family chose that propitious moment to step through the door. Gavin didn't know what to do, and his family, more silent than he'd ever heard the lot of them be, didn't help by simply staring.

Sara turned and let her head hit the wall with a dull thud.

Then his mother asked in a subdued tone, "She keeps her underclothes in the kitchen?"

SARA WANTED TO DIE. She thought, *If this were the Land of Oz, I could just sink beneath this sheet and melt away*. But it didn't happen. It was all well and good to plan a free-spirited affair with a gorgeous, virile man like Gavin, but it was quite another to have to face his mother—*his mother, for God's sake*—wrapped in nothing more than a sheet, the evidence of the affair plain for anyone to see. Only there wasn't an affair, dammit, not yet, because they'd interrupted. Hopefully his mother didn't know *that*.

She felt more than embarrassed, she felt…guilty, and she wouldn't tolerate it. She was a grown woman, and she could darn well do as she pleased.

She sucked in a deep breath, plastered a serene smile on her face, then turned to face the fascinated masses.

Jeez, there were a lot of them.

A dozen sets of eyes were trained on her. She lifted her chin and said a very proper, "Excuse me," then strolled down the hall to disappear into her bedroom. A minute later, Gavin joined her.

She stood with her back facing the door, staring out a window, but she knew it was him. He didn't say anything, and finally she turned to look at him. He leaned against the closed door, his arms crossed over his chest, a pair of her panties dangling from his right hand.

Without a word, Gavin held them out to her.

Sara closed her eyes. "Why am I always being humiliated around you?"

He didn't answer. Sara supposed that was because there wasn't an answer. When she opened her eyes, Gavin was still watching her, and still holding the panties out. She walked toward him, but when she would have taken them from his hand, he caught her wrist instead and pulled her close.

"I'm sorry."

Struggling against him for a mere instant, then giving up, Sara said, "There's no reason to apologize. It wasn't your fault."

"I started things this morning, when I knew my family

was coming. And I'm the one who invited them here in the first place."

"No, I started things." Then she peered up at him, giving him a weak smile. "And we both forgot they were coming."

"True enough." He tugged her closer and bent to kiss her neck. "You make me forget everything."

"I can't face them, Gavin."

"Of course you can." He framed her head with his palms and forced her to meet his gaze. "My family loves me, and that means they'll love you, too. No matter what. You have nothing to be embarrassed about."

Pressing her forehead to his chest, she groaned. She didn't understand him, or his reasoning. Surely his family wouldn't care about her just by association. "What did they think when you got my underwear?"

"I explained. It was no big deal."

"But they're all still laughing, right?"

"Naw. If I know my sisters, they're probably figuring some way to blame me entirely, while working up a good dose of sympathy for you."

"Why would they blame you?"

"Because I'm the baby brother, remember? They've always blamed me for everything."

Sara knew he was only distracting her, but she appreciated his efforts. "Even when you were innocent, I suppose."

"Of course. I got blamed the time Pam's bra ended up in the pool when she had her first boy-girl party. And Gina blamed me for scaring her boyfriend away one Halloween night." He said in an aside, "The guy was a real wimp."

"And what about your other sister?"

"Carol and I are closest in age. She just blames me for stealing all her girlfriends away."

"And did you?"

He shrugged. "I let them steal me away a couple of times." Then he chuckled. "But I never let any of them keep me for long."

"Maybe that's what Carol objected to."

"Yeah. They wouldn't come around her again after that."

"They were embarrassed. I can understand how they felt."

Gavin kissed her ear this time. "I'm letting you keep me, remember?" Then he added in a rush, "Besides, you're made of sterner stuff than they were. You're an iron woman. Shoot, I still remember the way you swung that rake…"

"Stop it, Gavin." But she was grinning. "All right. I suppose I can face them. But it won't be easy."

"You don't know my family."

Five minutes later, Sara discovered Gavin was right. He made the introductions with haste, barely giving Sara time to acknowledge each person.

"My oldest—nay, ancient, sister Pam, and her very brave husband, Gary. The two little rug rats who look alike are their six-year-old twins, Stevie and Stephanie. Then there's Gina, who's very obviously pregnant again, and her stallion of a husband, Sam." The other men cheered Sam and his potency in high good humor. Sara laughed with them. "The curly-headed seven-year-old is their son, Chris. And last is Carol, only two years older than me. She's married to Roy, and they have the little redheaded girl, Laurel, who's four.

And standing in the corner, smiling at me like I was still twelve, is my mom, Nora. The guy shaking his head—he does that a lot—is my dad, Hank."

There was no mention of her earlier entrance, and his sisters appeared to accept her easily enough. They weren't the kind to crowd a person, but they were open and accepting and as ready to grin as Gavin always seemed to be.

The brothers-in-law appeared devoted to their wives, attentive and loving. And the children were a boisterous handful. It was interesting for Sara to see the way they all seemed to work as a family. There was no real dissension, but the jokes and teasing were constant. Gina was especially tended to, her husband barely leaving her side, and Sara realized it was because the woman was pregnant. Sam strutted around her like the typical proud papa-to-be, never letting her out of his sight.

Sara knew it would take her a while to get all the names straight, but she found she was already looking forward to it.

Having Satan and the dog, which the kids lovingly named Tripod, gave her instant popularity with the children. And the animals seemed to wallow in their attention. Sara gave the kids a cat brush, and before long, Satan writhed on the ground in blissful ecstasy while they attempted to groom him. She saw the children chasing Tripod around a tree, but moments later they circled back, and Tripod had changed from the pursued to the pursuer. The kids squealed in playful excitement, and Sara could have sworn there was a smile on the little dog's furry face and a look of sheer rapture in her brown eyes as she flashed past.

"They're wonderful animals. How long have you had them?"

Sara turned to Gavin's mother. Nora was the kind of woman who never aged. Though there were lines on her face, and a few gray hairs mingling in with the dark, she was still attractive and still energetic. She made the perfect counterpoint to her Hank, who seemed an older version of Gavin. Both father and son shared a similar height and strength of build.

"I got them both from the shelter about a week ago. I knew the dog was wild, but I didn't think Satan was still this frisky." They both watched as the cat began chasing the dog and the kids.

"Cats are like men, honey. They never stop being frisky."

Sara chuckled, thinking of Gavin. "Amen to that." Then she caught herself, remembering that it was his mother she spoke to. Heat climbed up her neck. "Ah, I don't…"

"You're still embarrassed, aren't you? Please, don't be. We're all just so happy to see Gavin happy. Not that I ever doubted he would be. He's a hedonist by nature. Always has been. But his idea of happy and ours are very different."

Feeling uncertain, Sara said, "You want him to settle down?"

"Gavin told you? Never mind. Of course he did." Nora looked across the yard to where Gavin stood, tweaking his sister's hair, then dodging away from her playful slaps. "I was nothing short of shocked when he called to say he'd moved in with a woman."

Sara chewed her lip. Nora didn't exactly sound disapproving, but still… "He's lived with women before," Sara pointed out, subtly defending their living arrangements.

"Yes, but he never called to alert me to the situation, or

to tell me about the woman he was living with." She turned and smiled at Sara. "This is different. You're different."

Yeah, right. Gavin isn't sleeping with me. But no sooner had she formed the thought, she had to shake her head. Sleep, yes. Sex, no. But that might have changed if the Blake family had arrived an hour later. Gavin had definitely been ready to give in. And she was more than ready for the momentous occasion. Past ready. Desperate. On the verge of… Ah, but there was still the coming night, and Sara intended to force the issue, if it proved necessary.

"Great news, Sara." Gavin sauntered up, interrupting her thoughts with a warm kiss to her lips. Her gaze darted to his mother, who stood there wearing an indulgent smile for her only son. "The guys are going to help me move the rest of my stuff down here."

"The rest of your stuff?" She knew what that meant, but she could still hope.

"Yeah. My bed and dresser."

Her hope died. Gavin grinned at her crestfallen look, then gave her another kiss. "We'll be back in a few minutes."

Disappointment changed to chagrin when she caught his mother's amusement. Good grief. Fumbling through her explanations, Sara said, "He, ah…"

Nora waved away Sara's concerns. "I know my son very well, Sara. He's a rascal. Don't let it bother you." Then she added, "What do your parents think of your house?"

"They haven't seen it."

Nora merely blinked. "Oh?" But it was a very maternal inquiry, and Sara found herself drawn in.

"We're not really...close."

"Oh, that's too bad. They live far away?"

"No." There was something about Nora that invited confidence. Her questions were genuine, prompted by concern, not idle curiosity. Sara bit her lip, then blurted, "My parents live close, but they're not really interested in me or what I'm doing."

Nora studied Sara's face for a moment, then she shook her head. "Sometimes parents do the dumbest things. But you know, it's only because we're human. I can't tell you the number of mistakes I made with my children. Why, you could fill the Taj Mahal with my goofs."

Sara did a double take. "Gavin told me he had a wonderful childhood!"

"Oh, I'm sure he did. Still, there were plenty of times when he thought I was picking on him. All the kids have accused me of having a favorite, or treating them unfairly at one time or another. That's all part of being a child, I suppose. Kids view the world through a narrow lens, never noticing all the outlying problems that parents might have to deal with. Their feelings get hurt, and they think we don't care, when actually, we didn't even realize how they were feeling."

Sara thought of her parents' divorce, and how distracted they both became after that. Then she shook her head. "I understand what you're saying, Mrs. Blake. But my parents really didn't care."

"I can't believe that. No, you're a very nice girl, and children seldom get to be that way without some love and guidance."

The grin tugged at her lips, but Sara held it back. "What makes you so certain I'm a nice girl?"

"Gavin's with you, isn't he? And even though I have to admit to making mistakes, I know I didn't raise any dummies." She softened those words by asking, "Have you ever told your parents how you feel?"

"Well…no. There would be no point to it."

"Have you called them and invited them over? Do you try to go see them?"

Again, all Sara could do was shake her head.

"You know, honey, they could be thinking back on the past, seeing things now that they couldn't see then, and wondering if you could possibly still love them." Nora patted her cheek. "I have no idea what problems you had with your parents, but why don't you think about it? And remember that nobody's perfect, parents least of all."

Sara remembered those words the rest of the day. They kept coming back to her, over and over again. She realized she wanted to believe there might be some chance. She wanted the kind of relationship she'd just witnessed between Gavin and his family. That would be stretching it a bit, but perhaps there would be something, some closeness, to work with if she only initiated it.

She understood now why Gavin was so special, so understanding and accepting and confident. And seeing all that only made her want him more.

GAVIN HELPED BUCKLE his youngest niece into her car seat, then allowed her to give him a wet smacking kiss on his cheek. Carol stood on the sidewalk, saying her final goodbyes to Sara. Being closest in age, the two of them had really hit it off, and Gavin knew Carol would come calling again. All in all, he was pleased with the way Sara had been accepted.

His family had spent most of the afternoon with them, and each of his sisters had taken a turn grilling Sara for information. But Sara hadn't seemed uncomfortable with them. In fact, he'd seen her laughing out loud several times.

Lunch had consisted of takeout chicken, and they'd eaten picnic style on the back lawn. Satan had wandered from person to person, glutting himself on tidbits of food, then amusing everyone with his dexterity as he faced a mock battle with a chunk of chicken. He rolled on the ground, throwing the food in the air and then swatting it around. For a while there, it had seemed the chicken might actually win, but in the end, Satan proved the victor.

Tripod was just the opposite. She found a lap and refused to leave it. She was pampered and petted and hand-fed until Gavin feared she might pop.

When Sara had apologized for not having any lawn furniture, Gavin saw his mother's eyes light up and knew some would be arriving soon. He wondered how Sara would receive the gift, if she'd understand the spirit in which it was given.

The cars began driving away in a loud farewell ceremony of honking horns and cheerful children and waving hands. Carol embraced Sara, who looked somewhat startled by the gesture, but she returned the hug. Then Carol came to the curb with Gavin.

"Don't blow this one, brother."

Gavin grinned. "I don't intend to."

"Ah. So it is like that. Mom said so, but I wasn't sure."

Gavin looked back at Sara. She stood on the sidewalk, watching him and Carol. She was keeping herself apart, he realized. She refused to accept all of him. He hated it.

Smacking Carol's backside, he said, "Go on and get out of here. I have things to do."

"Uh-huh. In that big king-size bed you had Roy help you move?"

"Despite being married and a mother, you're too young to know about such things."

Carol merely snorted, then climbed into the car. She waved to Sara and Gavin as Roy pulled away from the curb.

When Gavin reached Sara's side again, she said, "Your sister is nice."

"Carol? She's a pain in the ass, but I love her." He put his arm around Sara's shoulders and started her toward the house. "So what about the rest of my family? Did they overwhelm you?"

"Of course. But then, you knew they would."

They passed the animals lying beneath a tree. Satan was sprawled on his back, his mouth open, snoring loud enough to scare away every bird in a five-mile radius. Tripod had her head resting on his belly. She watched lazily as the humans walked by, but didn't bother to follow. Gavin chuckled. "They look pooped."

"I think they both had more fun today than they're used to."

"And what about you?" They had reached the porch, and Gavin urged her up the steps. "Did you have fun?"

They stopped in the doorway. Sunlight slanted over the porch, diffused through the thick leaves of the tree Satan rested beneath. Gavin still had his arm around her shoulders, and he felt as much as saw her small shrug.

"Sara?" He felt concern, wondering for the first time if he'd done the right thing by bringing his family around so soon. It had seemed a perfect gambit, a way to prove to Sara that happy marriages did exist, that families could and should be a wonderful thing. But now, he wasn't so sure.

Sara took a small step toward him and he automatically put his arms around her, giving her comfort if that was what she needed. Maybe his plans had backfired. Maybe his family had only reminded her of what she didn't have, of how little her parents supposedly cared.

Hugging her tighter, feeling her body pressed to his from knees to chest, he stroked her hair. "What's wrong, honey? Did someone say or do something to upset you?"

She nodded, and Gavin felt his stomach tighten. "Tell me what happened." If one of his sisters had said something stupid to upset her, he'd…

"It was the men."

"My brothers-in-law?" Now that surprised him. They were all such laid-back, easygoing guys. He couldn't imagine them treating Sara with anything less than friendly respect. It had to be a misunderstanding. He cupped her chin, then tipped her head back so he could see her face. She wore the most wicked smile he'd ever seen on a woman.

"Your family is wonderful, Gavin. But I didn't appreciate the men fetching your bed. I hope you weren't actually planning on using it, because I'll have to say right now, up-front, I won't stand for it."

God, she was good. How any woman could look so innocent while she blatantly seduced a man was beyond him. Her cheeks were pink, but her eyes were direct, proving she didn't intend to back down.

That suited Gavin just fine.

"I wanted you to have a choice, babe." He searched her face, trying to read her expressions. He needed her to understand, to know how important this was to him. Sara wasn't just another convenient woman, she was *his* woman. Forever. "I didn't want you to make love with me just because circumstances had thrown us together."

"Circumstances didn't throw us together, you threw us together."

"I, uh, it wasn't exactly like that."

"Then why do you insist on sleeping with me every night?"

He ran a hand through his hair in vexation, then tried again to explain. "Because I wanted you to want me. But I don't want you to do something you'll regret later, and—"

"Gavin? Shut up." She went up on tiptoe to kiss him, and his lungs shut down. He was already hard, had been hard since she'd mentioned the damn bed, and the feel of her soft body shifting against his as her warm tongue stroked into his mouth nearly buckled his knees.

Pulling away a scant inch, she drew a deep, shaky breath, then swallowed. Her eyes still held his, and her tone was a husky, warning growl. "The only regrets will be yours when I murder you for being a tease. Please. Make love to me."

Gavin stared a moment, stunned by her blunt plea. "Now?" *Please, let her mean now.*

Without looking away, Sara slammed and locked the front door. "Right now."

His breath left him in a loud whoosh. He trembled. He shifted. He grinned. "Okay, woman, you've convinced me." Gavin grabbed her hand and started down the hall at a trot.

And as he tugged her down onto the bed, his body covering her, she groaned in relief. "It's about time."

chapter 8

SARA CURLED INTO GAVIN, feeling his heat, his hardness. His mouth was hungry on hers, his breath coming fast and uneven. His hands seemed to be everywhere at once, but it wasn't enough. She clutched at his back, holding on as he rolled on the bed, positioning her firmly beneath him, working himself between her thighs, thrusting against her.

His hands slid down to her hips and his fingers dug into her flesh. He panted in excitement. "I'm sorry, Sara. Too fast."

"No!" She was so afraid he'd draw back, quit again, that she wrapped her legs around him. "Stay with me, Gavin."

"Oh, I intend to." But he pried himself loose, pinning her arms over her head and levering himself upward. "We have to slow down. I don't have any protection in here and…" His head fell forward and he groaned.

"Gavin?"

"Don't move, sweetheart. I swear. This time I'll be right back. Don't you dare move." He shoved himself off the bed and jogged out of the room.

Sara lay there staring at the ceiling. One. Two. Three.

Four… Gavin was back. He set a box of condoms on the nightstand then turned to look at her. She remained perfectly still.

Fascinated, she watched his gaze going over her from her tangled hair to her feet. One of her sandals had fallen off, the other dangled from her toes. They had taken turns showering after his family arrived, and they were both dressed casually in shorts and T-shirts, but now Sara's shirt bunched up beneath her breasts and her shorts were unsnapped.

Gavin knelt on the bed, one large, hot hand coming to rest on her bare midriff. He stroked her, his hand trembling, his nostrils flaring as he struggled for breath. When he began slowly lowering her zipper, she brought her hands down to help him.

"No." Gavin caught her wrists and returned her arms to rest over her head. "Don't move. I mean it, Sara. You move and I'm done for."

"I can't just…"

"Yes, you can." He sounded very positive. Then he caught her T-shirt and pulled it up until he could twist it around her wrists. He held it there with one hand while he deftly unhooked the front closure on her bra. The material parted and her breasts were exposed, her nipples tight, a light flush heating her skin.

Gavin stared, then closed his eyes with a guttural groan. "Don't move."

"You already said that."

"I know."

He went back to her shorts and Sara, though more

excited than she'd ever thought imaginable, had to fight her embarrassment. "I had no idea you were so kinky, Gavin."

"This isn't kinky, babe. It's survival. I've wanted you for so damn long I can't remember not wanting you. And I've been disgustingly celibate for too many months. I'm working on a hair-trigger libido here. One wrong move, and…"

Stunned by his admission, Sara forgot to be embarrassed as he stripped her shorts down her legs and removed her one remaining sandal. She hadn't been with anyone, but then, there was no one she'd wanted. She'd never considered that Gavin had remained alone, too, since his breakup. She was amazed, and for the first time, she started to believe how much he might care for her. It seemed *un*believable, but also undeniable.

He traced his finger along the edge of her silky panties. Her breath constricted, her stomach muscles tightened. "Gavin? You've…you've really been celibate?"

"As chaste as a schoolgirl." His hot, intense gaze swept up her body, then settled on her face. "I didn't want anyone but you. Even before I broke things off with Karen, I was waiting for you. Just you, Sara."

Sara smiled, feeling oddly touched. She didn't know what to say, so she mumbled, "That's so sweet."

Gavin wasn't amused. He yanked her panties down, causing Sara to yelp. But before she could move he was over her, his mouth covering hers again, his tongue sliding in, hot and wet. His large palm smoothed over her breasts, pausing to lightly abrade her peaked nipples, then coasting down her belly and cupping over her mound.

"This is sweet, Sara." His fingers pushed inside her and she groaned. "Oh, yeah, very sweet."

For long, agonizing minutes Gavin tormented her. He wouldn't let her touch him at all, and that frustrated her. But how could she protest while he was making her squirm and beg and pant?

Gavin's mouth slid over her throat to her shoulder and then to her breast. He gently sucked her taut nipple into the heat of his mouth, and Sara felt her entire body clench. His fingers were still stroking over her, inside her, and she felt a wave of sizzling sensation begin. She fought it, but Gavin was relentless.

"Yes, honey." His tone was low and guttural, insistent. "Don't fight me, Sara. Not now."

Since she seemed to have very little choice in the matter, Sara gave in. Her climax was blinding, and she arched and twisted, hearing in the back of her mind all the soft, sultry words Gavin uttered to encourage her.

Limp, Sara was only vaguely aware of Gavin standing beside the bed removing his clothes. She opened her eyes a crack and surveyed his body. "That wasn't fair."

"Who ever told you love was fair?"

Love? Her heart skipped a beat and her emotions shattered. She didn't know if it was hope or fear or relief she felt, and since Gavin continued disrobing, she decided not to dwell on it. More than likely, it amounted to mere pillow talk. She wasn't overly familiar with the type of conversation appropriate at such a cataclysmic time.

Gavin's body demanded her attention, and her eyes

widened as he shucked his shorts down his legs, taking off his underwear at the same time. She was sated, but she'd have to be dead not to be moved by such a sight. He was strong and powerful and pulsing with arousal. She could have looked at him all day and been deliriously happy. But Gavin wasn't very accommodating. He faced her, his hands fisted at his sides, and gave her only a scant second to soak in the sight of his nude perfection before he climbed back into bed with her and reached for the condoms.

"Let me," Sara said.

But Gavin gave her a horrified look. "Not on your life. I'd never live through it."

"I wouldn't hurt you."

"No, you'd kill me." She frowned and he added, "I mean it, Sara. You keep those little hands to yourself. Maybe later, after the box is nearly empty, I'll let you play touchy-feely. But not right now."

He seemed so serious, she couldn't help but chuckle. "So you can play, but I can't?"

"Damn right." He slid the condom on, then turned toward her. "I'm sorry, babe, but I'm short on control right now."

"Then I'll hold you to your promise of later. Because I really am looking forward to touching you, Gavin."

His expression stilled with her words, his chest heaving, his jaw tight, then he growled suddenly, "Dammit!" And Sara knew she'd said too much.

She loved his loss of control. Gavin was like a wild man, starving for her. And here she'd thought he didn't want her! Ha! She had wasted a lot of time, she decided.

But then she couldn't think anymore. Gavin pulled her legs apart and said in a rough whisper, "Please tell me you're ready for me," and before she could answer, he pushed inside.

Frantically she tried to remind herself that sex was just sex, not love. But it didn't seem that way now. Not with Gavin staring down at her, his eyes so hot and filled with bursting emotion, his fingers twined with her own, gripping her, almost painful in their urgency.

"Sara," he breathed, and began to move.

Unbelievable the way the tension built again so soon. She cried out, but Gavin kissed her, his tongue deep in her mouth muffling the sound. When he came, he threw his head back and yelled like a crazy man. Sara touched him everywhere she could reach, stroking, kneading, then as he gave a great shudder she looked at his face and felt her own raging orgasm.

Very slowly, Gavin sank down onto her. She felt the harsh pounding of his heart against her breasts, felt his breath gusting against her sweat-damp skin as he tried to regulate his breathing. She was amazed. She was stunned.

Calm, confident, even-tempered Gavin was a wild man. Sara closed her eyes and hugged him close. She loved it.

MORNING SUN CAUSED his eyelids to twitch, and very warily, Gavin peered over at Sara. She was asleep, thank God. He felt numb all over, especially weak in the legs, and he wasn't certain he could do more than manage a shallow breath.

He'd planned, for so damn long, to make love with Sara and overwhelm her with his touted finesse.

Instead she'd damn near killed him.

She'd taken him seriously when he'd carried in the box of condoms. There couldn't be many left, probably only the ones he'd thrown beneath the bed, hiding them from her so she'd give him some rest. The little witch had been voracious. She certainly had more faith in his stamina than was warranted.

Many times he'd drifted into a deep sleep, only to jerk awake moments later, already hard, with her small hand stroking him or her mouth teasing him, or... But it had been wonderful. Exhausting, but wonderful. He muttered a quiet curse when he realized he was hard yet again.

He glanced at Sara's sprawled body and knew escape to be his only option. He had an hour before he needed to be on a job, and Sara had to go into work today, too. He sincerely hoped she had more energy than he did. His knees shook when he stood.

Satan and Tripod came together to the bedroom door when Gavin started out. The two pets had made a vicious ruckus last night when he and Sara had forgotten to let them back in. It had been the only reprieve Sara had given him, allowing him to feed the animals in the kitchen. But once that was done, Gavin found himself dragged back to the bedroom.

He grinned and shook his head. It hadn't taken Sara long at all to lose her inhibitions, and she was a glorious sight when she became demanding. He'd gladly play her sex slave again, just as soon as he had recuperated.

Picking up Satan and whistling softly to Tripod, he tiptoed out of the bedroom and into the hall, silently closing the door behind him. After giving the cat a few affectionate pats and rubbing Tripod behind the ears, he went into the bathroom to shower. He had just finished washing and was leaning back against the cool ceramic tile when the shower curtain opened and Sara stepped in. He gawked.

Sara slanted him a disgusted look, then stepped under the water. "Forget it, Gavin. I'm zonked."

Seeing that he was safe enough, he gave in to the urge to grin. She really did look exhausted, poor thing. He couldn't resist teasing her. "First wine, and now sex. You really do have this thing about overindulging, don't you?"

She pushed wet hair out of her face and glared at him. "Me? You're the one who wouldn't stop—"

"Oh, no, you don't. I was asleep, woman, and you—"

"You said I could touch you! But every single time I bumped you during the night you turned into a sex-crazed maniac!"

His fatigue miraculously disappeared while he watched the water sluice down her naked body. He picked up the soap and idly began working up a lather. "You have a way of *bumping* that sets a man off."

"*Everything* sets you off!"

"Well, what did you expect? I'd been deprived for too long. If you hadn't been so insistent on waiting…"

"Me!"

"Hush. Let me wash your back."

His hands went around her, then settled on her slick, wet skin. They smoothed over her shoulders, down the length of her spine, then lower. Sara said, "Gavin! That is not my back."

"That's okay." He kissed her throat, licking off a drop of water. "I dropped the soap anyway."

"Gavin…" Her voice dwindled to a throaty, demanding moan.

Twenty minutes later, they were both running late. Gavin finished dressing first, and he stopped on his way out the door to kiss Sara goodbye. She sat at the kitchen table, only half-dressed, still nursing a cup of coffee, and she barely managed a pucker.

He chuckled to himself as he headed for the office. He had papers to pick up, a few phone calls to make, he needed to meet the finishers at a house in less than an hour. His knees were shaky, his eyes burned from not enough sleep, and his heart felt full to bursting.

At this rate, Sara would cripple him within a week. But it was a week he anticipated with a good deal of excitement.

SHE WAS LATE, more than an hour and a half. Gavin was probably furious, since he had expected her home by six. Still, she sat in the car a few minutes longer, not opening the door, not looking at the house.

She heard the pitiful whining in the back seat and winced. Three pets was two more than Gavin had agreed to. Not that she felt she had to gain his permission for every little thing…but then, this wasn't a little thing. This was a very big thing. A very big, furry thing. With problems. *But what else could she have done?*

Sara saw the front door open, and then Gavin filled it. It was his habit to greet her at the front door each night after work, and she realized she'd already gotten used to it. He looked so good standing there, his hands on his hips, his brow furrowed in concern. He'd been worried about her? She hadn't considered that possibility. No one had worried about her in a very long time. He started down the steps, so she quickly came out of the car and met him on the sidewalk. She wrung her hands, trying to order her thoughts.

"Sara? What is it, what's the matter? Do you have any idea what time it is?"

His tone was sharp, a mixture of annoyance and worry. It was the first time he'd lost his temper with her since the day she'd brought home Tripod. She opened her mouth, ready to launch into her well-rehearsed explanations, and instead, she burst into tears. She was horrified by her own actions, but it had been such a horrendous afternoon.

Gavin grabbed her shoulders and shook her. "What the hell is the matter? Are you hurt? What happened?"

She shook her head, hiccuped, then tried again. "I'm sorry I'm late. I had to go by the shelter, and…Gavin, I have to tell you something."

He seemed to relax all at once. He pulled her close against his chest, and she didn't want to admit, even to herself, how wonderfully safe it felt. "Shh. Calm down, babe. Whatever it is, it'll be okay."

Then the sound of the sad, mournful whining reached their ears. Gavin froze for several heartbeats, then with a resigned sigh, he looked over her head to the car. Holding her shoulders, he pushed her back a ways to see her face. Sara bit her lip, knowing she looked guilty as sin, knowing she looked upset, but dammit all, there was nothing else she could have done. Gavin moved around her. Sara started talking ninety miles a minute. The problem was, she only had a fifty-mile-a-minute tongue, so most of what she said was garbled and nonsensical.

"It was the most terrible thing. Tragic. Just tragic. And so sad. You see, the old man died, and then the woman—his wife—just couldn't bear to go on without him, and she went into a decline. She's well over eighty, and she couldn't take care of herself, much less a dog. The family has its hands full looking after her, and the dog was simply wasting away. She misses everyone so much, and she's so unhappy. God, Gavin, I've never seen a more unhappy creature, and…"

Sara's explanation came to a screeching halt. Gavin opened the rear car door, shook his head, then began talking so softly, so calmly to the dog. When he lifted the collie out, holding her weight easily in his arms and started toward the house, Sara was speechless. She trotted after him.

"What are you doing?"

Gavin never slowed his pace. He crooned to the dog, but he turned his head enough to say, "She's upset. I'm taking her inside." The dog looked up at him, and Gavin asked, "What's her name?"

"Maggie."

He said the name, softly, slowly, making it sound like a compliment, and the dog stared at him as if captivated. Sara stepped through the doorway, holding the door for Gavin, and Satan and Tripod walked to her with rapt looks of curiosity. She took a brief moment to pat the animals, then rushed after Gavin. He took the dog to the kitchen and sat her on the floor by the sink, in the spot where the late-day sun coming through the window made a warm, golden pool on the tile.

Gavin knelt in front of Maggie, rubbing her laid-back ears. Maggie curled into a small semicircle, her entire countenance one of wary disbelief. "What's the matter, old girl? This is all pretty new, isn't it? But you're okay here."

His understanding, the gentle tone of his voice, brought on a fresh rush of tears. Sara felt her bottom lip begin to quiver and pulled it tightly between her teeth. Tripod sat back to watch the happenings from a distance, choosing to lean against Sara's leg. But Satan observed the situation with a jaundiced eye, then walked over and regally placed himself over Gavin's knee. The look he gave the dog was filled with possessive warning. Gavin chuckled, stroking the cat.

"Be nice now, Satan. You can see she's scared. Make her welcome."

Satan blinked, gave one of his rumbling, rusty purrs, and brushed against the dog. The dog's head snapped back as if startled, but Satan was relentless. Within moments, Maggie was splotched with Satan's yellow hair. But she didn't seem to mind, especially since Gavin was still petting her. Tripod moved closer and sniffed the dog, then flopped down beside her. She looked ready to go to sleep.

Sara sniffled, so touched by the scene she could barely keep her tears in check. Gavin heard the small sound and turned to her. "Why don't you go take your bath, honey? I'll look after Maggie, get her settled down for the night. In the morning, she'll feel better."

That did it. Sara wailed, covering her face with her hands. Only a second later, she felt Gavin pull her close. "Shh. It's all right now."

"I… I…know." She hiccuped, then made an effort to calm herself, but it was impossible. "I didn't know what to do. When Jess called me at work to tell me about Maggie, I just had to go and see her for myself. She wouldn't eat and she kept whimpering and she…well, she was so alone. So scared. You can't imagine what that's like, Gavin."

"Shh. It's all right now."

"I just had to bring her home."

"Of course you did. And now she'll feel loved again and everything will be fine."

After a loud, disgusting sniff, Sara wiped her eyes with the back of her hand. It was then she realized the kitchen smelled of cooked chicken. She looked around and saw a variety of pots and pans on the stove, and the table was set, complete with a lit candle. Or at least, it had been lit some time ago. The wick had long since burned down. Oh, no. Gavin had cooked dinner and she'd missed it. Again. He'd wasted another special meal on her.

"I'm so sorry." She wiped her eyes again, trying to rid herself of the insistent tears. She put her hands on his chest and looked up at him. "You went to all this trouble, and I wasn't even here in time to appreciate it."

After a long, intense look, Gavin glanced over his shoulder to where Maggie was allowing Satan to curl into

her side. The dog gave a single, loving lick to the cat, leaving
Satan's entire head damp and his fur ruffed in the wrong
direction. Satan closed his eyes and rumbled a ragged purr.
Tripod never stirred. Gavin turned back to Sara and kissed
her. "I'd say you were doing something more important.
And dinner isn't wasted. We can eat the chicken cold. In fact,
take your bath and I'll set us up a picnic outside. The
animals could use the night air."

Suddenly she couldn't breathe. Sara took a step back,
appalled, frightened, amazed. It wasn't a slow awareness, but
a burst of realization that nearly brought her to her knees.
She loved him. She didn't want to, didn't want to set herself
up for another disappointment, another hurt. But he gave
her no choice, damn him. How could she not love a man
who'd put the needs of an animal above his own?

The words felt choked as she forced them through her
throat. "Why are you doing this?"

Gavin knelt again by Maggie's side and stroked along her
back. This time the dog lifted her tail in a one-thump wag.

Gavin seemed to take an inordinate amount of time
before answering. Finally he looked up, his expression
blank of all emotion. "Did you really expect me to play the
tyrant and demand you take the dog back? Only a real
bastard would refuse to give that dog a little love. Ah, and
you were late, too. Should I have thrown a tantrum
because dinner was ruined? Would you have dealt better
with that?"

Sara shook her head, even as she said, "I don't know."

"You don't know me. Yet you keep comparing me to Ted

and your parents and every other person who ever let you down, and I don't mind telling you, it makes me mad as hell."

"I didn't—"

"Yes, you did. Why would you think I'd feel any less compassion for that dog than you do?"

"Because..." Sara swallowed. She drew in a ragged breath and started again. "Because you don't know what it means to be alone and scared and—" Her voice broke, but Gavin didn't make a move toward her. He continued to stroke the dog, and occasionally Satan when the cat demanded it. But his gaze never left her face, and through her tears, Sara saw his understanding. It was humiliating, because she had a feeling he knew her better than she knew herself.

"I'm going to go take my bath now."

Gavin nodded. "I'll get our dinner together. And Sara? When we're done eating, we're going to talk."

It sounded closer to a threat than a mere statement. Gavin watched her closely, as did Satan and Maggie. Even Tripod managed to stir herself enough to give a quick glance. Sara felt outnumbered, and after a huge sigh, she nodded agreement.

As if relieved by Sara's decision, Maggie laid her head on Gavin's thigh. The dog no longer looked so cautious or forlorn. And Satan seemed to be taking the addition of yet another pet in stride. That is, until he stood up and decided to mark Gavin as his own territory in the time-honored tradition of all male animals. Gavin jumped to his feet, but not in time.

Sara realized she no longer felt like crying. In fact, she

had to hold her mouth to stifle her laughter. She had just turned to leave the kitchen when she heard Gavin mutter, "I'll put ten bows on you, dammit! Do I *look* like a tree?"

chapter 9

FOR MOST OF HER LIFE, Sara had felt hollow. She hadn't realized that until now, when she felt ready to burst with an incredible wealth of emotion. She'd lived with emptiness so long, it was almost alarming to acknowledge the difference now. But feelings she'd never encountered before filled her, making her whole. She wanted to cry, she wanted to laugh.

She wanted to tell Gavin that she loved him.

But she didn't dare.

This was all too new and too fragile to put to the test so soon. As she sat through the dinner that Gavin had prepared, on the tablecloth he'd spread on the ground, she couldn't help but smile. He coddled Maggie, he calmed Tripod and he reassured Satan, all without thought. Simply because he was that kind of man—so different from any other person she'd ever known.

That, too, was frightening. How could a man like Gavin ever really care about her? She was so used to people turning away, or in Ted's case, running away. She wanted to surround herself with things that would be permanent. Like her house, her pets. But she couldn't make Gavin permanent. He would only stay if he chose to.

He looked up and caught her staring. She smiled, a sappy smile, she knew. Then she leaned over the food and kissed him. "Thank you."

He didn't question her sudden gratitude, or want an explanation for what she was thankful for. He merely nodded. "You're welcome."

"You're too good to me."

Gavin shot her a look, growled low enough to startle all three animals, then hauled Sara over the food, scattering plates and chicken and knocking over drinks. She found herself facedown over his lap, with his hand hovering over her backside.

"Gavin! What in the world…"

"What did you say, Sara?"

"Uh…" She wasn't certain what had prompted this barbarian mood of his, so she didn't know how to answer. But she did giggle.

His palm thwacked lightly on her upturned derriere. She tried, but couldn't quite stifle another giggle.

"That was what I wanted to talk to you about."

"My backside?"

"No, this damn habit you have of thinking I'm being too good to you."

"Oh." Her tone softened. "You really are— Ouch!"

"Did that sting?"

"You don't sound the least bit remorseful." She tried to rub her bottom, but he caught her hands and held them away.

"I'm not remorseful. Now let's try this again. Repeat after me."

"Yes, sir." She started to giggle again. She doubted, in her present mood and her newly acknowledged love, that Gavin could do anything to dampen her spirits or make her angry.

"Say, I deserve the very best there is."

"You are that, Gavin."

"My palm is itching, Sara. I think I may have a propensity for this type of thing. Don't tempt me."

"I deserve the very best."

"Much better." He began to massage her bottom. "Now say, I will stop keeping track of every nice thing Gavin does and accept his affection without remorse."

His roving, caressing hand made speech difficult. Sara squirmed over his knees. "Yeah, what you said."

"I want you to be happy, Sara."

All the teasing had gone out of his tone. When she tried to turn over, he helped her until she was cradled in his arms. She kissed his chin, his cheek. "I *am* happy. Very happy." She kissed his mouth, and the next thing she knew, she was lying on her back on the soft grass, with Gavin's weight pressing into her.

"You make me happy, too, babe. Believe that, will you?"

She didn't answer him. He didn't give her a chance to.

HE WAS READY TO KILL HER.

One animal had been enough. Two, he could have tolerated. Even three, given the circumstances, he'd have handled just fine. But five? He stared at the old, shivering poodle she held in her arms and felt his temper ready to snap.

"What's the matter with this one?"

Sara flinched slightly, and she had a little trouble meeting his direct gaze, but she finally muttered, "He's deaf."

Deaf. A deaf poodle. Just ducky. "Sara, I thought we agreed after the last dog—"

"I had to bring Melon home! No one would have wanted a pregnant dog. After she has her puppies, we'll find a home for them."

"And for this…this decrepit old soul? You know you won't want to part with any of them, Sara."

She hugged the poodle closer to her chest. "It's a good thing he can't hear you. And he's not decrepit. Just a little…"

"Ancient? Hell, I see gray hairs on him."

"That's the natural color of his coat."

"Yeah, right. What about his double chin? I swear, I've never seen a dog with a double chin before."

"He needs to be treated gently."

That was the thing about Sara. She seemed to have taken his words to heart two weeks ago. She was more relaxed around him, more accepting of him. But she still wanted to save every single animal that came into the shelter. Luckily the backyard held up, but they had to take regular duty with the scooper twice a day, and the pet-food bill grew daily. Gavin honestly hated to stem her enthusiasm for helping the animals, but enough was enough.

"Sara, this is not a halfway house for socially challenged animals. The last two you brought home weren't at the shelter long enough to be adopted."

"Because I know whoever took them wouldn't have

been as good to them as we are." The poodle lifted his grizzled head and gave Sara a slow lick on the chin. Gavin winced.

"Babe, listen to reason. When Melon has her pups we're going to be overrun with dogs. Poor Satan is liable to run away, Tripod will go into a nervous decline, Maggie will hide—"

He stopped abruptly when the poodle turned watery eyes in his direction, looking wounded to his very soul.

Dammit all.

He fought the inevitable for another three seconds, then stomped forward. "Here, give him to me. He's probably cold, even as warm as it is. I'll put him in on Maggie's blanket."

Sara's grateful smile wobbled. "Thank you."

Gavin managed to point an accusing finger, and his frown was downright mean. "That's enough out of you, lady."

She took his warning to heart and turned away, but he still caught sight of her smile. She trusted him now. But she still hadn't told him she cared.

He was about at the end of his patience.

After getting all the animals settled, Gavin located Sara in the laundry room and announced he had work to do. "The finishers are still up at the house. I want to go check on them, make certain they're on schedule. Tomorrow we'll be getting a new shipment of drywall and now that three of the houses are almost complete, I don't want to fall behind."

"It will be strange having neighbors, won't it?"

Gavin grinned. He knew Sara liked having the street to themselves, but she was also extremely proud every time he sold a house. So far, all the lots had been taken, with plans for the house styles already chosen. Within a year, all the buildings would be complete, and the street would become a neighborhood. Maybe, Gavin thought, someone moving in would want a dog.

He gave Sara a quick kiss. "We'll eat out tonight, okay?"

"I could cook if you want."

"No." He hoped he hadn't sounded too anxious, but in truth, Sara's cooking was almost inedible. "We deserve a night out."

"All right. I'll have all the housework done before you get home."

She was always so eager to please him, working extra hard to uphold her end of their bargain of sharing the chores. He shook his head, knowing better than to argue with her again. She was adamant that she always do her share. She worked so hard at making the relationship work, but she never gave him what he really wanted—a declaration of love.

SARA HURRIED THROUGH the house, making certain everything was tidy, sparing herself enough time to get ready for dinner. She wanted to look extra nice tonight, since Gavin was taking her out. She did her best never to look frumpy around him, though there wasn't anything she could do about her hair, which would always have a tendency to go its own way, regardless of her coercion. Gavin had told her once that he liked it for that very reason.

She was dabbing on a touch of makeup when the doorbell rang and all four dogs began barking at once. She had to shove animals aside to reach the doorknob, and when she opened it, she wished she hadn't bothered.

Her ex-fiancé, Ted, stood on the front porch, his hands shoved into his pockets, a suave smile on his handsome face. She took two steps back.

Her simple movement jump-started the outraged barking. All the animals seemed to vie for the greatest show of bluster, growling and snarling and forcing the hair on their backs to stand up. All but the poodle, who couldn't get his hair to oblige. But he made up for it by taking small, snapping bites of the air very near to Ted's leg.

"What the hell! Where did you get all these creatures?"

Sara had her hands full trying to calm the animals. "These are my pets. Hush, dogs!" They ignored her. While they had each openly accepted Gavin, not a single one of them seemed inclined to allow Ted past the front door.

Except for Satan.

Satan just sat and watched from a padded chair arm, his round eyes unblinking, his expression suspicious.

Ted tried to shout over the noise. "I'd like to talk to you, honey."

"I'm not your honey." Sara made a grab for Maggie, who was behaving in a very un Maggielike manner. She caught the dog's collar and began dragging her toward the kitchen, at the same time urging Tripod forward with the edge of her shoe. Ted stepped inside and stared.

"My God. That dog's missing a leg."

She ignored him and whistled for Melon, the only one of the bunch who would respond to such a command. The heavily pregnant animal lumbered behind, but she kept looking over her shoulder and growling at Ted. Since Melon was a singularly ugly bulldog, it was a sight to cause awe.

Ted called out, "The damn poodle is still threatening to bite me. Whistle for it."

"Won't do me any good," Sara yelled between bouts of barking. "He's deaf. Can't hear me anyway."

Ted stared at her in amazement. Then his expression suddenly softened. "My poor baby."

Sara closed the low gate to the kitchen and admonished the dogs to quiet down. Gavin had purchased the spring-action gate after having a night with Sara interrupted. Tripod and Maggie had decided to sleep with them, and Satan, of course, had refused to be left out. In truth, Sara wondered if Satan might not have led the troop.

She picked up the poodle and set him gently over the gate then turned back to Ted. "Now, what exactly did you need, Ted?"

He maintained his tender expression and pronounced, "You. I need you, Sara. And obviously you need me, too."

Sara stared. "What in the world are you blathering about?"

"It's plain to see, sweetheart." He shook his head in a pitying way and smiled again. "You're surrounding yourself by these pathetic creatures because you miss me. You need to be loved."

Sara felt as if someone had poleaxed her. *She needed to be loved?* It wasn't just permanency she craved? No, of course not. She did want to be loved. She wanted that so desperately, she'd been afraid to admit it, even to herself. She'd been doubly afraid to admit it to Gavin.

Then she stiffened her spine. No more. She wouldn't remain a coward. She loved Gavin and he deserved the truth, despite what his reaction might be. If he didn't care enough about her, if he couldn't learn to love her, then he might want to go now before her feelings began to suffocate him.

Sara paced. How to tell him? She couldn't very well just blurt it out...

Ted cleared his throat. "Sara?"

She glanced up, surprised to see Ted still standing there. He moved closer, and all the animals were quiet, as if waiting. Sara blinked at him in question.

"I'm sorry I hurt you, sweetheart. It was never my intention."

"No? That's strange. Did you honestly think I would appreciate having my fiancé in my bed with my neighbor's girlfriend?"

Ted made a *tsking* sound. "It wasn't exactly like that, Sara. I just got carried away. We both did. But we realize now what we might have thrown away by acting so—"

"We?" Sara felt her insides freeze, her lungs constrict. Ted took a step closer. Satan made an agile leap from the chair and sauntered slowly toward them.

"Karen and I." Ted glanced at the cat, then back to Sara's face. "I want to make it up to you, Sara. I want to come back to you."

A bubble of laughter took her by surprise. "That's absurd." She flapped her hand, dismissing the mere suggestion of such a ridiculous thing, then asked, "Did you say Karen? She's here?"

"Yes, of course." This obviously wasn't going the way Ted

had intended. "Listen to me, Sara. We can make a go of things. I'm ready now."

"I'm not." She forcibly kept her tone one of polite inquiry. "Where, exactly, is Karen?"

He heaved an impatient breath. "She went up to the empty house that worker boyfriend of hers is at. She saw him go inside the garage just as we turned on the street. She's hoping to patch things up with him."

Sara felt every protective, possessive instinct she owned come slamming to the surface. Karen with Gavin? Beautiful, tall, sexy Karen. Good grief.

She started to move around Ted, her steps anxious. "Excuse me, I have to go."

Ted turned, startled. "Go where?"

"After Gavin."

"Who the hell is Gavin?"

"The man you'll never be. Let yourself out, will you?"

"Now, wait a damn minute!"

With his raised tone, all the dogs howled in outrage. They leaned against the gate, snarling and yapping and doing their best to get through. Sara tried to ignore them all; her only thought was to get to Gavin and tell him her feelings before Karen had a chance to work on him. Not that she didn't trust Gavin, but this was too important to leave to chance.

But then Ted stupidly grabbed her arm to halt her exit, and all hell broke loose.

Satan roared out the most ferocious, menacing, hair-raising growl Sara had ever heard from him, and the gate in the kitchen collapsed from the combined weights of four enraged dogs. Ted flew from the house, high-pitched screams of fright signaling his terror. The animals took off in furious pursuit, Satan leading the way.

Sara watched it all in mingled amazement and horror, then she remembered Gavin. And Karen. And her love.

She thundered after the group, every step echoing her resolve.

GAVIN DID HIS BEST to free himself from Karen's grasping hold. The woman had no shame, especially given they were standing in the open garage. Twice now he'd told her it was over, that he'd meant it when he'd broken things off so long ago. Even without Sara in his life, he wouldn't take Karen back. She wasn't the type of woman he wanted or needed to be with.

He tried to be gentle, but Karen was deliberately obstinate about the whole thing. She refused to listen.

Gavin sighed in disgust as she once again threw herself against his chest and wrapped her arms around him. He propped his hands on his hips, allowing her, for the moment, to have her say. It wouldn't matter. He wanted Sara, and he'd have her eventually on his terms, no matter how long he had to wait, or how many pets he had to put up with. Sooner or later the woman would realize she loved him.

He could feel Karen cuddling closer and once again he clamped his hands on her forearms and prepared to pry her loose. Then they heard the noise.

Karen looked up just as Gavin leaned around her.

Racing down the middle of the street, looking much like

a bizarre circus parade, was Sara's ex-fiancé Ted and every pet Gavin had recently acquired. They made a huge amount of noise—a mixture of human horror and animal determination. Gavin started to chuckle.

Good old Satan led the group, galloping at full speed, his heavy body stiff with anger, his bent tail sticking out like a broken lance. All the dogs followed, even the aged poodle. As Gavin watched, Ted made a leap for a skinny little tree and hoisted himself upward.

Satan followed.

Ted wailed as the cat perched on the same branch, then sat back to watch. The cat didn't make another move, but he looked down at the loudly yapping dogs with faint approval.

Sara appeared.

She took one look at Karen draped in Gavin's arms and began a forceful, determined stride in their direction. She was breathing hard, and she looked as enraged as the animals.

Karen stiffened. "Oh my God."

Gavin allowed her to jump behind him and use him as a shield. Sara looked ready to explode with righteous anger. Gavin couldn't have been more pleased. There was no way he could mistake the jealousy in her eyes. Her lips were pulled back in a snarl and he could just see the tip of her crooked tooth.

He wanted very badly to kiss her.

When Sara got close enough, he grinned and reached into the garage for the plastic rake leaning against the wall, then offered it to her with a flourish. It was a subtle reminder, giving Sara the chance to collect herself before she did something she might regret later.

To his surprise she smiled, but it was a smile with evil intent. "I love you, Gavin."

For a long moment he couldn't move. Hell, he could barely breathe. Sara looked so stern, so forbidding. Her arms were held stiff at her sides, the rake in one fist, her legs braced apart. She'd said it like a command, and he nodded. "It's about damn time."

She took a step back, stunned. "Then I don't need the rake?"

"You don't need the rake."

She glanced at Karen who dared to peek over his shoulder. "You have about three seconds to make yourself scarce before I sic the animals on you."

Karen screamed, causing Gavin's ears to ring, and then she ran. Gavin started laughing and couldn't stop. Ted hollered for someone to help.

He and Sara both ignored him.

After fidgeting a moment, Sara took a small step closer. "I've been afraid to tell you."

"I know." Overwhelmed by tenderness Gavin touched her cheek. "I would have waited awhile longer before getting insistent."

"Insistent about what?"

"About hearing a declaration. About getting married." He didn't like his own feeling of insecurity, but he acknowledged it. "You will marry me, won't you?"

"I'll insist upon it."

Gavin pulled her close and began kissing her. It was only the honking of horns that forced him to pull away. "Oh, hell."

Sara followed his line of vision and then blinked in surprise. "Your family's coming to visit again?"

"Sort of. You see, you mentioned to Mom that you needed lawn furniture. That's probably what's in the truck."

Sara was stunned. "I can't accept lawn furniture from her!"

"Trust me, honey. She likes giving things. The whole family does. Do you think you'll mind being married to the spoiled, youngest child of the family?"

She gave him a slow, blinding smile that nearly melted his heart. "Are you kidding? I get you and lawn furniture? What more could any woman possibly want?"

epilogue

THEY ANNOUNCED THEIR intent to marry an hour later over coffee and cookies. It hadn't been easy to explain Ted, especially since he'd refused to come out of the tree. When he did come down, he had no way to leave; Karen had taken the car.

Gavin called for a cab, then explained to everyone that Ted preferred to wait on the curb—with Satan—until the cab arrived. Not a soul questioned that decision.

Sara had even more relatives to meet this time. It seemed his mother thought Gavin could use the extra support of the elders in the family, so there were two sets of grandparents tagging along. When the oldsters discovered Gavin had managed quite nicely on his own, they each claimed good genes as the deciding factor in his victory.

After Ted was finally picked up, the animals all wandered back to the house. Sara retold the story of how the pets had rallied together to come to her defense, and everyone was suitably impressed. Grandpa Blake showed a special fondness for the sweet-tempered Maggie. He claimed to have had a dog just like her in his youth.

Gavin's grandmother on his mother's side ended up with Tripod in her lap, throughout the entire visit praising the animal for her courage. And as Gavin watched them all interact, an idea came to mind.

"Does the retirement village allow you to have pets, Grandpa?"

"They do, and I know a lot of the folks in the village would love to have a good, dedicated dog. But most of them are on limited incomes and pets cost money."

Sara picked up on Gavin's train of thought immediately. "I have two friends who run a shelter. I bet they'd be willing to give the shots and checkups for free if the animals had a good place to stay. And Gavin and I could build a run of sorts right off the back door of each condo, so all the owner would have to do is hook the dog to a leash in the morning."

Gavin nodded. "It could be done. The village is set up with only ground-floor condos. If Jess and Lou would agree…"

"I'm certain they would." Sara looked so excited by the idea, Gavin knew she would be comfortable with the animals' living arrangements. They could personally select which homes the dogs and cats would go to.

All the elders agreed to take a pet from the shelter. They even seemed anxious about the idea. Sara promised to go first thing the next day and see what animals were available.

Gavin bided his time until he could get Sara alone in the kitchen for a few minutes, and then he pulled her close. She snuggled into him with a sigh of pleasure. "Thank you for coming up with such a wonderful plan, Gavin. It makes me so happy to know that a lot of the animals won't have to be alone anymore."

He squeezed her a little tighter. "They remind you of how you've felt for much of your life."

She nodded, then laid her cheek against his chest. "But at least I understand that now. And I think, if you don't mind, I'll try inviting my parents to the wedding."

"Of course I don't mind. Why don't we drive over and see them together? We can ask in person. You said they didn't live all that far away."

"Not too far." She stared up at him and sighed in wonder. "I really do love you, you know."

And he did know. He'd known all along she could give him what no other woman could. Herself.

He was just about to kiss her when he heard the rushing steps of a small army of children. They squealed in delight as they raced past Gavin and Sara in the kitchen, Satan hot on their heels. And as the cat flew past in graceful, playful pursuit, he looked up, and Gavin could have sworn he was grinning.

Sara laughed. "Your mother's right. He's just like you."

Gavin merely grinned.

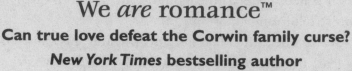
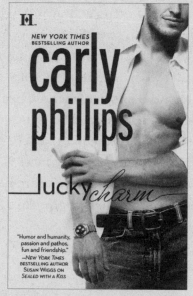

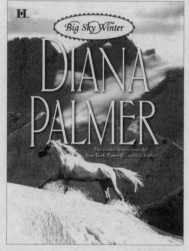